THE
BETA
BOYS

The Beta Boys

Copyright © 2023 Arin Mikailian

This is a work of fiction. It draws from the experiences of a group of high school boys growing up in Southern California during the early 2000s. Names and locations have been changed. The characters' motivations and the plot are a product of the author's imagination. The author acknowledges the trademarked status and trademark owners of various products, bands, and/or restaurants referenced in this work of fiction, which have been used without permission. The publication/use of these trademarks is not authorized, associated with, or sponsored by the trademark owners.

ISBN: 979-8-9890465-2-2

Cover by Guillaume Cornet

Book Design and Copyediting by Bodie Dykstra

For my dad and Uncle Hovik

A NOVEL

ARIN MIKAILIAN

FALL
SEMESTER

1

ROMAN

The high school party of a lifetime raged on: first-ever vodka shots, sprawling beats, dancing, rumors of making out, girls cackling in a huddle until one of them broke away crying, meatheads bumping shoulders as they sized each other up, seeing who'd be worthy of fight-of-the-night.

But Roman Vallancourt didn't care.

He heard whispers of hype about the event at school and pictured it from his cyber cave—aka his room. Sure, the party might have been a bit tantalizing, but to earn an invite, he'd have to talk to people, a lot of people, most of whom he didn't know. Death. Even the cost of being a wallflower was relatively high. Instead, he sank into the dependable padding of his desk chair, his feet muscles so calloused they no longer fell asleep amid marathons by a computer screen stretching past the rim of his afro. It was all he needed. He assumed a girl's touch couldn't be that much better. Like all of life's hurdles, caressing feminine skin could be procrastinated.

In his mind, he sat at his desk in a huge corner office like a thriving adult, a tech innovator earning passive income while wearing a T-shirt and shorts. He was proud to be alone on a Friday night in a room without posters—his mom didn't let him put any up. No need to dignify nudging elbows to make the most of his youth. After years of failed hobbies and participation trophies stacking up on his closet shelf, he found an extracurricular he didn't just tolerate; it consumed his adolescence like the child prodigies he saw on *60 Minutes.*

White words rained up his screen like commands in the archaic MS-DOS. But it wasn't boot-up jargon. Each line transmitted an expert opinion, friendly banter, or the occasional swear-fueled feud that got members kicked out, though most of the time, it was temporary. Nearly seven hundred users were signed onto #mswarez at the moment. Warez was slang for pirated software. The year before, Roman pledged allegiance to the popular DAL Net Internet Relay Chat channel—a go-to for finding leaked builds of the latest versions of Microsoft Windows and other pricey software brands.

The final build of Whistler, later renamed Windows XP, leaked onto #mswarez around the same time Roman joined. He had no such luck finding it when he first tried a different channel, #winwarez. Its users didn't even catch wind of it until hours after the leak. So Roman became a regular on #mswarez while #winwarez was cast as the loathed rival.

Screw those guys, Roman thought each time he heard the competition's name.

Either way, this was all old news. It was almost the fall of 2002, and everyone had moved onto the mysterious codename Longhorn. A handful of screenshots of it have been released so far. Users hotly anticipated the drop of the first build, and the hundreds-strong #mswarez army was ready to turn a leak into a flood. Many would tinker with a build's functionalities, find new features, and share screenshots of their discoveries. Being first meant a lot of bragging rights on the channel, but for Roman, he believed it would prepare him for a start at Microsoft as a lowly beta tester. Then, perhaps, he could ascend to a software engineer—a distant Plan B if he never discovered a billion-dollar idea like Bill Gates.

The umbrella term for the evening's activity on #mswarez was hacking, though Roman despised the clichés that word connoted, so he substituted the term with "H-wording."

"Uh, it's not like the movies," he told his best friend, Todd Tovmasian, the one time he feigned interest during an uneventful lunch break. "It's not like I'm going to type in shit fast and break into the White House. We're not, uh, really messing with people's lives."

A smart guy on the streets and on paper, Todd, short for Tadeh, shot back a raised eyebrow that touched the base of his spiked tips.

"Okay, bro," he'd say.

On the channel, Roman went by the nickname JaYnus, inspired by a much earlier OS build. He added the middle Y to try to avoid the rectal jokes. Other than the nicknames, the community was faceless. Roman, aka JaYnus, never started drama on the channel and often helped people troubleshoot. He couldn't imagine a hard-earned A+ on an exam being more rewarding than aiding a fellow expert. Not that he was a regular for high marks, despite his thick horn-rimmed glasses.

This was how it would appear on #mswarez:

[21:42] (ShawnM01): is there a way to edit the registry of an OS that won't start?

[21:42] (JaYnus): edit the boot.ini. And you know what to do with the other boot. ;)

After a year of dedicated volunteering, Roman yearned to be knighted an operator. Having ops meant he would get an "@" before his username, which would allow him to kick people out if they started drama. For his age-to-tech-knowledge ratio, he felt he was long overdue.

Sure, relatives suggested applying to MIT, Caltech, or just a state school with a decent computer science program, but the prospect made his soul gag. After all, Bill Gates might not have been Bill Gates if he hadn't dropped out of Harvard. The same went for Steve Jobs and Reed. Both men, free and untamed, changed the world.

Roman slid his glasses up his nose. His bumpy bridge was getting greasy. He coveted the #mswarez promotion more than anything, unlike the blue belt in Taekwondo that he was never bestowed, and the youth basketball tournament his old team, the Blue Panthers, never won. He never exuded a competitive spirit in intramurals, and his parents eventually stopped forcing him to go. In return, Roman cheered his parents on from within as their "Go Rome!" chants from the sideline devolved into tepid claps.

He envisioned the operator badge tugging at his shirt pocket, a constant reminder of his hard-earned promotion. If he earned it, he wanted to vet the patrons, like a bouncer, even make them register on NickServ to make sure they knew their computers. Only complex queries would be entertained, not basic cries of "Help! My Internet doesn't work!"

But for now, Roman's crowning achievement was a two-and-a-half-foot-tall full tower looking down at the surface of his desk with contempt. He overclocked the Athlon processor to achieve a staggering 2.3 GHz. Naturally, things got pretty hot, so with the birthday and Christmas money he saved up, he bought an expensive VapoChill phase-changing cooling rig that blew frigid sub-zero freon gas at a copper heat sink covering the processor chip. A hand-carved crevasse sealed with plexiglass allowed for a peek inside. The vertical pit of fans and processors orchestrated a whizzing like the interior of a plane in taxi on the runway. To mask it, he wore DJ headphones and blasted tracks from System of a Down's latest release, *Steal This Album!*—a suggestion he took up three weeks before it came out. The only sucky thing about his setup was how he'd stub his right toe against the tower at least four times a week. It was a small price for a humbler beginning than that of Michael Dell, another college dropout at nineteen who founded Dell Computers out of his garage.

Roman clicked and typed the night away in the hunching position his elders feared would stunt his growth. But at just under six feet, he'd done well for someone with two years of puberty left to go. His immense afro accentuated his height. The sea of curly locks obscured his monitor to anyone standing behind him, especially advantageous for a teenage boy. His backpack leaned against a small strip of wall between his closet and bedroom door and was to remain untouched the whole weekend.

The corded phone rang in his room, and he kept still, assuming it was for his mom, but he sighed and hung his head the moment he saw her reflection in a black, textless corner of his monitor.

Crap, he thought.

He swiveled around and lowered his headphones. Audrey, the cordless in her hand, was wearing pink muumuu pajamas. Her tone seamlessly shifted from intrigued to authoritarian.

"It's for you. It's a girl," she said. "And bring all of those cups downstairs."

Audrey had French roots, but it was Roman's dad who was a full-blooded French-speaking Montrealer. He stared his mom down until she backed out of his room. He swiveled back and picked up the phone.

"Oh my God, I'm so glad you're home right now," a girl said. "I know this is weird, but I got your number from Todd. He said you'd 'hundred percent' be able to help."

"Uh," Roman said. "Who's this?"

Another of his noticeable features was a deep speaking voice that put him ahead of the whistling cracks of most of his male classmates.

"Melineh," the girl said. "Shanazarian. You know, from Armistead's class?"

Roman remembered a girl who always wore sweats: a hoodie sweater over a sweater and bottomed with sweatpants, which made it hard to tell if she'd developed at all, so the gender difference didn't faze Roman much yet.

"Uh, yeah, I know you," Roman said as he offered up a Photoshop key to earn some return favors on the channel. "Your desk is close to the overhead, I think."

"So, until today, I was the overhead girl?" Melineh asked, then chuckled a bit.

Roman shut his eyes for a moment and exhaled as he mentally cursed Todd.

"Sorry," Roman said.

"That's okay," Melineh said. "I only knew you as the guy with the big hair. Didn't know you were a computer genius too."

"Uh, there's a big brain under the hair."

She giggled at the one joke he knew because his mom told it to relatives all the time to mask her hatred of Roman's slovenly do.

Melineh had a cute laugh, making it harder for Roman to get

this over with. He didn't even want to try to flirt. His life's work was more important. But the brain housing that mentality betrayed him and weaved a fantasy of Melineh whispering into his ear on a cooled bed. His daydreams of simply cupping boobs sure had matured.

Not now, though. Later.

Roman sought to make his tech support as bullet-point as possible.

"What's your problem?" he uttered. "I mean, uh, what's giving you trouble?"

"I don't know what happened, but my Internet stopped working and I need to get directions to my friend's party off MapQuest," Melineh said.

Roman's brain sighed at the only problem common folk ever bothered him about. Regardless, he readied to tap his mental troubleshooting guide to bring a quick end to this phone call.

"Since you're getting a DNS error, you have to check and see if the DHCP is enabled," Roman said.

"Huh?" she said. "What's that?"

"I mean, uh, I'll explain real quick."

Melineh wasn't the first girl to call him for help. Neither was it the first time Todd gave out Roman's number, much to his dismay. With a brief walkthrough, problem solved. She launched her America Online Instant Messenger, and Roman heard the dings of incoming communiqué over the phone.

Then things got weirder. Melineh wasn't saying goodbye. Roman clicked a pen, put it down, rubbed the back of his head, then picked the pen up again and clicked it some more. He dreaded having to take initiative, but he feared Todd busting his balls for not trying. Thing was, Roman couldn't think of anything to say; the blanks were real. The same Mother Nature that bombarded him with raging hormones had ground him to a mute halt. Roman swiveled away from the computer to better focus on finding something to talk about.

"So, are you going to the party?" Melineh asked out of the blue.

"Uh," Roman said, deciding to go with the first topic that came to mind. "Did you finish the study packet?"

Melineh chuckled. "No way! Mr. Armistead just gave it to us."

"Uh, same. I haven't started yet, either. Asymptotes are pretty tough."

But she didn't toss an agreeable lifebuoy. Roman, now aware of the pause, was certain Melineh had taken notice even earlier. He tried to think of something else to talk about.

"Well, thanks for helping me!" Melineh said.

"No problem," Roman said without hesitation.

"See ya!"

"Uh . . . See ya."

Roman beeped the phone off and slammed it onto its charging base. Sure, he had his silence back, but what a step backward. The last girl who called spent fifteen minutes talking with Roman about how she liked to customize her In-N-Out orders, though they never spoke again after they locked gazes in person and he jerked his eyes away without saying hello. Gone forever. It didn't matter. He was fine without a love life for now. But still, any progress negation was worse than botching a first attempt.

Breaking news: Roman was a virgin.

At least he had a lot of important work to do. Headphones back on.

[22:29] (Slam201): whats a bios lock?.. does it ask for a password or some shit on startup?

[22:29] (JaYnus): yeah, if you install it on a non-dell system

While Roman fielded questions like a press deputy, other channel surfers waited for the latest crack of Windows XP Plus to be leaked. A crack was a small third-party app that hacked premium software so it could be spread for free—the ideal teen price.

The member count on #mswarez ballooned to 983 as the night and hype progressed.

[23:16] (@Zodex01): what's with the lag? the crack was announced hours ago and still nothin. Does it ever take dis long?

[23:16] (Panga manga): take a sharpie and write winXPP on your butt and send to people as a crack.

Roman leaned in even more, regretting that he didn't pop in some Totino's pizza rolls earlier.

Oh wow, he just said that to an operator.

[23:16] *** Panga manga was kicked by @Zodex01 (banned: [flaming, drama])

Being kicked out applied to a username, not an IP address, so making a new one was the only handstamp required for re-entry. A kick served as more of a warning. Most usually came back and behaved themselves. You didn't want to be a hated guy on #mswarez and kiss any potential trades goodbye.

The head ops was the creator of #mswarez, Harry Link. Rumor had it he was *so* proud of his creation that he went by his real name. Other than letting people mooch advice, Roman had no idea how else to get ops. There were already fourteen of them.

Why not fifteen to nicely round things out? He'd often vent in all caps in a private chat box with a user named Betamaxer.

[22:56] (JaYnus): WHO GIVES A CRAP IF I HAVEN'T LEAKED ANYTHING?

[22:56] (Betamaxer): apparently people do lol

[22:56] (JaYnus): Do you know how hard that is? Sorry I don't have an in at Microsoft. You know how many people I've helped for nothing? Even when something leaks and it's out in the open, everyone comes to me asking for copies.

[22:56] (Betamaxer): Then start your own damn channel dude.

[22:56] (JaYnus): ha, yeah right

[22:56] (Betamaxer): i'll even join. I'm sure we can get a couple more people to come too

[22:56] (JaYnus): i dont wanna compete with Harry.

[22:56] (Betamaxer): someones got their head up their ass. you never will.

[22:57] (JaYnus): gee thanks.

[22:57] (Betamaxer): see, if someone talks to you like that on your own channel, you can kick them the hell out

[22:57] (JaYnus): Ok am i trying to invite a handful of people just to kick them out?

[22:57] (Betamaxer): whatever you wanna do. At least you can set the topics, talk about anything, keep out the noobs.

Roman started to think his own channel might be a pleasant diversion from all the hands-on projects of late that drained his birthday and leftover lunch money he stored in a shoebox in his closet.

Fresh off the sting of another awkward encounter with a girl, Roman countered with a few clicks and keystrokes to give birth to a virtual gathering place, one that could last for years or generations! Of course, he'd have to start small, first by inviting his closest #mswarez friends to join. It might have been meaningless to make oneself the head ops of a barren channel, but to see what it was like to have the "@" symbol next to his username, to be on the same level as Harry Link, might have been worthwhile. After birthing his channel, Roman stretched, yawned, and cracked his knees.

Over the weekend, he'd occasionally spot the blurred reflection of his parents and their shaking heads in his monitor as they passed by. Come Sunday night, Roman had to abide by the strictly enforced out-by-10:00-p.m. rule, but as a workaround, he dimmed his monitor, shut his bedroom door, and turned off the lights. A sacrifice he had to make was forgoing music so he could hear his parents when they left their bedroom for one reason or another.

Roman decided to call his channel #xwarez. So cool. He crossed his fingers and hoped that no one would think it was dedicated to porn.

Whatever. As long as I surpass #winwarez in every way. Screw those guys.

Roman tried recruiting knowledgeable members from #mswarez. He reasoned there was nothing wrong with carving out a clique from an established group of friends. Finally, with an even fifty members, Roman sensed he was ready to set the topic.

[23:11] (JaYnus): So, any predictions on what build 3683 will be like?
[23:11] (Samzar): Well, let me tell you what I think
[23:11] (Samzar): first,

The conversation stalled there. Everything went black—the screen and his room. Roman blinked slowly three times to make sure it wasn't his less-than-reputable vision.

It had to be a power outage, but when he looked out the window, he was puzzled by neighbors who still had their lights on. He hopped up to check on the rest of the house. A small crack of hallway light from beneath his parents' bedroom door perplexed him even further.

Then Audrey opened the door.

"So, you *were* awake?" she said. "You think I'm stupid? Well, good thing I finally noticed the fuse box is in our bedroom."

"I—I just had to go to the bathroom," Roman said.

"Just stop."

"Come on! This isn't fair! I paid for all this stuff."

"You mean your birthday and Christmas money? And the lunch money *we* gave you that you barely spend? No wonder you're all bones!"

Roman's father, Felix, in full wife-beater, Adidas shorts, and slippers, stepped into view and gave Audrey a high-five.

"Tu vois?" Felix asked his wife in a thick French accent. "Told you it would work."

"Get your act together," Audrey said as she closed her bedroom door. "Or your room is going to experience a lot of rolling blackouts."

Roman usually nodded off as the school bus scraped up the hill toward Herbert Lowell Wright Magnet High School. But this morning, panic shrank his lungs as he tried to steady papers on his lap in order to scribble clumsily deduced answers. For a boost of energy, he rode the surge of pride from signing up more than fifty people to #xwarez. The fond look back, however, was swapped for the latest threat from his parents. He stared at an assembly line of single-family homes out the window.

So, they can shut off my power at any time? This had to happen now? When I've got a channel to manage?

A big speed bump he should have known was coming threw his writing hand off the page, leaving behind a jagged skid mark.

Crap!

Roman focused on his pen and thought of other writing and drawing instruments, like a Photoshop brush—oh, how a few such strokes could solve everything. But he shook his head at the absurd idea.

Change of plans: he'd BS the rest of his work after meeting up with his friends on more stable ground.

An oval convoy of school buses finagled around the drop-off lane near a flagpole at half-mast. Roman hopped off and was welcomed by a sunny, blue, yet deceiving SoCal sky in the La Vista foothills, just north of Glendale. The piercing chill made him roll down his sweater sleeves. Fellow male classmates with hairless arms did the same while synchronizing an "ah, shit" as they were bruised by a pinching gust. Most girls knew better and wore their sleeves unfurled that morning. But in September, the early cold in Los Angeles County rarely lingered.

The torsos of the students bottlenecking through the school's teal entrance doors sported collared shirts, while their lower halves were nothing but khakis. Per school policy, jeans were prohibited. Roman took the rear entrance underneath a bricked alcove with teal-tinted windows above. He walked past the outdoor cafeteria with its concrete tables and neared the monolithic steps of the amphitheater.

Wright Magnet opened four years ago as an academic stirring pot of South Koreans, Armenians, Filipinos, and Hispanics. Roman was the only Quebecois import, as far as he knew. The "magnet" part of the school's name attracted thousands of applications every year from gloat-seeking parents. A random lottery system handpicked each freshman class. The academic requirement for admission was a joke, though. A prospective student only needed a 2.0 GPA. But Roman didn't care about any of Wright Magnet's selling points; he just wanted to go where his friends went.

Past a few students Roman didn't know by name, he came across the guy who always walked around with headphones and a CD player stretching the seams of his back pocket and, eventually, Melineh, who cradled a binder as she walked and talked with a friend. She hinted a smile at Roman, but memories of the awkward phone call crossed wires in his head and forced his line of sight the other way as they passed each other by. And that was that.

Relief that he didn't have to say anything flowed through him.

Then, a slap on the shoulder and the ensuing recoil revealed a cheery Alex Ter Alaverdian, who encroached on another chubby phase. His eager grin almost formed a perfect circle with his semi-unibrow—his most Armenian trait.

Roman had a few inches on his friend, one of the few he followed from middle school, where they met in eighth-grade history and bonded over sixteen-bit game talk.

"Thanks again for telling me how to fix the BIOS!" Alex said, referring to the critical component for running the PlayStation emulator, ePSXe. "You're really good at walking people through shit over the phone."

"No prob," Roman said.

"I'm already fifteen hours into *Chrono Cross*, not sure yet if it's better than *Chrono Trigger*, though. The soundtrack will be *super* tough to beat. Have you played it?"

"Uh, not yet."

Roman didn't play video games much anymore, but what was he going to do? Look for new friends at sixteen? He secretly severed all ties with modern gaming to focus his free time on #mswarez and now #xwarez.

"Well, it's freaking awesome!" Alex said, interrupting. "Especially if you've been out of the RPG scene. It's a good transition back or even an entry point into the genre, just like *Chrono Trigger*."

Roman nodded politely.

"You should be like one of those tech-support guys when you

grow up, the ones that help you with stuff over the phone," Alex continued.

Before Roman could retort with a verbal backhand because he knew he was skilled eons beyond some minimum-wage, script-reading dullard, he swung his backpack around and started pulling out his math homework. They approached the usual morning spot where Todd Tovmasian and his spiked tips waited with his backpack straps united at the center of his chest by interlocked fingers until it was time to exchange low-fives.

Roman sat on a stone bench, hoping the four minutes before the bell rang were enough time to finish everything.

"So, guess what?" Alex asked Todd.

"What now, bro?" Todd asked. He had a raspy voice, like a longtime smoker.

"I asked Melineh if she wanted to go mini-golfing this weekend. You know, that castle place in Sherman Oaks. After I told her I liked her."

Roman's ears perked up. Was it the same Melineh who called him the other night?

"Oh God, bro," Todd said as he winced.

"What's wrong?" Alex said.

"Nothing. Keep going."

"So, anyway, I asked her when we were talking on AIM."

"Oh *God*, bro."

"She said she couldn't go. But get this—she said she was sorry. I never even get a sorry."

"Bro, come on. You gotta stop sounding so desperate."

"What? How am I desperate? I'm approaching girls like the way you told me to."

"Not like a creep and confessing your love or whatever out of the blue. That's not what confidence is, bro."

"At least I'm getting them talking, and Melineh was nice. Someone else will be even nicer."

Roman's sense of hearing sharpened. He heard everyone's footsteps, then the isolated laughter from an adjacent group of Korean chicks.

"Just ease up a bit," Todd told Alex.

"Well, what else do you want me to do?" Alex asked, exchanging glances with both friends. "You guys rarely wanna hang out anymore. What kind of crew are we?"

Todd facepalmed.

"Oh, Jesus Christ, bro," he muttered.

A brood of burly dudes and their chatter of stick-shift cars and barbs questioning one another's straightness approached.

"Perfect timing!" Alex proclaimed and started running his fingertips together like a cartoonish miser. "So, Sako, where's my quarter?"

The group, all members sporting brand names and varying degrees of gel globs on their scalps, halted. Sako had lips that stuck out, a shiny, shaved head, and a thin, precise goatee. At first glance, he looked fat, but his stomach was rigid and never jiggled.

"Man," he thundered, "it's just a quarter!"

The air fell silent.

"I needed twenty-five cents to buy a freaking Powerade, and this guy was just there, so I asked him," Sako continued. "Two goddamn weeks ago!"

Everyone laughed at the measly debt, which snuffed out the last bits of concentration Roman had left to get his work done. Todd just smirked. Sako started walking away with his herd, but he whipped himself back for a brief moment and pointed at Todd.

"Four on four at four at the Y?" he said.

Todd nodded faintly.

"If you're short on cash, I can spot you," Todd told Alex after Sako walked away.

"I'm good, thanks," Alex said, shaking his head. "Why do you hang out with that guy anyway?"

"Bro, I'm trying to help you and that's all you care about?" Todd asked. "We just play b-ball sometimes."

By this point, the commotion was beyond too much for Roman.

"What about you?" Todd asked him. "You need help with that?"

"Do your thing, Mr. 4.2 GPA Photographic Memory," Alex said.

"Bro, why do you have to go there?" Todd asked with a lamenting tone.

"What? I'm just confirming that you're the best guy to help him."

Roman had tuned out. But instead of slipping into a fantasy of owning a futuristic cabin in the woods, he imagined himself seated at his computer, forging the document he knew would get his parents off his back. One didn't become a computer genius without knowing a thing or two about fabricating believable images.

Yet once again, he shook his head at such a thought.

"I gotta bounce," Roman told his friends. He shoved his math book into his backpack, rolled up his work, and shoved it under his armpit.

"Oh, okay," Alex said. "See ya! And remember! Spicy chicken sandwiches at lunch today!"

"Yes, we know," Todd said. "Just like every freaking Monday, bro."

Roman entered the main brick building and slid into a boys' bathroom. He dropped his backpack to the floor, scanned for a dry plot of tiles on which to settle, and tried to get back to work.

Todd peeked in moments later. He tilted his head back and pursed his lips. Roman called this look "the Chin."

"Wow," Todd said. "I've never seen you this desperate to do your work. Everything alright?"

"Yeah," Roman said as he flipped a page and imagined a nightmarish snapshot of his bedroom empty like a jail cell.

"Let me guess, all that forum shit ate up your free time? I don't know how you nerds can talk about computer shit all day."

"All night, too. And there's more to it than that."

"Amazing. I'll stick to shooting terrorists online and porn, thanks." Todd chuckled at his own joke. "What are you working on?"

"Graphing asymptotes. Don't think it's gonna be that hard."

"Not that hard, huh?"

Todd, too, dropped his backpack and sat next to Roman. Their friendship grew within standardized walls like these, not at parks or on bicycles. They lived on opposite ends of town, and hanging out often meant begging for a ride from parents fatigued after a long day at work. That was a Los Angeles adolescence.

"First off, you moron, you're *finding* the asymptote and you're *graphing* a rational function," Todd said.

"Crap," Roman said as he stifled his handwriting.

A kid stepped out of a bathroom stall, rinsed his hands, and left. Todd slanted himself and peered at the papers pressed against Roman's lap.

"Lemme help," Todd said.

"I'm good," Roman said. "You're gonna be late."

"I still owe you for that hard drive. My folks would have been pissed if they had to buy another one."

"I've got a bunch more in case, uh, you know, you decide to download more corrupted stuff off BearShare."

"Shut up, you lazy Frenchie."

Roman had no interest in a comeback.

"Fine," Todd said.

A friend's resignation was the hardest earned.

"By the way, did Melineh call you?" Todd asked. "Did you guys talk?"

Roman froze up and stared at the wall tiles.

"Come on, bro," Todd said. "You gotta give me something."

"Just helped her get her Internet set up," Roman said.

"That's it? You didn't get her number?"

"Why did you give her mine? Didn't you know that, uh, Alex liked her? I-I don't want any drama."

"What? Bro, I had no idea he liked her. He has a new crush every week."

Roman flipped the study packet over to the third page. "Don't worry about me."

Todd sighed as he pushed himself up from the bathroom floor. "You think the school would give us a day off on the one-year anniversary of the attacks."

Roman stayed focused on his lap papers.

"Fine, bro. I don't have time to argue," Todd said as he got up and tossed on his backpack. "I'll see you later."

"Later," Roman replied as his friend left the bathroom.

Roman started thinking about free will, how if anyone wanted to, they could go out into the streets to pillage. But those crimes were loud.

Despite having ditched professional wrestling as well in favor of computers, one of his favorite Photoshop pieces entailed inserting himself into a group photo of World Championship Wrestling's Wolfpac a few years ago: Kevin Nash, Scott Hall, the Macho Man, and Lex Luger. Roman masterfully heal-brushed himself over Sting, who he strongly believed had no business being a member and was always meant to fly solo. Roman took a dumb raised-eyebrow picture of himself in the bathroom and layered his head over Sting's, who stood next to Macho Man as they cheered their fists like beer steins, their biceps bursting.

Do it, brother! Roman, the wrestler, shouted. He had done everything except give himself a ringside name. *You know you've got this! Fake those grades! Fake them!*

And snap into a Slim Jim! Macho Man shouted. *Oh yeeeeeeeeah!*

Sheriff Vallancourt clomped around the Podunk town of Warezville on his patrol horse, Blackcomb, to ensure all was fine and dandy. Past the general store, he reined in his steed to get a peek inside. An old shopkeeper filled a bag with toffees for a young mother and her son.

Move along.

Sheriff Vallancourt and Blackcomb then came upon another humble structure.

Ah, the local schoolhouse. The kids must be getting out for the day.

The youngsters, their textbooks wrapped by little belts, poured onto the front steps of the red wooden schoolhouse. Unexpectedly, they stopped and dropped their books. In unison, they pointed their index fingers at the sheriff and started screaming.

"It's out! It's out!" they yelled.

Roman snapped back to his reality of a pair of purple Lakers shorts with the team's logo fading and the upward-racing text of his channel.

[16:04] (Betamaxer): It's out! 3683 has been leaked!
[16:04] (JaYnus): really? where?
[16:04] (dissomator): how the hell do we know before you?

Someone finally got their hands on the first build of Windows Longhorn. Roman opened another browser window to get into #mswarez, which had exploded to more than 2,200 online users. The chat text was scrolling so fast he couldn't spot a download link. He leaned in and squinted until he found one that worked and downloaded the beta.

Man, someone's gotta do a better job of organizing these download links, maybe on a website for #mswarez or something.

Roman snapped his fingers.

Aha! Another project!

He envisioned a polished website, an online database with meticulously aligned indices and immortal download links. First, #mswarez could get the suit-and-tie treatment, something so professional that word of mouth would land him some wealthy clients. Roman was willing to make peace with being a top-tier website developer if things came down to it. Easy six figures by his early twenties, he assumed. Not bad. Even if it took a few more years, he was determined to show his folks he wasn't wasting his time.

But for now, he crossed back over to his channel. His earlobes burned with confidence—363 members! Then 364! Some of the new members were even familiar handles from #mswarez. They were just like him; they loved real beta talk. These were quality additions, not just people begging for handouts.

[16:07] (NeOnE17): all these people here and none of you assholes have a working link anymore?

Roman spoke too soon, but being the founder of his channel, he took it upon himself to key and click a shareable download link into existence. Word on the cyber street must have traveled at light speed as a violent uptick of 112 users rushed into #xwarez. Roman would have dropped dead if he had to face down that many people in real life, but in this virtual case, he had never felt more alive. Sweat slathered his mouse, so he unclenched it and wiped his hand on his shorts. The initial reviews started pouring in.

[16:10] (moose&squirrel): Oh my god, the plex theme! What shade of blue is that?

[16:10] (teknojunky): it's about time! they were getting too family and wholesome with the color scheme, needed a futuristic look

[16:10] (dissomator): r u idiots kidding!?!?! i got dragged away from diablo 2 for windows with a new color?

Roman ran the latest build so he could pen his own critique. First to grab his attention was the new logo: a bull's skull with "Longhorn" written in what reminded him of an old-timey Western font. The photo album icon did a little dance, bouncing from side to side. It was intriguing, but he played it cool for appearances' sake.

[16:17] (JaYnus): yeah it's interesting, but i don't see how they're gonna keep it in the final version, there might be some rendering errors.

[16:17] (dissomator): shit, you're right.

[16:17] (moose&squirrel): yeah, how did I not see that

Roman clinked his imaginary champagne flute and adjusted his monocle.

Yes, Nigel. Quite.

The user count exploded—875! Alarms clangored in Roman's head; things had escalated to a break-the-glass-in-case-of-emergency scenario. Who knew if he'd ever see numbers like this again? Perhaps the best chance at winning operatorship from Harry was for Roman to show off his channel and propose a buyout so #mswarez could absorb #xwarez's membership base.

Roman shoved a finger in his itchy ear and ogled the blazing text. He decided the time was nigh to send Harry a private message, even though he was probably busy with his own channel. Roman opened a private message box and penned the most important message of his Internet Relay Chat career.

[16:29] (JaYnus): Hi, Harry! Would you like to have ops on my channel?

Roman smacked the enter key. He crossed his fingers and toes in hopes of getting an operator position in return. After all, favors between men of culture in this arena rarely went unreturned.

There was no immediate response, but Roman was okay with that. He warmed his palms with his breath. This was what life was all about—carving out one's own path, he mused. Nothing else mattered. Such was the case until he got a message. The potential weight made Roman lightheaded, but it was just a commoner.

(Betamaxer): Hey.
(Betamaxer): I finally got it. Wanna see?

The wrong person at the wrong time is the worst combination for an introvert, but at least the user emailed Roman a picture of himself hoisting an object the length of a cheese grater that was of great interest.

The young man with blonde Nordic bangs dangling down his forehead posed with a GeForce4 TI 4600 video card. With a fan right in the middle for cooling, it was highly sought after by PC gaming enthusiasts. Since a relevant discussion would be effort-less, Roman's mood perked up.

[19:02] (JaYnus): Damn, I was hoping you'd pull out the Voodoo3 3000

[19:02] (betamaxer): Pssh, I wish. The idiots making it can't figure out how to do it for cheap. We're never going to see it.

[19:02] (JaYnus): Yeah. It's stupid they got that far in development without thinking about it.

[19:02] (betamaxer): btw did you turn in mendoza's assignment?

Ms. Mendoza was their Spanish teacher and betamaxer, aka Jared Olson, was the only user Roman knew in real life. Roman, indeed, had forgotten about the conjugation assign-ment until now. Other than its champion robotics team, the only other way the school started living up to its name was by allowing students to turn in homework online for some classes. However, it didn't really improve Roman's odds of turning it in on time.

[19:03] (JaYnus): not yet. we got until midnight

[19:03] (betamaxer): yeah but remember how last time the web-site glitched?

[19:03] (JaYnus): but she still gave us credit at the end.

[19:03] (betamaxer): but what a potential loophole right? don't have much of a selling point at that point as a magnet school.

Roman wanted to share a virtual laugh with his friend, but instead, his synapses started firing at ludicrous speeds. Roman yawned and popped his ears. Then he cracked his knuckles, his left kneecap, his sense of ambition, then his patience in trying to become an operator. His eyelids receded, stretched by dumbfoundedness because he had never taken such loopholes so seriously. The verb that describes it: H-wording. It came with so many clichés that repelled Roman from ever bothering. But he also knew that building computers at home would only get him so far; it was a capped skill. Manipulating code, on the other hand, bending the will of pixels came with endless possibilities. If he mastered H-wording, maybe he could become a cybersecurity prodigy like his unofficial idol, Kevin Mitnick, one of the first famous H-worders who did just that. If Roman couldn't shake anything from the billion-dollar idea tree, if the last of the tech prodigies had already risen, he could make peace with being the best in an existing profession. Roman was confident that cybersecurity or coding was harder than hardware, so he would be paid handsomely for his protective services. At that point, why ever set foot in a classroom again? The world, in his view, ran on dropouts. The prospect almost aroused him. But even equipped with the bare bones basics about H-wording, mainly just testing for his own security levels, Roman knew his best chances would require an on-campus attempt.

"It's past seven and you haven't opened any of your books yet," Audrey said.

Roman twitched himself around to see his mother standing in the doorway again, this time showcasing her creepy, upside-down smile, which Roman called "angry teeth." She was a different mother at the moment, one who swapped shifts with a tender, macaroon-baking matriarch.

"I'll, I'll get to it in a sec," Roman replied.

"This is the only thing you have to do," Audrey continued. "You don't have to go to work. You don't have to clean the house. You don't do laundry. Do you think with marks like these you'll get into a good college? Do you think this lazy way of life will prepare you to take care of yourself when you move out? My *God*, you wouldn't last."

It couldn't have been a worse time for this spiel again, but Roman knew to just stay quiet and nod to prevent a futile debate. He turned his head toward his monitor in shame, mostly to keep up the act.

"You're going to be a loser," Audrey continued.

Roman had never heard his mom call him that before.

"What's so important that you do on your computer that it takes up all your time?" Audrey asked. "I know you're intelligent, but I've always told you: everything in moderation. You are addicted! Are you playing all those shooting games? Is that what you're doing? Are you going to shoot people at your school? Because you're so quiet? You want revenge like those kids we hear about in the news?"

"What?" Roman said, waving his hands in denial and shaking his head. "No! No! Of course not!"

Even Audrey seemed to think she went too far with that accusation and cleared her throat, then straightened her house sweater. With her being in the wrong, Roman was ready to capitalize with an argument, a thesis he never knew he was working on, about how his parents never even asked what he was up to and how nothing made him feel more alive.

"Your computer is supposed to help you with schoolwork, but you abuse it," Audrey started again. "Then you go and waste all of your gift money on this other computer junk. How about saving for a car when you finally get your driver's license?"

"Uh, it's not junk."

"Then what is it?"

"It's . . . It's . . . It's what I want to do."

Audrey's shoulders sank and she wore a look of disbelief. "You sound like a little kid."

"I mean, for life. Uh, for a living. It's not like video games."

Audrey snorted and rolled her eyes. "The way you're treating them, yes, they are. You don't know what balance is yet, but you're too old for us to punish you like a child. I'm serious this time. This is your last chance. If you don't get at least a 3.0 on your semester report card, we're clearing out your room!"

She tossed a piece of paper that was crinkled in her fist onto her son's desk before slamming the door behind her.

Roman got up for a second and saw his twelve-year-old brother Leon peeking from his room, his less impressive yet still blossoming schnoz resting over the side of his door.

"What did you do?" Leon asked meekly.

Roman threw his arms up like an attacking bear and jumped toward his little brother. "Shut the hell up!"

Leon, likely the only person who viewed the human twig Roman as a threat, obliged and slammed his door shut. Back on his chair, Roman saw a few more messages on his computer from Jared before he had logged off and when Audrey had interrupted.

[19:06] (betamaxer): like grades. You ever think about that?

[19:06] (betamaxer): you ever think about that?

[19:06] (betamaxer): imagine if we could mess with that shit, oh man.

[19:08] (betamaxer): hello, you there?

[19:09] (betamaxer): fine, see you later. happy jerking.

Roman noticed his reflection in the closet mirror. Then he picked up the piece of paper his mom chucked onto his desk. It was his quarterly report card that bore a 2.68 GPA. Despite possessing the necessary Photoshop skills, they were useless if he didn't have the key to the mailbox. So maybe a flight through the clouds was the last remaining battle plan.

Roman knew he wasn't intellectually disabled. If anything, he was convinced he was getting a jump-start on internships and apprenticeships—hell, in Third World countries, he'd already have a tech job, at least according to Alex. After all, Roman had installed Linux by himself in the seventh grade, then taught himself HTML and designed his first website the year after. Roman even knew the basics of how to H-word, simple key commands such as port-scanning and the like. They were nice and legal and often used as protective measures to ensure ports were secured.

Where was a better place to start than at his school? He couldn't believe he hadn't thought of this before. His attention switched to the dystopian ruins of old computer towers and monitors in the corner of his room. He mentally salivated at the prospect of remote grade editing and how much his room had in common with Michael Dell's old garage. He was surprised at the lack of hesitation. It must have been slain by the prospect of keeping his parents in the dark.

They don't care about anything I like! I have every right to cheat like this! I'll show them one day that I'm not wasting time!

Forget operatorhood. Succeeding in H-wording had so many real-world applications. It was the first time he was seeing the long term. H-wording would fit in somewhere on his résumé.

Having said that, he got a new message alert.

It was Harry.

This has to be it! Roman thought as he perfected his posture in one fell spasm. *He's gonna tell me how cool my channel is and make me an operator in return on #mswarez!*

He was so excited that he was already thinking of business card designs. The experience he'd acquire from being an operator surely would also be résumé-worthy. How else did the best and brightest of Silicon Valley get their jobs? Performing well on standardized tests? Roman saw no point in accomplishing the same thing as every other good student. He opened the message.

[00:12] (HarryLink) sure, thanks

That's it? God freaking dammit!

Roman shot up with rage, tempted to flip his keyboard over, but resisted after picturing his mom storming in again. After a deep, Zen-like breath and likening himself to Lakers head coach Phil Jackson, he sat back down. He let out a deep breath, and like most boys of his demographic when they were frustrated, his hands defaulted toward his pelvis so he could slip off his shorts. Roman clicked through several folders to get to his collection of incriminating .mpegs and .avis, hoping Jenna Jameson could sweep him away from all of this.

But who could think of such smut at a time like this? So many movies and TV shows romanticized H-wording, the click-clacks of a keyboard followed by a cheesy line like "I'm in." Before Roman knew it, he was marching toward his dad's office, roiling with excitement and drumming fists. When he peeked in, he was greeted by Felix's graying horseshoe. He was the third of his name, but chose to end the line with himself because he didn't want his son to be known as Felix the Quatre.

"Can I borrow your laptop tomorrow?" Roman asked. "Uh, it's for a school project. PowerPoint stuff. You know."

It was the first time he had made such a request, but he deemed it reasonable in exchange for in-house tech support and shifts as the designated toilet unclogger. Roman was a bit giddy at the chance of breaching an institution, a government one at that. Maybe H-worders were stereotyped in fiction for a reason.

"Only if you renew and update my antivirus," Felix said as he scribbled something down with a burgundy Montblanc pen. "And I mean before you give it back to me. Not when it expires and I have a gap in coverage."

Partially off the clock, he was again wearing a wife-beater, shorts, and horn-rimmed glasses like his son's.

"You got it," Roman said.

His mom must have been stalking him because she was waiting for him just outside.

"I'm gonna get started, I'm gonna get started," Roman told her. "I just need to call Todd."

She clung to a death stare for a few moments before looking toward the kitchen and walking past him without saying a word.

He had two months until the end of the semester. As he walked back to his room, Roman realized he couldn't just bring his dad's laptop to school to try to get on the school's intranet; he'd seen teachers and administrators confiscate cell phones. It had to be an after-hours thing, and since Roman had already failed his driving test twice, there was only one person he trusted to deliver him to campus after hours.

Back in his room, he picked up his phone and dialed. A motherly voice answered.

"Uh, hi, Mrs. Tovmasian," Roman said. "Is Todd home?"

"Is it really you, bro?" Todd said after being put on the line.

"Uh, yeah," Roman said.

"AIM down or something? Can't remember the last time you called. Everything alright?"

"Everything's good. Just wanted to see if you wanted to kick it on Friday or something."

"This friggin' guy. Were you visited by three ghosts last night? Or did the doctor diagnose you with AIDS and you've got a few months to live?"

"Uh, maybe a sleepover?"

"Wow, been a while since we did one of those. I'd hundred-percent be down, but I think I'm gonna be hanging with Lucy and a couple other friends that night."

"Oh." Roman paused and, frustratingly, took in the immediate hitch in his plan. "Okay. You're, uh, still trying to make that work?"

"'Still,' bro?"

"Uh, sorry. I meant good luck. I guess another time."

"Thanks, bro. And you forgot that the weekend also includes a Saturday. I'm down to hang then. Jesus Christ, bro. Without even realizing it, you try to get out of your own plans to spend time with humans."

4

"Are you gonna eat that?" Alex asked. "I'm not trying to be a fat ass and score some free food, but we're gonna be late for the movie."

Roman, from a daydream about his after-hours plan, warped back to the present, where he was holding an In-N-Out burger. "I will. Just not that hungry."

"Why else do you think he's so freakin' skinny?" Todd asked.

Roman dropped the half-eaten burger onto a red tray. Alex sat alone on one side of the booth and had already downed a double-double and a hamburger. Now, he was scraping the bottom of his tray of animal-style fries with a plastic fork. Alex wasn't invited, but Todd pulled a third-wheel move. Roman maligned the last-minute additions of people, but at least Alex was familiar and required no icebreakers.

Roman kept glancing outside at Todd's dad's old Audi. Roman had stuffed a duffel bag with an extra pair of socks, underwear, and Felix's laptop wrapped in sweaters in the trunk.

Todd yanked a tomato slice out of his protein burger wrapped in lettuce.

"I told them no freaking tomatoes."

"Really? Why?" Alex asked.

"They're gross in a sandwich. Too acidic."

"Well, I think having anything extra on that excuse of a burger you're eating is a plus."

"Gotta stay healthy, even when I'm eating unhealthy."

"Well, look who's an Olympic coach now that he's skinny."

Todd smirked. "While we're on the topic, how do you guys feel about hitting the gym after we wake up tomorrow?"

"Sounds fun, but I've got a family thing," Alex said. He and Roman looked at each other like they were on the same silent page.

"Pussies," Todd muttered before taking another bite.

"You know," Alex said, "I'd agree with you about the tomatoes if we were at one of those diners where they serve everything big, but In-N-Out always cuts them pretty thin."

Meat juice from his burger wrapper had leaked onto his wrist, so he licked it off.

Todd scoffed. "Okay, bro."

Alex threw down his fork and leaned back to stretch his arms over his seat. "This is awesome."

"What is?" Todd asked.

"I mean, the three of us, out together like this again. We don't do this enough."

"Why do you have to say it like that? You make it sound gay."

"Okay, fine," Alex said before turning to Roman. "I'm so miserable that you came, you piece of shit."

Roman, mulling a monsoon of hypotheticals about whether his plan would work, delayed responding with a half-hearted chuckle. He inspected the scenery, forgetting clocks weren't part of an In-N-Out's interior decor.

"Yes, Rome, they're called people," Todd said sarcastically.

Alex spoke with his mouth full of the last bite of his burger. "And *we're* going to be *people* who miss the first kill scene if you slowpokes don't hurry up and eat."

They headed to an eight o'clock screening of *Red Dragon*, the third installment of the Hannibal Lecter series, at the United Artists Theaters, a breezy five-minute drive from Wright Magnet, the venue for Roman's own feature presentation. They bought tickets to see *The Transporter*, rated PG-13, but ducked into the screening of the R-rated thriller. Alex was giddy and red when they took their seats.

"Relax, bro," Todd whispered to him. "Don't draw attention."

By the time the movie ended and they had left the theater, mild fog crowned streetlights with imperfect halos. Scattered clouds were purple in the night sky. The stable heat of a SoCal summer was long gone, but the boys needed nothing more than the light jackets they were already wearing. Todd and Alex had shoved their hands into their jacket pockets as they walked toward the parking lot while Roman hunched—surely unrelated to his nightly up-close screen stare-downs.

"I wished the movie was gorier than *Hannibal*," Alex said. "You got to see brains and shit in that one."

"You actually want to see *more* blood and guts?" Todd asked.

"Well, yeah, that's the whole point of a movie like that."

"You're sick, bro."

They both laughed.

"So, what now?" Alex asked. "Back to your place so I can kick both your asses in some *Goldeneye*?"

"Oh god, bro," Todd said. "That game is *so* old. When are you gonna upgrade to something like *FIFA*?"

"You don't *have* to just play the new ones, you know."

They were almost back to Todd's car. Roman couldn't procrastinate anymore—he had to force it out. "Uh, we're close to school," he stuttered, "why don't we head there?"

Todd scowled at him. "Why the hell would we do that?"

Besides the technical side of things, Roman hadn't thought that far ahead.

"What's going on underneath that tumbleweed you call hair?" Todd asked.

"I heard they turn off all the lights on campus at night," Roman said, talking out of his ass. "It'd . . . uh, might be trippy to see the stars without other lights getting in the way."

"Are you taking us on a camping trip, bro?" Todd asked. "Did you bring some marshmallows and graham crackers?"

"I just thought it'd be cool."

Todd glanced at Alex.

"I dunno," Alex said. "Might be fun. If we just stay in the car and sneak onto campus, it'll be like a real-life version of *Metal Gear Solid*."

"Oh God, bro," Todd said as he fanned his left hand through his jacket pocket.

The Audi coasted without much company along the sleepy suburb's main thoroughfare. Through the rearview mirror, Roman could see Alex's fixed stare on a "coming soon" sign for a new sandwich shop as it came and went. Then he started nodding off. Roman twiddled his thumbs in the front seat.

A few minutes later, Todd turned into the school's student parking lot. Alex convulsed out of a light snore. "Oh, man. We were cruising, right? Cool! Oh, shit. But I remember a story about this from the nineties. Didn't, like, the city ban cruising a couple of years ago?"

"Would you stop worrying, bro?" Todd replied in a short tone. "That's for cruising in places like Hollywood, where it's actually fun."

His headlights bore through the pitch-black darkness, revealing an array of empty parking spaces, a storm of dust particles, and a chain-link fence that lined the perimeter of the asphalt.

Roman squeezed his seat cushion, hoping his warmth would radiate toward the trunk and reach his duffel bag, reminding it its freedom was nigh. He had installed Sqandu, a port-scanner, that would peruse the hundreds of devices, like computers and fax machines on campus, for a port where data was exchanged.

Connecting to the school's unsecured wireless Internet network seemed like a promising start. Roman once saw his economics teacher connect to an unsecured network called "Wright Library" on a projection screen before downloading a PowerPoint lecture. So the closer he got to the library, the better the chance he'd have of his computer detecting the wireless network.

Meanwhile, Todd parked over four spaces.

"Look at us, guys. We're such rebels," he said.

"Can you give me one sec?" Roman said as he ogled the small flight of concrete steps that led up to the P.E. field. His friends responded with mild shock as he opened the door without warning and retreated toward the trunk.

"Todd," Roman called out. "Could you pop the trunk?"

"What for, bro?"

"Just real quick, please. I have to check something."

"This is so stupid," Todd said as he pressed a button to fling the trunk open. "I hope you brought some of those big jumbo marshmallows."

Roman grabbed his duffel bag, threw it over his shoulder, and slammed the trunk shut. He unzipped the bag and pulled out his dad's colossal HP laptop and rested it on the Audi. He scribbled his fingers across the trackpad until it woke up.

"Is that a laptop?" Todd asked.

Using the trackpad, Roman opened a dropdown menu to show the available unsecured networks, his mental fingers crossed for "Wright Library." But nothing. A blank list.

"Shit," Roman said to himself.

He closed the menu and opened it again. He refreshed over and over again. Still nothing. He had to get closer. Like a mother rushing to change her infant's diaper, he cradled the clunky laptop and made for the parking lot stairs.

"Where the hell is this guy going?" Todd asked as he got out of the car.

Roman steadied the laptop between his stomach and one of the beams bearing the load of the parking lot fence.

Refresh, refresh, refresh. Still nothing.

"Dammit," Roman said. "Freaking magnet school. You think they'd have a wider range."

He started cutting through the middle of the grass field, which would have gotten him called out for cheating while doing laps during P.E.

"Yo!" Todd shouted from a widening distance. "This might be considered trespassing." Roman looked back for a second to see his friend tailing him.

"You moron, at least turn down your monitor's brightness!" Todd shouted.

Each step on the lawn was crunchy and wet, radiating shivers through Roman's soles. He wanted to hold off on a response until he connected, at least. He stuck with a casual pace like he was leading a funeral procession on foot. He glanced back every few seconds until he saw Todd jogging and gaining on him.

"Jesus," Todd said, panting. "The one time you decide to be unpredictable, you pull shit like this?"

Refresh, refresh, refresh. Still nothing.

Roman's knees wobbled as he realized the craziness of his final goal; he felt like he was on stage in front of a yawning audience that just wanted him to fail already. But he was determined to H-word into whatever degree possible, so he could boost his grades, earn a bullet point on his curriculum vitae and a merit badge on his soul. Roman was convinced he was working harder toward his future than any other student; they were all just partaking in pre-established extracurricular activities while he was inventing his own!

Still, he couldn't help running out of breath so fast. He heard Todd's sneakers snap the grass blades. Roman upped his miles per hour with a determination he never showed his parents in any sport. He had almost cleared the field when he heard his friend yelling in his ear. It sent shivers down his back.

"The hell is wrong with you?" Todd demanded. "Let's go!" *Everything's dandy. Almost there. Almost there.*

But Roman's most nerdy trait outdid itself. Arriving at the edge of the field, his foot dipped into a small hole and his toes dug into a rickety fixture—a sprinkler.

Oh, those moments, he thought. *Those moments you realize you've messed up right before you actually do. Eternity, but still not long enough.*

If this trip played out in the worst way possible, it might set Roman's dad back about $1,500, but further at stake was his dad's trust. Roman couldn't believe he was this unprepared.

Down he went as he flung the laptop over his shoulder and,

like a reflex, shifted his hands toward the ground to break his fall. He managed to land in a push-up position and didn't suffer a scratch, but he postponed looking back. If the laptop had fallen onto the grass, there was a chance it could be salvaged. If it had fallen onto the concrete, it could have spat out its motherboard. Roman knew he couldn't spend the rest of his life on the ground, so he resolved to turn his head to see Todd clutching the laptop like he was presenting a long-sought bounty to royalty.

"Guess you can say I saved your work, bro," Todd said.

Roman let his forehead fall onto the P.E. field in relief. Then Alex arrived at the scene, struggling to catch his breath.

"Are we going to some secret LAN party?" he queried between deep wheezes as he gripped his kneecaps. "'Cause I suck at *Counterstrike.*"

Despite the failed attempt, Roman still felt a bit like his unofficial idol, Kevin Mitnick, who H-worded into companies like Motorola, Nokia, and Sun Microsystems. Mitnick had the technical skills up his sleeve, but none of it could have happened without social engineering—manipulating people to divulge sensitive information: fooling employees into thinking he was a badge-carrying co-worker, for example. Roman was willing to procrastinate that aspect for now, like it was everyday homework. Mitnick later dumped the black-hat life for the white, skyrocketing to a top name in computer security consulting—of course, after he was arrested by the FBI and served five years in prison.

But Roman likened his mission to shoplifting a pack of gum compared to H-worders trying to commit massive financial fraud. Other than editing grades, he didn't want to mess things up for people. On the contrary, he reassured himself that, in the long run, this effort would go toward helping others.

There's gotta be a job for someone who knows this stuff. Yeah, cyber-security has to pay big. Maybe that's an option.

It was the start of lunch break on Monday. Roman strolled down the hall as he gripped his backpack straps, thinking of how he could try H-wording from his room instead of on campus. His eyes darted between classrooms to his left and right. Each time one of the thick maple doors swung open, he got a peek at a teacher's computer on their desk. He started guesstimating. There were twenty-five or so classrooms on the first floor and likely the same on the second—each one housing Compaqs with unique IP addresses and, thus, a potential opening. Then there were the administrative offices stocked with computers beyond the check-in counter for visitors.

Roman recalled the basics: pinging and port-scanning were often the first steps in trying to do a simple H-word.

Numbed by concentration, Roman managed to glide-shuffle out of the path of hungry teens. He wondered where this hidden talent was when he played dodgeball in elementary school.

There was a lot of work to do. A plethora of IP addresses was a good thing: dozens, hundreds, or even thousands of chances.

Despite his passion for avoiding humans, Roman had to seek out someone who might have had vital information. He headed way past the trio of soda machines by the locker rooms toward the most fringe of hangout spots, where the skaters congregated. Jared pillared at the last bench before the faculty parking lot, along with the only skater boys at Wright Magnet, all of whom had also grown tall in the last year or two. Perhaps Jared had already tried H-wording and accumulated some time-saving insight. They all wore cargo shorts and formed a palette with their different-colored polos. These were the kids that the Armenians and Koreans avoided like the plague because they brought skateboards to school—a gateway to vandalism and a police record, at least according to immigrant parents.

Jared accepted a quick handshake and fist bump as he parted from his towering crew.

"I've never seen you out here," he told Roman. "Got some new toy to rub in my face?"

"No, no," Roman said with a soft head shake. He was almost bankrupt from the great splurge that included the seven-hundred-dollar VapoChill. "Do you remember that joke you made about getting in—I mean, uh, hacking into—the school's website?"

He sucked it up so he could utter the H-word just this once.

"I see. So, it was *you* that posted all those dicks on there," Jared said.

Roman's face went flush.

"Yo, just kidding," Jared said. "You didn't actually get in, did you? I mean, I knew you were the hardware king, but you got them breaking-and-entering skills too?"

"Well, uh, I dunno about that."

Jared raised his eyebrow. "So, you've tried?"

"I wanted to see if *you've* tried," Roman asked as he stuck out his chest a bit in an animalistic yet clueless attempt at social engineering. Jared's friends burst into laughter over an anecdote about farting on a sleeping sibling's face.

"I've only port-scanned the website's IP address when I was bored once," Jared said. "I got it using nslookup, but I couldn't find any other IPs."

"Do you know any of the ranges?"

"No way. I don't have the patience for that. Wouldn't you have to, like, guess that shit?"

"Yeah, I, uh . . . guess."

"Well, if you manage to get in, look for some nude pictures of that hot sub in adolescent skills."

"Uh . . . yeah, probably not gonna bother. Seems like too much work."

He lied so as not to draw further attention to his plans.

"Ah, don't be a quitter, man," Jared said. "If I could get in, I'd mess shit up. Who knows what we'd be able to do?"

Roman responded with a mild smile. "Yeah. Crazy fantasy."

"Well, gonna rejoin these idiots," Jared said. "See ya in Spanish."

The second after Roman walked away, Alex leaped out of nowhere into his face, startling him.

"It's spicy chicken day!" Alex said. "Let's go get some before they run out!"

"Uh, yeah."

They headed toward a blue food cart, the dispensary for Kenny Rogers Roasters sandwiches. Along the way, they came across a swarm of bros and their debate of whether it was tacky to swap stock Acura Integra taillights for Altezza lights. Todd had joined the group, as he did sometimes. Sako stood broader than all. The sun reflected off his shaved, shiny scalp as he bit off a huge chunk of his chicken sandwich.

"Just got the last one," he told Alex with a mouthful.

"Oh," Alex said, sounding grief-stricken. "Are you sure?"

Sako swallowed his food. "Bro, did you see how much he just sad tripped? Relax. I'm messing."

Sako chucked a few coins into the air. One of them grazed Alex's nose, making him flinch and sneeze.

"Bless you," Sako said. "There, I only owe you like twelve more cents now." He and a few others laughed. Then Sako looked Roman up and down and honed in on his afro. "Bro, when was the last time you got a freaking haircut? I don't even want to imagine what's going on down *there*."

"Hey!" Todd said, interrupting the follow-up laughs. "Let's go grab some Doritos."

They left. Roman was proud of himself for not feeling humiliated; people weren't getting to him as much anymore.

Alex rubbed his nose as a speck of snot leaked from one of his nostrils. "I'm gonna go to the bathroom and get a paper towel," he said. "Meet you at the cart?"

Roman nodded and they split up for the moment. His heart skipped a beat when someone tugged at his arm from behind. It was Todd.

"So, you're gonna tell me what the hell the other night was about?" he asked.

"Uh," Roman said.

"The P.E. field? We were all tired after that, so I let it go, but is everything alright? What were you up to?"

"I was just checking something."

"It didn't look like any old something. What was the laptop for?"

"Hey, Mr. New Guy!" Sako shouted from a few yards away. "Do you wanna get your stupid chips or what?"

"Can't believe he's still calling me that," Todd said.

He started hanging out with the school's most popular Armenian crew—at least among juniors—about a year ago. But Roman didn't mind because he knew Todd was growing as a person. He could never get in the way of that.

"I gotta go. We'll talk later," Todd said. "Just please don't tell me you have dead bodies under the P.E. field or something."

He jogged back to the flock of dudes.

Roman was left annoyed and confused.

Why does everyone think I'm going to kill people?

—

The ink of a school night brightened Roman's monitor. The screen fed like a river into his already damaged eyesight. The pain from his regularly scheduled toe stubbing subsided. His little brother was asleep, and his parents told him they were tired, so odds were low they'd barge in and demand a reset of their email passwords again.

Condensation from a glass of iced tea dripped onto a coaster. Roman put on his headphones and queued the first track off Tool's latest album, *Lateralus.* To be on the safe side, he booked a flight to Brazil with a brief layover in Russia by using www. switch.proxy.ru to spoof his IP address and make it look like he was embarking on the impending shady activity from São Paolo.

God, Brazilian women have great asses, he digressed. The task at hand encroached on jerk time, after all. The school website's IP address was 216.45.19.175. Roman opened Sqandu, so he could start where Jared left off: port-scanning the school website's IP on Port 80. And, as expected:

Port	State	Protocol	Service
80	closed	tcp	TCP

No duh, a magnet school would have taken the initiative to forge some formidable firewalls, Roman thought.

It was easy to look up a website's IP address, but other devices linked to the Internet, like fax machines and printers, weren't whipping open their trench coats and exposing their IPs. Just like how Mitnick pretty much started every heist, Roman had no option other than to start guessing.

IP addresses were often grouped together in sequential subnets, so Roman started counting upward from the school website's IP to find other working ones. He port-scanned 216.45.19.176, then .177, then 178, and so on. So far, each IP he guessed was valid, but they were coming back as closed. Roman hit about fifty dead ends. The task had gotten so repetitive that he felt nauseous. He pushed himself away from his keyboard.

He took a deep breath and reassessed. Everything so far was closed on Port 80. Roman tried dozens of other IPs, only to have the word "closed" burned into his inner eyelids each time he blinked. Sqandu stopped recognizing IPs past .344, but Roman knew there had to be more, given the number of devices he estimated. He started guessing again with numeral suffixes like .50, .100, .300. Some were legit, but the story was the same, as they'd keep retrieving a "closed" message.

Roman took another quick break and knuckled up his glasses, so he could drill his failing eyes. The most immediate damage could be done through Port 80, but there was one last option. Port 139, known as the direct host server message block, or SMB, could also yield the potential for breaking in, but necessitate additional steps that had to be taken in the real world. Roman started all over with the school website's IP address, 216.45.19.175, but this time he port-scanned via Port 139. Then, he was startled by the ding of an oncoming AIM message over Danny Carey's double-bass kicks. It was Todd.

kob34lyfe: everything ok? u ready to tell me now what the hell you were up to?

As much as Roman felt guilty for leaving Todd in the dark, he didn't have the energy to deal with him at the moment, so he minimized the message.

Just four IP addresses later, he got the first break of the night with 216.45.19.447.

Port	State	Protocol	Service
139	open	tcp	smb

He halfway leaped up from his seat, halting the millisecond before his headphones were yanked out of his computer.

As in open for friggin business! he thought.

It was time to hitch a ride on NetBus, a program that idled a few layers underneath other applications. NetBus was developed by the Swedes and afforded the ability to remotely control a Microsoft Windows computer system. Roman copy-pasted the IP address 216.45.19.447 into NetBus. He had no clue what to expect. Would there be an error message? Would indecipherable gibberish flood the screen? He hit *enter*.

A different yet more frustrating message appeared.

"Couldn't connect to local host."

Damn!

Roman grumbled at the prospect of another barrage of dead ends. He kept trying his luck on NetBus with other IPs open on Port 139.

One of the last tracks on *Lateralus*, "Triad," ended with a crushing crescendo. As it faded, the ringing that followed deafened Roman's ears more than the prior hours of heavy prog rock. He heard canned laughs, muffled by the carpet he squished between his toes, from an episode of *Frasier* his parents were watching downstairs. Roman chugged the last of his iced tea and let out a loud, crunchy burp, then covered his mouth halfway through the gaseous exhale to prevent any whining from his mom. Next, he tried 216.45.19.602.

"Couldn't connect to local host."

216.45.19.603.

"Couldn't connect to local host."

216.45.19.604.

"Couldn't connect to local host."

Come on, come on!

There had to be an opening somewhere, so Roman pleaded with the H-wording gods. With so many devices and connections, there had to be a crack. Even a hair's width would be enough.

Roman's backpack sat in its usual spot, the narrow partition between his front door and closet door. A notebook and a math book were strewn open on his desk for show.

Up next, he copy-pasted 216.35.19.617.

Roman spasmed with renewed attention as NetBus dropped him off somewhere he didn't expect. A new message popped up—well, it was more of a prompt, but still, it was exciting as all hell. His jaw dropped in disbelief. Something was close, so very close.

He imagined an ordinary morning for a teacher arriving to class before the start of the school day. First, the teacher would take a sip of hot coffee as she turned on her computer. Then, she'd be prompted to input her login credentials to gain access to lesson plans, work emails, and, potentially, her grade book. But in reality, this was no classroom. It was the bedroom of a sixteen-year-old who'd twice failed his driver's license test. The prompt was a little box soliciting two bits of information.

Username:

Password:

Nothing else could be accomplished that anticlimactic night unless Roman was able to miraculously guess a teacher's password—he assumed that was what the prompt requested. He made a few vain attempts, such as 'password1,' but they were met with the same message.

INCORRECT PASSWORD.

His frustration dimmed as he slid onto the coolness of an unmade bed, but the possibilities kept him awake. He also assumed the username must have been a teacher's email address, like the ones on syllabuses handed out at the start of the school year. But as far as passwords went . . . What would Mitnick do? This was nothing like building a computer from scratch, when Roman could visualize a final product spun by a gentle motor in a showroom of black ties and flashing cameras.

He was flat on his stomach like a docile spider, limbs extending off the edge of his bed. His thick glasses rested on his nightstand. A few rungs above legally blind, Roman barely decrypted 1:17 a.m. on his digital alarm clock. Its top edge reminded him of Todd's perfect spiky plane. That was another thing preventing sleep: an explanation about Sprinkler Gate. Roman owed his friend that much because, apparently, Todd wasn't going to let it go that easily. Roman cursed the honesty required of everlasting childhood friendships. He reeled in his arms and did a push-up, so he could roll out of bed. He took the restlessness as a sign to stay up. He put on his glasses and sat back down by the computer, then woke it up with a few shakes of the mouse. Everyone on his buddy list was away, including Todd and Alex.

It hit Roman that he couldn't sleep because of a nagging memory. He remembered something he read about on #mswarez that might help; it was about a small device he imagined as a dull version of a James Bond gadget. He saved countless hours of #mswarez on a notepad document, not for future blackmail, just reference. He scrolled through the first ten pages before giving himself a "duh" and using Ctrl+F. He recalled a night several months ago when a thousand users argued over the best bang-for-the-buck video card. Scattered in between were anecdotes about various web pranks. People would boast about their questionable but mostly harmless achievements all the time on #mswarez. Sifting through a great wall of typos and swear words, he found what he was looking for—a disgruntled user who worked at a clothing store and his tale of revenge against his dirtbag manager.

[01:22] (Reign316): the asshole. I do everything and then some. Even when i'm done with my work, folding and restocking, he doesn't let me stand still for one second. He wants me to sweep the floors! I'm not a freaking janitor!

[01:22] (Goatslinger): what did u do?

[01:22] (Reign316): the sickest thing ever. i plugged a key logger in the back of his computer and got his login info. when he was at lunch i logged in and i visited every porn site i could think of so the company could see his history and think it was him.

[01:23] (Goatslinger): you've got giant balls

[01:23] (Goatslinger): did they find out it was you? what happened?

[01:23] (Reign316): haha, they found out. HR hassled him all day. they didn't know it was me. even if they did it's just a stupid summer job.

It turned out that keyloggers could be bought on eBay, like everything else. Roman had forty bucks and change left over from the VapoChill splurge, barely enough to cover the device, plus shipping. He planned on heading to a local 7-Eleven the next day to pick up a money order, as he did for all his eBay purchases, since he was too young for a debit card. He'd also have to beat his mom to the front doorstep for a few days after school to intercept the package and prevent any nagging about another time-wasting tech toy.

But that peace of mind didn't stop Roman from flipping back to stomach over and over after returning to bed. Oddly, relief came when he pictured himself having a heart-to-heart with Todd about the night on the P.E. field.

Ugh! Fine! Fine!

After a final rush of cringe, Roman passed out.

—

Alex wasn't around for lunch the next day. Roman thought he might have been sick, which afforded the perfect opportunity.

Roman sat quietly atop a stone table next to Todd. The lack of small talk was typically blissful, but for once, Roman was ready to get something off his chest.

"I was trying to get on the school's Internet," he blurted out.

"What?" Todd asked, who was checking out some girls in the distance.

"That night. On the P.E. field."

"Wait," Todd said, "So, you were trying to get to school and hook up to an Internet cable?"

"No. It's a wireless network. It's called Wi-Fi."

"Wi-what?"

"Wi-Fi. It's like in the air."

"That's insane! Our school has that?"

"It's kind of a new thing. I can't even get it at my house yet."

"So, you're telling me one day I can have Internet wherever I take a laptop? I don't have to plug into a wall?"

"Uh, basically, but I don't know when that's gonna happen."

"Okay, so you were trying to get on the school's Wi-Fi, and then what, bro? What was that goddamn something you had to check, and why couldn't you do it back at my house?"

Roman spotted a leeway for some levity. "I didn't want to watch porn at your house."

The perverted arts only recently became a casual topic. A year or two ago, no guy wanted to admit that they jacked off.

"No, seriously," Todd said. "What were you trying to do?"

"Nothing, really. Just wanted to see if I could do it."

"Bullshit. You were at school trying to get on the Fi-Wi, and then what?"

"Wi-Fi."

"Whatever it's called, bro!"

Roman hesitated. He wasn't sure where he was going with

this. He kind of wanted to appease Todd, but at the same time, his friend's interest started to intrigue him.

"Were you trying to mess stuff up?" Todd asked in a mischievous tone.

"Huh?"

"Were you trying to hack into the school or something?" Roman cringed in response to the H-word.

"Well, uh . . ."

"I knew it!" Todd said. "What else would you be trying to do? That's what you geeks talk about on those forums. Freaking awesome! You must have pulled off a bunch of crazy shit by now."

"Actually, I've . . . um . . . never really broken into anything before."

Todd's grin and elevated eyebrows drooped in disappointment.

"I'm still trying to get in," Roman said.

"Man, I thought you were going to have some crazy story about hacking into a bank or something and stealing millions of dollars."

Roman pulled out his barren pockets at another lame joke attempt and was left with mysterious crumbs between his fingernails.

Todd didn't laugh. "Well, what did you want to do after you got in? What kind of shady shit are you up to?"

Roman was worried his friend would try to talk him out of his plans, especially if he hadn't let go of the night on the P.E. field yet.

"I have no idea what I'm going to be able to do," Roman uttered.

"Wait a minute. Are you gonna try to change grades or something?" Todd asked.

Roman was motionless.

"I mean, what else would you wanna do?" Todd added.

"Umm. I, uh . . . Maybe. I'm just trying to see if I can get access to the school's website. I'm just learning this stuff for now."

"Oh. That's it? Lame, bro! Thanks for dragging me onto campus late at night for nothing!"

"I-I was just trying to kind of test myself."

"Well, if you want to test yourself, hit the gym like me, gain some muscle, stand up straight."

Roman corrected his slouch to make himself look more prominent. The afro helped add some height too.

"It's gonna take more than that," Todd said.

Roman welcomed a breather where midday sounds flourished.

"So, what now?" Todd asked after the brief intermission. "Are you gonna try again?"

"Not like the other night on the P.E. field. There might be a different route from my room. I think I'm almost there."

"That's freaking crazy, bro. I didn't know you actually had it in you to do something bold like that. But aren't you scared at all of getting caught?"

"Uh, I mean, I think only someone on my level or higher monitoring this stuff would notice."

"Oh, *excuse me*, Bill Gates."

Roman took the jab as a bit of a compliment. "Plus, I'm using a proxy."

"So, where do you go from there?"

To Roman's surprise, his friend hung onto every word. He never thought anyone outside of #mswarez would be impressed by something so technical.

"I ordered something called a keylogger," Roman said. "When you plug it into a computer, it records all the keystrokes. I'm trying to figure out how I'm gonna do it."

"Get the hell out of here," Todd said as he shot the Chin. "So, *you're* the one who'll plug it in?"

"Yeah, when I figure out where."

"I know that. I meant you're the clumsiest person in the world. Who else would trip over a sprinkler head like that on the edge of a giant P.E. field?"

"There isn't a better way. Sometimes you have to do things in the real world. They call it social engineering."

"I see. So, you think you're gonna social engineer me into doing this for you, eh? Screw you, bro." Todd gave a raspy chuckle and then coughed.

Roman smiled faintly.

"Just kidding, bro," Todd said. "So, where do you want to try?"

"I've been thinking of starting with Wineman's class."

"The programming teacher? Why the hell there? If anyone notices the key thing, it'd be him."

"Yeah, but he logs in and out all the time. I can plug in the keylogger at the beginning of class and grab it on my way out. Except . . ."

Todd pointed his index finger at Roman's face, cutting him off. "Except you just remembered that the back of Wineman's computer faces the front door of the class."

Roman nodded and was disappointed in himself for failing to notice something so obvious.

"Listen. Alex always gives me a hard time because he thinks I got a 4.2 GPA just like that," Todd said as he snapped his fingers. "You know how, bro? Because I'm observant. While everyone else is jamming their heads inside books, memorizing everything, I pay attention to *why* each piece of info is important. And I do it fast. You know what? I've got an idea. How about my AP English teacher, Mrs. Crandle?"

"Does she even use the computer?" Roman asked. "She's pretty old."

"She barely uses it, but that's the point. She would never think to look behind her computer, and I have her every day. It would just be a waiting game until we can snatch the key thing back."

It was rare for Roman to hear something he didn't know he wanted to know.

"Do you remember that time I cheated at that carnival game back in elementary and won three goldfish?" Todd asked. "How I wore three different masks with the same black outfit, and they let me play that dart game three times, even though it said one prize per person?"

"But your mom made you flush those fish down the toilet after you got home."

"Doesn't matter, bro. I got them home. The goal was to win them. But I gotta ask, why do you even need a teacher's password to begin with?"

"Uh, well, I figure if I can find a working password, that's still a good step forward. That's still part of H-wor—I mean hacking."

"Bro, only you could make something exciting like this sound boring. But fine, whatever. If you need my help, I'm here. If it'll satisfy whatever nerd goal you have and get it out of your system."

Accidental social engineering, Roman thought. He'd take it.

He and Todd had to do a double-take when Alex appeared out of nowhere. He looked far from sick. On the contrary, it was the most glowing Roman had ever seen his friend, who strolled merrily alongside a girl—and a pretty one at that.

Tamar Sarkissian.

Almost Alex's height, she had long golden hair that wasn't

dyed like some of the other Armenian girls at school. Tamar spoke with a domestic yet foreign tone. Roman heard she moved to Southern California from Chicago less than a year ago. Her voice reminded him of a valley girl.

Alex delivered embellished takes on what a Persian-Armenian, or parskahye, obsessed with Japanese cars and partying sounded like. So, essentially, Todd.

"I drive a Honda Ceevic, bro," Alex said. "Let's go to a rave, bro." Tamar cracked up at the sing-songy pronunciation.

"I swear I didn't know that dialect even existed!" she exclaimed. "I wish we had your kind of Armenians back home."

Alex bolstered his smile. Roman and Todd locked their eyesights with him again and were the first to offer acknowledging nods.

"I don't sound like that, do I, bro?" Todd asked.

"Uh, no," Roman said. "Are they dating?"

Todd served up a fresh-baked Chin. "Yeah, they were hooking up on the beach, bro." Roman experienced a burst of jealousy at the thought of Alex losing his virginity before him. That's all Roman needed: to be the last of his male classmates to touch a girl. But, of course, he should have known better.

"I'm kidding, bro," Todd said. "Look how far they're standing apart. She's just being friendly."

"Great, now I'm going to notice every time you're trying to be observant," Roman said.

"I think it's good Alex has her around. He'll be distracted. He won't throw himself into our plan if he's gonna be busy with Tamar. He won't bug us."

"Our plan" already, huh? Well, at least it sounds like I've got a recruit who's willing to do the dirty legwork.

"So yeah, *Mario Tennis* is the only title that lags on the emulator for me, so if that ever happens, just turn down the resolution," Alex said to Tamar.

"I know!" she said. "I did the exact same thing with *Turok!*"

They trailed off toward the snack windows.

"So, *that's* what it is," Todd said. "She's a gamer."

Such a revelation sounded so strange, but also eye-opening in a good way.

A girl gamer? Roman pondered. This changed everything. Maybe there's a computer chick out there too. Maybe there's no excuse anymore. Maybe there never was.

Alex and Tamar vanished from sight. Roman was distracted by the injection of confidence at the prospect of titillating a girl with his PC IQ.

But let's not go nuts here.

"I bet Al's gotta table reserved for themselves and two spicy chickens," Todd joked.

Roman reverted to the task at hand. "So, you'd be up to . . . Why do you want to help?"

"I mean, it's not like it's a huge favor," Todd said. "You just want me to shove that logger thing in the back of a computer. Just put me at the front of the line if I need help with a computer again or a new part."

"Sure. Of course. So, you're, uh, pretty sure you can do it? You're not worried?"

"Why would I be?" Todd replied. "This will be like when I was a TA in the office last year. Do you know how many supplies I jacked? I'm set for life on Post-It notes and blue highlighters. Plus, if you're gonna steal a million dollars from the school, give me half."

They laughed for a sec.

"But when you have the password, you'll be done?" Todd

asked. "You'll get this hacking prank out of your system, then maybe you'll come to a party with me?"

Roman nodded while turning away from his friend. "When do you have Crandle's class?"

"After lunch."

"I could even do it after school," Todd said.

"Huh?"

"*Hundred* percent I'll do a better job than you did."

It didn't matter that Todd was the savior catcher from the other night; Roman felt confident enough to put his foot down.

"I can figure out a way to sneak into class when everyone's gone," Todd continued. "I bet I could—"

"No, no. Don't do, uh, don't do that," Roman said.

"What? Why?"

"We shouldn't do anything like that again after school."

Todd raised the Chin. "Fine, bro. I was kidding. Keep at it, though. You're getting there with your confidence."

The sun warming Roman's forehead annoyed him. Grains of sweat lined the southern border of his fro. Everyone on #mswarez did everything solo. Accepting his friend's help went against all of the channel's philosophies, but opening up to Todd felt like a group project where no one was lazy.

"I'll keep you posted," Roman told Todd. "I've gotta keep my eyes on the mail these next few days and wait for the package."

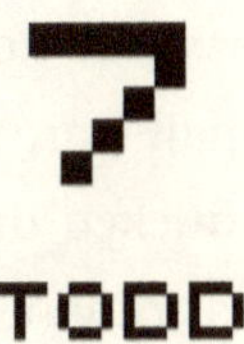

TODD

He wanted to scold Roman for wearing the same white, still some-how fading Champion sweatshirt with a green polo collar peter-ing out for the third day in a row. They approached each other in the hall between periods. Roman extended his hand at the agreed-upon spot, but the eraser-sized keylogger slipped from his grip. Todd shot out his arm and caught the device.

"Jesus Christ, how many times am I going to have to save your ass?" he asked Roman. Todd brought the keylogger up to his face and inspected it.

"So, this is it, huh?" he asked, then shoved it into his pocket. "Cool, no one's gonna notice. Don't worry."

Roman appeared more clammed up than usual, to the point that it started to weird Todd out.

"You alright?" Todd asked.

"You sure you wanna do this? I'm . . . I'm kinda nervous."

"Well, that's why I'm subbing in for your locomotor skills. Plus, after all you've done for me, risking viruses and shit and getting me all those burned CDs."

Roman arched his shoulders and raised his chin in a very Todd-like fashion. "I'd *never* get a virus."

"Jesus. Sorry, Lord Nerdenheimer the Fourth," Todd said as he fanned his hands sarcastically.

Roman accompanied him to AP English. With one hand, Todd gripped the rim of the classroom doorway before saying later to his friend. Suddenly, a small Korean girl with a cast of anime characters on her backpack ducked underneath his arm and into class. He had no time to assess rudeness.

"I'll meet you in the bathroom later," he told Roman.

In class, Todd was greeted with Mrs. Crandle's cursive handwriting all over the whiteboard from periods past. She wore a thick and long Mary Poppins-esque coat. The freshest ink marks were bullet points about *As I Lay Dying* by William Faulkner. "I forgot my copy," Todd said. "Can I grab one?"

"Of course!" Crandle said. "There's a few extra on the shelf by the window."

Her glasses reminded Todd of the ones Robin Williams wore in *Mrs. Doubtfire*. He approached a small double-decker case stacked with old paperbacks. He gauged the gap between his left hand and the backside of Mrs. Crandle's computer on the corner of her desk. Todd needed the scene to be as predictable and routine as his classmates' study habits, but something, or rather someone, wasn't in place. The small Korean girl, Eunice Kim, was at her desk when normally she'd be buttering up Mrs. Crandle at the start of class, fishing for validation of her interpretations of the current read. But instead of jovial ass-kissing, Eunice hung her head. Her jet-black hair, parted down the middle, poured onto her desk and hid her eyes, yet it was easy to tell she was crying. She reminded Todd of the monstrous girl villain from *The Ring*.

Of all the days she chose to act like a goth girl, he thought, looking over his shoulder. He squeezed the keylogger even tighter and fumbled with a few old books, pretending to browse for the most pristine copy. Todd overheard his classmates say something about Eunice.

"What happened to her?" a girl asked another girl.

"Is it true?" another one queried.

It seemed like the whole class was whispering about Eunice. Finally, one of her friends, Joy Lee, leaned from one desk over and said something to her in Korean. Eunice nodded.

"Caught cheating?" an Indian boy whispered to a fat kid.

Todd's interest was for sure piqued, but he had to stay focused. His torso eclipsed the gap between the bookcase and Crandle's computer. He tried to look as far back as his peripheral vision permitted. Two students walked in and dropped their heavy backpacks onto their desks. Todd believed the banging sound would somehow mask the unfurling of his left hand.

Remember the goldfish. Remember the goldfish.

He flicked his wrist, barely missing the slot and hitting the computer's casing: 0 for 1. The tardy bell rang. Audible concerns over Eunice started dying down. A panicked second flick resulted in a flawless dock.

Kobe! Swish!

Todd returned to his desk with a loaner copy and took a seat among the school's most prized possessions: honor students. For an hour, everyone got on their soapbox and fenced analyses about *As I Lay Dying*. Todd chose to forget about the keylogger, so he wouldn't radiate a nervous aura. He waited until class started winding down to deploy his strategy for Mrs. Crandle to log in to her computer.

"I'm sorry, Mrs. Crandle," Todd said as she smiled back. "I lost my copy of the essay prompt. Can you print me another one?"

She always handed out just the right amount of copies for the whole class, so Todd knew she had to be fresh out. She'd need to print another copy.

"A bit forgetful today, aren't we, Mr. T?" Mrs. Crandle asked.

Todd was so glad that no one outside of AP English knew his nickname. "Sorry."

"Not a problem."

Mrs. Crandle sauntered toward her desk. Todd watched her boot up the computer. Entering her credentials was next, but then he felt a piece of paper land on his shoulder. He turned around; it was Eunice.

"Here," she said. "You can have my copy. I'm almost done anyway."

Todd was stunned. "Um, thanks."

He took the prompt from her hand and noticed his classmates peering at him with judgmental leers for being so unprepared. He started to panic as Mrs. Crandle no longer had a reason to log in, but then Todd saw the reflection of a Microsoft desktop in her glasses. His spine shivered in relief.

"Oh, thank you, Eunice," Crandle said. "You saved me some paper!"

The bell rang. He got up, put the borrowed book back, and snatched the keylogger. He left the classroom and saw Roman enter the boys' bathroom, but Todd immediately didn't follow; his attention was reeled by a small gathering near the school's main office down the hall. A few Korean kids were huddled together. Eunice jogged toward them, hunching with a heavy backpack. Andy Yi crossed the administrative boundary into the hall, where she fell into his arms. But it was a quick embrace—he gently positioned her a step back. Andy said something in Korean. Eunice nodded, and they held hands as they walked toward the exit to the amphitheater.

Todd was startled when Joy appeared, standing next to him with a disapproving look on her face. She was as tall as Eunice but chubbier and often wore tight shirts that brandished a muffin top. Along with Todd, Eunice, and Joy were among the academic elites. They always placed in the end-of-year top tens and claimed all the academic awards. Despite having these accolades in common, they weren't even acquaintances, just competitors.

"What did Andy say?" Todd asked Joy.

Two slow blinks and a sigh later, she responded. "Just lunch detention."

"So, he *did* cheat or whatever?"

Joy paused and let out a long exhale through her nose. "He found a quiz."

She sounded frustrated; it was confusing. Todd assumed that if Andy got his hands on a quiz, he'd share it with his fellow Korean classmates, just like the Armenians would have, so what was the problem?

"They're so stupid," Joy said.

"What?" Todd asked.

Before he could get an answer, she was gone. Remembering that his *own* friend was waiting for him in a stinky bathroom, Todd retreated, unsure of how to process the scene he had just witnessed. Lunch detention for Todd seemed like a slap on the wrist for something like cheating on a quiz. Hacking into the school, however, would certainly warrant far worse. He joked to himself that it might be a good thing if Roman got caught with whatever he was up to. Perhaps getting into trouble would be the kick in the pants he needed to move from behind a computer to behind a girl—or at least ask one out.

Todd flung back the bathroom door and gave a greeting Chin to Roman, who leaned against the white tile walls, unsure of what to do with his hands until it was time for the quick exchange. But Todd didn't let go of the keylogger right away as Roman held onto the other end.

"Whatever you're doing, be careful," Todd said.

Roman stayed quiet.

"And if anything happens, I wasn't involved," Todd continued. "Okay?"

"Umm, sure. Of course."

Prolonging his grip for emphasis a few seconds more, Todd let go of the device. Roman shoved the keylogger into the front pocket of his backpack and zipped it up.

"I'm using a proxy. Hard to trace. No one's gonna notice . . ." Roman said.

"You know this is just a distraction," Todd said. "You're doing this so you don't have to do the things everyone else is doing. Did you even reach out to Melineh?"

"No."

"You're gonna blow your chance."

Roman didn't react. It dumbfounded Todd. He wished his friend would try. Not try harder, just try.

"I don't care," Roman said, sounding like he was losing his patience. "How can I feel anything if I didn't like her in the first place?"

"You can't know you like someone until you at least talk to them."

More silence.

"I don't get it," Todd said. "We're all running around with raging boners. You can't be *this* afraid of rejection, bro. Trust me, it took me a *bunch* of tries to get a kiss and start making out with chicks."

Roman seemed intent on staging a nonverbal protest until the subject changed.

"Fine, forget it," Todd said.

"Thanks a lot for doing this, though," Roman said.

Todd sighed. "No prob. Go do whatever alpha nerd stuff you gotta do. Then will you get this shit out of your system? Maybe come to a party with me this Saturday?"

"Why do you care so much about what I do with my free time?"

"Because free time can't always be alone time."

"Don't worry about me, man."

Todd just couldn't understand his friend anymore.

Dammit, bro, I'm barely gonna know anyone at this party. I want you there with me. You stuck by my side when I was struggling, when no one wanted to talk to me. I don't want to lose you as a friend down the road.

But those thoughts were miles away from Todd's lips. Brotherly affection was more than enough to start rumors. "I just want you to have fun," he said, his voice trembling with nostalgia. "I'm your friend. When I invite you to something, just come."

Roman took a few steps toward the sink and switched on the handles to wash his hands.

"Thanks again for your help," he said.

Todd shook his head and left the bathroom without saying bye.

—

ROMAN

The carpet beneath Roman's feet vibrated with Bob Saget's lame, muffled one-liners and accompanying laugh track. The TV sounds were assurances that his parents were glued to the couch, not that they'd understand the gibberish on Roman's screen if they barged in, but better safe than sorry. He heard fighting game music from his brother's room.

The normal setup. Iced tea, headphones, and track one of *Toxicity* by System of a Down. He felt capable of anything, a state of mind elusive until he nailed himself in the same spot every day. He flirted with the threshold, the login prompt, and even though he had yet to cross it, he wanted to pat himself on the back for getting this far.

You know what? Screw that! He thought. *I gotta go all the way!*

Roman plugged the keylogger into his computer, opened a browser window containing a notepad document, then opened that too. Everything Crandle typed during Todd's class appeared on-screen, word for word.

Even if this didn't work, he already had a new project lined up: a sorely needed website for #xwarez or #mswarez. It would be dedicated to nothing but betas and beta news. Such a masterful venture would do wonders for his résumé.

Roman furrowed his brow and re-focused on the screen. Crandle's first recorded keystroke combo was the initial Ctrl+Alt+Delete command to bring up the login prompt on her computer. Her login info was next:

ecrandle@gmsd.org
joycefan01

Who the hell is Joyce?

It didn't matter. Roman stepped off the imaginary NetBus and onto the doorstep to who knew where? He found himself gazing up at giant double doors made of ancient stone to ward off marauders. Crouching gargoyles from above guarded ornate patterns. The doors were shut long ago, never to be opened again, like the mausoleum of a Victorian-era family with no living relatives.

Roman rationalized that this break-in wasn't going to set off red flags compared to the number of times teachers must have logged in every day. They probably had remote access from home too.

Either way, whoever this Joyce was, Roman was glad she existed as he stabbed the key into the rusty lock and turned it—to his surprise, with unexpected ease. Dust plumes sprayed through the keyhole. One of the doors creaked ajar on its own; it even started to cower. The gargoyles started frowning in unison, and the earth shook. Patina chipped away. Roman tossed the key aside and wound his right leg. He landed a footprint on the crease where the double doors met, thrusting both of them back. Not bad for someone who hadn't played soccer since middle school P.E.

Something loaded on-screen—a large thumbnail composed of a sketch that read "A+" and, below, a message saying, "Welcome to Apollo." What he saw next made him look over both shoulders. Roman slid his headphones off. A few dozen names in alphabetical order came to the forefront, all of them Crandle's students. He recognized one of the names.

TOVMASIAN, TADEH

Roman opened tab after tab, each with titles such as attendance and tardies, but one herded his attention the most, one that said "grade book." Without hesitation, Roman clicked on it and began exploring the thinnest column, the one that was next to each student's name and was occupied by an A or an A-.

Earlier, when he thought about this moment, he pictured himself leaping out of his chair and discovering a hidden dance talent.

Instead, he was crippled, like he had contracted a petrifying curse from the stone gargoyles he had just demolished.

Whoa, whoa, whoa. This . . . This can't be real.

Roman was most comfortable exploring his friend's name, so he dragged the cursor over the box with an A reserved for Todd. Roman clicked and a blinking text cursor popped up to the right of the perfect goddamn grade, but with one backspace, it disappeared. He pressed the letter B and Todd's grade dropped. Roman changed it back to an A.

Holy shit!

ALEX

Alex knew of Tamar from her first day at Wright Magnet, but he hadn't said hello—placing her way out of his league was his default. She was around his height and a novelty for being an out-of-towner, but still bore the curves of local Armenian girls. Alex and Tamar sat in the same row in Algebra 2, when he first noticed her adorable profile and nose, which was small like a child's. He also knew how cold the weather had to be in order for her to wear her gray hoodie with pink stripes along its sleeves. Tamar remained eye candy until one day, Alex noticed a Nintendo 64 game cartridge on the floor at the end of class. He was taken aback as he bent over for a closer look.

What reckless fool would do this to a . . . He flipped the cartridge over to inspect the label, then his jaw dropped. *The Legend of Zelda? Ocarina of Time? How dare anyone do this to this masterpiece!*

Alex picked up the cartridge and tapped on the shoulder of the kid who sat in front of him as he shoved a math book into his backpack.

"Hey, Charlie," Alex said. "You dropped this."

"Not mine," Charlie said, glancing over his shoulder. "But I'll take it if you don't want it."

"It's mine," Tamar said as she came back into the classroom.

Alex froze with bewilderment before being smacked with the obvious—this had to be a prank, a top-tier one at that.

Bravo to whoever put this chick up to trying to fool me into being distracted so my pants could be pulled down or something. Well, I'm a little wiser as I approach seventeen, and jokes on you: I don't even wear tighty-whities anymore!

Alex, fraught with disbelief, started sliding the game into his backpack.

"Hey!" Tamar said, raising her voice. "I said that's *my* Zelda game!"

"Really?" Alex asked.

"Yeah, why's that so hard to believe?"

"No. No, it's not hard—I mean difficult."

She cracked a smile as Alex sighed and regretted his awkward phrasing.

"I'm going to my little cousin's house after school to play it with him," Tamar said.

Alex never thought he'd ever have a conversation about *Ocarina of Time* with a girl. Disney games? Maybe. But the sword-slashing, puzzle-solving, Tri-Force-seeking classic? Never in his wettest of dreams. Somehow, the next thing he knew, they were walking to the lunch area together.

"What's your favorite temple in the game?" Tamar asked.

This is really happening, Alex thought. He straightened his posture as his gaming acumen filled him with confidence.

"That's easy. Have you heard of the Spirit Temple?" he asked.

"Heard of it? It's the best one. Best puzzles and it's the most adventurous."

"Are you sure you don't prefer the Water Temple?" Alex asked with a sarcastic cadence that he felt fit like a glove.

"Are you kidding? I can't beat that without a walkthrough."

"A *walkthrough*? Come on."

"Okay, okay. Don't judge me. I took a peek at *GameFAQs* just to make sure I had the right order of adjusting the water levels."

Alex was stupefied.

She knows what GameFAQs is?

Alex had no idea what he was doing, but her questions were all within his comfort zone. This game talk would become a regular thing after class, but other, deeper, more personal topics started being broached. Well, mostly just jokes about his Persian-Armenian family; that type of mix was few and far between among Chicago's Armenian diaspora. Alex would recite common phrases spoken by his mom and dad: "koranam yes," meaning "I'd rather go blind," and "zets kootes," which literally translates to "you will eat a beating," a phrase directed at someone who defied their elders.

Soon after began the tradition of their weekly arcade hangouts. Video West was a white stucco shack in downtown Glendale, nestled between a nail salon and a stamp and coin shop. Most of the time, Tamar would meet him right outside; he never waited for her for more than a few minutes. Alex couldn't believe it: she was a punctual, pretty girl. He guessed he'd better call off what he anticipated would be an arduous road toward finding a soul mate, a road riddled with potholes of rejection.

On their latest scheduled hangout, Alex walked up to the arcade's entrance, but Tamar was not yet there. No biggie. He just wished he could hang out like this more often with Roman and Todd. Tamar filled the void despite the bit of added stress of feeling like he had to try hard to be cool.

Alex figured he'd get in a few practice rounds on *Mortal Kombat 2* before she showed up. But when he went inside, he saw Tamar from behind at the gaming cabinet. She was going crazy with the joystick and pulling off multi-button combos. Everything from seventies classics to a couple of co-op gun games lined the dim and poorly ventilated room.

Tamar's blonde strands stood out more than usual. There was no air-conditioning, just a lone fan on the floor, pointed in a direction benefiting whoever played *Ms. Pac-Man* or *Galaga*. There were two other boys in the arcade. One played *Marvel vs. Capcom* and another throttled combos on *Tekken 3*. As a joke, Alex wanted to scare Tamar and make her screw up her bout. Chants of *"Get over here"* and *"Finish him"* howled from the screen. Alex tiptoed until he was within "gotcha!" distance.

"Trying to learn combos without me?" he asked. "Cheater!"

Tamar didn't even flinch. Instead, she tore out her opponent's spine and held it up to the blood-raining sky.

"I only cheat after I beat the game the honest way," Tamar said, turning to Alex. "Plus, how am I cheating if I'm just practicing? Nothing stopped you from coming earlier and getting your training on."

Alex didn't have many qualms about cheating. If he got stuck in a video game, he'd whip out his Game Genie or GameShark and charge toward the ending credits with an undrainable health bar.

"Please, I've had this at home since I was eight," he said.

"But with an arcade setup?" Tamar asked.

"Everything from the Genesis Arcade Power Stick to the SNES Advantage."

"Doesn't matter, though. I'm still going to rape you."

Pfft.

Alex pulled out ten bucks' worth of singles his parents gave him. He used a machine to exchange the bills for enough quarters to make his pockets sag down to his testicles. With each step, the change and his nuts tapped each other like a Newton's cradle.

"Let's go, rapist," he said after returning with a fistful of quarters. "No, wait."

Tamar lost it and started cracking up. "Looks like it's not going to be hard to distract you. You'll do it to yourself."

"Alright, enough of that."

To show off, Alex called on Liu Kang to be his champion. It was the fighter he used the least, but he long ago memorized the combo for the character's fatality that entailed transforming into a dragon. Tamar elected Scorpion, the character often depicted on the cover art. Despite how adept she was at deploying the flaming skull finisher, Alex won this round. Next, she took him in *Tekken 3*. Then they scooted a cabinet over where he owned her in *Marvel vs. Capcom*.

"You should totally take C++ with me next semester," Tamar said in a positive tone despite having her ass handed to her. "We can learn how to program our own fighting games."

"Really?" Alex said.

"Well, not really. Maybe like Pong or something like that for now."

Alex spotted an onscreen reflection of Tamar trying to repress a toothy grin.

"I didn't know you wanted to be a game designer," Alex said.

"Might be worth checking out," Tamar said. "Just in case I don't want to end up an accountant or dentist like most Armenians."

Alex laughed. "You forgot mechanic."

Tamar snorted. "Don't think I'm hairy enough for that."

Alex slapped down a succession of button combos. "The

programming stuff seems really hard. If anything, I'd love to write epic RPG stories, like Hironobu Sakaguchi with *Final Fantasy* or Hideo Kojima with *Metal Gear Solid*."

"I'm pretty sure they started out as programmers too. Video game teams used to be really small back then."

"Guess there isn't a GameShark for the real world yet."

By the time their thumbs grew sore and bruised, they closed the session out with a less dexterity-intensive title. Alex let Tamar choose, and she went with *Donkey Kong*.

"This isn't my forte," she said. "But we haven't played it yet, so I'm sure we both equally suck."

"Excuses already, huh?" Alex asked.

Tamar pursed her lips. But to Alex's surprise, she dashed up those ramps and leaped over barrels like a summer Olympian, losing just a single life by the time she made it to the sixth level.

"Would you look at that," Tamar said.

Alex's jaw dropped in shock. He had always hated this game; timing jumps with Super Mario (the first appearance of the video game icon) was too difficult.

"You bamboozled me!" he exclaimed.

"I . . . what?" Tamar said as she raised a thin, natural brow.

"That's when someone lies about sucking at a game and then they kick everyone's ass."

"How dare you accuse me of being a bazboomler or whatever you called it," Tamar said as she adopted a Southern twang. "I demand satisfaction."

She breezed to the end of the eighth level, where she finally lost.

"I think that's enough," Tamar said. "Let's see you make it that far."

But Alex couldn't get past the halfway point on the first level.

The stupid hammer, designed to destroy the tumbling barrels, slowed down his jumping.

"Want me to teach you how to play?" Tamar asked.

"No, smart ass," Alex said.

"Oooh, is someone a sore loser?"

"No!"

"Oh, really? Tiny confession, there was an arcade on my block back in Chicago, and me and my friends knew how to rig machines for free games."

"So, you *are* a cheater after all!"

"It happened in another state. It doesn't count."

"Now look who's playing on god mode all of a sudden."

Another of Alex's Marios bit the dust. Losing badly, he almost summoned his inner five-year-old's crying power. He gave up before digging himself into a bigger hole.

"Alright, alright, you won," he said, swatting the joystick away. "Ready to go?"

They had stayed half an hour longer than usual at Video West on this hangout anyway.

"Okay," Tamar said and shrugged. She took a few steps toward the exit, her back to him. The angle instilled guilt in Alex. He noticed this was the farthest apart they'd been in a room since they stopped being strangers. He feared the distance would expand, that she'd keep going, away from this overgrown child who couldn't handle a little friendly competition and all the way home to an AIM buddy list filled with taller, broader, and smoother-talking guys.

I messed up, Alex thought as he took note of how much lighter his pockets felt. *I knew it was just a matter of time.*

But to his surprise, Tamar held the door open with a smile. Her face was tinted with a grid of alternating pinks and purples from

the cabinet screens. She kept looking at Alex, like she was trying to see past his unibrow and hints of man boob. They hadn't
kissed, nor had they held hands, but at least she appeared forgiv-
ing—still far more progress than the instant rejections of the past.
In a way, he still lost a small chunk of his sturdy innocence.

Alex's gut tingled. In the brief moment of clarity, he savored the depth of the scene like it was a work of art, a domestic
slice of life with titles like "Boy and Girl at Arcade #2" or "The
Unexpected Role Reversal Because She Opened the Door." The
thought of his parents yelling at him for showing up past ten
o'clock didn't register a microsecond of fear.

Let them shit their pants for once.

—

ROMAN

That same evening, Roman took a cosmic punch to the gut and
catapulted away from his monitor, knocking over his swivel chair
in the process. He tripped over a few cables and went butt-first
into a wall, then slid down to the floor. A cold flush came over
him, and dizziness spun his line of sight like a top. He got up,
only to collapse onto his bed while trying to catch his breath like
he had just run a twelve-minute mile in P.E. Snippets of scenarios
started pouring in at once.

*OhmygodIjustchangedgrades. IdiditIH-wordedIneverhavetodoschool
shitagain.*

He pawed at the floor, looking for his glasses, which had
fallen off.

ThisisinsaneIneverhavetodohomeworkagaintits.

A lucid nanosecond lassoed so many checkmarks: he could lie

to his folks, give himself good marks, keep his computers, pick up a valuable H-wording skill, and use the scores to get into a decent school as a backup. Hell, just getting his parents off his back so he could take on a couple more projects in search of a billion-dollar idea would be good enough. As his heart rate baselined, he got back up and grazed a lampshade with a stiff uppercut.

Another rush of adrenaline triggered the dawn of the gurgles. He knew he had seen something forbidden—like a blowjob in a porno at his friend's house when he was twelve. But the age of admittance was the sole rule-breaker in those cases. There would never be an appropriate occasion for witnessing what he had just accessed. The fear of being caught wrung his intestines. Roman ran out of his room. Normally quiet with his movements at this hour, he stomped his way to the bathroom while plotting.

His mom knocked on the bathroom door a few moments later. "Roman?" Audrey called from the other side. "Are you okay?"

Of course, the one time he made a peep at night, it brought her near point-blank.

"Yeah, yeah," Roman said.

He flushed and washed his hands. Audrey was in her nightie muumuu when he came out.

"If you're pushing too hard, that's not good," she said. "You need to eat more fruit. You don't eat enough fruit. Join Dad and me downstairs next time for some peaches and plums."

Roman nodded and went back into his room. He didn't care about lying to his parents. They never even tried to understand his hobby, how hard he bled for it, and that he dedicated the same number of joules toward it as the compulsive study habits of an honor roll student. He picked up his desk chair and sat back down.

He had also left the Apollo grade book open. Fortunately,

alarms weren't going off, and if he were detected, it would be traced to some IP in Brazil. To play it even safer, he decided to wait a couple of days to see if he heard any relevant gossip in the hallways at school. Or maybe Crandle's password would be changed if something fishy was suspected. Or perhaps Roman would be called to the office. He gulped. It was too late. An alteration had already been made—no more for now.

And after all that, he only had access to Crandle's grade book. Roman's chest tightened as the cruel realization started to set in.

I'm going to need six more passwords, he thought.

—

ALEX

While walking home, Alex wished he knew when to go for Tamar's hand, but at least their wrists bumped accidentally every now and then. The minimal contact triggered a hot pulse through Alex's body.

"You were so right about In-N-Out," Tamar said. "I finally went there with my parents last weekend. *Way* better than White Castle."

"White Castle?" Alex asked. "Never heard of it. Where's the closest one? I gotta check it out."

"Chicago," Tamar replied and giggled.

"Oh, okay. Might as well be on Mars."

Their wrists bumped again.

"I'd love to just travel and eat at a bunch of different places someday," Alex said.

"I'm sure you will," Tamar said.

The chat died down, so Alex went with his default

conversation starter of making fun of himself. "But I probably have to start hitting the gym or something if I'm gonna start doing something like that."

The last time he got on his parents' scale, Alex broke 180 pounds before running back to his room, naked.

"You're fine," Tamar said. "I like a little chub. Most girls do."

"Wait, so I don't have to get a six-pack?" Alex asked.

"Hell no. I mean, they look like they're fun to rub, but I love something to squeeze."

"Umm, that's cool."

These revelations were flipping Alex's worldview on its head.

"I, uh . . . It's still probably not a bad idea for me to lose a few pounds," he said, looking at her head on as he upwardly crossed his eyes. "And this unibrow isn't helping either."

"Don't worry about that," Tamar said. "Trust me, it adds character, just like big noses. I freaking love big noses. They're everywhere here in Glendale. Like that guy I always see you with. I think he's your friend. What's his name? The guy with the big curly hair."

"Uh, Roman?" Alex replied.

"Yes! He's got a shnozola and a half."

"Yeah. Big time, I guess."

On any other day, Alex knew he'd be brimming with jealousy, but not tonight. It helped to know that Roman was the only male he'd never have to worry about competing against for a girl. Now that's a friend.

Next thing he knew, Alex faced Tamar where the sidewalk met the slithering cobblestone walkway leading to her townhouse. It was unfamiliar territory, both in terms of physical location and encounters with the opposite sex.

Actually, forget sex—he just wanted to share the same side of a diner booth, for starters. After three hangouts, they'd only hugged twice. Maybe not all was lost for his first kiss that night. He assumed all Tamar had to do was lean in and plant one on his lips.

Wait, is that how this works? Yeah! This isn't going to be that hard.

Tamar locked onto his eyes longer than ever before. But Alex froze up. He clung to an eager smile and kept his hands to his side. Silent seconds passed. It was all too much pressure for him. Even though Alex and Tamar were about the same height, he felt like she was looking down at him with a taunting grin.

"Go home," she said as she crossed her arms.

Alex needed a joke to keep things going. "Hopefully, my mom went to bed so she won't ask if I want any of her crummy khoresht," he said and chuckled at himself.

"Okay," Tamar said. "Go home."

"Okay, same time next week!" Alex said, waving to her and his last chance for the night.

They parted ways, and she didn't look back.

—

ROMAN

Roman tore the plastic wrapping off a three-notebook set his parents bought him at the start of the school year and tossed one of them onto his bed. Despite the need for more passwords, he couldn't help but jump the gun and start crunching potential GPAs on his graphing calculator.

An A in Algebra 2 would be too unrealistic, but a B might be believable. An A in Cisco and P.E. would definitely fly. Roman's brain wrestled with the logistics over and over again. He vandalized a dozen wide-ruled pages with grade combos and GPA estimates. He randomly remembered that teachers had to file report card grades by midnight because Ms. Mendoza complained about staying up late one night to do so. The bedsheets grew hot and sticky with Roman's nervous sweat, so he got back on his feet and pinned the notebook against the wall and kept writing.

He clicked his pen repeatedly. Countless what-ifs snowballed in his mind until one clear solution emerged from the fog: above average but under the radar. Roman decided he'd shoot for a 3.4 GPA, an average his folks would be proud of without raising much suspicion.

This would be the comeback story of a lifetime, the phoenix of high school grades. His folks might buy into it since he was already spending every single night in his room instead of hanging out with troublemakers. Roman looked at his reflection in his closet door mirror. He zoned in on his dense glasses. Genetics already made him look the part. Why would it be so hard to believe he was a good student all of a sudden? It'd be just as respected as a growth spurt.

Unfortunately, everything pointed to Todd having to come out of retirement. Roman hated asking for favors, but Lord knew he didn't have the balls or the finesse to work the keylogger himself. He called his friend.

"You up for bowling this weekend?" Roman asked over the phone.

"Uh, I'll let you know," Todd said.

"Please, I really wanna go."

"Now? This one time? I'm trying to organize a group thing and Lucy might be there."

"I need to talk to you about the keylogger, about what I found."

"Why don't you just tell me now?"

"I don't want to say it over the phone or online."

"Well, you just said keylogger over the phone."

"Fuck."

"Shit."

"Can we just go?"

"Geez, alright. Fine. I'll try to get something going with Lucy next week. So we're doing Gem Village then?"

"Yeah. Can I get a ride?"

"Oh, come on, bro. Get your freaking license already. Sure."

Beneath the neon lights of the Gem Village sign, a patch of cool, conditioned air spiked Roman's face as he entered the at-capacity bowling alley along a stretch of car dealerships. He readjusted his glasses and was overwhelmed by the crashing of pins and girl clusters breaking into dance after a strike or even a gutter ball—it was a much more disheveled sight than the thousands of streaming comments on a typical #mswarez night.

Every lane was taken. Todd, now standing next to Roman, shrugged. "Guess we're not playing till morning. I'll go put our name down anyway."

A pair of hands landed on their shoulders.

"It's alright, guys," Alex said from behind. "We can kill some time as I kill you guys at the arcade."

He was already dropping quarters into a machine by the time Roman gave Todd a dirty look.

"What?" Todd said. "If Al knew we went bowling without him, he'd *actually* kill us."

Roman had fantasized about a *Mission: Impossible*-style

exchange in public where he'd recruit Todd for further H-wording operations, though that conjured up cringey images of nerds in movies saying, "I'm in." Roman was biting his nails, hoping Alex would soon be out of earshot. After forty-five minutes of Alex's unanswered ass-whoopings in *Street Fighter 2*, lane 17 freed up. The boys set down their Cokes and typed in their names on the scoring keypad. The competitive titles for the night, as they appeared on the TV above their lane, were TOD, ROM, and ALX.

"You're not cool enough for an X, Al," Todd said as the boys put on their bowling shoes.

Alex yanked his digits out of an alley ball and pointed at Todd. "It's going to be triple X soon."

Todd's eyebrows drooped. "You're kidding, bro. With Tamar?"

Alex beamed. "Things are going great so far. We're hanging out a lot, going to the arcade and stuff."

Todd extended the Chin. "That's awesome, man."

Alex eased up his grin like he was trying to play it cool.

"Sako hooked up with her, so I'm sure you don't have much more to go," Todd announced as he got up to readjust his pants.

Roman's ears perked up like an elf. He was a master at eluding drama, but a rumor about relations among students piqued *everyone's* interest. Todd was face-palming. Not a good sign.

"Shit," Todd muttered.

Roman turned to Alex, who clung to a dying grin until he let out the saddest, most whimpering chuckle ever.

"Yeah, that's something she would do," Alex said. "She . . ." He slid down his seat. "She . . ." He went pale. "She . . ."

Despite his wide-open eyes, it was hard to tell if he was still conscious until his breathing sped up and beads of sweat torrented down his face.

"Uh, you okay, bro?" Todd said as he got up and gently shook Alex's shoulder.

No response. This went way beyond any experience Roman had with rejection. Todd paced for a few moments, then strafed with a fresh Chin toward the cul-de-sac rack of bowling balls and picked up a fourteen-pounder.

"Come on, bros!" Todd said. "Let's do this!"

He had the inaugural throw of the night. It went in a straight line and struck nine pins. Then he crossed his arms over his crotch.

"Suck it!" he shouted at his opponents, but Alex didn't retort with the same D-Generation X slogan. He was still comatose. Roman went next and threw a seven. To his surprise, Alex snapped out of it and threw a six, missed the spare, and sat back down to resume his ragdoll state. Todd rubbed his hands together over the upward jet of air by the bowling balls. Roman was a bit mad at him for being so careless with such flammable gossip, but those thoughts were tossed aside when Todd started heading toward the bathroom. Roman followed and, on the way, looked back over at Alex, still slouching as he stared off into the oblivion that was lane 17. Roman felt bad leaving his friend behind, but an important task was at hand. He tapped Todd's shoulder to indicate they were going to relieve themselves together.

"Jesus Christ, man," Todd said. "Is all of our serious talk going to happen in a bathroom?"

They occupied neighboring urinals. Roman gawked at the ruby tiles inches from his face.

"So, we finally have a moment and you can't talk as usual?" Todd asked, looking down at his crotch.

"Uh, guess what I can do?" Roman blurted out.

"I don't know. You found out the principal is emailing dirty pictures of himself to the TAs?"

"Grades. I did it. I can do them . . . I mean, I can change them."

Todd's hand slipped off the flushing handle. He spat into the urinal and cracked a skeptical smile.

"Yeah, *freaking* right," he said.

"I'm serious," Roman said.

"Bullshit. No way. How?"

"Uh, all I did was find an opening on Port 139, and then I . . ." Roman stopped, figuring he'd spare his friend the boring semantics of the H-wording. "I found a database that can be accessed online. Then I tested it out by changing your English grade."

Todd, now washing his hands, spun around and flung drops of economy soap and water at Roman's shirt.

"The hell!" Todd said. "To what?"

"Uh, a B."

"What!" Todd shouted as he launched a fight-or-flight Chin.

"I changed it back! I changed it back!" Roman said as he used his hands to wipe off the drops. "I just wanted to try it out with someone I knew."

"Bro, why didn't you just change yours?"

"That's the thing. I could only do it with your grade—"

Todd cut him off and marched a lap around the tiny bathroom. "I can't believe this. Aren't they going to notice?"

"You mean the teachers?" Roman asked.

"No, the janitors. Of course, the freaking teachers, bro."

"Well, it's been a few days since I did it. I haven't heard anything."

Todd looked in every direction except for his friend's face.

Roman didn't think it'd be that hard to sign a contractor up for a full-time gig. "Uh, look," he said. "It's just one grade. It's not like we're changing a bunch. If they see that a few grades are off, they'll think someone made a mistake, and they'll fix it, and I'll see that they fixed it. Then I'll stop. Nobody's fault."

Todd did an inverse of the Chin and bowed his head, jaw slightly agape. "My God, bro. I didn't think you'd turn into an evil genius that fast."

"We can change more."

Roman was on the verge of propositioning the quid pro quo until a couple of guys walked into the bathroom.

Todd scratched the back of his head. "This is all too crazy. Let's get out of here. It smells like shit."

"Wait!" Roman said.

It wasn't the reaction Roman hoped for. Todd forced his way through a gaggle of fourteen-to-sixteen-year-olds on the way back to their lane. When they arrived, Alex was still draped over his seat.

"Maybe we should go," Roman suggested as Todd retied his shoelaces. "He looks sick. We can talk about our stuff later after we drop him off."

"What?" Todd said. "We paid for three full games, bro."

"Talk about what?" Alex said as he pulled himself up and flipped his frown upside down.

"Uh," Roman said. "Nothing. Just some other school stuff."

Alex slunk back down. Todd grabbed one of the eight-pound balls.

"Hey, Al!" he called. "Check this out!"

Todd charged toward the lane and flung the ball between his legs, a clownish act that still managed to knock down nine pins.

"Shit," Todd whispered to Roman. "I was going for a gutter ball to help him win or something."

Alex's semi-unibrow, eyes, and lips flatlined. The next time he moved was to wipe the sweat off his forehead, leaving a greasy blotch on the short sleeve of his gray polo. Todd and Roman looked at each other and decided the only thing left to do was keep playing.

At the stroke of eleven, the music got even louder. Roman positioned himself for another clueless toss until Todd started screaming into his ear over "Hot in Here" by Nelly.

"Can you change any more of mine?" Todd pulled his friend closer.

"What?" Roman asked.

"My grades, bro. I didn't mean to get nervous in the bathroom."

"Really? Uh, yeah, if you're down."

Finally! I did social engineering! Roman thought. *Even though I don't know what the hell I did!*

"I mean, I'm doing good this semester, but it could be better!" Todd shouted. "The top schools are ruthless. Plus, this might give me a better chance to spend more time with Lucy!"

"What does she have to do with this?"

Todd hesitated. "You're sure this is safe, right?" he continued yelling while asking.

"Don't worry about it. I got it covered!"

"It's just that the other day I saw Eunice . . . Her boyfriend . . ." Todd cut himself off.

"What?" Roman asked.

"Never mind! You're right! This is different!"

"I'm using a good proxy. Makes my computer look like it's thousands of miles away! Only thing is, I'm going to need your hel—"

"Can we please go, you guys?" Alex called from behind. He had finally gotten up. "I don't feel like playing anymore."

"There's just a few frames left, bro!" Todd said. "Come on!"

"Fine!" Alex shouted.

He hoisted Todd's fourteen-pounder above arched shoulders. Alex gazed at the pins. He approached and swung the ball so far back it almost flattened his cowlick. As the ball came down, he screamed, though the loud music drowned it out. The bowling ball flew over half the lane before it landed straight in the gutter. Todd laughed, but wiped his smile away when Alex, without hesitating, fetched another ball before his own came back and lobbed ferociously while the pins were still being reset. Alex's ball impaled the mechanical pinsetter and set off an echoing *thwack* that turned heads as far away as lane 8. The music stopped and a recording started playing over the music.

"Dear Gem Village patrons, we kindly ask that you please not throw your ball until the pins have been reset."

Roman wondered how often that happened to warrant such a recording. The pinsetter, now dented down the middle, stopped moving.

Todd herded his friends and made for the exit. "You picked a great time to turn into the Hulk, bro," he told Alex.

Outside, Roman and Todd trudged ahead and maintained a dozen-foot buffer between themselves and Alex.

"I hate AP history," Todd said. "If you could help me out there, oh man . . . Nothing but memorization."

"Well," Roman said. "The thing is, if you want me to change any more of yours—"

"Then you'll do it for me out of the kindness of your heart? Thanks, bro!"

"No, I . . . What I meant was . . ."

"Ugh. Let me guess. You were only able to get into Crandle's class. Shit. You're gonna ask me to do this again, aren't you?"

"Uh, yeah," Roman said, for once thankful for Todd's observant side. "Think you could do a couple of my classes too?"

"What?"

"I mean, we already have a lot of the same teachers. Armistead teaches your pre-calc class and my Algebra 2 class. I have regular econ with Hostetter, while you have AP econ with him. Then, like, one or two more of my classes you don't have."

"That's a lot of work, bro, but I got one password already. So, I should know what to expect."

"Like I said, I'll see if they change anything back. Plus, they hand back everything. Tests, essays, projects. We'd just say we threw them away already or something, so there will be like, no proof of what we actually got."

"Yeah," Todd said as his eyes lit up a bit. "Wow, bro, you're right! I mean, do you think if they see something's changed, they're going to actually lower it? You think they're going to look the student and his parents in the eye and say, 'Sorry, you were meant to get a B instead?' Imagine the lawsuits, the emotional distress. We might even be able to make some money off this."

Okay, Roman hadn't thought that far ahead. When they made it back to the car, he offered shotgun to Alex, who waved it off in favor of collapsing into the cushy backseat leather. They drove off.

"Look, Al, you don't have to feel bad, bro," Todd said after a short stretch of quiet. "I think they just hooked up once."

"Shh . . . Idon'twantotalkaboutit," Alex said in a rabid burst, minus the foaming of the mouth.

"She's spending time with you now. That's what matters," Todd said. "You just have to make it happen. Look, what does it matter after eventually you guys hook up?"

"Isaidshuttup!"

Roman had seen Alex get this angry once before when he broke an N64 controller by chucking it at the wall at ramming speed just because he couldn't beat his multiplayer kill count record in *Goldeneye*. The car pulled up to the Ter Alaverdian residence, a dingy apartment building.

"Have a good night, buddy," Todd said. "Everything will be fi—"

"Do you guys wanna come up and play some games?" Alex asked from the backseat. "Please? Maybe some *Goldeneye*? I'll go easy on you."

Roman and Todd looked at each other again.

"We kinda gotta get back home," Todd said.

"I'll let you guys use the golden gun," Alex said. "I won't even pick it up. Please?"

"Next time," Todd said. "We'll order some pizzas too. Or whatever."

Alex lowered his chin to his flabby chest. He seemed to accept the declined invitation.

"Sure." He paused and smiled. "Next time."

He got out and might have said goodnight before slamming the car door. Roman watched Alex power-walk toward the gate of his complex. His hunched posture made him appear headless, like a jilted folk creature in the night.

Todd started driving toward Roman's house.

Roman combed his fingers through his fro; sweat stuck to the base of his roots.

"I hope you're not going to give yourself a 4.0," Todd said. "'Cause that'll be a dead giveaway."

"No, just high enough so my folks will stop bugging me."

"Jesus, that's *all* you want? To stay in your room for months at a time until the brink of insanity, then randomly hit me up for burgers?" Todd sighed. "So, we're really going to do this?"

Roman started to feel like he was asking a bit much of his friend. But there was only one other person he could think of that could be trusted—or offer nothing but his loyalty just to feel like he was a part of something.

"If this is too much, I . . . maybe we can ask Alex if he wants to help too," he said.

"Are you kidding?" Todd asked with a chiding tone. "He has the biggest mouth ever. We'll get caught for sure. Sorry, I was just thinking things over. I've got this."

"Alright," Roman said.

A few minutes later, they arrived at Roman's house.

"Uh, you'll have time to get the passwords," he said. "I'll have until midnight when the grades are filed to change stuff. I found that out from my Spanish teacher."

"I guess this is an opportunity we can't pass up," Todd said as his friend unbuckled his seat belt. "If we can pull this off, I can definitely get into somewhere like Stanford. I need every GPA point I can get."

"Uh, but what about no 4.0?" Roman asked.

"I've gotten straight As since kindergarten. No offense, bro, but no one would ever believe you. I mean, they'd believe you could hack into a school, but get a 4.0?"

Roman was unsure if his friend had just insulted him.

"I didn't mean it that way, bro. See, you should be glad you're not the studying type of nerd. You'll never turn into a competitive loser. But whatever, I'm in."

10

TODD

He used to hate looking in the mirror and would twitch at the sight of his doughy folds when changing clothes or stepping out of the shower.

Now, he sighed as he reached for a small container of light tan ointment on his desk. It was near a few framed family photos and one of him and Roman from a birthday party two years ago—the one piece of evidence in Todd's room of his former physique. Roman looked the same, except his giant afro was dwarfed by Todd's familial girth, the Tovmasian barrel. Framed presidential awards and other prestigious plaques ran a lap around his bedroom walls.

Todd shut his blinds to shield his room from the afternoon sun. He stood at a ten-hut in just his boxer briefs as he faced down the marks in a mirror he dragged from his big sister's old bedroom. It was required to execute his plan of concealment. Grotesque streaks of blue and purple slithered around his now-toned waist, his shoulders, torso, upper thighs, and ass—all remnants of the summer of sixty-nine pounds. The streaks were thick and sewn together like a veiny spider web. Even with a strict diet of air and weekly marathons, they weren't going anywhere.

He had a few minutes before it was time to hit the books, so he twisted off the cap, lathered two of his fingers, and massaged the cream over the streaks until they vanished. He did a few turns and poses and cracked a smile similar to the one he had the first time he read 140 on a scale. No chick, especially not Lucy, could find him repulsive anymore—if only her goddamn parents let her hang out at night. Her schedule permitted the quickest of after-school ice cream runs, so quick a cone wouldn't even get a chance to melt under the Southland sun and drip onto Todd's shoes.

Barefoot at the moment, he started jogging in place. His sharp spikes were unwavering. Then he started sprinting in place, like the summer when everyone wondered what an overweight fourteen-year-old boy was doing at a gym at nine at night. He had barely convinced his parents to cut one hour of study time, so he'd have time to work out and a shot to live past forty.

Squinting at the reflection of his temple, the first glistening beads eked out of his pores. Todd shook his head a few times, but much to his dismay, the drops landed along his torso and wiped away the cream, revealing marks with the hue of a witch's mole.

Shit! None of these creams work!

He heard rapid steps ascend the staircase. Todd tossed on his T-shirt and basketball shorts just a few moments before his mother knocked on the door.

"Tadeh?" his mother, Seda, called from outside. "Are you okay?"

"I'm fine," Todd said. He had already caught his breath, another perk of losing weight. "I was getting a little tired. Ran in place to wake myself up. You can go. We're just wasting time now."

"If you're tired, then take a nap. It's okay."

"No!" he shouted.

"Or just come downstairs and eat," Seda said. "When are you going to stop doing this to yourself?"

"Dad said no quitting till eight. You know the rule."

"Fine."

Seda's steps faded downstairs. Back to the routine. Every part of Todd was perfectly still, except for his hands. He swooped his lead pencil like a beast while maintaining a heart rate of forty-two beats per minute—the same as a professional marathoner.

5:30 p.m. The nuzzling embrace of the odd and even functions of pre-calculus.

6:15 p.m. AP History. *Sit on my lap,* he thought.

7:30 p.m. Get started on the *As I Lay Dying* essay in English.

While most people set an alarm for the morning, Todd's went off at eight at night. He mentally chugged the final factoids of the evening, went to the bathroom to take an extra-long piss, and leaped downstairs for some dinner before heading to basketball with his friends at the YMCA. He caught a dense whiff of his grandmother's bamieh khoresht as he landed on his feet. From the couch, Aghavni observed the third of her progeny with a blanket over her lap.

"Bamieh? Hell yes!" Todd said.

She got up to serve her grandson a stew of lamb, tomato, and okra, not asking, "Enough?" until the fourth scoop. He raised his right palm on the fifth.

"What about rice?" Aghavni asked in Armenian.

"No rice. Just the khoresht," Todd said.

"Are you sure?"

"*Metzmom,* you know I rarely eat rice and bread now. But I will still eat and love everything else you cook."

Aghavni gave him an apprehensive look. "You're too skinny now. It's unhealthy."

In business attire, Seda did menial tasks around the kitchen. Todd sat at the dining table and blew on his hot dinner. After it cooled a bit, he went to town despite his grandma nagging him about constipation induced by eating too fast, but it wasn't fast enough. His dad set foot in the house. Next was his protruding gut.

"They approved the strip mall," Vigen Tovmasian said in a strong Middle Eastern accent to his wife. "Too close to residential. I don't care what the code allows. It's outdated. Stupid idiots."

He was a home architect by day and a member of the city planning commission on Wednesday evenings. Vigen was a bit shorter than Todd and had a thin patch of gray and white hair that thinly veiled a grouping of liver spots.

Todd regretted taking a minute longer to finish his dinner. His dad's commission meetings often went into the wee hours. Todd dropped his plate off by the kitchen sink and tried to duck out, but his dad cut him off as he kicked off his brown leather shoes.

"Where?" Vigen muttered without looking at his son.

"I finished everything," Todd said.

"Calculus?"

"Pre-calculus, as you know. Yes."

"When I was sixteen, I was already taking calculus."

"Well, I'm not enrolled in the Tehran Unified School District, Dad."

"What about the calculus course at Glendale College?" Vigen said. "Did you sign up for it?"

It would be a college transferable course, basically an extra period after school, two days a week, which would cross off two potential date days a week.

"Tomorrow," Todd said.

"Again tomorrow. Always tomorrow," Vigen said. "Seda jan, what are we going to do with him? We've told you a thousand times to register."

She shrugged from behind the kitchen counter.

"If you miss the registration, then you can't put the class on your college application," Vigen said. "If that happens, I won't let you drive either of our cars for a month."

"Dad, come on. I don't have the time to do all this."

And so began the futile routine. Vigen leaned his briefcase against an upright piano in the den. "Time?" He took off his coat and hung it in a closet by the front door. "That's what happens when you become a pretty boy. You have to maintain it."

"All the doctors said I had to lose weight."

"I was the same weight at your age, and I'm still fine," Vigen said, shoving his toes into a pair of brown slippers. "So are your brother and sister. And all of your uncles."

Todd rolled his eyes.

"What was I thinking?" Vigen continued. "We shouldn't have gotten you that gym membership."

"Dad, come on," Todd said. "I got healthy and kept my grades up. Nothing's changed."

"What's more important?" Vigen asked. "How many times you work out or your *real* work? Is it better to be a fit loser than a successful overweight man? Nobody cares about your weight if you're the best at what you do."

He moved to a spot under framed pictures of his first two children, Armen and Vaneh—both obese and lacking necks—in graduation caps and gowns from Caltech and Yale, respectively. Todd thought his dad was so selfish. He had arrived as a poor immigrant and got lucky by managing to raise two children who graduated from the best colleges in the country and had the audacity to demand the same of his third child.

"I can do both," Todd said. "I'm doing both."

"I won't know that until I see proof," Vigen said.

"You've seen proof. I lock myself in for four hours every day. I don't even go to the bathroom."

"Letters in the mail. Lots of them."

Todd was incensed, but the prospect of what was at Roman's fingertips elevated him to a restrained rage—best he saved that energy for the Y.

"Oh, you'll get your letters," he said with fists clenched at his waist, which bulged his biceps.

Maybe it wasn't the best time to propose a tweak to his study schedule, the first since he started hitting the gym over a year ago. All Todd wanted was to start an hour or two later so he could have a proper date with Lucy after school. After a few of those, maybe her folks would warm up to the idea of her dating someone. If Todd could get a 4.4, maybe even the unicorn that was a 4.5, he'd also have a stronger pitch for his dad about additional flexibility down the road, so he could live out at least a few quintessential teenage moments and avoid the path toward becoming weirdo loners like Roman and Alex.

Todd dropped to his tailbone and put on his Nikes. He grabbed his duffel bag and left.

"Be safe," his mother said as he closed the front door behind him. "I love you, Tadeh jan."

A few nights a week, Todd played basketball with Sako, Narbeh, Arbi, Arbo, and Artin. Soon after Todd dropped all that weight, started spiking his hair, and wearing trendier clothes, he found himself looped into the circle of the fittest and cockiest guys at school. He guessed it was what he wanted—shooting up the academic ladder and a social one could only be a good thing. It just took some time to get used to the shit-talking between his new friends.

"You ain't got shit, pussy," Arbo called out during the friendly game.

"You got lucky, bitch," Artin said after Narbeh shot a three-pointer over him. "I don't know who sucks harder, you or your girl."

"Don't be such a sore loser, gyote," Narbeh said, responding with the derogatory Armenian term for a homosexual.

The barbs were never more than skin deep and were met with laughs and, at most, a few shoulder-to-shoulder bumps. The rest of the time, they mimicked engine-revving sounds and re-purposed commentary from SportsCenter as their own expert opinions.

Although he was now among the supposed alphas, it never crossed Todd's mind to leave Roman and Alex behind; he'd join them for lunch whenever he could. Their social ineptness might have been annoying, but shit talk was directed toward video games or the bullshit obstacle of the day, never each other. No added stress, nothing to prove. It wasn't until recently that Todd became grateful for how obliviously considerate they were.

Sako thudded around the court, shirtless, eyeing a chance to jut out his trap. He didn't have a six-pack, but rather a toned gut with a faint dividing line down the middle. In fact, all the guys were shirtless except for Todd, who sported an away Kobe Bryant jersey. It was more of a matchup of spiky hair versus shaved heads. Despite the discrepancy in mass, Todd still had the wing-span to defend Sako as he backed up into him.

"Bro, you have the flattest chest here," Sako said, mocking him. "You ain't got tits to hide."

"You want me to strip *that* bad, bro?" Todd replied.

Sako smiled and spun himself around Todd, who kept up just enough to get his hands in the air and force a missed layup. Arbi rebounded and passed the ball to Todd. He dribbled down the court and faked his defender with a crossover that almost made him trip over his own feet. Todd drove in for a layup but was blocked by an airborne Sako, who didn't even raise an arm. Instead, he knocked Todd to the floor with his chest.

"My bad, bro," Sako said, offering his hand.

Regardless, Todd was starting to realize that Sako was kind of a dick.

"You alright?" Sako said.

From below, he had a triple chin.

Is this what Tamar saw? Todd asked himself. *Gross. Poor Alex.*

The guilt of being the stupid one to tell him about Tamar came back in spades. Todd understood now that he had to work fast to win over his own crush.

"Touch Lucy and I swear to god I'll kill you," he said under his breath, but thought he uttered that in his mind.

"Huh?" Sako grunted.

"I said that's a flagrant," Todd said, helping himself back up.

"Ha, not my fault you're bony as hell," Sako said, handing over the ball. "Sick cross, though."

—

Fueled by potential glory and Coke the next day, Todd sashayed into Mr. Hostetter's AP Economics class. He choreographed the term "nonchalant" into an elegant dance and performed a ballet in his brain. Heels together, Todd executed a plié that blossomed into a twirl and climaxed with an unfurling of the keylogger into the back of his teacher's computer.

Everyone had to shuffle around since they were working on group projects, and Todd acted fast to take a seat by Mr. Hostetter's computer. After the teacher logged in and tended to some emails, Todd did a movie theater date stretch to retrieve the keylogger. Easy. Handoff to Roman.

—

ROMAN

jhostetter@gmsd.edu
daddylovesmolly98

How cute, Roman thought. *Thanks, Molly. Daddy loves you too. No, that's too creepy. Just thanks.*

—

TODD

Test day in pre-calc. Old Mr. Armistead's nose was buried deep in the spine of a Tom Clancy novel. Todd made sure he was the first to hand in his exam so he'd be ahead of everyone else getting up and walking back and forth. Mr. Armistead's computer was situated at the apex of a boomerang-shaped desk with knick-knacks from places like Big Bear and Lake Tahoe keeping the ports company. *Ideal camouflage*, Todd thought. He placed his exam face down in front of Mr. Armistead, who hardly diverted his attention away from his book. Todd took a step closer to the computer, got on one knee to tie a shoe, and took note of how other students were still busy showing their work. He tugged the keylogger out of his pocket and swung up his arm to make the insertion.

Here's a souvenir from Hong Kong to add to your collection, Todd thought. *At least, I think that's where Rome ordered it from.*

The only problem was that the computer wasn't on. Todd walked by Mr. Armistead's class at the end of every period, and it wasn't until the last stroll of the day that he saw a booted-up screen. He strode in, pretending to be looking for he didn't even know what, and made the snatch after a quick crawl around the floor.

This is too easy. Forget the top twenty of the class; I'll be able to crack the top five! Handoff to Roman.

—

ROMAN

aarmistead@gmsd.edu
password

Of course, you old bastard.

—

TODD

Todd's erect Chin piloted his hot streak into Mr. Wineman's class during lunch the next day for an open house of Club Hodgepodge, an after-school club where students forged junk computer and electronic parts into franken-devices. Mr. Wineman was the computer programming, networking, and typing teacher. Todd didn't have a class with Wineman—he was one of Roman's teachers. No one else on staff had a more extensive collection of Hawaiian shirts. The subsequent snapshot was of a bunch of scrappy nerds. They stared right back at his wrinkle-free Tommy Hilfiger polo and spotless K-Swisses. Todd fudged himself between a fat kid in a fading green sweater and a short kid with a greasy combover.

The open house was also a recruiting tool to try and reel in some new talent onto the school's robotics team. All the desks were pushed outward to form a ring around the class. Piles of old monitors, towers, patch panels, routers, and vacuum tubes were strewn across a blue tarp. A robot the size of a small dog on its hind legs spun in place on four small wheels. Its graphite arms and hands clenched onto a small plastic ball.

"Everyone, meet Timmy," Wineman said as he held an RC remote in his hand. He wore glasses as thick as Roman's. "Well, this is actually Timmy 3. This one can do what its predecessors couldn't."

Timmy stopped spinning, brought its arms behind its head, and launched the ball through a hoop hanging above the whiteboard. Everyone started clapping, with Todd being the last to do so.

"And that's how we won county this year," Wineman said. "But it wasn't because of my accuracy. It was because Ranveer here made the clutch basket with his magnificent design and had help from his teammates."

Still in control, Wineman made Timmy rove in a loop of figure eights.

"And it's not just throwing balls we can perfect," Wineman continued. "There's a million potential applications for these kinds of robots, like a seeing-eye dog or a roving security guard equipped with surveillance cameras."

Timmy stopped in its tracks and faced the crowd.

"And *you* can be part of this too," Wineman said, pointing at the prospective members. "Who knows? Maybe next year we'll make a robot that can launch a perfect football spiral through a tire!"

This guy definitely molests the robotics team, Todd joked to himself.

Wineman walked over to his desk and wheeled an overhead monitor toward the center of the classroom. He pulled down a screen over the whiteboard and turned on the projector, which displayed a short list of safety tips for grounding electricity.

"I need to show you all something quick," Wineman said. "Since I'm going to let you try this stuff out today, I need to show you how to ground yourselves properly. And no, not the way your parents do when you screw up."

Todd thought the rows of bodies, especially the larger of the distracted nerds, were ideal for obstructing his wrist flicks. At a steady pace, he slid through the crowd until he arrived at Wineman's desk. Wineman had declined a school-issued computer and brought his own from home. As Todd reached into his pocket for the keylogger, his foot rubbed against something flimsy.

Oh, what's this?

His left foot hooked onto something.

"So, remember, everyone, your computer loves electricity flowing through it, but you won't," Wineman said.

Todd managed to free his foot, but at the cost of the projection suddenly vanishing and the whizzing of the overhead being swapped for a glaring mute. Todd heard *huh*s from the twenty or so nerds around him. Wineman traced the power cable with his eyes to an outlet near Todd, who was frozen in place with the key-logger enclosed in his fist. Todd scanned the room for a moment, then stopped to reduce implied guilt. Mr. Wineman's enthusiastic gleam morphed into the same probing stare every teacher had when seeking out a troublemaker.

Get lies ready, Todd thought. *Get ready to shove the keylogger up your ass if need be.*

"What are you up to over there, sir?" Wineman asked.

Todd lost count of the eyes peering at him. He was annoyed that he wasn't in trouble yet. He wanted it to be instant.

"I see what it is," Wineman said. "You've taken an interest in Big Bertha. It's kind of my own franken-computer. When the school ordered a bunch of new Compaqs, I told them I didn't need something new and shiny. So I made my own out of a 97 Acer shell, a 32-inch ViewSonic, and a Pentium 4. All of you here today can do something as cool as I did! What's your name, son?"

"Tadeh," Todd said, his voice cracking a bit.

"Well, Tadeh, you got bored with my presentation. I get it," Wineman said, waving him off with both hands. "If you want, come back after school, and I'll give you a good look inside, and that invitation goes for everyone. Now, would you mind plugging the overhead back in?"

Todd obliged without missing a beat. Even though he had failed, he stuck around for the rest of the open house to allay suspicion. After the bell rang, he sprinted out of the class with no intention of ever returning. The hallway must have rocketed to the steepest incline on his treadmill as he started sweating and struggling to catch his breath.

"I'm not doing Wineman," Todd told Roman as they walked to the student parking lot after school. Todd had promised him a ride home.

"Why?" Roman asked.

"Bro, that guy is freaking glued to his computer. There's no way the keylogger will go unnoticed."

"But, but our deal."

"Now I get why my friggin' dad told me to never do business with friends," Todd said.

Roman had a blank look on his face. Todd knew that although his friend wielded the almighty power of grade book revision, he could swing some of his own weight now.

"Isn't Wineman's class all about computers and shit?" Todd asked. "Doesn't this stuff come naturally to you?"

"It's the same reason why you hate government," Roman said. "Too much memorizing. He's the only one who gets to work with equipment during class. We rarely get to touch stuff."

"Stupid district. No wonder he does robotics shit at lunch and after school—in addition to being a loser with no life."

"You're not quitting, are you?"

They headed down the stairs to the parking lot. Lucy was picked up on Todd's hormonal sonar. He saw her behind the wheel of her silver 1985 BMW E30, the peak of Germany's post-war engineering reformation. The car was old but classy and in museum-quality condition. What Todd loved most was that the car was manual—it was love at first gear. Car culture to Armenian Americans is as vital as housing.

But Lucy wasn't backing out for the day just yet. Instead, she popped her hood and slipped out, her baby-blue toenails leading the way. She wore flip-flops, which she dragged across the asphalt.

Is she having car problems? Todd thought from a distance. *Rome, if Lucy needs my help, adios.*

A few spots over, the shortest junior in his class, Ed Pacheco, struggled to turn on his ancient Nissan Stanza. His engine wheezed as his circular glasses slid down his nose. His eyes were glued to his floor mat in apparent shame and humiliation. Todd, in good nature, would bug Roman about how even this shorter nerd with glasses managed to get his driver's license first. Then Sako roared by in a Toyota Supra with an aftermarket exhaust as big as a tuba.

"Hope your mom has Triple A, bro!" he shouted at Pacheco and cracked up with another dude in his car. Sako revved the Supra a few times before peeling out of the lot.

In spaghetti straps, Lucy went to her trunk and retrieved some jumper cables. On her way, Todd could have sworn she shook her head. Hopefully, she thought Sako was a jerk too.

Yes! Todd shouted in his head.

Or perhaps it was in a "boys will be boys" kind of way, indicating she wanted to be swept off her feet. Lucy's eyes always looked sleepy, open a quarter of the way, but she walked with wide-awake confidence to Ed's driver's side window.

"You've gotta pop your hood too," she told him with a smile. "It's the button by the penny tray right there."

Ed adjusted his glasses and popped the hood. Lucy linked the cars' batteries with the jumper clamps and turned on her car. Next, she signaled with her hand for Ed to turn the key. After a few coughs, the Stanza kicked over. They got back out and closed their hoods.

"Just make sure you get a new battery today," Lucy said. "But if the starter keeps giving you problems, go see my dad. He'll give you a discount."

She handed over a business card that she pulled out of her light pink, daytime clutch bag.

"Th-Thank you," Ed said.

"No problem. Drive safe!"

Todd was more enamored than ever. It wasn't the automotive skills or her cute baby fat love handles poking out just a bit from her top, but her lack of giving a shit for taking such a high-risk, no-reward gesture in an environment where all social classes had the same fragile footing.

Ed drove out of the parking lot. The boys hopped into Todd's car. Lucy saw him on her way out of the lot and waved. He waved back.

"I gotta learn how to jump-start a car," Roman said. "Useful shit."

Todd was still looking off into the distance until Lucy's old Bimmer was out of frame.

"Uh," Roman said. "You okay?"

Todd had figured out why her parents were so strict—it had to be because she was too nice, but someone had to be her rock someday. Even just a night out at the local Olive Garden would totally be worth it. Todd nodded, but was reluctant to reveal the bold idea he had to keep plans on track.

Later that afternoon, Todd borrowed a page from Roman's book and used a money order to buy something online. When the package arrived, the item resembled pens in a pocket protector, but the contents were much thinner than writing tools. Impatient to try it out, he dropped the sales receipt onto the floor of his front porch. In one hand, Todd held something he believed was a bogota rake and a tension wrench in the other. Both were tiny and puny and fit into the key slot of his front door lock. Todd rifled both of the tools in and out with great speed, but nothing was happening. From the bottom corner of his eye, he saw the sales receipt and the words it bore: "LOCK PICKING SET."

Each time he heard a car turn the corner onto his street, he'd stand up straight and pretend he was just getting home. Finally, he recognized the dulling silver of his mom's Lexus and gave up, resorting to the regular house key to get inside. But much like basketball or schoolwork, all it was going to take was some practice and studying.

He also remembered to pick up the receipt and hide it under his bed.

11

The second Alex stopped keeping busy, the crippling images seeped in.

Tamar hooked up with Sako, Tamar hooked up with Sako, Tamar hooked up with Sako. Spiraling into painful daydreams became routine. He'd envision them making out, steaming up any mirrors in the room, then the one-two of Sako undoing her bra, followed by the whisper of cotton panties being tugged down her thighs, and finally—

Alex refused to picture anymore.

This whole thing with Tamar was bullying by proxy. The security of being off campus was compromised. All this was compounded by the fact that Alex had yet to kiss a girl. Every moment, he coped with jealousy nipping at the back of his neck.

Homework became more difficult than ever before. Multiplying numbers became emblematic of Tamar and Sako doing it. Alex couldn't even watch porn without seeing their faces superimposed over the actors'. He went a week without masturbating until Alex was so backed up that it made the deed easier.

This, too, shall pass! Alex mentally shouted at his computer screen.

To help keep his mind occupied, he beat *Final Fantasy V* in just three days, a solid forty-hour commitment. Then he did it again. Next, it was onto a replay of *Chrono Trigger* and a quest to find all the hidden endings.

It had been a few weeks since Alex last went to the arcade with Tamar, pretty much since he learned of the bombshell from Todd. In the one brief AIM exchange he had with her, Alex chalked it up to having a big project to do. Other than that, he worked hard to avoid her. When the bell rang, he'd sprint out of the one class they had together and languish for breath on the way to his friends for lunch. They were the most reliable distraction, though Todd occasionally prodded about the latest.

"So, you're over it, right?" Todd asked one morning after they met up by the soda machines. "Onto the next one?"

"Yeah, for the most part," Alex said, lying, but he was believable enough to earn a Chin of respect in return.

It became more of a matter of self-hatred than getting over Tamar. He hated the soul he was born into. He hated how he couldn't learn from his mistakes.

But it was impossible to avert a good mood forever. Alex got a hankering for some Barq's root beer, so at lunch, he and Roman headed back to the trio of soda machines, where they came across an unexpected presence: Sako and a couple of other guys, including Todd, were lounging at a nearby bench. It was strange since they were usually atop the amphitheater.

Why does Todd have to hang out with him? Alex thought. *Does Sako have to take away everyone I like?*

Out of courtesy, Alex threw his head back toward Todd, who slanted his own with a forlorn expression. Befuddled for a second, Alex deposited three quarters into the soda machine and pressed the button displaying the Barq's logo. The bottle ricocheted its way down, but instead of a crashing sound where Alex would normally retrieve it, he heard a muddy *thud*. He looked down and saw that an efficient burst of a cold, creamy substance had splattered onto his black khakis. Before Alex could determine if he was dreaming or not, Sako's cadre erupted with laughter. Todd phoned in a few chuckles and tried looking away as he scratched the Chin. Roman stood like a statue and likely didn't want to get involved.

Sako jogged up and down a short sideline of high-fives from his friends. No further evidence was needed; Sako was previously known for a trending prank of flipping backpacks inside out. Alex bent down to get a closer look at the bottle to find it cratered in a potato boat. Everyone must have thought he had shat his pants.

But this was no time to run to the office and call his mom, begging her to come pick him up. Something snapped within. Perhaps his recent purchase wasn't a complete waste.

Still laughing, the pranksters didn't notice Alex dallying their way as he twisted the cap off his root beer bottle, which was slathered with spud mush on one side. Just three-quarters of its contents, Alex thought, so he could at least have something to wash down his lunch. In the end, the internal debate didn't matter because Alex emptied the entire bottle, dousing Sako's fashionable white JanSport with a brown canopy of soda. Sako, amid throwing his arms in the air, thrust toward Alex. He towered over Alex, broad like a triptych, ready to envelop.

"What the hell, bro?" Sako yelled.

His pupils were enflamed and ready to demolish like wrecking balls. But Alex didn't even bother getting into a defensive stance. He gazed up almost half a foot at Sako, stretching his grin to the point of a Glasgow smile while flaunting the furry arch above his eyes. Alex believed a fist-pummeling would be a blessing if it were the only kind of pain he'd suffer in life.

Everyone looked weirded out by the staring contest. Then Sako's friends started turning their laughs against him. With panicking wipes, he tried to get the stains off his backpack with a couple of used tissues he pulled out of his pocket.

"Shit! Shit! Shit!" he yelled. "It was just a prank, bro!"

Alex picked up a nearby unopened bottle of Sprite by its neck and raised it to the sky like a sword. Sako took a step back, tripped, and fell onto his ass as the bottle ascended. Alex wasn't quite sure where he was aiming—or, rather, what he was doing—but he wanted to cling to the thrill of dominance for as long as possible. It climaxed with a tap on his shoulder.

"Calm down," Todd whispered into his ear. "Good comeback, though."

Alex's insane grin dwindled back to normal. "Did she . . . Did she see?"

"What?" Todd asked.

He didn't get a chance to answer because, this time, Alex felt a tap on his other shoulder—it was the vice principal, Deborah Leininger, in her women's business suit, walkie-talkie in hand.

"How old are you?" she asked in a stern tone.

"Uh, sixteen," Alex said. "Seventeen in a couple months."

"Then start acting like it. You have lunch detention for three days."

"But . . . But he did it first!" Alex said, pointing at Sako, who put on a phony BS puppy-dog expression as he panhandled his friends for more tissues.

"Meet me at the bottom of the amphitheater tomorrow," Leininger said.

"Do I still get to eat lunch?" Alex asked.

But Leininger was already a dozen feet away and counting. Alex sauntered back to his friend.

"That . . . That was awesome," Roman said.

"Really?" Alex asked.

"Uh, yeah, except the part where you stared him down. That was kinda creepy."

"Did she see?"

"Sucks about lunch detention, though."

"Did *she* see?" Alex pleaded.

"Uh, who?"

"Who else?"

Roman did a quick scan of his surroundings. "I . . . I don't know. I didn't see her around."

"Dammit!"

Alex wound his leg, kicked a nearby trash can, and grabbed it to keep it from tipping over; he didn't need an extended sentence. In the process, some soda from a bottle shook free and glued his fingers together.

"Shit!" Alex shouted.

The next day, he roamed the amphitheater alone, picking up discarded bags of chips and shreds of lettuce as Sako and his brood pointed and laughed from underneath a green awning at the summit. Of course, Alex was humiliated, and he thought about spiraling an empty Sprite bottle he'd picked up toward Sako's head, but he was so tired, physically and mentally. He kneeled to tie his shoes, and before he could get up, he was blinded by sunlight reflecting off an aluminum wrapper.

"Here," Roman said.

He held a wrapped spicy chicken sandwich, still steaming.

"What's this?" Alex asked as he got back up. "Where's yours?"

Roman shook his head and let go of the sandwich. "I'm not hungry," he said.

"You sure?"

"Yeah."

Forget the Kenny Rogers sandwich; Alex was just glad someone was thinking about him. The gesture pinched his heart. He reached over and accepted the sandwich. He wanted to hug his friend, but knowing a group of immature lummoxes were watching, he held back.

Despite his well-known state of despair, Alex didn't want to lure pity. But this was one occasion where he needed to take any kind of attention as far as he could.

"Is everything okay?" he asked.

"Huh?" Roman said. "Yeah, I'm fine."

"I mean with you and Todd. And me. I feel like you guys are always talking about something, then change the subject when I show up."

Roman hesitated and darted his eyes around like he was watching a tennis match.

"No, we're good," he said. "Just homework and family stuff I don't wanna bore you with."

There wasn't enough time for Alex to determine if he was being truthful as he saw Leininger at the bottom of the amphitheater, pointing out various pieces of garbage left to pick up.

Alex inspected his left arm and peeled an Airheads wrapper

off his elbow. "I hope I never have to do this again," he said under his breath.

—

He couldn't hold out anymore; her absence was getting to him. The nostalgia of their hangouts struck a teary chord more than the ending of *The Legend of Zelda: A Link to the Past*.

"So, here you are, finally," Tamar said, standing by the entrance to Video West. "You been alright?"

She was the late one this time. She wore that gray hoodie with the pink stripes along the arms.

"Uh, just busy," Alex said. "Lots of projects that just came out of nowhere."

"Okay," she said, sounding unconvinced.

Alex slapped down button combos in *Street Fighter II: Champion Edition* like he was throwing nothing but bullseyes all night. He tried to resist glancing over at Tamar despite the allure of her baby nose, a sight more comforting than the dozen game-over screens he resoundingly dealt her.

"How did you get so good so fast?" Tamar asked. "Are you bringing girls here every night that I don't know about?"

"Can't I just be in the zone for once?" Alex replied curtly.

"Are you okay?" Tamar's nose, although tiny, blocked the countdown on the *game-over* screen. "You're acting weird. Does this have to do with you getting lunch detention?"

"How'd you know about that?" Alex asked.

"It was pretty hard to miss you in the middle of the amphitheater picking up trash."

"So, you saw *that*, huh?"

"What do you mean?"

"Uh, never mind."

The walk home would once again be the venue for an attempt. It was a quiet stroll. They slowed to a halt at the sidewalk slab where he'd usually say goodnight. Tamar started waving and yawned.

"Wait, before you go, do you have a second?" Alex asked.

"Sure, what's on your mind this time?" she asked, followed by a light chuckle.

Alex's gaze shifted toward the freshly cut grass behind her.

This is the way it's done, he thought. *Get it all out. Don't use words like "crush" or phrases like "I like you." You're more mature now. You're ready.*

"I'm sorry if I've been weird tonight. I don't want to sound like an idiot," Alex said. "It's just been so great hanging out with you. I mean, I don't think I've ever had so much fun with a girl—I mean, with a gamer—at an arcade. I feel like, with all that time we're spending together, well . . . What I'm trying to say is that there could be more of that. Lots more at arcades and stuff."

Tamar giggled a few times, but it didn't faze him.

No rejection yet. She isn't walking away. Keep going.

"I'm crazy about you," Alex said.

But in return, the giggles escalated to a few hearty laughs. "What's so funny?" Alex asked. "I'm not trying to be funny!"

"No, no, I'm sorry. I'm not laughing in that way. It's just that you get exactly like this when you think you're about to beat me and then I own you."

"Believe it or not, for once, I'm serious, Tamar!"

"I know you are."

"And I want you to know that you're an amazing person, that

I'm so lucky to get to spend time with you. Every second of it, I forget about everything. I feel like a man without ever having to set foot in the gym once."

She raised a puzzled eyebrow in response to that last qualifier.

No evidence of rejection. She isn't running away. Keep going.

"Well, thank you," Tamar said. "I mean, I'm flattered, and I think you're cute."

Keep going! Keep going! Keep going!

"But I don't know," she continued. "I don't think I'm . . . I mean, this is so out of the blue."

"What do you mean?" Alex said.

"I thought we were just hanging out."

It was like the momentum of an avalanche had stopped halfway down the mountain.

"I get it. It's because I'm not like Sako," he said.

"I'm not following," Tamar said.

"Everyone knows about you two, apparently!"

She sighed as she raised her palm to her forehead. "That asshole."

Alex didn't understand how a lover could be described as such.

"Look, there was so much going through my head at the time," Tamar continued. "I was getting used to a new school in a different part of the country. Sako was just there at the moment. He was the first guy to introduce himself, and he showed me around."

"I can take you to better places!" Alex said.

"Alex!" Tamar said, stifling the moment. "Sako was a blip on the radar!"

"It's because he's big and strong, right? That's all you guys care about."

"No, Alex, if you're worried about who I care more about,

there's no contest. I deeply care about you. He and I don't even talk anymore. We've both moved on."

Alex wasn't ready for a compliment, let alone one so uplifting that it somehow elevated him over his archenemy.

"I guess that makes me feel a bit better," he said. But the maturity would only last for a few measly moments. "So, does that mean you'll go out with me?"

Tamar sighed. "I don't know. You're putting me on the spot!"

The burst of frustration shut Alex up.

"So that's it?" Tamar asked. "You're just asking me out 'cause you think I'm easy or something? That's really scummy, Alex."

"No!" he exclaimed. "It's not that at all!"

"And here I am thinking you were different."

"No, Tamar, I still want to be with you. Doesn't matter what happened in the past. I'm sorry I even brought it up."

"God, I hate it when people get so judgey about stuff like this."

"I'm not judging. I just felt . . . inferior."

"Do you think that's how I look at you? You think that's why I like hanging out with you?"

"So, does that mean you'll at least think about it?"

"Alex, can we call it a night?"

"Can we talk tomorrow or something?"

"*Alex,* something like what you're asking for isn't meant to start from a moment like this. It doesn't feel right."

Tamar looked off to the side, past the intersection, which was uncharacteristic of her. Then she glanced down at her feet, which was even weirder.

"Something's gone," Tamar continued. "That's what it is, to be honest. There was something in the beginning about you, but now, it's gone."

Her apology sealed the deal as well as most of Alex's nostrils.

"I'm sorry," Tamar continued.

The thought of pursuing someone new made this broad, quiet street claustrophobic. Tamar raised her head to look at him.

"But you're still a super-fun person," she said. "Chat on AIM later?"

"For sure!" Alex replied, reinvigorated by another opportunity.

"Good."

Tamar initiated a hug, not just a quick one-arm-over-the-shoulder. It was full-frontal; she rested her chin on his shoulder, oh so briefly, for the first time.

"Goodnight," Tamar said.

"See ya."

Alex, hands in his pockets, started heading home. He pictured himself as the lead in one of the romantic comedies his mom would watch. In it, he was the protagonist who would devise a zany ploy to win over the girl. But the movie ended before it started and was replaced with a reality show of him bending over and wheezing, wondering why he was first to be voted off the island.

At least all the other girls were quick with their emphatic no's. At this point, he couldn't wait to get home and just cry. He felt he had earned a good wailing. It'd been a while; the last time was when he plummeted off his cousin's bike and scraped his knee.

Waterfall tears erupted the second he stepped into his house and saw that his parents were already upstairs in bed. Then in the bathroom. Then in the shower. Then in his room. Then in his bed.

There was one common thread through all the girls who rejected him; they were all gone.

Out of sight, out of mind. The next day, he and Tamar did indeed chat on AIM.

S0lidsnacK85: I don't want anything to do with you.

P3achy_Zelda85: So that's it? You never want to talk to me again?

S0lidsnacK85: itll make things easier. I can't and dont want to go on being friends

P3achy_Zelda85: Whatever works Alex. Whatever works.

12

TODD

Roman ate lunch quietly as usual, but Alex's staredown with a patch of crabgrass and refusal to speak was downright rude—not even a generic take on the prior night's Lakers game or an unrequested rental review. After all, Todd could have opted for the top of the amphitheater and watched other dudes show off their new tennis shoes instead of a front row to this mopey duo.

"Listen," Todd said. "Don't let your life fall apart over her."

Alex's first response was a pale face, the lower bristles of his unibrow having grown into gothic bangs. "Easy for you to say. This is all your fault. You threw me off by telling me about the whole Sako thing."

"Bro, I'm trying to encourage you now. Plus, we go to a small school. People are gonna have histories."

"So, you wouldn't care if Sako did stuff with Lucy?"

"Hey!" Todd barked. "Come on. You don't think girls rejected me when I was twice as big as you? I'm the same guy I was back then, except no one listened to me. No chick would even look my way!"

Alex looked down at his shoes. "I'm, I'm sorry . . ."

"All good, bro," Todd said.

"I'm sorry I'm always wrong!" Alex got up and threw what was left of his sandwich in the trash, tossed on his backpack, and marched away.

Todd threw up his hands and groaned. "Oh, Jesus Christ, bro. I'm so sick of this shit. Not just him, but you too." He pointed at Roman, who had just shoved a Pringle into his head.

"Uh," he said with a full mouth.

"Both of you guys need to grow the hell up," Todd said. "You can't be bitter about shit forever."

Later that day, Todd meandered around Ms. Mendoza's desk as a couple of students lined up with questions in preparation for the Spanish 5-6 semester final. Her computer screen was asleep, which meant she had to log in at some point. While she busied herself wiping the whiteboard clean, Todd popped in the keylogger and returned to his desk.

He swung by to retrieve the device at the start of tutorial period, a sort of group study and the final class of the day. With so many minds preoccupied, Todd thought no better time to make the grab.

He took a seat next to a blonde girl. She was the only roadblock between himself and the device, but she was reading a video game magazine, so no biggie. Todd leaned back into his chair as far as he could to attempt the suavest of movie-theater stretches, but his grasp was just a few hairs short of the keylogger. He winced, and the hind legs of his chair trembled while pawing at the device, brushing it with his middle finger until gravity won. As he started falling over, he grabbed the right shoulder of the blonde girl, who turned to him in shock. It was then that Todd noticed the girl was Tamar. She paired a smile with a condescending stare.

"Um, can I help you?" Tamar said and laughed playfully.

In the second and a half before he responded, Todd noticed her petite nose. "Oh, sorry. Just stretching and, uh, really needed it."

"Okay." Tamar sounded confused, but entertained.

Reeling in his arm, Todd kept cool until he saw Alex looking in from the hallway. Alex's eyelids had vanished, and his forehead went blood red.

"Oh shit," Todd said. "Gotta go."

He leaped to his feet and dashed after him.

"Al!" Todd shouted. "Al! It's not what you think!"

Alex sprinted off. Todd remembered he was keylogger-less. He looked back and forth between the computer and his friend, stumbling into the distance. At the last second, Todd chose to fall back into class and found himself face-to-face with Tamar again at the doorway.

"You dropped this," she said, keylogger in her hand.

Todd snatched it. "Thanks for giving me back my eraser. See ya."

He started turning away.

"It's just that I've never seen an eraser with a USB connector," Tamar said, then chuckled.

"Oh, that, those are just . . . uh . . . some staples I stuck in there. You know what it's like being bored and—"

"You're welcome."

Todd simpered. When he broke free, it was too late. Alex was long gone.

"Ah, fuck me," Todd said as he bent over, coughed, and slammed his fists against his knees, causing him to spring up in place.

He met up with Roman after school near the departing buses.

"Here you go," Todd said, handing him the keylogger. "Just

because of your stupid Spanish grade, Alex now thinks I'm trying to make moves on Tamar."

"Huh?" Roman said. "What the hell? Why?"

"She was in the way, bro. I had to reach around to grab the little thing, and I lost my balance."

"What? How could you let that happen?"

"Hey, screw you, bro! I'm the one running around like Forrest Gump here this whole time!"

"But you got the password, right?"

"Yeah, yeah, yeah. It should be there. Of course, that's *all* you're worried about. Now, excuse me while I go into hiding. I don't wanna be known as the guy beaten to death with a soda bottle."

—

ROMAN

He gawked at the Apollo grade book, fingers perched on the keys like a parrot in a pet shop window. He perused the recorded keystrokes for Ms. Mendoza's new password. It was teachachica0.

The clock on his screen read 11:52 p.m. Anxious, he stood up fast and stubbed his right toe, but the adrenaline suppressed the pain and gave him a clear mind to decide he'd start engaging in three more minutes.

Roman leaned into his computer until his lenses pecked the monitor. He grabbed a sheet of notebook paper near his keyboard and examined it carefully. The grade calculations he had made resembled typed words, but they were handwritten with quantum precision. Roman went over the math with one word in mind: believability, which bankrolled the easiest edit—an A in P.E. He had no idea how he was getting a B. An A in Cisco and a B+ in government could be easy sells as well.

One last manic switch back to #mswarez to kill a few agonizing minutes.

[23:53] (@Zodex07): so yeah, I think it's well and secured, nothing pinged back from Port 80
[23:53] (kandyraverr88): that's good, nice and secure

Nice and secure? Roman thought. Time to anonymously dispense some sage "H-wording" advice.

[23:53] (JaYnus): try port 139 next time if u wanna get in
[23:53] (kandyraverr88): 139? What you talking about man?
[23:54] (@Zodex07): i'm just testing security at my dad's office… the hell you think we're doin?
[23:54] (kandyraverr88): we're not hackin here duude lmao
[23:54] (@Zodex07): lol 139? amateur hour or what? you install a hidden camera to record passwords being typed too?

Straight away, Roman put an end to the mockery by "x-ing" out of the channel's chat box.

Amateur hour? I'll show some guy I've never met before amateur hour.

11:55 p.m.

Oh shit! No more wasting time.

He got his digits in gear. The ensuing clickety-clacks were robotic and underwhelming at face value, but drumroll, please—his new GPA was a grand total of 3.4, his highest ever. He couldn't believe all the heist work boiled down to these grains of input. No wonder that's all they showed in the movies.

He opened a fresh window so he could alter Todd's grades. His were easy since just a few B+'s had to be upgraded to an A– and an A- to an A. It might have seemed like a negligible nudge, but AP grades carried more weight. It wasn't until recently that Todd told him one could get a 4.0 without getting straight A's if enrolled in AP classes—that was why an A in an AP class could bump a GPA well above a 4.0. After Roman's doing, Todd was now poised to get a 4.35.

An AIM ding. Speak of the devil.

kob34lyfe: did u do it?
JaYnus: i'm working on it
kob34lyfe: bro, there's like a few minutes to midnight
JaYnus: need to do it at the last possible second
kob34lyfe: ok
kob34lyfe: after you're done with this go get ur freaking license

Roman muttered "this freaking guy" under his breath and replied with an impulse from his burning temple.

JaYnus: let's see. do you think an F in an AP class would actually count as a C?
kob34lyfe: ok ok sorry sorry. do ur thing. thanks
kob34lyfe: l8er
kob34lyfe: btw the hell am i gonna do about al. i tried IM'ing him, no response.
kob34lyfe: i wanna make sure he'll be calm next time I see him
kob34lyfe: that's why I didn't join you guys for lunch today and hung with sako and stuff instead.
JaYnus: he didn't bring it up either when I saw him today.
kob34lyfe: great. you couldn't ask him how he felt?

JaYnus: he didn't seem like he wanted to go there.
kob34lyfe: well try if you can tomorrow.

Roman was too busy to keep talking. The time was nigh. While he had Todd's grades open, he took the final step by dragging the cursor over "import grades." One last breath before he took the plunge. He clicked. It was done.

Roman then moved the cursor over to his own grades and clicked "import grades." It was done.

No error messages. He looked out his window. No police sirens blaring toward his house. A strong wave of goosebumps shimmied up his spine. Roman threw back his arms and slumped like he meant it. The digital alarm clock on his nightstand read 11:58 p.m. He had never felt so fulfilled and mature. Roman envisioned a Venn diagram encompassing his professional growth, personal growth, and satisfied parents. Now, with nothing to do but wait, he figured to get started on another project, building a website for his #xwarez, but drowsiness flooded his head. Calling it an early-ish night started to feel right until the sight of a familiar name in the grade book perked him up.

ALAVERDIAN, ALEX TER

They had three of the same teachers, and Alex was going to get C's in their classes.

This poor guy, Roman thought.

Nothing ever worked out for him save his proclivity for finding the crispiest spicy chickens out of a pile of soggy ones. Roman hated to admit it, but he, just a little, enjoyed seeing Todd squirm, even if he never imagined it. Todd was always an exemplary student used to nothing less than clockwork acclaim. He was lucky;

he was one of those with a photographic memory who never had to open a book. It was like an unending stream of answers divinely siphoned into his brain. But that was what made Todd the perfect partner; no one would suspect him. Well, maybe, except for Alex, who now likely considered Todd a conniving backstabber of the highest order.

Shit.

There was no way Roman could deal with a friendship divorce and be forced to take sides.

ALAVERDIAN, ALEX TER

There was his name again. Roman was stuck on it.

ALAVERDIAN, ALEX TER

Roman massaged his right cheek. Other than treating him to the occasional spicy chicken sandwich, Roman knew of only one other way he could cheer up his friend or, at the very least, get on his good side if he snapped again.

Roman dragged the cursor over Alex's row for his Algebra 2 class.

He'd be the only other person. I can handle it.

A few more clicks and clacks later, his friend was poised to receive a B+ in the class. Followed by an A- in English. And a B in Spanish.

Roman was growing firmer in his belief that all of life's problems could be solved with the click of a mouse. He even thought of names for the philosophy, like clickism or magic . . . solving . . . box. Creativity wasn't his strong suit.

13

Rejuvenated smiles mingled in the hall following finals and a four-day weekend, but Roman stressed like he had shown up on exam day without once opening a book. Plus, he pictured himself naked throughout the ordeal.

He crossed paths with Alex, who was slouching through the hallway.

"Have you seen Todd?" Alex asked after raising his head.

"Uh, no, not yet," Roman said.

"Are you sure? You're not covering for him, are you?"

"No, I haven't seen him."

"I need to talk to him."

"I'm sure he'll be around later."

"Okay. I'm gonna go grab some fifty-cent leftover pizza from yesterday. Wanna come?"

"Did you get your grades yet?" Roman asked.

"Huh? What? Why?"

"Um . . . I wanna see how we did in P.E."

"All we did was walk around the field the whole semester. I'm sure we didn't get less than a B."

"Can you just call me when you do?"

"Alright, sure. Weird. Now let's go knock down some Domino's."

Roman wished he could witness his folks unseal the report card peppered with his virtual fingertips. But until it arrived and he had confirmation his effort had worked, he resolved to head elsewhere after school. Monday, he went to Alex's house to play some *Goldeneye*—Roman was never happier to die fourteen times in a row. Then he called his mom to ask what was for dinner.

"Beef Stroganoff," Audrey said.

If things had gone the other way, she would have spoken in loveless spurts, meaning the plan had failed. If that were the case, Roman would hang up and call back later after his mom cooled down and start negotiating the terms of surrender.

He went to Alex's house again on Tuesday. Still nothing in the mail.

Wednesday. Not wanting to burden Alex's parents with host duties any further, Roman headed to a park down the street from Wright Magnet after school. He lay down on a picnic table under a giant oak tree and dreamed of rescuing the last burrito on Earth until he was catapulted back to reality by the horn of Todd's mom's old Lexus SUV. Roman hopped in, and in a rare move, they didn't shake hands. Todd seemed tense and didn't make eye contact.

"You didn't get it yet?" he asked.

"I would have told you," Roman said.

"This is insane. It's never taken this long for me."

"It's only Wednesday. Hoping it doesn't come as late as Saturday."

"Saturday? Bro, you're killing me!"

Todd palmed his face with both hands. His raspy delivery shattered into whining cracks. "I can't believe we did something so crazy like this! The hell was I thinking? I can't wait anymore!"

What's he so scared about? He's still gonna get higher than a 4.0 . . . I hope.

"I just grabbed In-N-Out with Lucy and a couple of her friends," Todd continued. "We're *this* close to finally getting a one-on-one date. This boost we've been working on will clinch it for me."

"What?" Roman asked. "What does she have to do with this?"

"Her folks don't let her go out on the weekends, as far as I know, and I . . . ah, never mind. I don't wanna bore you with this crap. Hope you weren't waiting too long."

"No worries. Thanks for the ride."

After they pulled into a 76 downhill at the corner of the block, Roman used the public Pacific Bell phone to call his house.

Audrey answered. "Going to be late again? I made cassoulet."

Thursday morning: a bombshell by the kitchen island. Audrey told Roman she had a doctor's appointment in the afternoon and wanted him home to let in an air-conditioning repairman.

"What?" Roman asked. "Why can't Leon just let him in?"

"Because he's too young to be left home alone with a stranger," Audrey said, dropping a banana into her brown bag lunch. "Plus, you haven't been home after school all week. Where are you going? Are we going to have trouble keeping you in this house now too?"

To smother the rising suspicion, Roman obliged and cold-wheezed up his hill after school at an urgent pace. He spotted a portly man in white overalls leaning against a van parked in front of the Vallancourt residence. He was dozing but somehow still had a toolbox in hand.

"Sorry," Roman said, trying to catch his breath.

"Ees okay," the repairman said, squinting back to reality.

Despite his mom's orders, Roman was ready to jet the second he let the repairman inside. Roman skipped up the front steps, wrestled with his keys, and dropped them when he whipped them out of his pocket. A few blurry hand motions later, Roman pointed the repairman in the direction of the air-conditioner. A peek out the door, and as he hoped, he saw his brother turn the corner onto their street on his way home from school. But just behind him was Audrey's silver Honda Accord.

The hell, man? Roman shouted internally. *What about her stupid appointment?*

Panic-stricken, he surveyed the immediate neighborhood; cross streets might as well have been dead ends. He was trapped, options low, the moments where the best H-worders thrived, but all contingencies pointed toward running back into the house. He stumbled over a row of shoes by the front door and ran to the rear patio, beads of sweat grazing down his head. In the yard to the right, an elderly woman napped in a hammock, and to the left, a man in a braided sun hat snipped bushes with hedge clippers. Only one place left to go, Roman sprinted up the stairs to his room; at least his door had a lock. If worst came to worst, he could hole himself up in his 175-square-foot box—a man-made desert island where he could subsist off half-drank cups of room-temperature iced tea. If his folks saw a 2.5 GPA or under and unplugged his Internet, he intended to break off a piece of his closet door mirror and use it to signal Morse code to the outside world via sunlight. Roman imploded into his swivel chair and gripped the armrests. His hands kept slipping off because of his sweat, now cold. The chinking of Audrey's keys onto the marble kitchen countertop induced a spasm. Then he heard nothing. No tearing of an envelope. He wondered how loud paper could be. Roman shook his mouse to awaken his computer as a momentary distraction. A thousand scenarios of why his mother was silent played over and over again until—

"*Roman!*" his mother screamed from downstairs in an unheard-of register.

It sounded unearthly, like someone had frightened a banshee. Something pinched in the left side of Roman's chest. Then he noticed the door; he had left it open!

He was about to leap from his chair and slam the door in his mother's face when he heard a loud ding through his headphones. Roman glanced at the screen. It was an AIM message from Todd.

kob34lyfe: You did it. You goddamn nerd.

Unable to process what that meant, Roman swiveled toward his bedroom door, still intent on slamming it, but Audrey was already there, envelope in hand. She was smiling and flexed elusive dimples, clear indications that he had misinterpreted her death cry.

—

Audrey canceled plans to cook dinner and instead made an urgent phone call to Felix to pick up some of Roman's favorite Chinese food, Wok Tok, on the way home from work. Chicken chow mein, fried rice, kung pao chicken, orange chicken, and Mongolian beef were splayed on the table in plastic to-go trays. Any other night, Roman would have usually tossed food onto his plate and run back upstairs, but the occasion called for a family dinner. The moment was serene until his mother broke the silence.

"A 3.6!" Audrey said. "Can you believe it? I was in a bad mood because I had to come home to use the bathroom and be late for my appointment, but that all changed when I got this great news! Why didn't you tell us earlier you were doing better at school?"

"He got his modesty from your father," Felix said in the final chews of some kung pao, elbow on the table, signaling a V with his chopsticks.

"Tell us, Roman, how did you do it?" Audrey asked.

He took a swig of unsweetened iced tea as he pondered how his calculations were a little off.

A 3.6? Oh well, no biggie, he thought as he gulped. *I'll get it right next time.*

"Uh, I just spent more time on my homework and stuff," Roman said, knitting clumps of chow mein together.

"See!" Audrey said. "I knew you could do it!"

"You shouldn't be afraid to brag," Felix told Roman with a mouth full of orange chicken, making it even harder to understand his accent. "You have to in the business world. You have to sell yourself if you want to succeed or else how will people know to trust you?"

He patted Roman on the shoulder. Roman felt him clenching for meat, but Felix only scraped his clavicle.

"It just drives me crazy that you were the last one to realize you had it in you," Felix said.

"He's not *that* smart!" Leon quipped from across the table. His afro was a fledgling bush compared to Roman's.

Audrey gave him an admonishing sneer as Roman let sweet, savory, and crunchy sensations do the tango in his mouth. Orange chicken had never tasted better.

There was just one last item on the agenda that Roman was

procrastinating: a request for free-range isolation, round the clock. In the meantime, he was stunned by how much his family was enjoying dinner for once.

So, all I had to do was get good grades? So dumb. I give even less of a shit about lying to them now.

"I had a good day too," Felix announced. "I finally got my project approved by the city council."

"The strip mall?" Audrey asked with gleeful curiosity after setting down her glass of Diet Sprite. "Just look at my big boys!"

Even Roman knew some details about his father's lengthy struggle to get the project approved.

"It was on TV," Felix said. "Do you want to see?"

Leon hopped toward the living room as Felix grabbed the remote. Roman and Audrey followed.

"I was hoping to surprise you, but our son's surprise outdid mine," Felix joked.

Roman looked away as his father tried to make eye contact. Felix turned on the TV, and a previously recorded version of himself appeared on-screen. He was at a podium, standing in front of a curving array of renderings and maps on display boards.

"I had to make the project smaller, twice," Felix said, talking over the broadcast. "In return, none of the stores can stay open past eight at night. Your friend's dad, that idiot Vigen, said this intruded too much into the neighborhood just because a few old people came and complained about noise and traffic. I can't believe you're still friends with his son. That jerk preferred an empty lot forever. What a waste!"

Leon, elbows on the back of a sofa and jaw nestled between his fists, awed at the public broadcast, though after two minutes in, he let out a deep yawn. Felix's project was approved four-to-one, with Vigen casting the sole dissenting vote.

"Good job, Dad!" Leon said. "Are you going to be on TV every night?"

"I hope not," Felix said, then sighed. "Four years. I fought all those NIMBYs and finally won."

"What's a NIMBY?"

"They're people who hate progress. But I waited. I kept pushing. A lot of those older people who complained started dying, believe it or not. Younger people started moving into the neighborhood, and they were fine with it. NIMBYs are old people who don't want anything to change. Just goes to show you: don't ever give up. Just like your big brother."

Roman forced himself to stay glued to the screen. He wanted this phony-baloney moment with his family to be over with so he could head back to his room. But before he could, he had to try and push his luck further.

Everyone started heading back to the dining table. On the way, Felix stopped by the kitchen counter and picked up Roman's report card to take a closer look before smacking it back down with pride, the tassels of his horseshoe whipping back and forth.

"So, what do you want for this?" he asked. "A new video game?"

Finally, a segue. The ball was in Roman's court. He had mentally rehearsed each word to ensure not a single stumble. "Can I stay up until midnight from now on?"

His parents looked at each other. Audrey shook her head at her husband.

"So you can go back to what you were before?" she asked. "You worked so hard to get here, and we're very proud of you, but this shouldn't be a one-time thing. You should always be working this hard. I thought you would have learned that from doing so well. I'm sorry, but no."

"Come on, why?" Roman asked. "I'm not even gonna apply to a college. I'm gonna go straight to GCC."

"But you still need to know how to be a good student for college," Felix said. "At least you're learning that now."

Roman repressed the boiling rage. After all that running around he put Todd through, the coveted extra free time was denied, but at least his computer gear would stay put for now. He made peace with working on side projects with the status quo free time, especially now that he was certain he'd never have to open a book at home and still give himself a plausible grade at the end of the next semester.

"Okay," Roman muttered.

There was still the matter of the freebie dangling in front of him. He just wanted to be left alone, not to extort.

"Uh, I'll think of something else later," Roman said.

—

On the night of "mission accomplished," Roman had another major first: he passed out on his chair moments after rebooting his computer. Perhaps it was a reward from his body to his brain. The ringing of his bedroom phone woke him up around eight at night, but as usual, he didn't answer. The back of his afro had flattened. He pawed at it to comb it back out.

"Roman!" Audrey called from downstairs. "It's for you!"

Oh no, Roman thought as he reluctantly answered the phone. *Not another clueless moron who wants help.*

But it was Alex. "I got a 3.3!" He shouted over the phone.

"Wow," Roman said. "That's, uh, great. Congrats."

"That's what you wanted to know, right?"

"Uh, yeah. I'll see you tomorrow. Later."

"But why—"

Roman hung up and scratched his nose.

"Your friend did well too?" Audrey asked.

Roman was startled when he saw her standing in his doorway. He stared at his mother long enough for her to get the message.

"Okay," Audrey said as she backed out and winked one eye. "Remember, I'm proud of you."

She shut the door behind her.

—

The next afternoon, Roman and Alex strolled around the P.E. field, foreheads dry. Their classmates kicked a soccer ball back and forth across the grass like an aggressive tide. The boys were mum for the moment. Roman wondered how he'd explain his friend's grades.

"Has Todd talked about me?" Alex asked. "He's avoiding me, isn't he?"

This might have been the opening Roman needed. "Uh . . . I think I gotta tell you something."

"'Bout what?" Alex asked.

"It's about your grades."

"Weird, right? Everyone must have bombed the final or something; must have been some crazy curve."

"Or maybe I had something to do with it. I mean, or maybe I planned something . . . or I could have already planned something."

"Wait, what?" Alex asked. "What are you saying?"

"I did it."

"Did what?"

"The grades. They were me. I mean, I . . . I . . . changed them for you."

"Oh, my God!" Alex belted out in shock. "You're kidding, right? How?"

Roman shushed him. "Keep it down."

"Of course!" Alex said, toning down his voice. "Why the hell am I even asking, Mr. Computer Genius?"

"I guess."

"That's insane! It's like something out of a movie, like *The Matrix* or something. So, you really hacked into the school?"

Hearing the H-word aloud made Roman cringe a little. "Shh!" he said with the accompanying finger-to-lip move.

"Oh, shit. Sorry, sorry," Alex whispered in kind. "How the hell did you do it?"

"Well, it wasn't just me. Todd helped too."

"What!" Alex shrieked as the kids playing soccer nearby turned their heads. Alex covered his mouth and spoke through his fingers. "Oh man, that makes so much sense now! So *that's* what you guys were talking about all the time! I thought you guys were talking shit about me or something."

What began as a trigonometry word problem was simplified to a kindergarten one plus one: it couldn't be any clearer now.

"So, when you saw Todd, uh, reach behind Tamar, he was just trying to grab the keylogger," Roman said. "It's a thing you plug into a computer and it records passwords."

Alex's brow exploded to the heavens, then fell back to earth.

"But don't tell anyone!" Roman demanded.

"Oh my god! I can't believe I got so mad at Todd."

Roman was a little disappointed Alex had already gotten over the grandeur of the H-wording scheme. "It's okay. I think we're good. He was worried you were gonna kill him or something."

"What kind of friend have I been? Todd's right, as usual. I'm too paranoid."

"Kinda. Maybe."

Roman gulped his saliva. He was relieved that his friends wouldn't be heading toward a fatal duel.

"But I don't get why you didn't tell me about all this earlier," Alex said.

"I mean," Roman said. "Didn't want too many people to know. You know?"

"But why . . . why would you do something like this for me?"

Why indeed? After all that lying and sneaking around, telling the truth for once seemed the most appealing choice.

"I dunno," Roman said. "I guess . . . I guess . . . I just felt bad."

"You felt bad for me?" Alex asked after a few silent moments. "You did this just because you felt sorry for me?"

"Uh, no, I meant . . ." Roman said.

"Am I that sad to you guys?"

"I guess it's because we're—"

"You're one of my best friends too!" Alex proclaimed, cutting in with speedy gratitude. "Anything I can ever do for you, just let me know. Any game you want to borrow, just ask: N64, PS2, GameCube. I'll pick the best spicy chicken out for you, the superest crispiest ones."

Roman wasn't sure if such a skill was up to par with his "H-wording," but he politely nodded anyway.

The P.E. teacher blew the whistle. Everyone jogged back to the locker rooms.

As Roman pulled his polo shirt over his head and let it drop onto his torso, Alex turned the corner from another row of lockers.

Roman wasn't sure how much more gratitude he could handle.

"Do you have a second?" Alex asked.

"Uh, sure."

Roman, still pantsless, put his glasses back on and was taken aback by Alex's dilated pupils.

"I know you've done something awesome for me, and I'm super grateful," Alex said.

"No problem. Just, uh, remember—only me, you, and Todd know."

Alex had that same look in his eye when he directed his rage at Sako as he readied to strike him with a bottle of Barq's. Given his friend's recent unpredictable nature, Roman backed up a little more.

"You have to drop his grades," Alex said. "Sako's grades. Like an anvil."

"What?"

Roman scanned the locker room to make sure no one heard anything.

"I . . . I don't think I can," Roman said.

"Why?" Alex asked.

Roman scratched the back of his head.

This is what you get, he thought. *You help one person and everyone wants to start mooching off you.*

Alex offered prayerful hands, but Roman didn't think he'd ever be arrogant enough to consider himself a God.

"I'm not trying to screw with people," Roman said. "Sako would complain to the school about his grades being messed up right away. It'd mess everything up for us."

Alex inched closer as Roman held his ground.

"Please, Rome!" Alex said while on the verge of tears. "I just can't let that guy win. I've been losing to guys like him my whole life."

Alex tossed his hands in the air. "I get it, I get it. I moved too slow with Tamar. Sorry for not losing my virginity at fourteen, everyone! We don't all get our first kisses at summer camp when we're eight!"

"Maybe Todd's right," Roman said. "Maybe you should move on. Find a new chick."

"So, you're telling me to man up? Just like everyone else?"

"I didn't say that."

Alex kicked a column of lockers. He coughed once and kicked them again. Roman flinched.

"Everyone tells me to be a man," Alex said. "Man up, don't complain, don't cry, don't show emotion, keep it in, be a man. Every time I try, I get shut down, so for once, I wanna take a shortcut. Messing with Sako like this will make me feel like a man!"

Roman had had enough of the pity party. He wasn't going to let anyone perturb his life's work thus far.

"You know what I had to do to get here?" Roman asked, asserting with his paper-thin chest. "Todd and I started this months ago. I'm not gonna screw it up just because you wanna get back at someone."

Alex looked down at the floor.

"I'll do this again for you," Roman continued. "Any class you want. Next semester. Just let me know."

He took a few steps back to grab his pants that hung on a wooden bench and put them back on.

"Let's go," he said after he finished getting dressed. The day almost out, Roman thought he could at least accompany his friend to the buses. Instead, he heard another plea from behind.

"Then at least let me help," Alex said. "Is there anything I can do?"

Roman turned around. "Todd and I took care of everything already."

"I can help too." Alex's face was still red and oily from P.E. "Please. I wanna work with you guys. I know I'm meant to be a part of this. I have nothing else goin for me."

Come to think of it, Roman did have two new classes for the spring semester, meaning two new passwords he'd need. But he wasn't even sure if Alex would be any less clumsy than himself. A drip of sweat from Roman's highest curl dropped onto his right lens.

"I dunno," he said. "We'll talk about it later."

Roman left the locker room as the day's final bell rang. Alex stayed behind. Just past the front gate, Roman spotted Todd walking with a girl. It was Lucy. She had long black hair down to a thin waist, despite little love handle dollops. Her eyes were barely open. Roman thought it was kind of cute. Good for Todd, he thought. Roman was somewhat fearless of Lucy's type in an untraditional way; he assumed he was cut from their field of vision by default. If there was no need to ever communicate with an out-of-his-league girl, what was the point of feeling shy? As Roman approached them, he started extending Todd a low five and caught a few of their trailing words.

"You learned how to drive stick first?" Todd said.

"I *only* know stick," Lucy said. "Want me to teach you?"

"Hey! I know how. So does that invite extend to letting me drive your old E30?"

"Just 'cause you called it old, I'm gonna think about it. For a long time." They laughed.

Roman and Todd made eye contact for a nanosecond, but Todd kept going. Roman looked over his shoulder, a bit baffled. This wasn't just a good old-fashioned awkward moment.

But just like every day after school, the weight of being around people slunk Roman in front of his monitors for hours. For once,

#mswarez and #xwarez were background noise. He was ready to embark on his next project: a legitimate Web presence for #xwarez, one that would push his skills to their limits. He believed the website could be a kickass hub for the latest leaks and an index for every version of Microsoft Windows, like a human evolution chart. It would be a perfect balance: in public, as in the forums, he'd boast about his intricate yet user-friendly site, while behind the scenes, he'd be an H-wording ninja.

Roman dusted off a few desktop icons untouched for some time. He placed the site-making ingredients on the table: notepad, terminal, and Dreamweaver.

Roman pressed his fro against his chair's headrest. He took a deep breath and reminisced about the steam rising from the asphalt grates on a family trip to New York City a few years back. That's not a thing in Los Angeles.

Further into the Big Apple's past, he disappeared into a sea of fedoras and overcoats on an early winter's day. The clomping of business shoes spoke louder than voices. He slid into an empty alley but didn't know if he was hiding or trying to meet someone. Didn't matter. He leaned against wet bricks and lit a match to awaken his cigarette.

A hacker? Fine, call me that if you want, toots.

A small puff of white drifted past his lips, where it hovered until another exhale dragged it past the scope of the film camera lens. There was no point in denying the title anymore. He was well behind the screen and the computer parts—he was one with the pulses.

—

"You got in, didn't you?" Jared whispered as he leaned in toward Roman, startling him.

"Huh?" Roman said.

"You got into the school system, didn't you?"

An audience of nerds exploded with applause. Jared was the only one who seemed unimpressed. Roman had brought his computer to school, along with the crowd-pleaser: his VapoChill, a miniature fan with tubes that sprawled like monstrous tentacles crawling up a skyscraper, all backlit by a bulb that glowed like a radioactive blueberry raspberry Icee. Once in a while, Mr. Wineman's after-school club corralled members to see who could get a crummy 1999 eMachine running the fastest, a geekified version of a street race. This week, Roman pushed the piece of crap to 1.2 GHz, while Jared's pitiful Pentium setup couldn't even crack 800 MHz.

"I knew you were gonna kick my ass," Jared said.

"Too bad your divorced parents couldn't get you better parts," a Korean kid with glasses called out.

"Shut up!" Jared shot back. "Both your folks are goddamn surgeons. You can afford NASA equipment. You're just too pussy to compete."

The small ring of dorky roasters laughed. Everyone packed their gear into their backpacks and duffel bags to head home for the day, except Roman, who was fixed on Jared. As students left, Mr. Wineman huffed and puffed as he dragged desks back to the standard lecture format.

"It's okay, boys. I don't need any help," he said sarcastically.

Roman approached Jared as his bangs hung dangerously close to the zipper of his duffel bag.

"How else would you know port 139 could work?" Jared asked without looking up.

"Uh," Roman said.

"I was on the forum the other day. I saw what you said. Why else would you bring up 139?"

"I mean, uh, I was just sayin'."

"I knew you were a genius already, but now you're like a freaking god!"

Roman's lips quivered.

You know what? Best to play it safe. Just downplay the significance. It's not like you stole the school's funding or something.

"Yeah," Roman said. "Uh . . . just got into something called Apollo. No biggie."

Jared twitched, and his eyes were bugging out of his head. "What?"

Uh oh. Didn't know he knew what that was.

"You mean the grade book?" Jared continued.

"Gotta go," Roman said.

He tossed bags crammed with his gear over one shoulder and shoved the icy VapoChill under his left arm, which crystallized streaks of deodorant.

"Whoa, whoa," Jared said, following Roman as he cut out of the classroom. "You can't just leave me hanging like that. You seriously got into the grade book?"

Roman flung himself around to ensure that comment didn't prick up other ears in the vicinity. He got lucky.

"Dude," Jared said. "You're insane."

"Please," Roman said.

"How?"

"Don't."

Jared ran his hands through his middle-parted hair.

"No-nobody," Roman said. "Please, nobody."

There was a glimmer in Jared's eye; it reminded Roman of the stable green light on his personal router—everyone knew that meant a solid connection.

"Dude," Jared said. "Are you seriously asking me that?"

—

Back home, Roman slid down his chair, feeling a little numb and trying to assure himself he still had everything under control.

His mind on grades, he popped into Apollo instead of his channel, figuring it would be novel to see the smartest and dumbest students on the same level since it was the start of a brand-new semester.

Before long, the averages would push them further apart, the minority groomed for the showroom, and the rest would become entrails in the trough.

Roman started with a teacher's login he already knew by heart. Mr. Hostetter's class.

jhostetter@gmsd.edu
daddylovesmolly98

An unexpected prompt:

INCORRECT PASSWORD

Roman thought he had accidentally misspelled something and tried again.

INCORRECT PASSWORD

Again, but with other teachers' logins.

INCORRECT PASSWORD
INCORRECT PASSWORD
INCORRECT PASSWORD

INCORRECT PASSWORD
INCORRECT PASSWORD
INCORRECT PASSWORD
INCORRECT PASSWORD

Shit.

SPRING SEMESTER

14

ROMAN

Roman gawked at a few screenshots of the upcoming version of Windows XP. So far, the previews revealed a sharper baby blue for the plex theme, a new search interface, and the mega-anticipated WIM imaging format. Roman pressed his knuckles against his sandpaper chin, thanks to his first crop of stubble. He addressed the winter weather by donning an old Lakers hoodie with peeling serifs along the team's name.

This better be a good update, he thought.

A few nights ago, some guy named Melvin Bing materialized on #mswarez and posted the first images of the latest build of an upcoming version of build 4008, which was likely to drop any day now. Since then, Roman proudly launched irc.xwarez.net, where he shared the screenshots with the Web, as well as a link to the #xwarez channel, so users could discuss. He also posted more recent builds like 3683 on the website, but also ones dating back to the original beta, Microsoft Windows 1.0, strictly for nostalgia. But when a build of 4008 finally leaked, it was a huge letdown.

[20:23] (JaYnus): the DCE is broken
[20:23] (s0lidsnack): so is the media player
[20:23] (betamaxer): at least we get a preview of explorer, even if it's just 6.05
[20:23] (teknojunky): i hope this doesn't mean they might reset

However, not all was lost. Even though build 4008 was a bust, Roman's website lured over sixty thousand visitors on the day of the leak. He had no clue such a clamoring fan base existed outside his own microcosm. Out of those visitors, roughly a thousand joined the #xwarez channel. Roman was dumbfounded. He wondered how monetizing clicks, which he equated to a humble paper route at this point in his career, would pay out.

A private message notification on #mswarez caught his attention. It was someone he hadn't heard from in months.

[20:24] (HarryLink): Hey man, great job on the website. i'm not even pissed that it's kindda biting off my name
[20:24] (JaYnus): oh. my bad.
[20:24] (HarryLink): don't worry about it. u want to combine channels? I'll give you ops.

"Ops" as in operator.

Roman's initial reaction was to try and correct his atrophied posture after sitting for so many hours. He hobbled and winced in pain, but ultimately powered through and started shadow boxing.

"Yes!" Roman said. "Hell yes! You like that? Jaynus the operator? I'm gonna kick all you newbies and freeloaders out!"

After KO-ing a few air pockets, he buttressed his lower back with his fists. Then he leaned into his computer and typed to accept the promotion.

[20:25] (JaYnus): wow. thanks!

[20:25] (HarryLink): I'd show u around now, but I'm a little busy. I'll onboard you over the next few days.

[20:25] (JaYnus): sounds good harry. i'm really looking forward to it.

[20:25] (HarryLink): just have a valid credit card ready.

Scratching his sideburns incessantly, Roman was trying to figure out how to get his hands on his dad's American Express without him knowing.

[20:27] (JaYnus): sure.

[20:27] (HarryLink): just kidding. had you there. you're gonna have to see through bullshit to be a good op, but we'll work on it.

Roman exhaled a head-lightening breath.

A newfound sense of pride started blooming, but he couldn't help dwelling on the mystery of why the school passwords didn't work anymore. At least there was some reassurance in that Principal Harold Grubner hadn't stopped him yet at school, had Roman stare down the barrel of his quadruple chin, and said, "You need to come with me."

Roman's most educated guess was a mandatory password reset at the start of the spring semester for the entire teaching staff. But he hadn't shared that theory with his friends yet, let alone the loss of access. Todd, by this point, was regularly lunching with Lucy, which Roman didn't mind—a friend's progress, one must never interfere, yada yada.

But a few days later, Todd decided to grace his friends with his presence. "So, everything's good to go, right?" He asked Roman with a half-eaten sandwich in one hand and a discreet tone. "My first AP history exam is next week."

"Uh," Roman said.

"There's barely any flavor!" Alex proclaimed from a stone bench nearly across from the blue lunch cart.

It was spicy chicken day, but for unknown reasons, cold-cut sandwiches were being sold instead.

"Just a few bologna slices, lettuce, and tomatoes on a cold roll," Alex continued. "Where's the sauce? At least spicy chickens had that Cajun breading."

"Okay, bro," Todd said, looking over his shoulder.

Roman also wasn't in the mood for Alex's gustatory hot takes.

Roman stripped off his sandwich wrapper in a slow, cylindrical unspooling. The sun, magnified by his lenses, made his eyes water to the point where he yanked off his glasses and drilled his sockets with his knuckles.

"You okay?" Todd asked. "You're being quiet, even for you."

"I have a problem," Roman said as he slid his glasses back on.

But even before he could take his next breath, Todd got in his face and began muttering hypotheticals. "Did you lose the passwords? Were you caught? Did they tighten security?"

"Without tons of mustard, deli sandwiches suck," Alex said before noticing how abnormally close his friends' faces were to one another. "Whoa, are you guys okay? What's up? Got another super secret you guys wanna share?"

Roman couldn't bring himself to ask Todd to do all that legwork again. Todd had clinched academic perfection and got his girl, while Alex said his parents had honored their promise of double game rentals from Blockbuster every weekend. Roman felt his friends' rewards were charged on his livelihood, and the debt had to be paid by all.

"The passwords don't work anymore," he said.

Todd spiked his sandwich into a nearby trash can. "Goddammit!"

"Too many tomatoes in your sandwich?" Alex asked.

"Don't try to be funny. You wanted to be a part of this, right?"

Alex stood up and clapped his hands together once. "Wow! Really? We're gonna do some *Metal Gear Solid* stuff?"

Todd responded by raising a Chin of frustration. "You think this is fun? Rome, why the hell did you give freebies out? I did all the work!"

"Uh," Roman said. "I dunno. I—"

He spotted the portly Principal Grubner waddling like a penguin with a manila folder under its wing as he led a trail of suits who looked like school district employees. Although he could have moonlighted as a mall Santa, there was never anything jolly about Grubner's cloaked muffin top and shiny scalp.

The principal! Grubner has to have access to the grades.

If there was anything he'd learned from Kevin Mitnick, it was that one had to start somewhere, even with a guess. Roman's assumption of the year was that Grubner must have access to every student's files like some kind of fail-safe, some final override authority if necessary. He wasn't double-checking every single grade before they were all sent to the printer. Roman so much hated being back at square one.

"Earth to Rome," Todd said.

Grubner led his guests into the auditeria. Roman stayed locked onto the line of boring adults until the auditeria door closed behind the last of them.

"Now," he said without much bravado.

His friends bore blank expressions.

"Now!" Roman said as he hopped to his feet. "We gotta go now!"

"What do you mean?" Alex asked. "I was gonna get another sandwich. I'm gonna try extra mustard this time. By the way, Todd, do you have an extra quarter I could use to buy another sandwich?"

"*Kooft ara* your sandwich, man."

Roman stood up and power-walked past his friends. "Come on," he told them.

"Where the hell are you going?" Todd asked.

"We gotta get Grubner's password. He's gotta have access to everyone's records."

"Whoa, whoa, whoa. Right now, bro?"

"You mean the principal's office?" Alex asked and appeared a bit panicked. "Isn't that gonna be the hardest one to get?"

"I just saw Grubner go into the auditeria with a bunch of other people," Roman said. "It's gotta be some kind of huge meeting. Come."

They started jogging together and went past the building entrance closest to Grubner's second-floor office.

But Roman kept quiet until they reached the edge of the lunch hangout zone near the teachers' parking lot. Out of the row of dudes wearing studded belts and cargo pants, Roman tapped Jared's shoulder and pulled him aside.

"He's the one I told," Roman said, pointing to Jared.

Jared shook Todd's hand. "Uh, hi. So, you're like one of the main guys in all of this? Badass."

"You want that A– in CISCO this semester?" Roman asked. "Then we need your help."

"Hell yeah!"

Todd shrugged and seemed confused. "How the hell are you guys so bad in computer classes?"

"Hi, by the way," Alex said, "I'm Alex!"

Out of character, Roman interrupted them by karate-chopping the air between them. "Guys, we have a perfect chance now. Grubner's in a meeting or something. Todd, here's the keylogger."

He pulled it out of a small pocket of his backpack.

"Can you go with him and make sure the coast is clear?" Roman asked Alex.

"We're really doing this?" Alex asked. "Well, if we're doing it together, then it's more like a *Final Fantasy* quest, now that I think about it."

"Okay, whatever, bro," Todd said, interrupting. "Listen, I've worked as a TA before in the main office. I've never seen anyone lock a door in the admin office unless they leave for the day."

Finally, his observant side was coming in handy.

"So, you want me to be a lookout too?" Jared asked.

"Actually," Roman said, "I, uh, need you to keep an eye on Grubner. He might be in that meeting for all of lunch. Who knows?"

"If I see him come out, then what?"

Roman had never done so much real-world, real-time thinking; it was thrilling, but the natural high was dampened by the self-reminder that he was dealing with people. "Uh, the second Grubner leaves, can you run to the main office? Like, really fast to give the guys a heads-up?"

"I don't think I have to push myself that hard to beat that fat ass," Jared said.

"Great."

"What are you gonna be doing during all this?"

Roman couldn't hold his lips back from smirking.

"Jack shit, as usual," Todd answered.

"Yup," Roman said. "I got really hungry out of nowhere. Gonna grab some chips."

"Ooh," Alex said. "Flamin' Hots?"

Todd grabbed and dragged him by the shoulders. "Oh, for God's sake, bro, let's go."

Everyone split up.

—

TODD

"Listen," Todd told Alex. "Forget what Rome said. I need you to go to my car. There's a gym bag in the trunk. Grab it and meet me at the front office. Here are my keys."

"But—"

"I'm not an idiot. I don't need you as a lookout right now. I'll know when someone's coming."

"Okay, I guess."

Alex turned and headed the other way. Todd, calm and poised, went inside the main building and headed to the second floor. He flipped his head back every now and again to acquaintances as he made his way to the threshold of the main office, where he saw Grubner's office door six yards deep. It was shut, but Todd wasn't so sure if it was locked. He wanted to see if Alex was nearby. Todd dashed outside and didn't have to scan long before Alex came into view. He was hurdling over the monolithic steps of the amphitheater while carrying a dark blue gym bag. Todd wondered why the hell he wasn't taking the normal stairway that adjoined the amphitheater. As Alex stamped down on the fourth step, he lost his balance and fell onto his side.

"Shit!" Todd said.

He took a mild, instinctual leap to check on his friend, but stopped short as a few other students moved in. Tamar was one of them. But as soon as Alex looked up at her, he convulsed to his feet and jostled through the observers on his way toward the regular stairway.

Good, he's fine, Todd thought.

He walked back to the office. It was lunch, so fewer employees had to be back there. He gave himself ten seconds to sprint to Grubner's office and plug in the keylogger. No one was at the main counter, but the soundtrack of the nine-to-five blasted all around him. Keyboard strokes, telecom bleeps, and fax machine bloops. He realized he'd gone to check on Alex because finding a way into Grubner's office was too hard. He didn't know what to do with himself.

"What do you need?" asked Ms. Weaver, the senior administrative assistant.

"Uh, nothing," Todd said as he stared at the H.L. Wright Magnet-branded clock on a wide partition obstructing most of the back office. "Just checking the time."

Likely having developed a thick sixth sense to lying students, Ms. Weaver raised an eyebrow, but cautiously sat back down at her desk, where she was out of sight thanks to the grossly tall front counter.

Alex came around the corner, heaving, and dropped the gym bag.

"Bro, what are you, stupid?" Todd asked. "Why did you go up those gigantic steps?"

"I thought . . ." Alex said, panting. "I thought it'd be faster."

"Either way, forget it. We're not going to try now."

"Huh?"

Todd nudged Alex down the hall and grabbed the gym bag from him. It was filled with basketball sneakers and rolled-up socks, but that's not what he was interested in. He unzipped it and retrieved two tiny tools he held in his palm close to his body.

"What the hell are those?" Alex asked jokingly. "Bobby pins or something?"

"This one has to be a secret between you and me," Todd said.

"Why?"

"It's gonna help us get back into school later."

Alex was now a degree paler. "Todd," he said, sounding scared. "Seriously, what *are* those?"

Jared's blond mid-parted hair flapped into Todd's peripheral vision.

"You've got lots of time," Jared said as he tried to catch his breath. "He's giving a PowerPoint about some kind of new senior project he wants to start next year or something."

"You're kinda late," Todd told him.

Jared shrugged. "Sorry, I'm not a ninja yet like you guys! At least I know he's not coming for now."

"Either way, this isn't gonna work," Todd said. "We gotta try again later."

"Todd," Alex said. "I asked a question."

Todd looked both of them over. "It's gotta be tonight."

—

The last glimpse of the sunset warmed Todd's hairline while Lucy's lips cooled his own. They were in his dad's car, parked in a vacant cul-de-sac. Todd was in the driver's seat while she sat next to him. He ran his hands up and down her arms.

"It'd be easier if you came on my side," Todd said.

"That can wait," Lucy said, gently pulling away.

Todd was fine with that. He just wanted a few more minutes alone before he had to go, just a few more to fortify his memory of the scene.

—

Todd and Alex walked up the stairs from the student parking lot toward the P.E. field and their ultimate destination, the main building. They stopped momentarily by the chain-link fence surrounding the field. The main building's exterior hanging flood lights were as motionless as the bricks they illuminated. As far as Todd knew, the only surveillance cameras were pointed at the school's main entrance and the locker room entrances.

The night air was silent enough to hear a fly sneeze. Todd sported a black baseball cap, while Alex stretched a hoodie so far over his head that it censored his unibrow.

"Everything's gonna be alright," Todd said.

Alex turned to him with fear and uncertainty in his eyes. "I can't believe we're gonna do this. This is crazy! Please don't make me! Running around school during the day is one thing, but this—"

"You wanted to help, right? This is how you gotta do your part. Don't expect me to feel sorry for you."

Alex's panting sped up.

"Come on, I'm still doing the hard work," Todd continued. "You're just coming along, so if we're spotted, we can split up."

"I don't know if I can," Alex said.

"Really? Mr. I Don't Have Anything to Live for Because the Girl I Liked Didn't Like Me? You sounded ready when we talked about this on AIM."

"Please, Todd."

Todd couldn't believe he was about to use the B-word. "We're a brotherhood now. You, me, Rome. We're brothers. Not sure yet about that guy over there."

He tilted his head toward the parking lot, where Jared waited in his Honda Prelude. Todd could have driven himself and Alex, but he thought it was smarter to have Jared drive his own car in case they were spotted fleeing the scene.

"Us three, bro," Todd continued. "We're beating the system!"

Todd punched the chain-link fence, almost buying into his own claptrap. It was enough for Alex to inhale a contact high of pride. Todd thought they were about to snarl and howl in solidarity. They started jogging across the PE field.

"This really *is* like *Metal Gear Solid*," Alex said.

"Bro, I've been playing nothing but the *FIFA* games for like the last two years," Todd said.

They neared one of the fading teal doors leading into the main building. He picked this entry point because it had the most basic-looking lock. Todd pulled out the bogota rake from his pocket. He inserted the rake into the lock and pulled it in and out as Alex observed. Todd started losing his patience and escalated to a haphazard rhythm until he turned the tool like a key. They locked in surprised reactions as they heard the unlatching.

"Where did you learn that?" Alex asked.

"Shut up a sec," Todd whispered back.

He creaked the door back with a dainty nudge. Alex's jaw hung open in wonderment. The hallway was still like a remote lake, ready to thrust waves at the drop of a pebble. The boys heel-toed into the building as blue nightshade tinted their backs. It was a straight shot to Grubner's office, but Todd feared that sprinting would make too much noise, and there might be janitors about.

They puttered past classroom after classroom. But Todd couldn't help revving into a brisk trot, at which point he kicked off his sneakers to cut the noise baggage and chucked them at Alex.

"Hang onto those!" Todd said.

"Gross!" Alex said as he fumbled with the shoes, trying to avoid touching the undersides.

Todd exhaled through whatever gap his anxious teeth-grinding afforded.

He thought of Lucy kicking sand on a beach.

A creak from ten o'clock. Was someone opening a door?

Todd pictured a high-rise office at a top-tier law firm.

A creak from four o'clock and more from other directions. They whizzed by his head like bullets, reminding him of that time he watched *Saving Private Ryan* with his uncle's surround-sound system. Todd pulled further ahead of his friend. He didn't care if cops would cut him off with guns pointed.

Shoot me! Todd thought. *I'm not gonna slow down, goddammit. Just shoot me!*

Todd wielded the wimpy rake yet eased into a sensual insertion at the last second. He fiddled as his entire body pressed against Grubner's office door. He shut his eyes to concentrate and imagined his heels peeking over a narrow mountain ledge, wondering if a shift of a toe would deprive him of a final step on Earth before his fall.

The rake turned.

Todd leaned into Grubner's hearty maple office door. Before heading inside, he looked back toward Alex, who had taken refuge in the alcove of a boy's bathroom entrance. Todd managed to read his lips, which were transmitting, "Oh God, oh God, oh God," as he held tennis shoes away from his face like they were a stinky diaper.

With Grubner's door vanquished, Todd dragged his feet across the principal's carpet, past a desk chair and file rack. The next stab was the trusty old keylogger into the back of Grubner's computer, which was situated an inch or two from the wall; there was no real reason for anyone to look back there if they weren't a diligent duster. Todd shut the office door behind him and fiddled again with the rake to lock it. He walked toward Alex, who was still cowering in the alcove.

"You did great," Todd said.

Alex shot back a grin, which was contagious, and Todd couldn't help but copy, knowing he was almost in the clear, plus the twofer of making his friend feel like he was a part of something. But the warm, cornball moment gave way to tachycardic shakes as the buzzing of what sounded like RC cars zoomed through Todd's ears. Before he could see what it was, he found himself on the floor. Like a broken compass, he gazed in random directions into the dark hallway until he zoned in on something stocky on its side, wheels spinning in the air.

"What the hell was that?" Alex squealed as he tried to keep his voice down.

"Shhhh!" Todd said, still on his ass, trying to concentrate. "It's that . . . It's that robot from Wineman's club! Club Podge or whatever!"

"Shit! Did we break it?"

Alex kneeled to inspect the robot as Todd got back on his feet.

"What's it doing here?" Alex asked. "And what's all this stuff on it?"

The robot was wearing a helmet, and its torso was enwreathed by kneepads and some other blocky items they couldn't make out.

"Let's just get out of here!" Todd said.

Alex turned the robot onto its wheels again and it continued moseying on. It wasn't until the boys were hopping down the ice-cold amphitheater steps that Todd realized he was still in his socks. He signaled for Alex to return his shoes, then started hopping and stumbling to get them on as they started crossing the PE field again.

"Why'd you take them off?" Alex asked.

"I saw it in a movie," Todd said.

When they got to the parking lot staircase, there was no guiding headlight. They dashed down the steps and kept peering around the darkness.

"Where the hell is he?" Todd whispered.

"I don't know!" Alex shouted. "He couldn't have just run off, right?"

A pair of headlights flipped on and stole the boys' attention. Then they were both punched by the sound waves of a car horn. Jared laughed like a madman from his lowered driver's side window as he zoomed toward Todd and Alex from the other side of the parking lot.

"Dude, shoulda seen your faces," he said after he rolled to a stop.

"The hell is wrong with you?" Todd demanded as he and Alex got in the car. "This isn't a game, you idiot!"

"Relax! I was just messing. Got bored."

"Just drive!"

"Fine, man. Take it easy!"

They cruised to a red light at the bottom of the hill, where Alex provided an abridged recap. "Everything worked out fine, I guess, but that robot was a trip."

"Robot?" Jared asked, his eyes darting back and forth between the road and the rearview mirror.

"We saw that robot from Mr. Wineman's class or whatever just randomly rolling through the hall," Todd said. "No idea why."

"You mean the one from Club Hodgepodge?"

"Yeah. Were you and Rome in Virgins Anonymous together?"

"Shit! That's Timmy! I used to be on the robotics team. Mr. Wineman said one day he was gonna start letting it roam around the hall at night 'cause it could be a good security tool someday or some shit. The robotics team hooked up a ton of batteries that would each kick in after the used ones died."

"What the hell? Are you serious, bro?" Todd asked.

"It didn't see you, did it?"

"Uh, why?"

"Um," Alex said. "It ran into us."

"What!" Jared exclaimed. "So, it saw you, then?"

"What do you mean it *saw* us?" Todd asked. "Did you guys install eyes on that thing or what?"

"Wineman always talked about mounting a small camera on its head. He thinks it could be like surveillance or security or something like that."

"Shit!" Alex said.

"Why didn't you tell us?" Todd demanded.

"I didn't know Wineman was gonna actually use that thing tonight!" Jared retorted.

"I knew I saw something on that thing!" Alex's face dropped into his hands. "You told me this was gonna be easy, Todd!"

"Hang on a sec," Todd said. "Are you sure it was recording?"

"I have no idea," Jared said.

"Well, we can't risk it."

"So, what do you wanna do?"

"What kind of camera was it?"

"It was nothing professional, just like those small home-movie camcorders they sell at Best Buy."

"Then that means we gotta switch tapes just to be sure," Todd said.

"What?" Alex said. "I don't want to go back in there. Please, Todd."

"Switch the tapes with what?" Jared said.

"Let's go to the Rite Aid on Foothill," Todd said.

They cruised down the dead suburban boulevard, where Rite Aid was the one place still open. Lacking an interest in amateur cinematography, the boys didn't know what kind of tape they needed, so they grabbed multiple sizes: mini DV, micro MV, and Hi8. Todd carried the tapes and led the trio to the checkout, where he dropped them in front of a cashier, who reviewed the dark-dressed boys in the dead of night with great suspicion. Alex was licking a cone of rainbow sherbet ice cream that came out of nowhere.

"What?" Alex asked. "How often do you get to eat something that's pink, green, and orange?"

Jared placed a small package of candy on top of the tapes. "I'll take this Fun Dip too."

After a speedy and swerving return to campus, Todd and Alex retraced their steps until they found Timmy chugging along like a mascot that would give the Energizer Bunny stiff competition. Without needing coaching, Alex latched onto Timmy's base and picked him up. Todd cupped the robot's head in one hand and confirmed that, indeed, it was fixed with a camera. The boys synchronized glances of relief. Todd ejected the tape and fished through his pockets to find the right-sized replacement. He sighed when the first cassette he pulled out was the right one and swapped it out. With the task complete, Alex returned the robot to the floor. But there was something off. Literally, Timmy's head was still in Todd's hand.

"It wasn't me!" Alex whispered with teary-eyed panic. "It wasn't me!"

"Ah, crap!" Todd said. "Let's just leave it! Let's just leave it!"

He reeled Alex by the shoulder as he was running toward the door leading to the amphitheater. They skipped down the large stone steps. Their stomps pulsed through the dining area, un-nerving Todd.

"We can't just leave the robot like that!" Alex said. He was already out of breath despite going downhill.

"They'll just think it crashed or something. They'll know what to do. They built it. They can fix it." Todd lunged off the last concrete slab and landed in a sprint. "Remember, don't tell Rome about this," he said over his shoulder. "We did this during school or whatever."

They jogged back to Jared's car.

"You guys did it?" Jared asked as the boys hopped in.

Todd and Alex looked at each other, then the former nodded.

—

The following morning, Todd carried himself like any other day down the hall before the first-period bell rang. He ran into Alex, who certainly wasn't as fresh as a daisy. He had blue eye bags, which Todd had never seen before. That was weird since Alex was known for marathon gaming nights.

"Did you sleep alright?" Todd asked.

Alex shook his head. "I was really scared."

"Don't worry, bro. You can nap after school."

"Thanks, Mom."

Todd smiled lightly. "Just looking out for you."

"No, I seriously forgot where I was for a sec."

"Whatever, bro. Just don't knock out for too long because we gotta come back—"

A staggering shriek from a few classrooms over wiped Alex's bloodshot eyes clean. They jogged over to see what was up. A few other kids were already at the rim of the door, peeking in.

Inside lay Timmy, a headless, mechanical corpse on a blue tarp atop a few desks pushed together. Mr. Wineman was hugging an Indian student who was sobbing into his Hawaiian shirt.

"I don't know what to tell ya, Ranveer," Wineman said. "We built that thing rock solid. Never thought it would lose its balance like that."

A group of nerds—one chubby, one with glasses, one chubby with glasses, and another with greasy hair—encircled Timmy in mourning. To Todd, it looked borderline satanic.

"Does this mean no county this year?" one of the robotics team members asked.

Wineman bowed and slowly shook his head. "It's this week-end. There isn't enough time. We'd have to start from scratch."

Ranveer recoiled from Mr. Wineman and wiped the tears off his cheeks. Alex turned to Todd with watery eyes, as if he were among those who had lost a friend. Todd, on the other hand, was beaming like a murderous clown.

This has nothing to do with us. Move along, he tried conveying to Alex via telepathy.

And away they strolled into another day of high school in America as government-funding stats until they returned that night and evaded becoming criminal stats once again.

The morning after, Alex napped as he sat upright against

a metal load-bearing post in the minutes leading up to the first bell. Todd, mouth agape with a lock-jawed yawn and baggy eyes, handed over the keylogger to Roman by the soda machines.

"You better freaking get me into Stanford yesterday," Todd said to him.

—

ROMAN

It wasn't until after a few hours of moderating at home that Roman shifted his body in his seat and felt a small, but blocky thing jab him in his pocket. He plugged in the keylogger, opened a notepad document, and scoured for the one string of letters that mattered.

hgrubner@gmsd.edu
animalstyleplease

You freakin' fat ass.
But this time, past the virtual doors he'd kicked down so many times, he plummeted into a tesseract. Each corner housed younger versions of himself and less bushy hair staring right back.

Meanwhile, in the real world, there were a few more onscreen tabs: 2001–02, 2000–01, 1999–00. Roman sifted through them, and bad academic memories started coming back to him in droves: a C– in geoscience in ninth grade, a C in Spanish in his sophomore year. Roman wanted to see how his friends had done in the past. He dove further into the archives and saw that Alex could just never get over the B– hump in math. The one thing these older grades shared with the newer ones was that they, too, could now be backspaced. Feeling somewhat giddy, Roman boosted his math marks in previous grades to A's. No sirens.

The anaphylactic nausea from Roman's first break-in last semester was absent. His bowels were still. Despite no stomach issues, something still hurt. Only then did Roman notice his curled-in toes drilling into the bedroom wall. They had never touched before.

We own the school, he thought.

15
ROMAN

They weren't to be messed with, a slow-motion unit, their foot-steps occasionally syncing with the drumbeat of the Rage Against the Machine cruncher "Calm Like a Bomb" that played in Roman's head.

That was until Alex broke off and jigged past the trio of soda machines like a street orphan eager to show off the fruits of his pickpocketing. Todd raised a finger to his lips and shushed. Alex complied for a second, but then showed off his unremarkable wingspan. It was infectious, as Todd couldn't hold back, either, and high-fived him before man-hugging and slapping his back a couple of times. Roman hunched over with a nimble grin, the most emotion he had exerted on a weekday morning.

"What did I tell you, bro?" Todd said. "Do you think I'd make you go through all that for nothing? Of course, it was gonna pay off."

"Well, we had no choice. *He* practically made us," Alex said as he tilted his head playfully toward Roman, who shrugged.

But then a blonde blur on a skateboard kamikazed into Todd,

dragging them both into a soda machine and a blown-up projection of a Coke bottle.

"The hell you doing, bro?" Todd shouted.

"Oh, my bad," Jared said. "I just thought we were celebrating. Sorry."

"What's with you and trying to do *Jackass* shit?"

"Hey, if it wasn't for me, you wouldn't have made it to Rite Aid!"

"Rite Aid?" Roman asked.

"Uh," Todd said. "Nothing, just ice cream after we finished. Anyway, great job, guys! I told you if we waited for the right window, we could get it done during the day."

"I'm so happy," Alex said. "If I don't do well in Algebra 2, I gotta go to summer school. But that's not gonna happen now!"

It would have been a likely outcome for Roman too.

"And now that we can change old grades, too, I think I'm gonna apply to DigiPen," Alex said.

"Digi—what?" Todd asked. "The hell is that?"

"It's this school up in Washington where they teach you how to make video games. I wanna be a game designer and tell long stories like they do in Japanese RPGs."

"You have a chance to get into a good school, and you want to go somewhere no one's heard of? What do you even need to get in?"

"A 2.5."

"What? A monkey can get a 2.5. What the hell are we doing all this for?"

"Well, my folks also promised me double game rentals from Blockbuster every weekend for a month."

Todd slapped his Chin downward in disbelief. "After all that, you want to go to a place called Digimon."

"DigiPen," Alex said.

"Whatever, bro."

As for Roman, he was confident H-wording would be his launchpad into a tech career, but admittance to a decent school couldn't hurt if he needed more time for that billion-dollar idea. Not to mention, dropping out of college would feel freaking sweet. Plus, Roman figured if there was any lecture that wouldn't put him to sleep, it'd be from a computer science professor.

"Uh, I was thinking of CSUN, maybe," Roman said out of nowhere.

Todd raised a Chin of pleasant surprise. "Well, did someone *finally* talk about college plans for the first time?"

"Yeah, 'cause it's only like twenty minutes away."

"I see. So, while I've been narrowing down my schools based on who's got the best odds of getting me into a good law school, you've gone with the easiest commute. Man, you guys don't know what kind of opportunity we have here."

Alex and Roman looked at each other in silence.

"I don't think I'm gonna apply anywhere if that helps, Roman," Jared said. "I might go work for my dad out of state for a while. He's in construction, and he'll probably just find a place to put me."

"You guys serious, bro? None of you are gonna apply to a good school?"

No relevant response.

"This shit is fun, though," Jared said. "We're getting back at these shitty ass teachers."

"Relax, prankster boy," Todd said. "We're not starting a revolution here."

"Whatever. At least hacking into the school is so much safer than what Eunice and her friends are doing."

He reeled the boys' startled attention.

"What do you mean?" Todd asked. "I thought it was just her boyfriend?"

"It's a whole syndicate," Jared said with a sarcastic tone. "I mean, I dunno. Maybe not. But I've heard they've gotten a couple of tests since her boyfriend got caught that one time. I think they're all TAs or something."

Roman and Todd exchanged gawks.

"What's the big deal?" Alex asked, looking confused. "Eunice's boyfriend is stupid for getting caught. But we're not like that. We're freaking ninjas! Right, guys?"

Todd zoned out. The rest were quiet too.

"What?" Alex said. "What did I get wrong this time?"

"If other people are cheating," Todd said, "it could trigger something."

Roman froze up with fear and confusion.

Todd drove his fist into The Chin and looked like he was reading rows of text in the air. "Teachers. If people keep getting caught cheating, teachers are gonna start paying closer attention to the records."

"Holy crap," Jared said. "I didn't think of it that way."

"What should we do, Rome?" Todd asked.

Factoring in more people was harder than calculating asymptotes. "Uh, well, I wanna keep going," Roman said.

Todd sighed. "No duh, you do, bro. Any suggestions on what to do about the Korean chick?"

"Uh," Roman said. He wasn't quite Kevin Mitnick in his prime yet.

Todd scratched the back of his head while he circled a lap in place. "Oh god, bro. Do I have to do everything?"

"Well, you guys are both in the elite student club, right?" Jared asked. "You know each other?"

"Yeah, yeah," Todd said with another deflating exhale.

"Well, there you go," Jared said. "That's your in."

"Fine, fine. I'll think of a plan, as freaking usual. I'll let you guys know. I'll see you on the field trip." Todd low-fived everyone and bumped elbows.

—

The whole junior class visited the Japanese American National Museum in Little Tokyo. It was sunny and shadowless outside by the end of the tour. The teachers led students to the outdoor Japanese Village Plaza for lunch. Most were carrying the jackets they brought for the now-expired morning chill. Todd walked hand in hand with Lucy. Her friends were a few clicking heels behind. They'd take turns catapulting up to the couple to deliver a gossipy rumor about some other chick, then retreat. Being the first in a serious relationship, Lucy was their queen. Her crown: a pink visor. Roman observed disapprovingly from several heads behind because Todd didn't seem to be doing anything about the Eunice situation. Sure, Roman was grateful for his friend's help, but this was no time to gallivant around with a girl, something billions of other males throughout human history had done.

Alongside Roman was a breathless diatribe from Alex about why RPGs and their grandiose plots were way more rewarding than any button-masher. When the words cut off, Roman noticed Alex had dropped to the very back of the roving crowd and was fixed on something ahead. Roman followed his friend's line of sight, which led to Tamar's flowing golden hair. She was walking between two other guys, neither of whom was Sako, who could be heard nearby spouting a bigoted impression of a Japanese accent.

The students passed through a mid-block terrace lined with sushi restaurants, ramen joints, and discount stores. Much more familiar with Americanized Chinese food than Japanese cuisine, Roman opted for a bakery that sold ham and cheese sandwiches. His classmates had taken up most of the benches by then, but Roman had no issue staking out a shady spot against a blank restaurant wall and its canopy runoff. After the first bite of his sandwich, he spotted Alex again, this time with a group of Korean students, as he bit off a chunk of a green ball Roman assumed was wasabi.

Shit! He's gonna freaking die!

But after a few big chews, Alex bellowed a deep, satisfied groan. "*How* have I not had mochi until now?"

Relieved, Roman was just glad Alex could find others to get along with. He took another bite as birds chirped and humans laughed in harmony.

I wish we did more field trips, he thought. *I didn't know LA had cool places like this.*

Then he caught Jared out of the corner of his eye. He was talking to a girl who hadn't crossed Roman's mind in a while: Melineh Shanazarian. Roman hadn't said a word to her since that awkward phone call months ago.

"So, if you ever need help with your grades, just let me know," Jared told Melineh in a flirty tone. "I'll take care of it for you."

—

Fatigued juniors, eyelids heavy from bus lag, trudged back onto campus after the field trip. The day wasn't over yet. Seventh period and tutorial still loomed. But Roman was wide awake and his fingers trembled with nervous rage as he tapped on Jared's shoulder when he trailed a group of skater dudes laughing obnoxiously. Jared told them he'd catch up while Roman clung to a stone face in an outdoor corridor by the math and science building.

"Uh-oh," Jared asked. "What crazy stuff did you pull now? Oh, by the way, I was looking for a rip on IRC and saw you're an operator now. Congrats on the promotion, dude."

The compliment choked Roman up on the inside. He never thought he'd earn praise for being a semi-bigshot online in the real world. "Uh, yeah . . . Thanks."

"Kick anyone out yet?" Jared asked. "I know how much you were itching to do that."

"A couple, yeah. But they're still onboarding me and stuff."

"Did they make you sacrifice a goat or something?" Jared said and chuckled.

"The girl you were talking to," Roman said, interrupting.

"What? When?"

"Today."

"Which one?"

Okay, you're not a player. "Melineh, I think her name is."

"Oh yeah," Jared said. "Cute Armenian chick. Kinda has hair like you."

"Um . . . I guess."

"Oh, my bad. Didn't mean to make it sound weird."

"I heard what you told her. About the grades."

The lump Jared swallowed was audible.

"Why . . . why would you do that?" Roman asked.

He had filed his grievance. Jared bowed his head, letting his blond bangs shield his eyes.

He better feel ashamed! Roman shouted in his head. *Everything guys do is in the name of getting chicks. No one will remember that.*

"After everything I went over?" he continued.

It surprised Roman how fast one could inject guilt. Finally, he learned something useful from his parents.

"Okay, okay, you're right, but think about it for a sec," Jared said. "Think about all the girls we can get with something like this."

Familiar faces arose behind Jared's shoulders—some bullies Roman hadn't seen since middle school and, naturally, his parents. Both were groups that wouldn't even let him get in the first word. None of them was going to stop him.

"What were you even gonna do?" Roman asked. "Ask me to change them for random chicks? What if I said no?"

"Look. Don't get mad. But . . ."

"Uh, if you want girls, work on your game," Roman said. "But you can't . . . you can't have this." He had a faint memory of saying that, nor could he recall seeing Jared slide down the wall into a squatting position, his bangs hanging like a curtain without a stage.

"I promise I won't do something like that again," Jared pleaded, then raised his head.

Still firmly within his comfort zone, albeit a bit woozy, Roman knew what to leverage.

"It's not like anyone else knows about the robot," Jared said.

"Huh?" Roman replied.

Jared twitched, and his bangs shook hard. "Oh, uh, nothing, never mind."

"Just let me know what grades you want at the end of the semester, and I got you," Roman continued.

Jared obliged with a few quick nods, eyes on the ground, but it wasn't good enough.

"But don't try anything like this again or tell *anyone* . . . or . . . or I'll change Grubner's password or make some kind of glitch so the school will know something's wrong," Roman said. "They'll make it even harder to break into. No one will get . . . uh . . . anything."

"OK, OK, dude. No need for the nuclear option," Jared said. "I'll back off."

There was no farewell flipping of heads toward each other. Jared was left behind in silence.

Todd was waiting in the wings.

"I think that's the most badass I've ever seen you, bro," he said to Roman. "Save that energy for a chick next time."

Before they went on with their day, Roman's knees started giving way. Inside a hallway, he lost his balance and leaned against the popcorn wall to level himself and ended up scraping his forearm.

Todd caught him before he could hit the floor. "Oh, that's right. That was your first time threatening someone, *period*. Jesus, it's like I'm watching a baby learning how to walk."

"What . . . what did Jared mean about a robot?" Roman asked, sounding dizzy.

"How the hell would I know, bro? Maybe he was trying to seduce a robot too? Some of you nerds take your passion way too far. Just let it go."

—

TODD

The day after, Lucy's left hand was more than enough reason to be alive, even if it was just a brief escort from her English class to

Algebra 2. But somehow, Todd was thinking about another girl. In an imaginary college-ruled notebook, he scribbled ideas on how to get Eunice out of the picture. Not even a fantasy could fix his atrocious handwriting.

"Is it test time?" Lucy said.

"Huh? What?" Todd said.

"You always zone out when you're about to take one. It's like a dorky meditation."

"I was just daydreaming about . . . I was trying to think of a Baskin-Robbins flavor that sounded like a girl's name that I'd want after school to make you jealous, but I couldn't."

Lucy snorted. "Dum-dum."

Todd wondered how such inconsequential drivel meant the world to him and how he could even think about talking to another girl behind her back.

When he took his seat in AP English behind Eunice, he went limp and let an idea guide his limbs to tear out a sheet of paper and scribbled a message on it: *I can help you out. I won't get caught. Meet me by the three Coke machines at three.*

He rolled up the paper, pretended it was the keylogger, and casually slipped it into one of Eunice's unzipped backpack pockets. His forehead plummeted to his desk in shame.

This is the stupidest thing I've ever done, he lamented. *A note?*

Like someone as promising as Eunice would fall for such a third-grade gesture, but at least the note was anonymous, Todd reasoned. No harm, no foul. If she showed up and he didn't, it'd be five minutes of her life wasted.

But there she was, arms crossed, leaning against one of the soda machines at the meet-up point even before Todd arrived.

"Let's get this straight," she said as Todd walked up to her. "I'm not gonna go out with you."

"Huh?" Todd said.

"Everyone thinks Nathan got with me because he stole a few quizzes. Jesus, I'm not for sale, okay? People are so dumb."

Todd let her cool down until the time to play was ripe. "Then why did you come?" he asked craftily before reverting to his normal tone to avoid sounding flirty.

Eunice looked him up and down. "I thought you were one of the goody-two-shoes, even after you got skinny. Why would you do this?"

"Why else?"

Eunice rolled her eyes. She seemed to get it. "I just need AP chem tests. I'm not even really cheating. I just want a heads-up. I hate it when that old fart Gossard throws in a random question from the book or something we barely talked about."

"Yeah, I know the feeling. Where you thinking? USC? UCLA?"

"CalArts."

"CalArts?"

Eunice slid the backpack off her left shoulder to show the meticulous etchings of the cast of *Cowboy Bebop*, as if it were lifted from celluloid. Todd couldn't believe it wasn't imported from Japan. "That's really cool," he said. Todd only knew of the anime because Alex wouldn't shut the hell up about it after watching the entire series on Cartoon Network's Adult Swim.

"I need time to make an awesome portfolio," Eunice said. "The admissions office is going to care more about that than what I get in stupid chem."

"Then let me get you what you need," Todd said. "I don't need your boyfriend getting caught again."

Eunice looked away. "Nathan just got careless once, okay?"

"He was a TA, right?" Todd asked. "For Gossard?"

Eunice nodded without looking Todd in the eye.

The things some guys will do for girls, Todd thought. *And here I am, slave to a Roman.*

"It was just *one* time," Eunice said. "One time. Nathan was digging through a drawer he wasn't supposed to be in. I have no idea how he didn't see Gossard coming from behind."

"Well, before you try for Gossard or anyone else again, let me try to get you a copy," Todd said.

"But what will you do differently?" Eunice asked.

Well, as a former T.A. himself, Todd knew that a lot of teachers reused tests from previous years. They just mixed up the order of the questions to throw off Scantron memorizers.

"What makes you think you won't get caught?" Eunice asked.

"I just won't," Todd said. "The most important thing is I'll make sure this never gets back to you."

Eunice lowered her protective arms. "By Thursday?"

Todd thought all he needed was one night, and he had three to work with. "Uh, yeah. Sure."

"If you get what I need, I'll make sure none of my friends try," Eunice said. "And I'm still not gonna go out with you if that's what you're still hoping for."

Todd arched his back. "I'm seeing someone. Do you know Lucy?"

Eunice didn't seem impressed or interested at all. "You know where we hang?"

"Uh, by the M5?" Todd asked.

Eunice nodded. But Todd wasn't certain yet if they had inked the deal.

"You know," Eunice eventually said, "everyone would flip a shit if we did go out."

"Yeah, they definitely would," Todd said.

They shared a genuine but foreboding laugh.

"What about your friend?" Todd asked. "Joy didn't seem too happy with your boyfriend being caught."

"Don't worry about her," Eunice said. "If she thinks it's just me and my friends, she won't say shit."

Todd nodded, although he was two-thirds confident about what she meant.

"So, Thursday it is," he said. "Then you'll have more time to draw Power Rangers and stuff."

"That's not even an anime," Eunice said. "God, how are you in AP?"

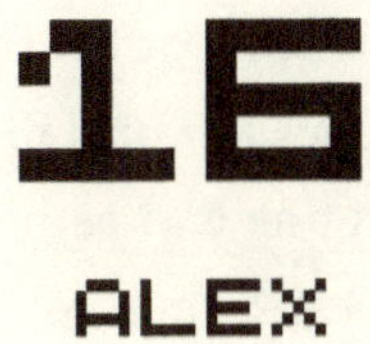

With the summoned blade swings known as Knights of the Round, Cloud Strife dispatched the final boss of *Final Fantasy VII*, Sephiroth, the one-winged angel, into polygonal shards.

The end.

Roll a bunch of Japanese names.

Butt on the floor, legs crossed, Alex chucked the PlayStation controller aside and groaned while stretching out his limbs.

Now what?

He was fixated on the crusting plate that an hour ago housed two stovetop burgers prepared by his mother. A bit more health-conscious in his later teens, he skipped a Klondike bar for dessert in favor of a sliced Gala apple, courtesy of his mom once again.

Alex didn't believe in gamer's remorse. Each slain title would be a conversation starter with grinning nerds later in life. The only remorse would come from delaying the start of another adventure or lagging in making the first move on a girl and losing her forever because one's a hopeless loser who'll never learn. Alex hung his head—he became a flash vortex, hungry for everyone's pain to feel normal. He craved a spotlight in the dark, but the twitching SquareSoft logo on his 13-inch CRT T.V. had to do.

The self-imposed no-contact order with Tamar wasn't working as well as he had hoped. Sure, trimming interactions lowered the chances of further false hope or hearing about a new guy she could be dating, but flashbacks of his failure still singed his brain from time to time. It wasn't as bad as his flaming corneas at the moment. Alex rubbed his eyes, then reviewed the long-standing line of PlayStation jewel cases bookended by a vertical stack of R.L. Stine's *Goosebumps*, untouched since the sixth grade. There was one unplayed title left: *Star Ocean: The Second Story*. The commercial for it boasted eighty-six possible endings, a colossal amount of hours he wouldn't have to risk being rejected by girls. Plus, with Todd busy with his new, presto-instant oatmeal girlfriend, no peer was left to criticize Alex's life choices.

Alex had settled on being more like Roman, monogamous to a screen, even if it cramped his Indian style. As he popped up to grab the new game, a Charley horse detonated in the deep meat of his right thigh. He gripped the afflicted drumstick and fell back to the floor, wondering if the frequency of such pains would increase with age, which was interrupted by another thought of whether Roman's dual monitors technically made him a polygamist.

Alex's biggest obstacle with Tamar was the two classes they had together, but at least she sat a few rows behind him in both. Their humanities teacher had assigned a research paper: each student had to write about the governments of their South American country of choice. Unfortunately, that meant daily trips to the library where computer seating was assigned and, of course, Alex and Tamar across from each other.

Luckily, his Compaq obstructed her face, except for when she chatted with the girl next to her, who wouldn't shut the hell up. Tamar's petite nose was still a magnet to Alex's side-eye. So much for researching Pinochet's military dictatorship that day.

Suddenly, two-thirds of an AIM message ding blared through Tamar's speakers before she muted her computer. Alex angled his head and saw her hands covering her mouth and her cheeks had turned red.

Her neighbor giggled and slapped her arm. The tee-hees had to be boy talk-related.

Who's she talking to? Alex asked himself. *Has to be a guy. Which guy? Are they planning on hanging out? Are they having a post-hookup recap?*

Alex stared at the home keys for the duration of the prolonged brain fart. He was experiencing a complete breakdown of out of sight, out of mind. It turned out that letting go of the past was just as hard as getting the girl.

In harmony, the zany ploys from a dozen romantic comedies told him to get up, casually walk past Tamar and glance over her shoulder to see who she was instant messaging. It'd be pretty easy to discern a masculine screen name from a girl's. Then, per the romcom joke-per-minute rule, he'd trip over his feet, shrug and smile at her after she decided to see what the commotion was with no follow-up questions.

But the split-second eye contact he made with her when he stood up to stretch his arms shoved him right back down. Alex focused on the rear casing of Tamar's computer, specifically the ports, which morphed into expanding whirlpools trying to suck him in.

Pulling off pranks required just as many balls as approaching random girls.

Alex slept much better as of late, knowing that his password-harvesting days were over, and he could coast until it was time to flip the tassel over on his mortarboard.

The ports on the back of Tamar's computer started whispering to each other, keeping a secret from Alex. They were muted lip movements of her typed words. Then the USB port, where the keylogger would go, started licking its lips. Alex sure hoped the port was a female.

Tamar started typing incessantly. She definitely had the words per minute to become a game programmer someday. A zanier ploy than the movies projected within Alex's brain as he ogled the P.C. orifices.

The sun's reflection off his computer neighbor's watch reminded Alex of the safety net that was daytime versus breaking into school at night. He couldn't imagine what would happen if he and Todd were caught after hours. Still, exiting his adolescence without a first love felt worse. There had to be a consolation prize at least.

I can only be happy if I know she isn't.

Alex felt his heartbeat in his earlobes as he scurried to find Todd before they all met up with Roman for lunch. Alex strode so upright that his shoulder blades trailed the rest of his body. He thought about how he'd try to snag Todd from Lucy for a few minutes, only to see him crop up out of nowhere by the outdoor dining tables and advance with an assertive Chin until they were face to face.

"Look, bro," Todd said. "I know we had a close call, but we gotta come back one more time."

"Let me try," Alex said.

Todd tilted his head like a curious puppy. "Huh?"

"Give me the key thing."

"Ha, nice one, bro."

"Which class? Let me try . . . I mean do it. I'll do it."

Todd hesitated. "Didn't you pretty much crap your pants last time we went?"

"I was the one who noticed the camera on Timmy. I'm good for something."

Todd looked away and scratched the back of his head. "Thing is, bro, I don't need passwords this time. I need a copy of a test."

"Maybe I can get it off the computer," Alex replied promptly. "Teachers gotta print them out from somewhere. Less risk."

"You're . . . you're right," Todd said, sounding confused. "Wait, *you're* right?"

"I am?" Alex said, then cleared his throat. "I mean. Just let me try. Anything so we don't have to come back at night again. Who do you need?"

"Mr. Gossard," Todd said, sounding skeptical.

"I have him for physics."

"This tactical genius. It's for AP physics, just so you know."

"Wait, why do you want to jack tests now?"

"Look, long story short, bro, it's for Eunice. It's the only way she's gonna stay put and not do shit."

"What!" Alex exclaimed. "Did you tell her what we're up to?"

"Bro, she doesn't even know you exist. I'm pretending to be a lone wolf here. Actually, more like a lamb, a sacrificial lamb. Do I got to 'bah' for you, too, bro?"

"Do you want my help or not?"

"I thought you were traumatized from last time."

"Uh, if it means I have a better chance at getting into DigiPen, I'll do it."

"Jesus Christ, bro. Still can't believe you want to go to that ITT Tech B.S."

"This isn't daytime TV crap, man," Alex said, barely hanging onto a thread of patience. "DigiPen is a real school. Not everyone wants to go to Stanford or whatever, like you."

Todd sized him up a few times. "Only reason I'm giving you this is because I don't want to come back at night either. I'm worried the robotics team replaced Timmy with RoboCop by now or something. But if you get caught . . ."

He didn't finish his sentence. He pulled the keylogger out of his pocket and handed it over to Alex, who cut him off.

"I won't."

"And just like the other stuff we've done, not a word about this to Rome."

Alex hustled far ahead of his humanities classmates the following day toward the library, hoping he radiated overachiever vibes rather than sinister ones. While the class was still a colorful blob through the library's front window, Alex whipped out the keylogger and half expected to miss the port by a mile and even drop it, resulting in an awkward manhunt between people's feet for the device, but it fit into the port like a glove.

He sat and logged onto his computer, trying to avoid eye contact with his classmates as they filed in. He expected a ring of them pointing at the keylogger because he feared nothing else in this library of a few thousand stacked books and dozens of chairs could go askew. But everyone had logged on and was minding their own business. Forgetting Tamar was even there for the rest of class was cruise control.

When the lunch bell rang and Alex was the last person left—save the curly-haired librarian in a cardigan who popped open her Tupperware at the front desk—he snatched the keylogger and plugged it into his computer.

"Just one more second," he called out to her. "Forwarding myself some links."

The librarian nodded while munching on a scoop of macaroni salad.

Alex rushed to open the Word file containing all of Tamar's keystrokes, but then looked out the window at the wrinkled American and California state flags pressed against the flagpole on this windless day. It wasn't the patriotic stars and stripes he could roughly make out that delayed the invasion of privacy, but rather an attempt to dodge his reflection in the computer screen. The Alex he saw in the mirror every day was a gamer on good days and on bad days, a harmless loser. But from now on, he'd also be staring back at a creepy guy.

Ah, screw it. Just this once. We all have our moments, even the cool guys! Don't tell me Todd never obsessed over Lucy!

Alex couldn't wait to see the trivial boy-girl chat with sex as the unspoken goal. It'd justify a week of pizza for lunch and an excess of porn sessions. Oh, how much time to pass by indulging in pleasure!

He dug his peepers into the screen expecting to read, "I love you" or "Shakey's tonight?"—that's what he'd say, anyway—but the text was rather flabbergasting. Gibberish and weird symbols abound, such as:

```
int: assigned x=x1+
(version_compare) Snake(unsigned x1, unsigned short y1)
cout:x=x1+
nbd:distribution_int_distribution<ent> distribution(=high)
```

Alex couldn't make any sense of it. It reminded him of Roman's computer jargon. Alex stroked his hairless chin at the potential revelation.

She's . . . She's trying to change grades too?

Well, maybe not that far, but it sure seemed like she was trying to stir something up on a school computer.

Although Alex was relieved at the absence of flirtatious dialogue, this confusing body of text was still alarming. He logged out and felt around for the computer's power-down button until he found it, then tossed his backpack over one shoulder and hid the keylogger in his clenched fist. He mused that if he and Tamar were still friends, he could have learned a thing or two from Roman and amassed a few more conversation starters and sustainers for her. It would have been great.

Alex expected his moral compass to guide him down the amphitheater toward his friends to report Tamar's suspicious activity, but she was blocking the staircase, joined by vacuous co-eds Alex would never talk to, though he knew why she hung out with those types: new student syndrome, a drive to amass a high-volume of friends—if you're an extrovert that is.

Tamar leaned against the handrail and crossed her left hand over her right elbow. She was wearing a khaki skirt. Alex had never seen her thighs, which were meaty and tan. He now categorized her as a woman, which retroactively made their past hangouts make him feel more capable.

Two future frat boys named Arbi and Arbo, wearing pink polos and shorts at half-knee, synopsized a near-fight at a weekend kickback.

A believer of fate as the governor of planetary orbits, something told Alex this could be his last chance: if Tamar was a budding computer geek, then man, did he have an impressive bombshell to drop. Maybe Jared was onto something in trying to swoon girls with promises of 4.0s. If there was one life lesson Alex had learned from Tamar, it's that passion had the power to bring and keep people together. Not the lusty type of passion, but rather, the goal-encompassing one. The type of common goal that buried all hatchets for the sake of humanity's progress, or all the way down to a good conversation in this case.

He knew he could do it again.

All he needed was a confident greeting. Even if the hacking wasn't Alex's doing, he knew he could pad the story out with his twilight adventures with Todd—it all sounded easier than joining a gym.

The romcom framing in Alex's mind tagged out for an action film, where he'd be chased by a pair of Slavic goons in tracksuits for some reason, while Tamar was a window-shopping ingénue he'd run into and seize her attention by the elbows.

"You're the only one that can help me," Alex'd say, or more relevantly: "You're the only one I can trust with this."

But then Alex remembered the little thing of saying he never wanted to speak to her again. It was on AIM, too, so the record would always be clearer than a downplayed memory.

In reality, Alex stood there like a walleyed cow for so long, Tamar finally noticed, but she didn't wave hello. The day's heat reminded Alex of the stuffy nights at Video West. But Tamar wasn't smiling like that time she held the door open for him. Instead, she started reminding Alex of all the other girls.

Uh oh. I hope she doesn't think I'm an annoying creep now. Ah, crap, I might be.

Alex was clueless about what to say. The keylogger would have to serve as the conversation starter since his sweat lubed it through his knuckles like a tiny middle finger. He didn't even notice until Tamar's glance dropped to his hand and darted back and forth with his face like she was trying to put two and two together.

Then Alex remembered that story of the time she gave the keylogger back to Todd.

"And then he yacked on her shoes!" Arbi or Arbo yelled.

A burst of laughter and disgusted groans sent Alex on another seldom sprint to the hallway in the main building. He didn't know why, but he ran up to the second floor, far from the crowds and pressed his back against the hallway wall to catch his breath. When he did, there was nothing but blood loyalty swimming through his veins. Alex went back to the library during tutorial period and printed the transcription of Tamar's typing and chased Roman down before he got on his bus.

"Oh, that's *Snake*, right?" Roman asked the second Alex showed him the printout, pointing at it with a Flamin' Hot Cheeto.

"Huh? You mean the game character?" Alex replied. "Solid Snake?"

"No, the game, *Snake*."

"The one with the worm or whatever that keeps growing the more you eat?"

"Yeah. That's some good C++ right there. I didn't know you were taking it. I mean, no one asks me about this stuff, but that looks like really good code."

"Uh," Alex said. "Thanks. Been working on it for a while. Glad it looks good."

He couldn't remember the last time his friend was dead set on keeping up a conversation.

"Show me code whenever," Roman said. "I'll let you know how to make it better. But seems like you got it."

—

Amid prime evening gaming hours—pretty much any time before sleep—Alex was on his right side in bed, stirring the crumbs from a slice of Napoleon his mom bought from an Armenian bakery.

He didn't expect such a heavy dose of existential dread that day, especially one that'd cast such oppressive doubt to get him rethinking his career choice. Graphics of *any* era now seemed intimidating. Even some good old *Super Mario 3* was too daunting a tapestry of coded numbers and letters to wrap his head around. How on Earth was he going to be a game programmer if he couldn't recognize the bones of one of the most rudimentary titles like *Snake*?

Those numbers and letters; it's like cracked out Algebra. I suck at math. I'm never gonna be able to do it.

Alex discovered a small cream deposit in the dipped rim of his plate and combed it with his fork, which he slipped into his mouth. The sweetness was mild. Kudos to the baker for their restraint, he thought. A good baker knows how to craft a delectable pastry to satisfy a dessert craving without making a customer feel disgusted afterward or regret their gamble with diabetes. No, Alex liked the first description better. He flip-flopped on his opinion.

The Tamar situation wasn't scrubbing off either. He perceived their latest crossing of paths as a tease of closure since it was capped off by group laughter. He realized all he had to do was stay patient and finish up that paper on Pinochet, then they'd return to their respective classroom rows, and she'd only see the back of his head from then on. Never was he more motivated to complete an assignment, regardless of the availability of hacked grades.

And, of course, there was no way she'd know what the keylogger was, even if she'd seen it before. She wasn't *that* tech-savvy! Not as much as Roman, at least.

Let the great powdered sugar hunt begin!

Alex shoved the fork back into his mouth to claim the final specks of white. Nothing like a comfort dish to distract the brain.

His favorite part of the Napoleon was the air pockets dividing the crusty flakes and custard. Who would have thought voidness could be a key ingredient? Well, he supposed so for donuts. The Napoleon was from a place called Heritage Bakery. Alex thought the dessert to be of quality enough to be the eatery's heritage. He couldn't quite figure out how to explain it any better. For now. Love of food was easy and words were hard, but he had this inexplicable urge to learn.

An AIM ding from his computer startled him. Alex rolled out of bed and onto his desk chair to see if he had gotten a message from Todd.

kob34lyfe: i knew you didn't get it. otherwise you would have bragged about to me 86 times by now.

Ah, crap, Alex thought.

At least he felt like he had gotten better at seeing in the dark school hallway and smiled, thinking he had leveled up like in an RPG. He even played a battle victory jingle in his head and smirked.

"The hell are you so happy about?" Todd asked as he looked over his shoulder.

"Nothing," Alex said.

Todd led the way again with the bogota rake to jimmy themselves into Mr. Gossard's classroom.

"All that 'Splinter Cell' you play," he whispered to Alex, who observed from over his shoulder, "You think you would have learned something about stealth and get the login info."

"I haven't played 'Splinter Cell,'" Alex whispered back, "I don't have an Xbox. But I've played the hell out of *Metal Gear Solid 2* on the PS2, though. It's almost the . . ."

"Whatever, bro!" Todd said as he fiddled with the rake. "I'm joking and this guy's doing a live review column. I'm just glad you didn't get caught."

Alex took a little longer than usual to respond. "Uh, yep. No way."

The door unlocked and ushered the boys in toward Mr. Gossard's computers. Alex stared at Todd's right hand, expecting him to swap the rake for the keylogger.

"I wanna try something different this time," Todd whispered.

He dropped to his knees and shoved the rake into a small lock on the top drawer of a stumpy rolling cabinet.

No way, Alex thought. *Can a desk lock work like a door lock?*

At last, the drawer spat out like a mocking tongue. Todd wasted no time rifling through the papers inside until he gasped with delight.

"This is it!" He muttered, holding up a pair of papers stapled together. "Gimme the backpack."

Alex slipped it off and handed it over. Todd unzipped it and pulled out a Polaroid camera and snapped a few pictures of the test.

"Told you this was an even better idea," Todd said. "Now we don't have to come back and get the keylogger." He shoved the test back into the drawer. "Just this one trip and we're done. Let's get the hell outta here."

Now he was talking Alex's language. He tossed the backpack over his shoulder with a smile, which was wiped away after he heard accented banter from down the hall.

The boys sprang to their feet and gazed in every direction except the exits. They focused on a double-door storage locker at the back of the classroom. Alex surprised himself when he beat Todd there and pulled one of the locker doors open so they could hide.

Inside, they were nose to nose. As fast as Alex's heart raced and his mind filled with fear, there was still a tiny crevice reserved for self-pity.

Can't believe the closest mouth I've ever been to is Todd's.

They tried to slow their breathing to achieve some kind of claustrophobic zen. Alex heard someone open one of the doors to Mr. Gossard's classroom. Their embrace tightened as Todd had no choice but to rely on a weird angle and press his hands down on Alex's shoulder like mannequins crammed into a crowded warehouse. Todd held his breath. Alex, on the other hand, held catatonic because his mind was still elsewhere. All he could see in the dark were flickers of Tamar's extra blonde strands and her indifferent face from earlier. She must have hated him by now.

Alex heard the shuffling of feet from outside the locker. It sounded like someone was walking up and down each row of desks, but he took solace in the worst-case scenario: yelling grown-ups if he and Todd were caught. At the end of the day, it didn't seem like that big of a deal. They'd get in some trouble, followed by a likely moratorium on Blockbuster rentals. But his racing imagination also couldn't help animate a scene of his friends getting booted from school by Principal Grubner.

A new school? A breath of fresh, forest air—oh, the prospect of a blank slate. New faces wouldn't know of his old shame. It was all so titillating.

But Todd looked down at Alex with a shell-shocked glance.

Oh yeah. My friends.

Although a seeping odor of stale Pine-Sol reminded Alex of home, Todd wasn't ready to go.

"Little longer," he whispered, his elbows trembling. "Just gotta be a hundred percent sure."

By the time that percentage was achieved, Alex's heart rate had dropped to that of a turtle. They hadn't heard a dead giveaway like a toilet flush in what seemed like forever. When they finally let themselves out, they were certain the mystery entrant must have been a janitor because of how well the floor now glistened in the moonlight. Alex spotted the classroom clock, which read a quarter to eleven.

Dragging his feet, Todd stretched his arms, cracked one side of his neck, and yawned without accompanying foley.

Alex burped quietly and blew the air out of his mouth. "I'll take an all-nighter in there with you versus a robot any day," he told Todd.

Todd responded with an incredulous shrug. "Once again, you make everything sound gay."

—

TODD

The sun blurred Todd's vision and blanked his brain the next morning as he passed through the snack area, barely remembering his destination. His eye bags were as veiny blue as his secret stretch marks. Looking for something to stabilize his line of sight, he scanned for the familiar and spotted Alex sleeping upright on their morning bench, back against a metal pillar, while Roman, sitting next to him, was nostril-deep in an issue of *Maximum PC*. The shock of seeing Roman reading something, let alone what seemed like a paid subscription magazine, woke Todd up a bit.

Todd approached a long-decommissioned utility cart with *M5* spray-painted between its headlights. A few of Eunice's friends were chatting and sitting on the edge of the flatbed, including Joy, who was doing homework and swatted at one of the girls who had scooched too close. Two Korean boys leaned against one side of the cart. Todd was a few dozen yards away, hoping it would be enough for Eunice to detect him on her radar, which she did. Todd reached into his pocket and pulled out a handful of Polaroids of the upcoming AP chem test. Eunice was smart enough to sneak off before her friends saw him coming. Eunice snatched the photos and flipped through them, but said nothing at first. She flipped through them again, and still no words.

"What is it?" Todd asked.

Eunice raised her eyes to meet his.

"Don't tell me they're not bright enough," Todd said.

Before he knew it, she threw her arms around his neck and drew him in for a big hug. Their flat tummies pressed against each other.

"I didn't think you'd actually do it," she said. "You're not a creep. You're *not* a creep."

"Uh, thanks?" Todd said. He took a few steps back to end the embrace and looked over his shoulder to ensure Lucy hadn't spotted the interaction.

"We'll stop," Eunice said. "So, you'll do this for us from now on?"

Great, Todd thought. Looking down at her, his delirious smile resembled a checkmark.

Before he could respond, Eunice tugged open one of her khaki pockets and dropped the Polaroids inside. She smiled at him before returning to her friends, who were still talking among themselves and paid no mind to the exchange. It was all the gratitude Todd needed. He swallowed his spit and took a deep breath as he turned around. Still no Lucy. Instead, straight ahead at the morning Danish line, there was her friend Marina, mouth agape as she gave up her spot and fled like prey to warn the pack.

17

ROMAN

His username finally prefixed with an "@," Roman spent marathon nights moderating #mswarez. The channel acquired his own, #xwarez, but he still had a carnal drive. He sat in the dark with a thick blanket over his head and the monitor to shield any light from escaping through the door crack and alerting his folks, especially at two in the morning. Despite the occasional sweat bead stinging his right eye, it was worth it to have the power of kicking people out. Most boots were warnings so users would get their act together before having their IP address blocked. Spamming was one of the common reasons.

[01:02] (Dr^Meister01): Tired of jerkoff floods taking out your connection? Now you can fight back!!! Strikeback will trace the attacker to their host as well as built in ctcp/time/version/packet options. Dont let this happen again, protect yourself TodaY!!! get it here --> http://www.geocities.com/w238zip93.html

^Dr^Meister01 was kicked by |JaYnus| (Advertising is not permitted in #mswarez.)

Breaking the rules also extended to excessively typing text in alternating colors. Sure, it seemed innocent, but IRC was a delicate forum. Colored text took up eight bits of information, so a thousand-letter message with alternating hues, caps and italics would amount to twelve times the amount of transmitted data. Too much data meant bigger packets, which led to the greatest enemy of free speech in the Internet age: a slow server. Roman didn't quite view himself as a freedom fighter, but kicking out bots was noble enough.

[03:26] (Phoeni<X>01): HAHAHAHHAHAHAHAHAHAHAHAHAH
[03:26] *** Phoeni<X> was kicked by JaYnus (Too many damn caps! Plus, blue and red? Come on.)

Then there were the annoying users who'd beg for cracks or ask stupid-easy questions like how to get faster Internet. It wouldn't take much of that to get booted.

But like exploring every crevice of a new beta leak, the novelty of operatorhood began to wane. Sure, it was fun to boot people, but helping #mswarez become an exclusive club where PC devotees and potential professional connections could be herded under one roof was the bigger picture. He messaged Harry Link about proposing some foundational changes.

[21:13] (@HarryLink): are u serious?
[21:13] (@JaYnus): yes, no more guests.
[21:13] (@HarryLink): but our numbers will take a hit
[21:13] (@JaYnus): do they really matter that much? we should be known as the expert community for like networking and stuff. we'll attract the best users

[21:13] (@HarryLink): i mean i don't like newbz either, but this is all just for fun.

[21:13] (@JaYnus): just think about having everyone register with NickServ first if they wanna get in

[21:14] (@HarryLink): do you have any idea how long that's going to take? not to mention someone will have to spend their entire time on the forum kicking guests

[21:14] (@JaYnus): we'll tell them to come back with a username, that's gotta be enough to keep some moochers and shit talkers like those #winwarez assholes from coming back. It might even trim bot numbers.

[21:14] (@HarryLink): so you're willing to tell EVERYONE to sign up with nickserv?

[21:14] (@JaYnus): we're already setting an example, people like you and me. we've had our usernames forever, people will begin to identify with theirs if they register.

[21:14] (@HarryLink): alright, give it a shot for a couple nights.

Roman wasted no time being proactive about the purge.

[20:02] *** Guest58933 was kicked by |JaYnus| (kicked: [exp/nick] Guests IDs are not permitted in #betas, please register with NickServ and rejoin.)

Roman rinsed and repeated a few hundred times until think-tank roundtables became more frequent.

[21:49] (mixethman): im running 2532 now someone pls send me moo.dll

[22:06] (dazb6901): rtm is the final code, Retail may have a few extra bug fixes but it's the same code

[23:12] (WPA01): on mIRC, it is dcc options, dcc ports, set first and last to match open ports, make same if only one open port
[23:16] (jazzfone): do you think bill gates could throw a pizza party so huge it'd close a whole Domino's store for the night?

Well, at least the dialogue was more relevant. Things were so peacetime that Roman felt like Sheriff Vallancourt again. It'd been some time, he reckoned, since he had patrolled his Podunk. After a leisurely stroll, he found himself on a park bench. He removed a sandwich from a brown bag that his wife, Monica Bellucci, had packed for him.

But then screeches fell from the sky, like poor car brakes, and explosions trapped him where he sat. Packets dropped in swarms. Someone had intruded #mswarez and typed *HELLO ASSHOLES* and other profane strings of gibberish over and over again in all caps and in red, blue, and yellow.

The hell? Roman thought. *These children. I'll have them all kicked out before they know it.*

[00:35] (moose&squirrel): It's those Winwarez assholes!
[00:35] (daXgage): those losers still have their lame ass channel?
[00:35] (Dissomator): I thought people were being vetted now, WTF?
[00:36] (@JaYnus): we're gradually doing that, just give me a sec
[00:36] (mixethman): Are they really trying a DOS attack? How amateur is that.

Roman agreed. Just what did these goofballs think they were going to do? He cracked his knuckles and readied to boot them with a single roundhouse kick. The user count was 842. But then, a waterfall of rainbow letters torrented down the screen. By the time Roman exhaled, there were only 421 users left. Half of the sheriff's town had vanished, as if it had been flattened by a giant's footstep.

Did they just cause a netsplit? The hell?

[21:36] (mixethman): Did we just get netsplitted?

[21:36] (Dissomator010): just because you guys never leak before we do. Screw you guys.

[21:36] (moose&squirrel): you pussies! newb cockcucking pussies!

[21:37] (mswarezsucksdix): mswarez sucks! mswarez is gay!

[21:37] (Dissomator010): real clever name there douche

[21:37] (Dissomator010): Dude this means goddamn war.

[21:37] (moose&squirrel): Yeah! Let's get them back and DDOS the HELL out of them!

[21:37] (@HarryLink): Really guys? This is no big deal. We can recover in a few minutes. Just give everyone a chance to come back.

But for Roman, it was the principle of the thing. He couldn't stomach being outfoxed by a poser. Unacceptable.

The sheriff adjusted his ten-gallon hat and reached into his holster as he looked upon his town from a jagged mesa off in the outskirts. Plus, it was raining.

Not on my watch, buckaroos.

Scratch that. Roman thought a military general would be more appropriate for this showdown, so he swapped the western attire for the green Marine Corps uniform that the berating Sergeant Hartman wore in *Full Metal Jacket*.

In the real world, he opened an application called Rootkit. He port-scanned for #winwarez's IP address, then started typing in a combo of letters and numbers.

General Vallancourt inspected the ranks, lapping them as the bombing went unabated outside of their base. Rifles pressed against their chests, none of the soldiers blinked. A #winwarez infantry unit might have executed a denial-of-service attack, but #mswarez had plans to retaliate with a meteoric *distributed* denial-of-service or DDOS attack.

"Now listen here, maggots," the high-ranking French-Canadian virgin said. "You've trained long for this, and zero day is here, but you're only putrid patriot wannabes until you've risked your life for that giant green lady. She puts up with bird shit all day, so you can deal with a few lines of colorful capital letters."

His motivating words echoed up the hangar walls.

"You will fight, and you will win!" General Vallancourt shouted with a generic Southern accent. "Our bounty will be the bodies of our enemies, freedom, and socks!"

Roman was pulled back to the present day after he saw his mom's nose peeking over the threshold of his barely ajar door.

"I need to wash your socks," Audrey said.

In just two breaths, Roman scooped them off the floor and out of his hamper, tossed them into the laundry basket held in his mother's arms, and slammed the door, barely missing her face.

"Careful, you idiot!" she yelled from the hallway.

Plop and swivel back to the screen. With the help of Rootkit, Roman conscripted more than ten thousand bots via botnet. These bots, unlike the spamming kind, were facsimiles of private citizens recruited through malware to stealthily hijack personal computers and have them disseminate packets. When executed in such regimental bulk, it could do some instant and major damage.

Roman logged into #winwarez's channel just to see the calamity unfold. He double-checked the IP address for #winwarez's channel and typed it: *[69.83.121.44] -t -l 65500.*

Now he was a mile high, piloting a fighter jet. He looked out the window to confirm his target below, an enemy base with nuclear missiles ready to launch, while suicidal combatants stuck their tongues out toward the sky and went, "Na, na, na, na, na, na."

Savages. It's us or them.

He dropped the bomb.

The #winwarez channel window vanished. Roman returned to #mswarez.

[00:42] (@JaYnus): I got em.

[00:42] (moose&squirrel): What?

[00:42] (@JaYnus): Their whole channel is down.

[00:42] (XOR_DIP): Alright Jaynus! You're the man!

[00:42] (Dissomator010): Heinous Jaynus! how's that for a new nickname?

[00:42] (@JaYnus): haha that's great man

[00:42] (duudamaan2001): Dude, you're the future of this channel.

Roman started doing a graceless version of the Macarena that rotted into a spoiled cabbage patch. He expected a freeze-frame ending like in every eighties rerun he watched on mornings off from school, but instead, he received a private message.

[00:43] (@HarryLink): Why did you do that?

[00:43] (@JaYnus): Cause they messed with us. All I did was get them back.

[00:43] (@HarryLink): Great, now you're gonna start a prank war.

[00:43] (@JaYnus): but we're better, we'll always get them back harder.

[00:43] (@HarryLink): I thought you were trying to have a legit presence. With your website we have a chance to be a source.

I have big plans. We won't be taken seriously if we're doing child's play stuff like ddos attacks.

[00:43] (@HarryLink): that's not even real hacking, so don't feel too impressed if that's what you're trying to do.

[00:43] (@HarryLink): Anyone could have done what you did.

Talk about stolen thunder. Anyone could do it? Roman wanted to show off his H-wording skills like a child with a fancy new bike or video game system. He viewed himself as the most textbook H-worder and deserved to gloat and diss anyone thinking they had accomplished something grander. But he just took it. It was short-lived either way.

[00:44] (@HarryLink): Let those idiots come back and do what they want. Just don't fight back. They'll get bored.

[00:44] (@HarryLink): I like what I'm seeing with your NickServ filter tho. Let's get working on implementing that and scoping out the IPs that carried out the DOS attack and we can just ban them outright.

[00:44] (@JaYnus): I'm down. I'll get right on it.

Incoming messages were silent on IRC, so Roman shuddered when he heard an AIM ding. It was Todd.

kob34lyfe: yo
JaYnus: what's up
kob34lyfe: good news. Eunice is gonna stop
JaYnus: oh awesome.
kob34lyfe: yeah, i'm good at chem, gonna help her study.
JaYnus: cool
kob34lyfe: but one more thing
kob34lyfe: ok don't get mad

JaYnus: what?

kob34lyfe: remember how you let one slide for Jared?

JaYnus: I don't want to talk about this stuff online

kob34lyfe: It's real quick. I won't get specific

JaYnus: fine

kob34lyfe: well, i kinda had to tell Lucy about our shit.

Roman wanted to respond with even more F-bombs than the explosives he dropped on #winwarez.

JaYnus: wtf. why?

kob34lyfe: her friend marina saw me talking to Eunice. i had to tell lucy man. there's no way getting around a girl who thinks you're cheating… You gotta tell the truth…

JaYnus: what!?!?

kob34lyfe: obviously I can't let Lucy think I'm just helping EUnice study, that's like the prime makeout scenario, so I had to tie it back to you

JaYnus: the hell man!

kob34lyfe: it's fine, it's fine, bro. she's not gonna say anything

JaYnus: how can you get away with sneaking around with the keylogger and then get caught by freaking one of her friends of all people?

kob34lyfe: whoa careful about what we're talking about.

JaYnus: shit shit shit shit shit shit shit

kob34lyfe: we'll talk more later.

And later, the next morning, as Roman bit off a piece of a crusty, day-old Danish a few yards from the snack lines, Todd jogged up to him. He was clean-shaven in an ironed button-down shirt, but a nervous face sapped the stylishness.

"You got your girl," Roman said, his mouth full of pastry. "Why . . . why is she my problem?"

A crumb flew off his lips and landed on Todd's shoulder. He didn't seem to care. Roman held off on low-fiving back because his hands were sticky.

"Whoa, bro," Todd said. "Who's this guy thinking he's a badass? Could you cut me a little slack, for God's sake? After how much I've put my neck out there for you?"

As usual, he was right, or at least he sounded right. Of course, this guy was going to make a good lawyer.

"Get this, Lucy doesn't actually want you to change anything," Todd continued. "She just wants to see it. As in, see you do it. Can we come over tomorrow after school? We're both free then."

"Why?" Roman asked.

"I'll just play it off like it's a prank or something. Shit, after she sees it, she'll probably wanna get in on it. Would you mind changing a few grades for her?"

There wasn't much of a choice. A satisfied girl was much more desired than a scornful one in this case. At least Roman knew that much about the opposite gender, which he only knew thanks to ancestral DNA.

"Fine," he said. "Just try to come before six. That's when the forum starts getting packed."

"Will do," Todd said. "I wouldn't ever wanna interrupt your computer cult. Oh, and, uh, I got a ninety-two on my latest pre-calc test. Can you bump it to a ninety-five?"

"Fine."

"Thanks, bro. Everything else alright?"

The only thing comparable to a love life, Roman didn't know why it felt so natural to blurt out a recent achievement. "I'm actually an operator now. They finally made me one. That's why I don't wanna get on there too late."

"Finally," Todd said, then elevated The Chin slightly. "Whatever that means."

They low-fived and parted ways.

Roman never cared about the student bulletin board that looked like an explosion of pinned flyers for tutoring and time-wasting clubs. But on the way to first period, he noticed one fresh sheet from the corner of his horn-rimmed glasses. It was an imprinted logo. It was for Torch & Lehigh, the school's academic honor society. It included a list of names of those who had made the cut based on prior semester grades. Roman hesitated to give his full attention because he remembered the 3.5 GPA requirement for a student to be admitted to Torch & Lehigh. Then he remembered how he accidentally gave himself a 3.6 GPA last semester. Then he saw his name toward the end of the list. An initiation by pizza party was also listed on the announcement. No one turns down free pizza.

18

Before Roman knew it, he was standing before Mr. West, an AP history teacher who had scouring-pad-like gray hair.

"Last name?" Mr. West asked as he flipped through a few pages on a clipboard.

"Vallancourt," Roman said.

"Haven't heard that one before. Definitely won't forget that name."

Great, Roman thought.

Inside, dozens of honor students self-regulated into small groups. There wasn't a decibel of awkwardness. Cadences were confident, even from those with braces. Laughs were hearty, postures upright, and eyes never on the floor. Roman thought at least there would be a couple of antisocial nerds occupying a corner or two to balance things out. But of course, everyone had to be a Todd clone. Everyone had to be extroverted as hell. Being this kind of person went way beyond studying all night. If only Roman could brag about his extracurriculars at home.

"Grab a slice and join us," Todd said into his ear.

"Huh?" Roman replied. "Join who?"

"I'm gonna hang with a couple guys from AP government."

"But I dunno what to say."

"Just grab a few slices and join me. Geez. You wanna blend in, don't you?"

Todd took a few steps back because of a girl who elbowed his funny bone a little too hard. It was Eunice. Her face was framed by her swooping jet-black trim. Her expression was emotionless but clearly directed at Todd, who tossed back an all-purpose Chin. The overachievers sure had a weird language.

Everyone looked familiar, but Roman couldn't put a name to most faces. He prided himself on avoiding so many people for years. No history, no drama. The only people he recognized were teachers like Mr. Armistead. Despite being old and his ear whiskers paddling in the air, his memory seemed fine when he looked confused after seeing Roman, who had never earned anything higher than a B– in math. An evasion plan came to mind. Each time one of his teachers got to within twenty-five feet—or three Shaqs—he'd stroll to another grouping of floor tiles. Perhaps this wouldn't be that hard of a social engineering exercise after all. He heard pangs about *Joe Millionaire* and Ruben Studdard versus Clay Aiken on *American Idol* as he slid past a few clusters of students. Then someone said they were grateful that *Kingdom Hearts* wasn't a turn-based RPG.

Oh, Alex would have loved to have been here for that.

Thinking it best to end the lagging, Roman made his way toward the pizza boxes. While he filed through them in search of one with just plain cheese, another hand landed on his shoulder. This time, it was Mr. Wineman in his trademark khaki short-shorts, Hawaiian shirt, and handlebar mustache.

"It's you!" Wineman said. "Hope to see you again at Hodgepodge. Think you'll one-up your own VapoChill by then?"

"Uh, maybe," Roman said.

"Well, I'll buy a front-row ticket right now if that's the case!"

Roman offered a hint of friendly teeth until he could walk away. Even though Wineman could be annoying, he sympathized with his loss of Timmy, which was a techie project after all. Not enough, however, to offer condolences. Roman couldn't believe a robotics team rivalry could escalate to breaking and entering. From the corner of his horn-rimmed frame, he spotted Todd gesturing for him to come over already. Finally, pizza time. Roman snagged two big cheese slices, reasoning the more he had to eat, the less he'd have to talk. This wasn't going to be so bad.

Just let Todd do all the talking.

But when Roman turned around, he was struck by a blockade of flesh that almost knocked the plate of pizza out of his grip. He was further startled after noticing the flesh was attached to Principal Grubner.

"Oh, I'm sorry about that," he said with genteel delivery.

They stared at each other in silence for a few sweaty seconds. Roman felt naked and translucent.

"Are you okay?" Grubner asked. He was wearing a white-collared shirt paired with a blue pinstripe tie.

"Uh, yeah," Roman said.

"Always look both ways. That's not just meant for crossing the street."

Of course, teachers find any excuse to caution, Roman thought in a split second. To him, they were all pathetic losers who drew validation from talking down to kids. Back to Roman's paralyzing fear.

Grubner pulled a clipboard from an alcove of flab forged by his arm and man boob. He flipped through a few pages. One of them momentarily raised his tie by accident. Then he looked Roman up and down.

"What's your name, son?" Grubner asked. "I recognize your hair, but I don't think I've run into you before."

Roman looked over at Todd for any kind of guidance, but his friend had literally turned his back on him. "My name is Roman. Val—Vallancourt."

"Interesting," Grubner said. "Just when I thought last names couldn't get trickier than Armenian ones. Where's that from?"

"Canada. Uh, Quebec."

Uncharacteristically, Roman craved small talk. He wished Grubner would ask a follow-up query about Montreal, where Roman had visited relatives and could speak about it with a six-out-of-ten confidence level, but mostly, it'd be trivia about the Tim Hortons menu. Anything to end this scrutiny. Grubner inspected the papers again. Sweat started macheting through Roman's fro.

He's not looking up grades, is he? They don't keep stuff like that so close to their chest, do they?

Grubner looked Roman straight in the eyes and smirked.

"Have a good lunch," the principal said before waddling over to a group of students.

Roman felt like the auditeria was shrinking around him. He scanned the room once more to ensure Grubner didn't see him pull an Irish exit. Outside, Roman jogged to the stone benches past the spicy chicken cart and laid down his plate of uneaten pizza.

His heart raced and his joints burned with terror. His brain searched for a panic button.

Stop this now. End the H-wording altogether.

After a few exhales, Roman hoped Todd would start spouting reassurances from behind like a trainer in a boxer's corner. But it was just Alex, for whom Roman had accurately calculated an under-the-radar 3.4 GPA, excluding him from the luncheon.

"Ah, dude," Alex said. "You didn't have to bring me pizza."

By this point, Roman had lost his appetite and didn't care. "Just take it," he muttered.

"Oh no, I was just kidding. If anything, I owe you after that spicy chicken you gave me."

"It's fine. I'm not hungry anymore." Roman pushed the plate toward Alex across a stone bench.

"I never understood how one simply loses their appetite, but I'll die before I turn down free pizza," Alex said.

He snatched the plate and started going to town on his first slice. "Thanks, buddy! Listen, if you want any game from Blockbuster, lemme know. I'll pick 'em up on Friday and give them to you on Monday or something, so you'll at least get a couple days."

"Yeah, okay," said Roman, who was getting antsy. "I'll let you know."

"Man, did I luck out in the friend department. I got someone who gives me free pizza and fixes my grades."

Fixing grades—other people's grades. Roman shattered the glass casing housing the panic button with a headbutt.

Back home, the Apollo grade book was spreadeagled onscreen, but there were no lackluster test grades to tweak for now. Roman analyzed the numbers like he was about to execute a major Wall Street trade. The Grubner run-in got him thinking this H-wording heist was way beyond a simple prank—there needed to be a fail-safe, a firewall more dependable than relying on spoofing his own IP address, which Roman considered amateurish by this point. Something needed to blur the line between a glitch and his S-tier H-wording. At random, Roman picked a student's name on-screen—Martin Jambazian—and hovered the cursor over it in the grade book. He clicked and tapped a few keys to boost Algebra 2 quiz scores and raise his overall grade from eighty-three to eighty-four.

Out of superstition, Roman held his breath to see if any alerts popped up. None did.

Oops, did I do that?

Not that he was proud of himself for doing a Steve Urkel impression.

Another name, another name.

Roman scanned the grade book for someone non-Armenian to avoid raising suspicion of a race-based scam. A Filipino kid would do for the sake of diversity.

Miguel Tuazon? No, no, no. He's not getting a seventy-three. He's getting a seventy-five. Oops, I did it again.

Roman would rather confess to every iota of H-wording to a sold-out stadium before admitting he liked that Britney Spears song. He'd even sung it to himself in the shower once, but never again after Leon opened the door because he needed toothpaste.

Roman flipped through a few other classes and picked another student.

What do we have here, Michelle Mnatsakanyan? A ninety-two in U.S. history? Make that a ninety-three, 'cause I don't have a reason to not like you yet.

Teachers would assuredly blame the inconsistencies on a bad day, a streak of brain farts, a good old-fashioned computer error, or those margins of error Roman kept hearing about on CNN during the 2000 presidential election.

Remembering that the whole goal was to make himself appear like a diligent student, he boosted a recent history quiz from a seventy-nine to an eighty-five.

He tweaked a few more scores and decided he'd wait a few days to see if they were changed back—if not, the security plan would have succeeded.

Roman stretched and pushed his chest out. It was the afternoon that would keep on giving, as Harry Link sent a private message with details of big plans he'd kept under wraps until now.

[17:51] (@HarryLink): you're lucky that I'm letting you do this after the stunt you pulled with winwarez, it's mostly cause you live in LA.

[17:51] (@HarryLink): so after the convention's over for the day, i need you to hang around, listen for any gossip, maybe you'll even run into Bill gates at a bar or something.

Harry was talking about the upcoming Professional Developers Conference at the Los Angeles Convention Center this summer. The event would draw in the biggest tech names and upcoming products in the PC world.

[17:51] (@JaYnus): but i'm not 21
[17:51] (@HarryLink): how old are you
[17:51] (@JaYnus): almost 17
[17:51] (@HarryLink): ur kidding
[17:51] (@JaYnus): is that a problem? I mean is it gonna be an issue?
[17:52] (@HarryLink): I'm surrounded by freaking kids lol
[17:52] (@HarryLink): I'm more than twice ur age lol. u kids are getting into this stuff way too early man. don't you have homework to do?

[17:52] (@HarryLink): Ok, i'm not even gonna think about bars, what's the longest you can stick around for??

[17:52] (@JaYnus): i can ask my parents to pick me up whenever, i think

[17:52] (@HarryLink): … your parents … my god i feel old. are you sure? Can I trust you with this?

[17:52](@JaYnus): of course, i'll get a lot of good pics and shit to post on the site.

[17:52] (@HarryLink): great! I'll hit you up with more details soon

[17:52](@HarryLink): you'll generate way more money than you're making now on your site.

Despite the good news, something suddenly obliterated the feng shui in his room. Only the presence of humans could do this much damage, and this time, it was two of them: Todd and Lucy stood at the doorframe, staring at his crotch for some reason. That was when Roman remembered he was still in a pair of purple Laker boxers. Lucy giggled.

"Seriously, bro?" Todd said.

Roman jolted out of his chair and tripped over a shoe, landing on his bed, luckily back-first. He sat upright and pedaled his legs through a nearby pair of khakis.

"Roman, your friends are here!" Audrey yelled from downstairs.

"I thought you heard us come in, bro," Todd said.

Todd was in a black button-down shirt and black jeans, while Lucy wore a blue denim jacket over a white tank top, a black skirt, and black high heels. Armenians liked to dress nicely when going to someone's house, regardless of the occasion, Roman recalled.

"Uh, hi," he said. He got back up, only to sit in his chair again, then swiveled to his monitor. "Give me a sec."

Audrey unexpectedly walked in wearing a house robe and placed a check made out for $348.65 next to his mouse.

"Is this for you?" she asked.

With tens of thousands of visitors heading to the #mswarez website every day, Roman had capitalized on Google AdSense, which he used to place ads on his website. He got paid by the page view and even more if a visitor clicked on an ad.

He didn't think he'd do this well with his first pass with passive income. He wished he could shove the check within a hair of his mom's face to prove that his passion wasn't a waste of time, that this was just the beginning, that by some carefree day, he'd start getting checks with commas.

"Yeah," Roman said. "It's mine."

"Did you get a job?" Audrey asked.

Roman cleared his throat and spoke a little louder than usual so everyone heard. Todd and Lucy were respectful and quiet.

"When I got some free time from studying," Roman said, "I designed a website. I'm making money off ads."

"But you don't even have a checking account," Audrey said, now whispering and bringing the check close enough to Roman's neck to accidentally nick him. "What are you going to do with this?"

Roman was getting ticked that she wasn't seeing the bigger picture.

"Whatever, man," he said without looking at his mother. "I'll figure it out."

"Okay, okay," Audrey said. "Here, let me cash it for you at the bank so you can waste more money on more computer junk."

Great, Roman thought. *Now I gotta fight her for my own money.*

Audrey smiled at the guests. "Do you kids want anything? Hungry? Thirsty?"

"No, thank you, Mrs. Vallancourt," Todd said.

Audrey looked Lucy up and down and shot Todd a wink. "Nice jacket," she said. "Nice shoes. Nice everything! Todd, you're a lucky guy!"

Todd pursed his lips and bobbed his head.

"Aww, thank you," Lucy said.

"Alright, I'll get out of your way," Audrey said as she tugged the ends of her robe knot. "Let me know the second you guys change your mind."

She left Roman's room.

"Your mom is so cute," Lucy told Roman, who stayed glued to his screen in silence.

"You gonna do your thing?" Todd asked.

"Yeah," Roman said.

Arriving at the Apollo grade book was now pure muscle memory. But it wasn't fast enough for Lucy not to notice the huge, disassembled computer tower in a corner of the room and the stacks of motherboards and other PC guts shoved into another corner.

"You build computers?" she asked.

"Yeah," Roman said.

"That's so cool!"

"Tell me one of your classes," Roman said, looking over his shoulder. Todd sighed.

"One of my classes?" Lucy said.

"Yeah. Which one?"

"Algebra 2. Do Algebra 2," Todd said.

Within a few seconds, Roman had her name onscreen: *HAMBARSOUMIAN, LUSINEH*. She had a B in the class. Lucy squinted as she leaned toward the screen. Her hair was almost interwoven with Roman's locks.

"What is this?" she asked her boyfriend. "Is this the study aid you were telling me about?"

"Study aid?" Roman asked.

"Okay, okay," Todd said. "Luce, listen. I didn't think you'd understand until I showed you."

Roman's eyelids receded. He twitched toward the monitor, thinking his narrow shoulders would block what was onscreen.

Goddammit, Todd. You mean you didn't actually tell her? You told me she was cool with it!

Lucy dropped her arms to her sides and retreated a few steps. "You're cheating?"

"No! No! No!" Todd replied. "Just think of it like we're giving ourselves extra credit," Todd said.

"No wonder you're Mr. Top 20!"

Todd waxed the air in the direction of the monitor. "All of this is insurance. It'll guarantee that I'll get into the best schools."

His life's work aside, all Roman could do in the middle of an argument was impersonate a statue. This just couldn't be the end—it couldn't.

"Why did you even tell me about this?" Lucy asked.

"Because you saw me with Eunice," Todd said.

"You think I'm that paranoid? It's just a hug. I hug your friends when I see them after you guys play basketball."

"I just wanted to make sure you believed me."

"Believed you?" she scoffed. "Have you guys thought about what would happen if you got caught? They're gonna suspend or even expel you!"

The boys said nothing. A weather report about partially cloudy skies on Thursday reverberated off the stairway ceiling.

Todd brushed his right hand over Lucy's shoulder.

"We're not gonna get caught. This is the last semester we're doing this. Then I apply to college, and I'm done. No one's going to care how well I do in my senior year. Then I'm gone, and nobody will give a shit about stupid high school ever again. Tell her, Rome. Tell her how you do it, bro."

Roman was in the middle of an ear pick.

"Umm. Yeah, I use a proxy to fake my location," he said, still facing the monitor and catching a few reflections of body language. "There's no way the school can find out."

Lucy inched a step back and sounded even more repulsed. "I knew you guys were close friends, but not pulling off criminal stuff like this!"

Roman's ethics were finally confronted by public opinion. Minus an elevated heart rate at the notion that things might be spiraling out of control, the molecules governing his sense of morality were unfazed.

This? he thought, referring to the grade book. *All this is just job training.*

Todd's body was mostly calm, except for his fingers typing on his thighs. "We already got away with it last semester. We'll be fine. We can help you, too, if you want. Any grade you'd like to change?"

But Lucy had rejected the conversation in favor of staring out the half-shut Venetian blinds. Todd slid behind her and massaged her index finger with his thumb.

"Should I . . . Do you want me to step out?" Roman asked as he swiveled in his chair.

Todd raised a wagging finger at him. "It's your house, bro. We'll go." But he didn't leave before whispering into Lucy's ear, which Roman overheard, "I've told you how my folks are. Look where all this has gotten us."

Lucy sounded stuffed up. She gradually turned around. "You cared that much about me? To do all this?"

Todd flipped the Chin. "Are you kidding me?" he said, cupping her elbows. "Just about everything I do is 'cause I care about you. Except when I play *FIFA*."

A gentle cackle from Lucy. She hugged Todd. Roman wanted to yank out a red card from his pocket and blow a whistle from atop the Swedish Alps. There was to be no philandering in his sanctuary, not even if Roman was the offender, but he may have also just witnessed the smoothest social engineering he'd ever seen.

"I just don't want anything bad to happen to you," Lucy told Todd.

"Nothing will. Are you kidding me?" he replied. "Especially with this computer genius over there."

Roman made eye contact with Lucy as she rested her chin on Todd's shoulder.

"You're like a mad scientist," she said. "And I totally dig the fro too. We should invite him to Alina's party."

"Uh, sure," Todd said. "But, Rome, you gotta dress better than that, bud."

Lucy now had a carefree smile, the kind Roman saw girls give stone-faced guys hanging out at the mall.

"Just don't get caught," Lucy said.

As the embrace ate away at Roman's patience, she caught another glimpse of the grade book.

"Wait," she said. "What am I saying? This is crazy . . . telling you not to get caught."

"Babe," Todd said. He sounded more annoyed than worried now.

"I can't do this, having to always worry about it."

"There's nothing to worry about! All the hard work is done."

Lucy broke free. "Can I go home? I'm sorry, Roman. I don't mean to be rude."

She marched out of the room and headed downstairs.

Oh, shit.

Roman flew out of his chair and grabbed Todd's elbow sleeve as he tried to leave. "You didn't tell me she was gonna get mad," Roman said. "She's not gonna tell anyone, is she?"

"No, bro, she'd never do that. Don't worry about it. I'll handle it."

Todd tried to pull away, but another question came to Roman's mind. "Wait, why were you hugging Eunice?"

Todd's pupils moved back and forth like the platen of a typewriter. "I told you already." He followed Lucy.

Roman overheard an exchange of swift goodbyes downstairs, followed by the shutting of the front door.

"You couldn't offer them a glass of water?" Audrey shouted from downstairs.

19

The Lucy situation ended with an armistice. No breakup, but no makeup make-outs either, not even a mall date. So, Todd gave her space for the next few days by relocating his lunch appointment with Alex and Roman to the top of the amphitheater, where they lucked out and claimed a bench. Sako's crew of revving sounds, overblown laughs, and shit-talking barged from a few cliques over.

"Why do we have to be up here?" Alex asked.

"Will you just get over it already?" Todd replied. As he shoved a brown rye chip from a bag of Chex Mix into his mouth, he gazed down the giant steps at Lucy with her group of girlfriends, all of them shaded by the light blue metal awning spanning the boys' and girls' locker room entrances. It wasn't far from the soda machines where Todd and his friends usually hung out in the mornings.

"I don't get it," Alex said. "If you guys fought, why aren't you trying to make up right now?"

"You stupid, bro?" Todd retorted. "Of course, I'm gonna

try to do that. I'm just letting her cool off. Don't wanna sound desperate."

"Why does everything sound desperate to you?"

"Shut up."

Todd spent the rest of lunch trying to read Lucy's lips. Her friends' lips too. He knew it was dumb and stalkery. They were too far away, anyway. All he could decipher was that Teni, one of Lucy's friends, had lipstick on her teeth.

She's trying hard to find a distraction, he thought. *But that means she's gotta be thinking about me too.*

Seated on a bench, Roman leaned forward and asked, "She's not going to say anything, right?"

"Or what the hell are you gonna do? Kick her ass?" Todd said. "Give me a break."

The day's only hopeful moment was after the bell that ended lunch. Todd was heading toward one of the main building entrances. That was when he believed he saw Lucy levitating his way, divinely possessed and ready to forgive.

"I missed you," Todd blurted out.

But once the sun's glare cleared up, he was face-to-face with Eunice.

"The hell?" she said. "Uh-uh, you're not making moves, are you?"

"No, no. Just thought you were . . . Ugh, never mind. What's up?"

"You know Mr. Fields, right?"

"AP gov? Yeah. Had him last semester."

"That's who I need next."

"Fine. When?"

"By tomorrow."

"What? That's not enough time!"

"I wanted to tell you earlier, but you haven't been at your usual lunch spot this whole week!"

After school, Todd restarted AIM on his computer over and over again—no word from Lucy. The thought of reverting to the single life was revolting. There was nothing else on Earth he wanted to do more than share a piece of furniture with her, maybe along with a protein double-double from In-N-Out, animal style, no tomatoes.

At least he and Alex only had one class to visit that night. Alex waited by the door of Mr. Fields's AP government class as a lookout while Todd inspected a drawer cart by the teacher's desk. The top drawer had a lock. He remembered another TA saying Mr. Fields reused the same tests every year, and if they were stored somewhere in class, it'd be this drawer. Todd slid in the bogota rake and fiddled, but the drawer wouldn't budge. Alex beckoned with his hands to vamoose. Todd ignored him and fiddled on with no progress. He remembered himself at the gym over a year ago, jumping rope, sweating balls, his folds clapping.

Present-day, skinny Todd pressed his right foot against the drawer to add some leverage.

"Come on," he grumbled.

He was proud of achieving his goal of fifty push-ups in a row. It was the same stamina and patience that'd get that big admittance packet in the mail from Stanford.

Whatever. Doesn't matter. Lucy will never kiss you again.

"Goddammit!" he said in a loud whisper.

Todd put his right foot down, but an irrational synapse wound it up like a punter.

Shit. Too late.

The small storage unit flew across the room. Todd shut his eyes to heighten his hearing in preparation for impact. He wasn't sure if it was so violent that a shockwave had knocked him unconscious, as he had heard nothing. Upon opening his eyes, he saw Alex gripping one of the edges with both hands.

"Are you crazy?" Alex asked, panic-stricken.

"How did you get there so fast?" Todd asked.

"I have no clue! And what the hell is wrong with you, man?"

"I'm sorry! Relax!"

"Why the hell did you do that?"

"I don't know! I don't know!"

Teeth clenched, Alex rolled the cabinet back to its spot.

"I'm sick of this," Alex said. "If you can't open that thing, then forget the test. Let's get out of here. We've had too many close calls."

"But bro!"

Alex raised a finger. "That Eunice chick is being so selfish. She'll survive without one test."

"Bro."

Alex got into his friend's face. "I don't give a shit about me, but I don't want you to mess up your chances by doing something stupid."

Todd was speechless and apparently a sheep to leadership as he tailed a storming Alex out of the classroom.

They passed by the same class the following morning with Roman in tow before the first bell of the day. Alex had bags under his eyes again.

"Couldn't sleep?" Todd asked.

"I didn't mean to snap at you like that," Alex uttered.

"Don't worry about it. I won't snap like that again, either. Thanks for keeping me in check, buddy."

Their low-bumping fists met by their waists.

"But yeah," Alex said. "I couldn't sleep, so I stayed up and beat *Metal Gear Solid 2* on hard mode."

"You'll sleep fine tonight," Todd said.

But a complete stranger emerging from Mr. Fields' AP government class staggered Todd's optimism. Two years into high school, he pretty much knew all the adults on campus, at least by face. But this new person, the glint off his badge assumed to be janitorial in nature, was the final confirmation. Todd engaged in immediate eye contact because if it was over, he wanted to know right away. But the throng of bottlenecking students reeled the tall and youthful officer's attention as they tried to get a peek at what had transpired.

"Everyone just back up a couple of steps," the young officer said.

His shoulders were wide, like they could support a three-ring circus. Todd swore every police officer and firefighter rolled off the assembly line just like that. Then a much shorter, chubbier officer stepped out of the classroom and took off a pair of plastic gloves before readjusting his belt. Todd caught at least one word via lipreading.

"Nothing," the gloved officer uttered to Principal Grubner, who was standing there with a clipboard cradled against his man boobs. The news didn't alter his stoic demeanor.

"Nothing was stolen?" he asked. "Bart, get over here."

Mr. Fields, in a brown-patterned vest over a cream shirt, inched toward the principal. Grubner massaged the wrinkles on his forehead. "Did someone actually break in, or is your anal retentiveness acting up again?"

"There's a scratch on my rolling cabinet I've never seen before," Mr. Fields said, pointing at the fixture in question.

The chubby officer scrutinized them and seemed unimpressed. "Next time, call us when something's actually been stolen."

Todd felt something land on his shoulder. Luckily, it wasn't one of the officer's hands from behind ready to greet him with a pair of handcuffs. Instead, it was Alex's head. Todd jabbed his elbow into his friend's ribs and commandeered him like a ventriloquist all the way outside, past the boys' locker room. They crossed paths with Roman, who followed them to an expansive asphalt limbo between the P.E. field and the faculty parking lot.

"What's wrong?" Roman asked.

"Can you chill, bro?" Todd told Alex.

Alex was winded and didn't respond.

"Uh, everything okay?" Roman asked.

"Yeah, yeah, we're fine," Todd said, fanning a hand at his friend.

"Don't tell me we're fine!" Alex countered. "I told you something like this would happen!"

"We're fine because I know we're fine," Todd said. "Are you gonna calm down now, bro?"

Todd turned his back to Alex and adjusted the collar of his gray Fila polo.

"We would be fine if you chilled the hell out last night and didn't mess with that lock so much!" Alex said.

"Shut up!" Todd spun around and thrust his palm to within a few inches of his friend's mouth.

"Lock?" Roman asked.

"I'm sorry, Todd," Alex said. "But we can't do this anymore. It's way too risky."

"Yes, we can, bro." Todd leaned closer to Alex and whispered, "This is just a hiccup. It was my bad, I admit it. And blame Mr.

Fields for being super anal about his furniture placement. But like I said, I won't lose my cool like that again."

"'Yes, we can?' Are you crazy?" Alex asked, speaking over Todd's shoulder. "Rome, listen, we've—"

"You know what, Al?" Todd said. "Rome and I saved your freaking life." Todd backed off a few feet and pointed at Alex. "We brought you into something cool so you wouldn't sad trip about Tamar forever."

"Rome, we've been breaking into school at night!" Alex shouted.

Todd groaned violently. Despite a widening of the eyes, all Roman did was hunch his posture.

"First time was just to get Grubner's password. Then we started stealing tests for Eunice," Alex continued.

"Okay, bro!" Todd said. "That's enough!"

"We broke in with a lockpick! Todd ordered it online."

"Al!"

"You, uh . . . You . . ." Roman said. "What?"

Todd got in his face to try to cork the ongoing outburst.

"The hell can you even say? After all the times I risked my ass going running around like a goddamn Soviet spy. I'm the *only* reason we've made it this far."

Roman's eyes widened more, magnified by his thick lenses.

"Oh, wake up, bro," Todd said. "This isn't like you hacking at home while scratching your balls. I've had to get my hands dirty. I've done a kickass job. Eunice has no idea what we're really doing."

"But Lucy does now," Alex said.

"Come on, bro. One thing at a time. I told you, don't worry about her."

"Don't worry about it? She's ignoring you! Even I know when a girl is pissed. What's stopping her from telling on us?"

"A girl can be pissed and still care about you. God knows if you'll learn that on your own someday."

"Look, guys," Alex said as he got between Todd and Roman. "This was fun in the beginning. I thought this was gonna be like a prank or something, but I don't want us to get arrested! I can't even imagine what our folks would do to us."

The first-period bell rang, but no one seemed to care about being tardy.

"Bro," Todd said, "the cops are gonna leave and forget about this. They've got bigger fish to fry. People break into schools all the time and try to steal shit to pawn or whatever. They have no idea it has anything to do with the hacking. I heard them. They have no clue what's going on."

"We weren't even using gloves or anything. They're gonna find our fingerprints!"

"Hey, smart guy, have you ever given your fingerprints before? Then there's no way they're going to have them on file. That's for keeping track of convicted felons and shit. I could go jizz all over that classroom, and they'd never know it was me!"

Todd coughed and spat onto the concrete. He must have shut his friends up. "See? Mock trial experience, baby. You really think I'm gonna let something bad happen to you guys?"

Alex did a few panicked heel turns. He walked toward a brick wall and pressed his backpack against it while covering his face with his hands. "I don't even care about grades anymore, man. I just thought we'd have a few secret hangouts like we're a club or something. Like, we'd pick up some Shakey's and play some *GoldenEye* multiplayer."

"Bro, the PS2, GameCube, and Xbox are out. Why are you still obsessing over the N64?" Todd asked.

"The classics are still fun," Alex said, slowly lowering his hands.

"Jesus Christ, why am I even asking? Is that all you wanna do? Play games? Haven't you toughened up from this shit at all?"

"I don't want anything bad to happen to us. You guys are . . . I . . . You mean so . . ."

As long as Alex didn't start crying.

"Tell you what, bro," Todd said as he chewed on a hangnail and took a few steps in his direction. "We'll take a little break with the after-school activities for a few weeks. Maybe I can figure out how to get tests during the day in the meantime."

Alex was now using his hands to emphasize a few key words. "Todd, do you hear yourself? The police *were* here. We could have been arrested, and you wanna try again?"

"You know what, bro? I'm sick of trying to motivate you. I'm so sick of it."

Alex looked dehydrated and pale. "You're being . . . you're being a shitty friend!" he whimpered. "No matter what you think, you don't care what happens to us, but I care about what happens to you!"

Todd scoffed and rolled his eyes. "You're never going to get anywhere if you're gonna whine about having to work hard and the shortcuts you're gonna need to take. You have to take short-cuts sometimes."

Alex used one of his sleeves to wipe his nose. Todd squinted in disbelief and rage.

"Me? A shitty friend? Look at all the changes I've made to bet-ter myself," Todd said. "I could be hanging out with Sako and those popular guys all the time. I could have left you guys, just like, overnight and never spoken to you again. But I didn't. What does that tell you?"

Alex slightly lowered his head.

"Yeah, that's what I thought," Todd said, then looked at Roman.

Time to put out another fire before it was even lit.

"And you're not too far off," Todd continued. "You're not gonna become a millionaire hiding behind—"

"The police were here 'cause of you guys?" Roman said, interrupting. He pressed his palms down on his afro, making his hair look like a hedge trimmed to resemble the letter W.

Todd, on his toes since the start of the school year, pounced into his friend's face. "Oh, that's good, Rome. Let me have it, bro! Go ahead, snap. Now it's your turn. You've been waiting to do this, just waiting for the right moment to finally do it. I can take it."

"I think—" Roman said.

"That's it, bro," Todd said.

"—we're done."

"Let me . . . Wait. What?"

"I said I'm, uh, done. I'm not changing any more."

"Yes!" Alex said. "Let's have a retirement party at In-N-Out!"

Todd started waving his hands around like he was trying to prove to an officer he was unarmed. "Wait, wait, wait, Rome. Let's think about this. We've all got plans here!"

"I've been thinking lately," Roman said. "Going to that Torch & Lehigh pizza party made me nervous."

"Yeah, but you did great. You did fine. No one's gonna suspect anything."

"I gotta change a few more things. In the records. To cover our tracks. But other than that, we're done."

"What are you talking about?" Todd asked.

"I can't believe . . . I can't believe you guys did all that shit! I-I told you, don't go after school."

"Oh, come on, man. I helped bring your dream to life. You're lucky to have a friend like me, especially since you're socially handicapped."

"I'm sorry, Rome!" Alex said. "I didn't mean to keep this from you!"

"Rome, please," Todd pleaded.

"You're a 4.0 genius," Alex told Todd. "You'll get in anywhere."

"You get to make this call just because you know what keys on the keyboard to press," Todd told Roman. "If I knew how to hack, man . . ."

"You . . . you think you're the only one that worked hard on something twenty-four-seven?" Roman replied.

"Yeah!" Alex said. "What Rome's trying to say is you guys are crazy smart in your own ways."

"Shut up, Al," Todd said. "You still couldn't have done all this without me."

But the attempted stinger didn't land, as Roman seemed to enjoy scratching his right butt cheek.

"Bro. Come on," Todd said. "What am I supposed to tell Eunice now?"

"I'm sure you'll figure out something," Alex said.

"Hey! Who said you're off the hook here, bro? Help me brainstorm."

"Me? I dunno. Just tell her you couldn't find it. I don't think it'll do much good if she tells on you. Won't that make it harder to steal tests?"

Todd couldn't believe it: the virgin kings had somehow checked him. Alex aligned himself with Roman shoulder to shoulder and disdained expression to disdained expression.

"Don't look at me like that!" Todd demanded. "There's no way you can pin this all on me! Screw you guys!"

He marched away, and it was cathartic. He knew he was right, like a flawless argument penetrating the jury box, followed by the sound of a cash register bell and a unanimous multimillion-dollar verdict.

Todd didn't say a word or a "sup" to anyone on the way to class. No biggie. Snack was a different story, though, when he bought a bag of Flamin' Hot Cheetos from a vending machine and turned around to find nobody waiting for him, just a bunch of his peers laughing at their respective snack tables. His internal compass was warped. Not knowing where to go, he took a seat on a stone bench next to the vending machine. No one ever sat there. Who'd want to have front-row access to kids running up to the vending machine all day? Not even the most outgoing of card-carrying extroverts. Todd tore open the bag of chips and stared into its half-emptiness. He didn't know which way to look. He ate a chip and tasted the salt, but not the flavor. Two girls walked by and giggled. Todd felt like the laughs were toward his direction. No friends, no Lucy. He felt like a freshman at a new school in a new state.

God dammit, he thought.

Like all great philosophers, Todd had an epiphany as he bought a chalupa from one of the lunch windows during lunch. It took a single, extra-bright neuron to outshine his enduring thought process: *Chances are, there's always going to be somebody above you.*

That one hurt a lot.

But maybe being somebody's somebody meant you'd still get to be somebody.

Todd trudged past his munching peers and chucked the quarter-eaten chalupa into a trash can on the way past tuned-out chatter so he could hear Roman's and Alex's voices as soon as possible. They were eating cold-cut sandwiches. When Todd got close enough, they all locked stares. He felt shorter, probably because he had gotten down on one knee. All that was missing was a sword, a quiver, and for Roman to have royal blood.

"I'm really sorry," Todd said.

"It's okay," Alex said. "Just—"

"Not you, dumbass," Todd said.

His friends' expressions hadn't changed.

"Fine," Todd said. "You too. Rome, I . . . I . . . didn't mean to disrespect you by going behind your back like that. If anything, it's because I believed in you so much. I wanted to do anything I could to make sure you succeeded."

He glanced over at Alex, who displayed a hangdog face. Roman, on the other hand, reminded Todd of pixelated stadium attendees from his *FIFA* games.

Dude, come on.

"Uh, cool," Roman said. "Thanks."

"Oh. That's it? We're good?"

Todd was expecting a customary low-five, but his friend had other plans.

"End of the semester," Roman blurted.

"Huh?" Todd replied.

"I'll change them again at the end of the year. Just like last semester."

"Really!" Todd exclaimed.

"Yeah. Guess I, uh, overreacted. We can still boost our shit without them knowing, I think."

"Ah, geez," Alex said. "So, we're not done? We gotta do more sneaky stuff?"

"No. I'll just wait till the last minute to change shit like last time. I got all the passwords. Guess I can't really be pissed at you guys. You got them, after all."

"Oh, thank God," Alex said. "Finally, I can sleep."

Todd chuckled.

"And you know what else?" Alex said. "I think I need good grades more than ever cause I wanna get into a tougher school than DigiPen."

"No way, where?" Todd asked.

"Not exactly sure, but it's gotta be somewhere that teaches journalism, I guess. I . . . I wanna be a food critic."

Todd lit up with excitement. "No way! That's freaking amazing, bro. You're so cut out for that!"

Roman perked up a light smile. "Yeah. Totally a great fit."

"Really?" Alex asked as he grinned from ear to ear. "Thanks, guys! I was thinking I could even be a game critic too!"

"Bro, forget college!" Todd said. "Start practicing now! I've bet you've got a billion opinions to get off your chest."

"Yeah, I do."

"Write for the school paper or something!"

Roman nodded while smiling faintly. "Yeah."

Todd sprang to his feet, raised the Chin, and offered Alex a hearty high five and a hug. Alex, and even Roman, grinned to the max.

"Thanks, man!" Alex said.

But as the moment waned, the boys sat back down and sighed in unison.

"I guess the only thing left is Eunice," Todd said. "I'll talk to her in fifth period. I think I can get her to be okay with it. She dumped this on me last minute, after all."

—

Instead, Eunice shoved all the papers and books off her desk in the middle of pre-calc. Students gazed over their shoulders to assess the commotion, but went right back to work after Eunice gave each of them a death stare. Even the teacher, Mr. Dimmer, looked over and didn't say anything.

"What do you mean you couldn't get it?" Eunice asked, roiling.

Todd sat next to her during a period of group study. He was a little flummoxed by her brazen littering. "I . . . I tried! I didn't have enough time!"

"You promised me. AP gov sucks. It's not fair. He throws in questions from the book, and we never talk about that stuff in class! I'm never going to need any of that trash."

Todd felt more uneasy than when he saw the police officers. Nothing was scarier than a hysterical perfectionist.

"You sure you looked all over the class?" Eunice asked.

"It just wasn't there," Todd said. "I cleared that room from top to bottom and didn't find anything."

"I guess that means I'll have to get Nathan or one of his friends to try again."

"How? You don't even have the right tools."

Todd gasped and covered his mouth with both hands. Next, he wanted to slap himself for letting something like that slip. He forgot who he was talking to. Eunice's pupils sank to a lower quadrant. She was processing something; Todd knew the look when someone was trying to do the math in their head. Eunice looked like she had solved a Calculus II problem, like it was two plus two.

"The police car," she said.

Oh, shit.

"That's why you couldn't get it," Eunice continued. "You were almost caught."

"No! Not at all!" Todd said.

"Nathan just got caught by a teacher. You're *trying* to get arrested?"

"That wasn't me that broke into the school. Someone else must have broken in to steal some tech gear or something."

"Just forget it."

Right before the end of class, Eunice gathered her belongings and slid out of her seat. "You've ruined it for everyone."

"Wait," Todd conceded. "So, you'll forget about me and all of this?"

The bell rang.

"Stupid boys," Eunice said without looking at Todd. "You can't do anything right."

Todd interpreted that as the World Cup winner of reluctant yeses. Eunice was the first out of the classroom, leaving just as the teacher was making an announcement.

"Oh, almost forgot!" Mr. Dimmer said. He got up and taped a piece of paper to a corner of the whiteboard. "Thought you'd like to see your grades heading into the midterm next week."

An unexpected update, to say the least. Todd scurried to the sheet and squinted. The grades were posted alongside student ID numbers to protect anonymity, but the AP class was so small that everyone was able to discern who was who. Everyone had some level of A, of course, and Todd sat firmly at a ninety-six. The figure encompassed the past few test scores Roman had bumped up, thus giving Todd the highest grade in the class.

Oh, shit.

He turned around to see Joy, arms crossed, focused on the posted grades behind him. Unlike the minimally stylish Eunice, Joy was always plain. She barely wore makeup. Her khakis were always worn high, which almost hid a protruding tummy. After inspecting the scores, she looked back at Todd.

"Good job," she said.

Todd sighed in relief. No suspicion, after all. That was until a fuzzy scalp grazed Todd's shoulder. Tiny Ed Pacheco had cut in out of nowhere.

"Good job?" he yelled at Todd with a series of cracks in his voice. "How the hell are you doing so well?" He planted his hands on Todd's shoulders and started shaking him with restraint. "How the hell did you climb so high? I'm sick of your type! Gotta be perfect at everything? Gotta get the girl too? She's the only one who was ever nice to me!"

"Calm down, you psycho!" Todd said. He shoved Pacheco a little harder than he would have liked because the little guy fell hard on his ass.

Pacheco tried to pick himself up until Todd lifted him by his polo collar until they were face to face. Todd's ensuing words exploded with rabid ferocity as he spat onto Pacheco's upper lip with each syllable.

"Nobody owes you anything!" Todd shouted with buggy eyes. "You don't know what I do outside of here! You don't know what I do!"

Honor societies and good attendance didn't matter in situations like this, as even the school's best and brightest shouted,

"Fight, fight, fight!" Their classmates formed a ring around Todd and Pacheco.

"Hey! Hey!" Mr. Dimmer shouted as he hit his knee on the underside of the desk while trying to get up. He inserted himself between Pacheco and Todd to break up the scuffle. Out of the corner of his eye, Todd saw Joy leave the classroom.

Pacheco wiped the spit off his face. Mr. Dimmer ordered Todd and Pacheco to report to Vice Principal Leininger's office. They'd end up playing the "academic pressure card" and were each let off with just two days' lunch detention. Todd was glad Grubner was off that week because he was often stricter and could have suspended him, derailing his college prospects altogether. Luckily, there was a rumor going around that Leininger was a fan of doling out lunch detention because it saved on the janitorial budget. If Roman and Alex saw Todd carrying out his sentence, he'd attribute it to excessive peeling out in the student parking lot after school.

Todd and Pacheco went opposite ways once they left Leininger's office. Massaging his temple a few times, Todd asked himself what could possibly come next. The answer was Lucy walking alone. Todd was certain he had burned through his protective layer of Old Spice by now, so he didn't want to get too close. Lucy, wearing a white polo and a khaki skirt like a Wimbledon darling, seemed receptive to a greeting.

"Hi," Todd said.

"Hey," Lucy said.

Realizing that oncoming students weren't making this easier, Todd and Lucy took a few steps toward a hallway wall.

"I haven't been ignoring you," he said.

"I know. Pretty hard to miss your eyes on me all around school," Lucy said.

"I . . . I just wanted to give you some space. I—"

"What took you so long? You were fine with letting me worry?"

Todd thought and thought. Then thought some more. It had only been four seconds, but it was too long for comfort. He kept things simple and let genuine sentiments flow.

"Roman's my best friend," Todd said. "Sometimes it can take a while to change someone's mind about something they're passionate about."

She had every right to be snippy, and he knew that.

"Oh, really?" Lucy asked, sounding sarcastic. "Interesting."

"We were just kids, and we did dumb kid shit," Todd continued. "I don't want to be a kid anymore."

Lucy squinted, and with those sleepy eyes, it appeared she had lost a tussle with narcolepsy, but a few up-and-down scans of Todd showed otherwise.

"I have to pee," she said. She removed her backpack and stabbed it playfully into Todd's stomach before heading to the girls' bathroom a door over.

Cradling Lucy's backpack with one arm, he waited until she shut the bathroom door behind her to raise a free fist into the sky in victory.

—

The entire neighborhood smelled like one big barbecue. Even the oncoming wind couldn't tone it down. Most likely, it was the start of fire season in the Southland. Todd tried to catch a few gliding embers with his hand out the window at a red light. The dusk air was parched. He wore a black blazer over his finest white button-down tucked into a pair of black slacks. He pulled his dad's Audi over in front of a house and rolled up his window. A fruity aroma took over the cabin. Even though it was the mass-produced Dark Kiss by Bath & Body Works, it smelled one-of-a-kind coming off Lucy. She looked over at the familiar house as the front door opened. She turned back to Todd, this time with a goofy duckface. He wanted to kiss her, but the rustling of the back door stalled the moment.

"You don't know how long I had to argue with him over the phone to get him to come out," Todd said.

He unlocked the car door.

"Hey," Roman said as he got in and buckled up.

"Yo, bro," Todd said.

"Hi, Roman!" Lucy said. "Are you excited for Alina's party?"

Todd looked back at Roman with the smile of a QVC salesman. "Before we go, I was telling Luce how relaxed we are now since we gave up the hacking," he said. "All of it. And that we're completely done, right?"

ROMAN

Of course, Roman didn't expect such a question. He was so pissed that Todd kept throwing these curveballs and trying to pass them off as life lessons.

So, this was the big H-wording thing that Todd could only talk about at the party? If Roman had known he would be put on the spot, he would have turned down the invite. The audacity of cheating Roman out of a Friday night at home, the one night he could stay up late without his folks nagging. He wasn't sure if Lucy knew they intended to change grades again at the end of the semester.

Todd kept winking his left eye like he was having a stroke while Roman sensed his own twitching. Lucy, oblivious, was somehow beaming with her half-shut eyes.

Roman faked a smile that hurt his jaw. "Yeah, uh, we're done."

"Yep," Todd said. "See, Luce? He's a changed man. Ready to go, br—"

"Why should I do nerdy computer stuff when I could go to parties?" Roman continued.

"Uh, right on, bro," Todd said.

"And, you know, try to talk to a bunch of girls all night. What else am I supposed to be doing at my age?"

"Oh my god, Roman, I love it!" Lucy said, then elbowed Todd. "Let's see who we can introduce him to tonight."

"Sure," Todd said. "Sure, babe."

Shit, Roman thought. *That's the last time I try being sarcastic.*

The setting sun shone off Lucy's silver sequin dress. Roman, just a few notches below in fashion sense, tossed on his light gray polo and black jeans from when he was fourteen.

Alina lived in the Belmont Historic District, one of the wealthier Glendale neighborhoods. Roman felt like a pet dog in the back seat as he stared at Todd's and Lucy's hands knitted together atop the gearshift.

Roman kept behind them as they walked up the front steps to Alina's house, which resembled a La-Z-Boy armchair reclined into the hills. The anger concentrated on Todd was morphing into fear of how many people were inside. A pair of grand doors, kind of like the ones Roman imagined kicking down the first time he H-worded into the school, were answered by the host, who wore a beige blouse, a floral wrap skirt, and a bare midriff. Alina took turns hugging Lucy and Todd, while Roman's intuition indicated a hearty handshake was the next logical step in the greeting sequence. Alina obliged and giggled.

"Nice to meet you," she said. "Snacks and drinks in the kitchen."

The next thing to greet Roman was a winding staircase. Then he saw a fuzzy reflection of his fro on the marble floor. He held his breath as he scoped the scene. All the other guys either had spiked hair, slicked-back hair, or clean-shaven heads. There were small groups scattered between the foyer and the distant sliding patio door, where Lucy and Todd were heading. Everyone was talking; their words came naturally, but it sounded fake, like they were regurgitating a script.

Out of shits to give in a time that was a personal best, Roman sneaked a detour to a living room. He dropped onto the couch, praying a TV would already be on, but it wasn't. Alina strung by more guests in the hall with hellos until she noticed him.

"I've got a few of your kind here," she joked, approaching. "I'm guessing I can't force you to get to know them?"

Roman said nothing, which was another way of saying yes.

"You can invite a friend if you want," Alina said.

"Um, I'm good, thank you."

"Go ahead, as long as they're not gonna start trouble."

"Uh, okay," Roman said.

Alina was already making small talk again in the hall. Roman spotted a wall clock. Eight-thirty.

There's only one person to call at a time like this: the gamed crusader!

He came across a cordless phone and dialed. Of course, Alex sounded thrilled, but he made one requirement very clear.

"Is she there?" Alex asked over the phone.

"Who?" Roman asked.

"You know, man."

Roman hadn't seen Tamar, but he was desperate enough to double-check. The cordless phone pressed against his chest, he hustled through a few nearby rooms. He spotted some blondes, but none of the strands belonged to the girl in question.

"She's for sure not here," Roman told Alex. "I checked."

Alex's dad dropped him off at the party about twenty minutes later. Roman was elated; he had found Doritos Cooler Ranch in a fitting blue plastic bowl, and his friend had just arrived.

So much weight was lifted off Roman's shoulders that he

straightened his back to lead a parade march, patriotically waving the American flag. Then, of course, Todd had to open his mouth when he bumped into them near a platter of deli cuts, hummus, pita chips, seven-layer dip, and a few bottles of Grey Goose vodka.

"Are you kidding me?" Todd asked, looking them over. "Okay, Rome, glad you could stop by and have fun with everyone for five minutes."

Roman and Alex smiled and cheered their red solo cups filled with Pepsi and exited through the patio doors. Just off the deck, a gravel footpath led to a roaring fire pit in the middle of a lush green backyard. Roman made a quick mental note to be mindful of any sprinklers.

A bean arch stood as a gateway to the backyard from the driveway. Two speakers blaring hip-hop were pressed against the base of a blue jacaranda tree. If he took the people and noises out of the picture, Roman thought the scene could make for a serene desktop background.

Todd sat on a wooden lawn chair by the flames as Lucy perched on the armrest. He had one arm around her waist and leaned toward the fire pit to ash a cigarette. Roman had never seen him smoke. Either way, he was itching for a one-sided conversation.

"Uh, are you playing anything good right now?" Roman asked Alex.

Alex unzipped his hoodie and stretched out its pockets with his hands each time he tried to make a cogent point. "Roman, my friend, have you heard of a little game called *Xenogears*?"

"No, sir, I have not. Tell me more."

"Well, I've finished the entire *Final Fantasy* series, so I've been on a quest to play all of SquareSoft's other RPGs. SquareSoft's peak was in the mid- to late nineties, you know, when they'd release almost one *Final Fantasy* game per year, alongside another masterful non-canonical title. Case in point, *Final Fantasy III* in 1994, known as *Final Fantasy VI* in Japan, and *Chrono Trigger* in 1995."

They lapped the fire pit.

"And what did you think of *Xenogears*?" Roman asked.

"It may seem trivial, but I'm a big fan of the fact I can see my entire party running together onscreen, not just the main protagonist's sprite—it adds more to the sense of adventure. You'd be surprised how rare that is. Anyway, I just finished disc one of *Xenogears*, which was ridiculously long and—"

Roman yearned to hear more, but pointless party chatter clogged his ears. There was no way Alex had already finished. Roman conducted a visual sweep of the crowd.

Tamar came into view underneath the bean arch.

She wore an olive-green sweater dress draped from her left shoulder. She tugged it from the bottom to straighten it out. She surveyed the attendees and hopped to Todd and Lucy.

"Oh, so *this* Todd is your boyfriend?" Tamar said. "How's it going, Mr. Keylogger?"

Roman lost his balance and dug his right foot deep into the gravel. He remembered Todd's story about the unintentional fresh-getting with Tamar when trying to snatch the keylogger from the back of a computer, but he had no clue she knew what the device was. Roman locked eyes with Todd, whose pupils were trembling.

"She's coming," Alex said.

"What?" Roman asked.

His mind fogged by fret, he didn't realize Tamar was already standing in front of them.

"Oh, hi," she said, sounding like she was pretending to be surprised.

"Sorry, I should have said hi first or something," Alex said.

"I didn't know you knew Alina," Tamar said, interrupting.

"I don't. I just sneak around neighborhoods looking for parties to crash and deli platters to freeload off of."

Tamar chuckled. Alex must have been zoned out when she mentioned the keylogger. Over Tamar's shoulder, toward the fire pit, Todd and Lucy were no longer sitting there. Sensing Alex was on the verge of a long catching-up session, Roman retreated into the house to look for Todd and pick his brain about what to do about Tamar.

But Alex limped from behind. "Where you goin'?"

"I thought you guys, uh, needed a minute," Roman said.

"Some of her other friends came up to her and started talking. I had to slip away."

"Did you hear what she said?"

"I didn't know she was gonna show up. I'm not ready to see her again!"

Roman was in no mood to play sympathetic virgin. "Did you hear what she said to Todd?"

"Hi?"

"No. She said something about the keylogger. I need to talk to Todd."

"Oh, crap. Really? She knows what it is?"

"We need to figure out what we're gonna do. Who knows who else she's mentioned it to?"

"You think she knows what we're doing with it, though?"

Someone said, "bro," prompting Roman to spin around to a pool of eight other Armenian dudes with gel in their hair, none of whom were Todd.

"Do you think I was wrong to just stop talking to her?" Alex asked, snatching Roman's attention back.

"What?"

"What if Tamar gets a boyfriend soon? Why should I put up with that and still be friends with her?"

"Um, I dunno. Let's go look for Todd."

Roman tried walking away, only to be grabbed by the arm.

"You know what's the worst part?" Alex asked. "I couldn't even kiss her in my dreams. Each time I tried to, she backed away and turned back time with her index finger, counterclockwise, like it was a magic wand. Maybe it's 'cause I just spent too much time watching her hands playing arcade games. I dunno."

Nice. My friend has lost his mind.

"Nothing destroys your confidence like a dream where you can't do what you want," Alex said.

Roman anxiously scratched behind his left ear. "We gotta find Todd."

His foot was halfway out the balcony door.

"She'd never tell on you guys. You know that?" Alex continued from behind.

"Huh?" Roman said as he turned around.

"She knows some embarrassing stuff about me that no one else knows about. She doesn't start rumors."

Back on the patio, Roman saw way more people than before. He scanned for a spiky head, but again recognized no one.

"*Ara!*" someone called out. It was one of the few Armenian words Roman understood: it was the equivalent of "bro."

"*Ara!*" a short Armenian guy said again as he walked toward Roman with open arms. He was a familiar face from school, wearing brown leather shoes and a brown leather jacket. "*Ara,* let me ask you some-ting. You're not Armenian, right?" He put a hand on Roman's shoulder. "So, how is your nose bigger than mine?"

The brown-shoe guy said, then cracked up with a few of his surrounding friends.

"*Ara*, stop messing with him," another Armenian guy said. "You're gonna scare him away." This one was wearing a black Adidas tracksuit and had a penciled mustache. Likely no older than seventeen, he already had a bald spot.

Roman stabbed his hands into his pockets and hoped this person would soon turn his attention elsewhere. Instead, Adidas guy reeled Roman in by the shoulder with such vigor that he expected a peck on the cheek.

"We're gonna do a toast, *ara*," the Adidas guy said. "Join."

He dollied Roman to the top of the deck. A flood of faces from below confronted him. The Adidas guy raised his red cup to the night.

"*Engehrner!*" he shouted.

Roman had no clue what that meant, but at least he could tell it wasn't his name. So far, so good.

"Arshavir!" a few voices yelled back at the Adidas toaster.

"*Ay bozee tgha!*" another voice shouted, triggering a wave of laughter.

"Hey!" replied Adidas guy, whose name was now allegedly Arshavir. With a stern face, he shook his index finger at the guy who called him out. Then Arshavir loosened up and resumed his toast. "It's nights like this I'm forever happy I have friends like you!"

He earned an uplifting "huzzah" from the underage revelers, who all raised their solo cups in kind. Arshavir squeezed Roman even tighter. Roman thought this was a lump sum of the karma for turning down past invites from Todd.

"Thank you again, Alina, for hosting," Arshavir continued as he surveyed the crowd. "And cheers to this guy. What's your name again, *ara*?"

"Uh, Roman," Roman said while in a vertical fetal position.

"Ro-man!" Arshavir yelled. He raised his cup again. "To Roman-tik! Look at this guy, already dressed for school. You're gonna bang so many bitches, bro!"

A girl next to Arshavir slapped his right arm. The onlookers cracked up again. During this brief intermission, Roman spotted Alex in the crowd, trapped in a circle of other Armenian chaps who toasted with paper shot cups.

"It's just that I've never . . . I've never . . ." Alex said.

They all took a swig. Alex grimaced away from the circle.

Arshavir raised his cup again. "Anyway, to Ro-man!"

"To Ro-man!" the crowd shouted back.

Roman fought to hang onto his aching smile, which seemed more difficult than hanging onto the edge of a cliff with his pinky during a hailstorm. He kept reminding himself that extroverts get bored easily. They were insatiable zombies. Everyone would move on to roasting someone else in a second . . . just a second. He pictured his room frozen in time forever. Sanctuary.

Breathe. Just breathe. It's almost over.

"This guy," Arshavir shouted. "This guy. He's gonna help all of us!"

Roman's mentally framed image of his room shattered into pieces, some sharp enough to stab right through his heart, which started racing. It also might have been Arshavir's resisting arm. But Roman managed to slither out of his clutches and ran back into the house.

"Hey, where are you going, Roman-tik?" Arshavir yelled.

"Let him go. You embarrassed him," a girl said.

"What embarrass, *ara*? I'm trying to be a good Armenian ambassador."

Roman dashed into the kitchen, hunching over like he'd been

kicked in the gut in a vain attempt to blend his afro into the background. However, the girls giggling at this scrawny nerd fleeing from the apex of teen networking tarnished his plan. He turned at every unoccupied corner until he was dizzy.

Being the focus of school gossip—at a school party. Death. It must have started with Tamar, Roman thought. She must have spilled the beans! Damn Armenians and their light-speed rumor mill! With no Todd around, Roman felt helpless. But the inability to leave yet gave him an idea: the grade book. Changing more grades at a different location could confuse someone trying to trace the H-wording.

Alex stumbled back into view. "Do you know what it feels like to be drunk?"

"Huh?" Roman asked. "How many shots did you take?"

"Half of half of one. I think. But I spit it back out. My uncle gave me one last Christmas as a joke, and it burned my throat like crazy, so I didn't want to do a full one."

"You're fine, you're fine. Now, let's go. I need to get to a computer."

"Now? Why?"

"Uh, long story. We just gotta cover our tracks."

Alex rolled his eyes. "Ugh, fine."

They loitered in the foyer until enough backs were turned to them. They ran upstairs and peeked behind three bedroom doors until Roman found a green Jello-toned iMac stationed under a degree from USC's Gould School of Law. He parked his butt onto a swivel chair and twirled once. Amid the revolution, he saw Alex staring in from the threshold.

"Uh, lemme know when someone's coming," Roman said.

Turning to the screen, he booted MSN Explorer and was

instantly back at the Apollo login page. Not hearing a door shut in the background, Roman swiveled again to see Alex unmoved.

"Uh," Roman asked. "You okay?"

"I . . . I can't do this right now," Alex said. "I'm sorry. I'm gonna go try to find her. You got this."

He closed the door behind him.

Roman heard ringing in his ears, which was weird because he was so accustomed to silence. Must have been intuition to act fast.

He spotted a digital clock on a nightstand next to a king-sized bed: 10:29 p.m. Besides the law degree, the bedroom window was a snapshot of an idyllic cul-de-sac. Around it hung commendations from various bar associations. This was VIP solitude.

One day.

Roman perused the grade book and settled to bump up every fourth student until he had changed twenty-four of them with a margin of error no greater than two. He stretched for half a minute as a self-pat on the back, but another glance at the clock informed him it was only 10:37 p.m., lots of party left.

That's only how long it took? Maybe if I do the whole junior class, it'll be time to leave when I'm done.

But he resisted, thinking that making too big a change at once would be much more noticeable. For a second, parties didn't seem so hard anymore. Hell, if regularly attending parties could create a network of decoy H-wording sources, kind of like a real-world version of a DDOS attack, Roman would gladly rage with local Armenians every weekend. Everything would culminate with a repeat of good grades and a trip to the Professional Developer's Conference in the summer. Roman couldn't wait.

Satisfied, Roman shut down the computer and started leaving the bedroom. The second he opened the door, a girl was there.

In his mind, he checked the boxes: almost sharing a room with a girl, standing within kissing distance of a girl, smelling her breath. It was enough accumulated experience to justify avoiding girls for another six months.

Roman remembered her. She was thin and had that unmistakable curly hair like his own. Melineh Shanazarian.

"Oh," she said. "Didn't know someone was in here."

"No, uh, I'm not in here," Roman said. "I mean, I'm going."

"What's going on?" a girl called from down the hall.

Behind Melineh, down the hall, stood Alina, who, in return, saw them in close quarters. The paparazzi photo. The scandal. The rumors.

"Uh, I just had to—" Roman said.

An adjacent door cracked open. Someone said "shit," but instead of pulling it shut, they conceded. Todd emerged, the Chin sky-high. Lucy peeked her head over his shoulder.

"Were you able to finally go to the bathroom?" Todd asked Roman.

All involved parties turned to him.

"Sorry," Todd continued. "My friend likes a little too much privacy."

Melineh and Lucy giggled.

"Guilty," Melineh said. "That's why I came up here."

"Okay, and what are *you* two doing up here too?" Alina asked as she approached the quartet.

"Nothing, nothing, just girl drama. She needed a minute," Todd said. "All settled."

From the corner of his eye, Roman saw Lucy elbow Todd in his lower back.

"Come on, guys," Alina stressed. "No guests upstairs."

They all apologized and started heading back down to the party.

Todd and Lucy were just ahead, hand in hand. Roman was getting annoyed because Melineh kept parallel to him. Lucy took a quick break from Todd to shoot them a smile meant to be of record.

Oh no, Roman thought. Even he knew that was the matchmaker's gaze. But more concerning was when Melineh uttered something unintelligible, paired with a finger pointing at Roman. She deferred to Lucy, who absorbed the momentum and converted it into a quick head shake. Lucy adjusted her bangs and flashed a mischievous smile at Roman. "So, Mel, how do you know each other?"

"Oh," she said. "This one time, he helped me with an Internet problem I was having. I had that problem a few more times, but I remembered what he taught me, and I was able to fix it again."

"Wow!" Lucy exclaimed. "When was this?"

"Um, a while ago," Melineh said. "Your boyfriend gave me his number. He said Rome would 'hundred percent' help me."

"We should all have lunch together this week at school!"

"Yeah! Totally! Where do you usually hang out?"

By now, Roman was beyond antsy to the point it was liberating. He had no memory of Melineh's reaction as he ditched them and rushed ahead. He didn't care. His life was more important.

"Oh, okay," Lucy said.

He did, however, log that response. Roman dragged Todd with him until he found a sparsely populated spot by the stacked washer-dryer combo.

"Bro, what's your problem?" Todd asked. "Can you try and have just one ounce of fun?"

"We're in the clear," Roman said.

"Huh, what?"

"I changed like a bunch of grades. I think if I keep doing this, we'll be in the clear."

"What? That's your plan to cover our tracks? Are you nuts, bro?"

"Uh, not like by much. Like by a couple of points, so if teachers suspect something fishy, they'll think a glitch did it."

Todd combed a hand through his spikes. "I gotta say, bro, that makes the most sense of anything you've ever told me. At least with computer shit."

"I changed them on Alina's parents' computer."

"Of course. Why else would you be standing in the bedroom with Melineh right there?"

"She just showed up out of nowhere."

"I know, bro. Relax, I'm not gonna give you that much credit. But why that computer?"

"It was the only one I could find," Roman emphasized. "You heard what Tamar said, right? About the keylogger?"

"Yeah, but we didn't have to take care of it tonight. Just have fun."

"How does she know what it is?"

"I dunno, man. She's a gamer. Wouldn't be surprised if she was into computer shit too. She's weird. Oh, wait. Al's not around, is he?"

Roman looked around. "I dunno where he went."

"How many did you change?" Todd asked.

"Like twenty-five."

"Whoa, bro."

"Just to be safe. Then, some guy toasted outside, saying I'm going to help all of them. What the hell does that mean?"

"So what?" Todd asked.

"What else would anyone know me for?"

"Maybe 'cause you're my friend?"

"Huh?"

"Bro, just 'cause you don't give a damn about my Armo friends doesn't mean they don't know you. They know who I hang out with, and probably at some point, I told them you're a computer genius that can burn games and shit. Just like everyone knows Lucy and how I have a huge dick. Speaking of which—" Todd leaned closer to Roman's ear. "First hand job, bro."

"Oh," Roman said. "Yeah?"

Todd nodded. "Don't tell anyone, though. Not even Al."

"Oh, okay. I won't. And, uh, nice, I guess."

"You *guess*, bro?"

Roman smirked. "Well, guess it sounds like I had an easier time getting you to run around the school for me."

"Hey!" Todd said. "See, I know you have charm in there, bro. Save some of it for the chicks outside."

Feeling a bit more at ease, Roman walked outside with Todd.

"You gotta invite me to more parties. Uh, might be the only way I can change even grades more down the road," Roman said.

Todd gave him a skeptical Chin. "Ah, I see how it is. You're afraid to tell me you're having a good time."

"Uh, no, no."

Out on the deck again, a cloud of cigarette smoke slapped Roman. The cheering crowd had broken up into smaller cliques.

Todd chinned toward an unoccupied corner of the backyard without saying a word. He didn't need to. An ominous breeze whistled through the branches of the jacaranda tree. Its leaves quivered toward the direction of a lone toolshed propped up against a fence. The small structure, crowned with a fluorescent bulb, cast a spotlight on a pair of legs. The knees bent, bringing most of Alex's head and body into the light so he could tie his shoes. He got back up and walked in small circles a few times while muttering to himself. Then Roman swore he saw him start doing some lunges. Todd walked calmly back to the fire pit, where Lucy slipped on a coat over her shoulder while chatting up another girl Roman didn't know.

Tamar sat on the edge of a lawn chair, conversing with another couple. Whatever Alex was planning on doing, Roman didn't want to witness it; he'd experienced enough embarrassment for the year.

Todd, with a Beck's in hand, was waving to Roman to join. While Roman didn't want to, his friend was joined by four others. It'd be the ideal climate for playing the good listener. But on the way, a literal roadblock eroded his path. Roman was face-to-face with the hairy chest of Sako, who had left the majority of his silk burgundy shirt unbuttoned. His cologne couldn't mask his sweaty musk. Roman coughed. Sako had a beer in one hand and a red plastic cup in the other. "Bro, you're the computer genius, right?"

"Uh," Roman said.

Sako's blinks were half a second apart, and he slurred his speech. "Oh yeah, you're Mr. French guy. Can I ask you a . . . le favor?"

"Um . . ."

"He's not gonna do anything for you," Alex said.

Roman had no clue when his friend came into frame. Alex's hands were tucked into his hoodie pockets. He stuck out his chest like a grand ship's figurehead.

Sako grunted and took a step back to secure his footing. "The hell asked you, bro?"

"I said he doesn't owe you anything," Alex said.

Roman was a little impressed by his friend's restraint. At first. Sako took a step toward Roman, and Alex copied.

"Get the hell out of here, bro," Sako said. "The computer genius can make his own decisions."

Roman wasn't sure if it was intentional, but Sako stepped on one of Alex's feet, which triggered more than a simple reflex.

"No!" Alex screamed. He grabbed Sako's collar with both hands. "I said he'll never do anything for you!"

So much for growing up, Roman thought as he withdrew himself like a skillfully executed martial arts defensive move.

Shaken and wide-eyed, Sako dropped both of his drinks. He grabbed hold of Alex's grip and tried to shake him off. "What the hell, bro? I just had a Photoshop question. Why the hell do you care about that? Why do you got shit against me out of nowhere?"

Alex let out a series of short groans as he struggled to regain momentum.

"I'm done with this!" Sako shouted.

Sako lifted Alex by his shoulders with ease and carried him for a few yards. Alex kicked the air, occasionally making contact with Sako's shins. Sako lost his balance and dumped Alex onto the bean arch, which collapsed without hesitation. It sounded like a Christmas tree falling over. Alex got right back up, apparently in zero pain as he seethed, but before the episode of *Armenian Gladiators* continued, most of the partygoers were cracking up at him. Alex's clothes and hair were riddled with flower petals. Even Sako joined in.

"Oh my god!" Alina shouted as she emerged from the crowd. "What did you do? Who even are you?"

"I'm so sorry!" Alex told her.

The laughter died down, and someone tapped Roman on the shoulder. It was that Arshavir guy. "Hey, sorry about earlier, man. I didn't mean to make you uncomfortable. I just wanted to be nice because I wanted to ask if you could help me download the new *Lord of the Rings* movie."

Photoshop? Roman thought. *Lord of the Rings? That's all? Of course, Todd was right as usual. I've never been happier to be a computer nerd.*

"Uh," he said to Arshavir. "Yeah. Sure. Later."

Then Roman's eyes were drawn to the side of the house, as were everyone else's at that exact moment. The wall was a dance floor of flashing blue and red lights. Todd was already on his way out with Lucy in tow as she struggled to maintain her high-heeled footing.

"Well, that was fun," Todd said. "Went on longer than usual. Till next time, guys! Come on, Rome!"

"What's going on?" Roman asked as he caught up. "Where's everyone going?"

"Bro, the fiends are here. Party's over."

Sako jogged by with hefty breaths and a few other dudes who loaded into a Mercedes SUV that sped off. Two cops paced in front of their squad car parked in the driveway.

"Come on, come on," one of them said, guiding everyone toward the street with a pointed baton. "Got a lot of complaints. You're all done."

Roman was in a euphoric mood, knowing he might get away with his H-wording heist. As a bonus, he was leaving the dreaded party.

"I can drive," Lucy said as they approached Todd's car. "I didn't have anything to drink."

"You sure, babe?" Todd asked.

"Don't forget about me!" Alex called from behind, swatting the last of the petals off his clothes. "I'm here! Can I get a ride too? I don't wanna ask Alina if I could use her phone after what just happened."

"Sure," Lucy said. "I've got room for one more."

She beeped off the car alarm as the boys opened their respective doors.

"I can take him home," a girl called out.

It was Tamar, underneath a streetlight, hands clasped at her waistline.

"I drove," she said. "I can give him a ride if it'll save you guys some time."

"Um," Alex said.

"Sure!" Lucy said as she lit up.

She hopped into the driver's seat of Todd's dad's car, and Roman returned to the back seat, but before he shut the door, Todd ran around the car and low-fived Alex. Roman overheard them.

"Find out what she knows about the keylogger," Todd said. "But don't make it obvious."

Alex took a few seconds before nodding, then disappeared into the march of teens still leaving the party.

Todd sat up front and reclined his seat.

"You guys hungry?" Lucy asked as she pulled away from the curb.

"Hungry and tired, babe," Todd said. "But more hungry."

"I think I know what you guys want," Lucy said with a good-natured smile.

She drove downhill for a while until she made a left onto a major street and merged onto the southbound State Route 2 freeway. It was a quiet drive and, for Roman, the highlight of the party. He leaned to his left and saw that Todd had passed out.

"You guys are really done, right?" Lucy asked.

Caught off guard, Roman glanced at the rearview mirror. Lucy spread her eyes wide open like a starved owl. She was probing him. It was unsettling, but two could play this silent stare-off.

"Uh, yeah, we're done," Roman said. He probed right back until Lucy's attention shifted back to the road.

A few minutes later, they arrived at the butt of a quarter-mile line for In-N-Out. Eventually, an exuberant employee with a greasy forehead tapped a pen on Lucy's window.

"You know, Roman," she said, meeting him eye to eye in the rearview again, "if you want to get girls, don't be a dick to them."

"I know," Roman said.

Lucy lowered her window.

"Good evening, folks!" the In-N-Out employee said. "What can I get ya?"

Roman stared at Lucy's right hand on the steering wheel and reminded himself not to shake it goodnight.

Tamar's Jetta, on the other hand, was the only car originating from the party that didn't join the long winding line for In-N-Out.

"It's . . . it's good to see you," Alex said from the front passenger seat.

"You too," Tamar replied as she signaled for a lane change. "Did you lose weight?"

Alex didn't think so. There were a few recent days of intermittent fasting in order to enhance the flavor of an upcoming lasagna night at home, but his pants fit the same.

"Uh, maybe," Alex said.

Tamar flicked part of her golden hair behind her right ear.

The whooshing of a few passing cars briefly overtook the conversation.

"Uh, when did you get your license?" Alex asked.

"'Bout a month ago," Tamar said.

"Cool."

After some time of not speaking to one another, it wasn't

so easy slipping into jokes and conversation. A quiet minute went by.

"Uh, so who've you been hanging with lately?" Alex asked.

"Just the guys at the top of the amphitheater," Tamar said. "Edgar, Armen, Arbi, Arbo, Arvin, Norvan. I've been hanging with a couple of girls, too, believe it or not."

"Like who?" Alex asked.

"I'm not sure if you know them, but Armineh and Gohar."

That's great! Alex thought. No one had secured the whole of her attention. He knew of the girls Tamar had mentioned, but was way too intimidated by their upkeep to ever try talking to them.

"So, if you're Little Miss Popular now, does that mean you're not getting enough gaming time?" Alex asked. "I bet you're losing your touch without me."

"Hey, let's not get cocky. I've already beaten *Wind Waker.*"

She was referring to *The Legend of Zelda: The Wind Waker.*

"Really?" Alex asked.

"Not my fault you got a PS2 instead of a GameCube," Tamar said condescendingly.

Alex smiled. "Too many kiddy games on the GameCube. It's the same franchise characters over and over again. Where's the innovation?"

"Wow, does that mean you're too mature for gaming now?" Tamar kidded.

"You know what I meant," Alex said.

The road to old times was rougher than the patchy one that lay ahead. After another quiet minute and desperate to change topics, Todd's directive to investigate came to mind, but Alex couldn't think of a way to bring that up either. It just had to be now?

"You alright?" Tamar asked.

Alex wasn't sure when he'd share another late night with a girl again. It took about seventeen years of existence to take one out. Who knew when the next time would be? Drawing out the night as long as possible was paramount.

Within the oncoming traffic, a faint neon blur of two primary colors grew brighter and clearer. Yellow elongated bulbs spelling out a brand name against a blue backdrop signaled to Alex like those guys waving batons on a tarmac. Clear for takeoff.

"Um," Alex said. "Are you in a rush to get back home?"

"I mean, eventually, I have to, yeah."

"Do you wanna see what's new?"

At a red light, Alex indicated his unibrow toward a strip mall.

"Now?" Tamar asked.

"Real quick. Haven't had a chance to go this weekend."

"Uh, I guess. I haven't been there in a while either."

Tamar pulled her car into the parking lot. Dusk summer heat loitered still, but even more comforting was the aroma of plastic-wrapped DVD cases and buttered popcorn when they walked inside the corner strip mall's anchor store. Other air pockets hinted at whiffs of Red Vines and the fading blue carpet's date with a wet dry vac.

Ah, Blockbuster.

"We close in fifteen," a pimply-faced teenager in a blue polo, yellow collar combo said from behind a boxy computer.

Alex yielded and swung back his head. "We'll be real quick."

Tamar beat him to one of the video game aisles and inspected the back covers of some GameCube titles.

Alex was aghast after he turned a very familiar corner and saw nothing but lime green-rimmed cases.

Nothing but Xbox games? He thought. *What the?*

Alex called out to the employee. "Excuse me, where are the N64 games?"

The pimply-faced teenager shrugged. "Those were old. We got rid of them."

Alex breathed in and death rattled, but sucked it all back up when he ended up on the same aisle as Tamar, who was still browsing GameCube titles alone. Alex approached her and took note of a game case she picked up.

"*Eternal Darkness?*" Alex asked.

"Did you play it?" Tamar asked back.

"No, but I read about it in EGM. Think it was one of the first M-rated games on the GameCube."

"Oh, did you read last month's article about *Metal Gear Solid 3?*" Tamar asked.

"Yeah."

Now they were both browsing, occasionally grabbing a game and checking out its back cover.

"So, what do you think?" Tamar asked.

"Well, my first thought was, why the hell are they setting it in the past? *MGS2* ended on such a big cliffhanger, and now they're sending the story back to the Vietnam era?"

"I'm sure they'll answer some stuff. Hideo Kojima is a genius."

"An evil genius who makes me wait forever for answers."

Alex thought he had the last word, which was self-gratifying, only to have it enveloped by the touch of something smooth and living—thankfully, unlike a horror movie monster hiding under a bed. A delayed flinch later, he witnessed his hand over Tamar's hand over a copy of *Tony Hawk's Pro Skater 4.*

She spread her left thumb, which Alex, out of human legacy, massaged up and down a few times with his index finger. Tamar tucked her chin into her chest. Alex could have sworn her eyes were closed.

This isn't that hard!

He wasn't sure who de-initiated, but they detached and faced each other in the middle of the aisle. Alex expected a twenty-something couple laughing at him from down the aisle, but was happily disappointed by shelves of non-judgmental rentals and the humming of a muted TV set hanging from the ceiling.

Tamar cleared her throat and straightened her dress again. "So, what was that about?"

"What was that about?" Alex asked.

"The fight."

"Oh. You saw that?"

"Uh, pretty sure we all did. What happened?"

Uh-oh. Alex detected a projecting tone. Of course, the super-brief brawl was over jealousy. But seeing that bald oaf encroach on his friendship turf was the breaking point.

"Uh, Sako was messing with my friend," Alex said. "I think he was drunk."

"I see," Tamar said, sounding unconvinced.

"He started it."

"You sure?"

"Yes."

Alex couldn't resist the urge to do what he suspected was the right thing. "I'm sorry I was so weird. I didn't mean . . . I didn't mean to . . . to treat you like shit. I really wouldn't be surprised if you hated me at one point."

"Alex," Tamar said.

The best moments he'd had this past year blurred his vision, along with some salty water. Alex flexed his cornea to hold the droplets back.

"No matter what . . . I couldn't picture my life without you in it somehow," he said.

Tamar stared down at the shag. "I can tell you meant that. I don't hate you, if that's what you're wondering."

"Really?" Alex said, sounding a bit too eager, before catching himself and dialing things back. "I mean, really?"

"Just chill out a little. It's like you're always on eggshells, and it's putting me on eggshells. I knew you weren't being you."

"Until I do something evil like eat the last slice of pizza or something like that?"

Tamar sighed. Alex realized he probably shouldn't be kicking his mood back and forth so much. "No, you're right, you're right."

It was loud and clear: she didn't want anything beyond historical precedent.

"So, wanna head back to the arcade soon?" Alex asked. "Haven't been back to Video West since the last time we went."

Tamar looked to the game shelf on her right. "Maybe."

"So, maybe I can call you tomorrow or whenever, and you'll have a better idea then?" Alex asked.

Tamar sighed again. "Alex, let's just get used to talking again for now. See each other around school before we hang out like that again."

"Uh," Alex said, "sure."

With an urge to keep one of his hands busy, Alex leaned his palm into the top shelf to his left, expecting to discuss a watered-down hangout schedule.

"I'm tired," Tamar said.

"Oh, uh," Alex said, "Okay."

Passing the front counter, the teen cashier saw their empty hands and grunted something under his breath. Tamar was about to sit down in her car when Alex remembered this outing was technically a mission ordered by Todd.

"So, uh, you know my friend Todd, right?" Alex asked.

Tamar stopped getting into the car. "Okay, so I didn't know you guys were that close."

"Huh?"

They were separated by the Jetta's roof.

"I've been wanting to ask you, what are you guys doing?" Tamar asked.

"Um."

"That keylogger thing. I saw it with Todd and then you. What are you guys doing?"

"Huh? How, how do you know what it is?"

"That little thing looked weird. It was smaller than the USB drives I've seen."

"Why'd you announce it like that at the party?" Alex asked.

"I thought it was cool after I researched it. I didn't think it'd weird Todd and Lucy out."

"Did you . . . did you tell anyone else about it?"

Tamar shook her head. "Why would I?"

Oh, how her ethics were as upstanding as his own, Alex thought. He hesitated while processing what to say next.

"Uh oh," Tamar said. "This must be big."

Alex shook his head with gusto. "No, uh, it's more of like a prank . . . on the school."

Tamar snickered. "So, what are you doing? Changing grades or something?"

Alex thought his feet were burrowing into the parking lot asphalt. "Um . . . what? How do you . . ."

The three-second pause was more than incriminating. Tamar grazed her palm across her forehead, sweeping wisps of her hair into the night. "Holy shit, why else would you need the keylogger?"

Alex ping-ponged his eyes over Tamar's accusatory stare.

"That's incredible!" she said.

Alex wished he could process thoughts faster than a PS2. He worried about being sniffed out, but was simultaneously aroused by something he could offer that no other dude could.

"You're like *so* ahead of me and my programming!" Tamar proclaimed.

"Well . . ." Alex said. "I'm not the . . ."

Tamar slid a step toward him with a coy cadence. "Can you get me straight A's?"

"Huh?"

"I'm kidding, I'm kidding, but you gotta tell me everything! You have to tell me how you did it!"

"Well, uh, it's not all me."

"That's right. So, it's you, Todd, and who else?"

"I-I don't think I can say any more."

"Oh, my god. How can you be a tease for the first time ever right *now*?"

"Uh . . ."

"Come on! How'd you do it? You can't just stop there."

There was nothing Alex wanted to do more than mimic the expository cut scenes in an RPG strictly told through text, but his party was counting on him. He wasn't going to be the one to betray them, even if it would have been the best character arc. He smashed the pause button and kept mum. "I-I just can't. At least not for now. Maybe, maybe later?"

Tamar went stone-faced. She sat behind the wheel and started the car. Alex got it in too. Tamar adjusted the rearview mirror and cleared her throat. "So, you want to start hanging out again, but you don't trust me."

Alex snapped his buckled-up torso toward her. "No, no, it's not that, I swear!"

"Why even tell me about this then? What do you want from me?"

Tamar looked like she was posing for an ID picture under a military dictatorship that had made smiles punishable by death. She was bereft of the glow she used to inject into Alex's life. He had an out-of-body experience. He saw their backs as they played at an arcade cabinet. The game didn't matter. That moment. Forever.

And infinite quarters.

"You can't tell anyone," Alex said. "It's true."

—

The Monday morning hall reeked of 409. It didn't help that he came upon a hand-holding pair of freshmen he recognized from the orientation crowd on the first day of school. How did these kids learn to do that before learning the Pythagorean theorem? After all he had gone through, Alex only had an impromptu, half-assed thumb war to show for. At this point, he was definitely going to jerk off to the sequence after school and not feel bad about it.

An announcement blared through the PA system: Bus 106 had just arrived.

Avoiding and running away from problems worked so well for Alex, or so he hoped. Maybe something else had to change, he pondered.

Maybe it had to be the scenery.

What that actually meant was on the tip of Alex's tongue. There was just another year of high school until everyone went their own way, starting over at different colleges as freshly minted adults, unaware of each other's embarrassing teen moments. But another year felt like a century.

Alex stopped dead in his tracks by the main office en route to first period. One of the school secretaries answered a phone behind a glossy wooden desk. His brain was tired, so burnt out from obsessing over a single girl.

Alex started limping like Frankenstein's monster toward the office.

Wait, what am I doing? he thought.

He wasn't sure what was controlling his body, but whatever it was didn't feel much remorse. Another banal step, but deep inside, he tripped over unfiltered thoughts.

You're going to turn you and your friends in. It's the only way you can make a clean break from all of this.

Alex yipped with sadness and followed up with a phony cough. All he wanted was the normal high school experience. Forget losing his virginity; a few kisses to reminisce over would have been good enough. Why was it so easy for everyone else?

As he caught up with his surroundings' pace, his stomach churned. This wouldn't be like using a cheat code in a game; there'd be no continues for himself or his friends.

Straight ahead, a bustling office. Any employee would do.

Just start simple. Say someone's been cheating and you know. Then, at the very end, say you were dragged into this.

All that remained was a straight shot of a dozen checkered floor tiles demarcating the well of the front desk from the rest of the hall.

Alex knew how to play the victim well. He'd get his uncle to change the channel when his cousins watched *Beavis and Butthead* because the animated blood scared him.

You're doing the right thing. You'll be out of here in no time with a fresh start.

A few more steps. Just one black tile stood between him and

the front desk. A greying secretary wearing low-hanging bifo-cals flipped through a collated book while she was on the phone. She raised a dour finger to Alex without stating an estimated wait time.

He spotted a group of laughing Korean students walking by. In fact, every student in the vicinity was paired up. Alex thought about their histories; the stories they shared and the ones waiting to be written.

"Hey!" Todd said, swooping in from behind with a labored cheeriness. "How's it going, bro?"

Alex was a big, meaty bag of novocaine. "I'm okay."

"Good weekend?"

"Yeah."

"So . . . how'd it go with you know who?"

A run-in with Todd was the last thing Alex needed. The sec-retary was still glued to the phone. Alex cleared his throat. "She doesn't know."

"Doesn't know?" Todd asked. "Bro, she knew what the key-logger was."

"She doesn't know . . . she doesn't know what we're doing."

Todd squinted and raised the Chin.

"Like you said," Alex said, "she's just a weird chick who's into games. She knows computer stuff too."

"How do you know she's not gonna tell anyone about the keylogger, though, bro? She announced it at the party like it was someone's birthday."

The elevated Chin reeled a lanky hickey past his collar. Alex was tired of having to answer to people who've experienced all the pleasures he's never enjoyed. He also craved hot wings for lunch, followed by a craving to clip Todd the person, not Todd the friend, in that uppity Chin. After all, he dragged Alex into this mess, and he's still making demands? The only thing faster than a fist to the face was a lie.

"Look," Alex said, "I just told her we're playing a prank."

"Prank? What do you mean prank?" Todd demanded. "That's the kind of rumor that gets people caught!"

"You mean caught like how Sako got into trouble when you saw him put the potato boat in the soda machine and didn't tell me about it?"

"The hell does that have to do with anything right now? You're still not over that?"

Alex scratched his forehead. "She thinks it's a prank we're playing in the computer lab or something, okay? You know, randomly opening other people's CD drives. Rome has our asses covered. What's to worry about? I had to tell her something."

Todd took a few patient breaths and kept his Chin elevated.

"Come on. That was it, I swear," Alex said. "Can you have faith in me for once?"

"Alright, bro, alright. But if she's the reason we ever go down, knock on wood, *meres arev*, I'm gonna chain you in my garage so you never see an In-N-Out again."

"Just kill me at that point instead."

They laughed.

Alex was so relieved and proud of himself—despite also feeling like a suicide bomber—for he was about to shake off Todd!

Still on the phone, the secretary nodded like his mom's parting sentiments as she wrapped up multi-hour calls with her cousins. Alex brimmed with shameful glee at the notion of running away from it all, regardless of the price tag.

Almost time. I guess.

"Anyway, you'll never guess what I found," Todd continued.

Alex didn't realize his friend was still there. "Huh?"

"My folks made me clean out my closet this weekend to get rid of some old junk," Todd continued.

The secretary hung up.

"My old Sega Dreamcast!" Todd said with a twinkle in his eye that seemed genuine. It stood out more than his announcement.

"What?" Alex asked with excitement. "Dreamcast?"

Todd pursed his lips and bobbed his head.

"I didn't know you had one," Alex said.

He remembered the day it came out: 9/9/99. The same day as *Final Fantasy VIII*, which he owned, but the Dreamcast was the console version of the girl that got away. Alex had minimal experience with Sega's last gasp in the console wars, even though it preceded the GameCube, Xbox, and PlayStation 2.

"First thing that came to mind was you and Rome," Todd said. "Maybe we can order some pizza too. Been a minute since we chilled, anyway."

But still, Alex perceived Todd as a dead man walking. Next, he imagined Roman's corpse on an autopsy table, a white blanket covering all but a toe tag and his afro.

The fleshy levees struggled to hold back Alex's pooling tears. Borderline crying twice in less than a week. No good. Alex managed to wipe his eyes with the short sleeve of his polo. Then he sniffed back and swallowed some phlegm.

"You okay, bro?" Todd asked.

"Yeah, just allergies. Couldn't get a sneeze out."

"I was gonna say you're bipolar as hell, bro."

Alex feigned a light grin. "Do you have *Crazy Taxi*?" His voice cracked, then he gurgled snot.

"Uh, I gotta double-check," Todd said. "I think I saw a driving game in there, but I'm not a hundred percent."

"The . . . the multiplayer is really fun."

"I gotta go, bro," Todd said, patting Alex's shoulder before springing away. Alex looked back, and of course, Lucy had entered the picture. Alas, the sole woman in Alex's life had crossed her arms and stationed a red pen over her left ear that matched her mood.

"What do you want?" the secretary asked.

The majority of the student body funneled around him ahead of first period, including Tamar, who shot him a smile, the kind any of his friends could tender. But what was the point? Sure, he had only confirmed the hacking and reserved the leverage of a ton of minutiae, including the leveling-up arc of breaking and entering any Japanese class system programmer would just die to have for their thief character, but Alex knew his own title was to be forever friend—no particularly useful skills other than level 99 listening.

She had won again.

Alex felt like a mix of a baby and a moron.

On the plus side, Alex's soul read Tamar's trustworthiness like it was some kind of ambient Braille.

The way no one came close to bumping into Tamar, she might as well have parted the traffic like Moses, no matter how much Alex wanted to dispel her myth and repel from the school forever. He wasn't sure if Moses had followers, students, or disciples, so he stopped with the religious analogies and, hello, focused on the contrasting dark hair of Tamar's commute buddy.

He also wasn't sure if her name was Ani, Anahit or Astghik. At the fault of the school's dress code, her gray polo and beige khakis made her look tomboyish, but he reneged his opinion at the sight of a thin, brunette stalk growing out of a green scrunchy, peaked with a bobbing frond. It was kind of cute. She noticed Alex, then signaled to Tamar like a catcher to a pitcher. Tamar waved at him without much zest before whispering something into green scrunchy girl's ear. Scrunchy girl's lips were parted like a calm fish's mouth, but it was kind of cute. Scrunchy girl locked glances with Alex, then addressed Tamar again. Scrunchy girl said something, drowned out by the congested hall. Tamar finally nodded at her. Both girls smiled at him as they crossed his path and kept going.

Alex assumed Tamar told scrunchy girl good things about him, how cool he was, which could be omitted as long as there was an oral highlight reel of his arcade skills. Other girls had to be turned on by that, too, right?

In a desperate search for affirmation, Alex daydreamed of lunch—not the meal, but the block of time. Even Todd factored into the fantasy, surreptitiously elbowing one of Alex's love handles and whispering into his ear, "This could lead to meeting other chicks, bro."

But still, not her.

If this was all supposed to be so easy, why didn't natural selection breed awkwardness, lack of self-confidence or just general dating ineptness out of humans?

While referencing his inner *Darwin for Dummies*, Alex heard gentle paddles of a hammered dulcimer accompanied by monkish chants as he sat down in Spanish class.

Maybe . . . maybe I can do it again, he thought. *With someone new.*

He had to. He believed he owed his friends that much for sticking by his side and putting up with his emotional flare-ups and unsolicited food critiques, albeit they're both from the heart. Just like in any RPG, experience earned is forever. Time to grow up. Time to stop overreacting to everything.

All Alex wanted now during Spanish class was some zone-outage. Oh, the tranquil ignorance.

None of his spacing out was perturbed until he saw something curious from the thin window sliver built into the classroom door. It was a middle-aged woman, Vice Principal Leininger, Alex realized just then. She kept pointing at him, then at the floor out in the hall. Strange. Alex couldn't recall threatening anyone with a soda bottle as of late.

THE LOST
SEMESTER

ROMAN

Roman's fro was gauze in his ear canals as daydreams of upgrading his glasses to something more Silicon Valley chic a few months before the prestigious Professional Developers Conference drowned out Mr. Armistead's algebraic ramblings—until the teacher singled him out.

"I think she wants *you*," said Mr. Armistead in a tan blazer. He leaned his pelvis into an overhead and pointed out to the hall with a green marker.

Puzzled by the feminine pronoun, Roman turned to the door and saw Vice Principal Leininger through a sliver of glass, staring back, pointing to the ground over and over like her finger was a blinking cursor. His first instinct was to keep his hands busy, so he gripped the corners of his desk. Then, a relieving memory: his mom mentioned an upcoming doctor's appointment, so he must have forgotten to go outside to wait to be picked up, and Leininger was dispatched as a reminder. So, like a good little boy, Roman calmly stood up and walked out of the classroom.

"Get your things, please," Leininger told him as he crossed the threshold.

So, it *was* a doctor's appointment after all! Roman shifted back into class, paying no attention to the two dozen heads of his peers drawn his way. He packed up and left. Leininger led Roman down an empty hallway, minus one kid clutching a hall pass, who ran inside a boys' bathroom. No way anything was wrong. In fact, Roman imagined his mom grabbing some McDonald's after the appointment, if the extinction of his appetite as his stomach wrung itself of metabolic enzymes was nothing but a false flag.

But instead of turning toward the school's entrance, Leininger guided Roman past the main office's front desk to what seemed like the closed door of a conference room.

At least it wasn't Grubner's office, but the ensuing frame was just as frightening.

Leininger opened the door, and there were his friends: Todd on one side of the conference table and Alex on the other.

Something told Roman they didn't have doctor appointments as well.

The boys locked quivering pupils. Todd and Alex were two mutes with pale, stiff cheeks. The malady must have been contagious as Roman noticed his hands turn a little mayonnaise.

"Have a seat," Leininger said.

She sounded like she was underwater. Roman complied at a satisfactory pace, taking a seat between his two friends.

"No talking," Leininger said as she shut the door behind her.

But before the boys could even try to disobey, the door swung back, held open by Principal Grubner, his mouth agape. Sweaty combover strands stuck to his shiny scalp. He looked as lost and confused as the boys.

"Are you Roman?" Grubner asked, trying to catch his breath. Perhaps Grubner had forgotten their awkward encounter in the auditeria.

"Uh, yeah," Roman said.

"Follow me, please."

Roman took one last look over his shoulder at his friends on the way. Though silent, he could hear the roars of their panicked stares.

This time, Roman was led down an unfamiliar hall with green carpeting. He had never seen this part of the school before. He had a flashback to the night when he first port-scanned the school's IP address and wished he had given up in favor of an early porn session. They arrived in Grubner's office, where the principal took a seat behind his desk, glasses at the tip of his nose.

"Sit," Grubner told Roman, whose shoulders were uneven. Roman obliged again.

Grubner tapped various parts of a piece of paper with a pen. Leininger came out of nowhere and stood next to him. Roman started breathing harder, fogging up his glasses.

Grubner mumbled to himself. Roman couldn't even stutter. He wanted to skip ahead to his punishment.

Out with it already, he thought. *Out with the life sentence of lunch detentions!*

But he didn't have to think too deeply to realize he likely faced much more than that.

He had a split-second urge to punch Grubner in the face and run for the rest of his life.

"Mr. Vallancourt," the principal said, still fixed on the paper. "What grade did you earn in Spanish 3-4 last semester?"

Roman's mind was so clouded with fear that he couldn't debate whether it was a trick question.

Did they want the real grade or my edit? My mom, my mom, my mom. My daaaaad.

He hunched beyond belief and chose to go with the inflated grade. "I got a . . . B+."

Grubner checked something off on the paper. "I see. And what about Algebra 2?"

"An A-, I think," Roman said.

Grubner's cadence didn't exude the joy of grilling litterers or girls wearing super short skirts. He kind of sounded like he was ready to apologize.

"Are you sure?" Grubner asked. "Please be honest with me."

Roman half-shook his head like a batter changing the course of his swing at the last second.

"How did you do it?" Grubner asked.

Roman's breaths grew constrained. Now, he wasn't getting enough air out. He didn't know if he had said anything incriminating. He couldn't believe it. This was all over a few grades. It's high school. Who cared? All Roman thought he deserved was a few "stay in schools" or "dope is for dopes" and bada bing, bada boom, "stay in the category of building you're already in."

Still, he dared not look Grubner in the eye until the most pragmatic answer came to mind.

"I . . . I didn't hurt anyone," Roman said.

"That's not what I asked," the principal replied promptly. "How did you do it?"

Like always, procrastination made anything seem doable, but only if other humans weren't involved. Petrification commenced. This was worse than having to introduce himself to an audience of a thousand girls.

"I . . . I didn't," Roman said.

All the time that he could have practiced pickup lines in the mirror, like every other teenage boy. He could have at least re-hearsed for an interrogation. The futility of fetishizing the past.

Grubner took off his glasses and flung them onto his desk.

"Look," he said. "Don't make this harder than it's already been on all of us."

Roman was too far in pants-shitting mode to decipher that statement. What else was there for a scolded child to say to a grown-up?

"I'm sorry," Roman said.

Grubner responded by crossing his arms and slanting his flabby self toward Leininger. He used one of his hands to cover his mouth and whispered something to her. Leininger nodded, then they left the office long enough for Roman to memorize the pattern of the buzzing melodies of the fluorescent lighting from above. It was a welcome distraction from the possibility of no longer being wel-comed at H.L. Wright Magnet High School or his own home.

Someone returned to the office, but it wasn't Grubner or Leininger. Instead, a man of average height with slicked-back hair and dark green suspenders fortifying a swollen gut pulled up next to Roman on a spare seat.

Roman next noticed a handgun and a golden badge at the gen-tleman's waist. He spoke with a disarming tone.

"Hello there," the man said. "I'm Detective Leland with the Glendale Police Department. Boy, you must have done quite a number for me to be here."

Roman stared at him, but not as an act of non-violent resis-tance or exercising the Fifth Amendment. He was worried that looking elsewhere would earn drawn guns.

What . . . the . . . hell . . . is . . . going . . . on?

Grubner's college degrees hanging on the wall behind Leland started swapping places, like a game of Tetris.

"Look, kid," Leland said. "Roman, right? I'm glad that no one's hurt, but you did something. Can we talk about it?"

Even with standard fare room temperature, beads of cold sweat slid down Roman's sideburns.

Leland scratched the tip of his nose and surveyed him with a condescending look. "You know, you don't look like the kids I normally deal with. Hell, you might even be the first one I've seen who wears glasses that thick."

Leland pulled his chair closer to Roman. "But from what your teachers and principal have told me, you've messed things up quite a bit."

Roman angled his head down toward Leland's brown, shiny loafers.

"How . . . how do they know?" Roman asked.

Leland shook his head. "I can't get into that."

He leaned back in his chair. "But it's true? You and your friends hacked into the school and changed your grades? And your class-mates' grades too?"

Roman was mid-gulp when he cleared his throat. He coughed a few times. "But I didn't hurt anyone. I didn't hurt anyone!"

"I know you didn't," Leland said. "Believe me, I can tell you're a good kid, and to be honest, I have no clue how you did it. I'm actually a little impressed."

Roman grew frustrated in waiting for a stern talking to when Leland got up and showed him the door.

"Come on," the detective said. "Let's get you back with your friends."

A tidal flush of relief almost overwhelmed Roman. Perhaps the impending lecture was reserved for a group setting.

Back in the conference room, he sat between Todd and Alex again, but not for long, as moments later, Grubner returned. The principal let out a deep sigh. "I'm afraid I'm going to have to suspend you all for now. I'll call your parents soon to discuss what's next."

Todd stared Grubner down in statuesque denial.

Roman coughed once. *Just suspension?* The fates had bargained for a favorable settlement! Sure, his parents would yell a lot, and there'd be some revocation of privileges and pastimes, but—

"Let's go, boys," Detective Leland said as he returned. He traded places with Grubner, who ducked out moments earlier.

Three more men came in--uniformed men with buzz cuts and clanking belts. They had badges, too, but they wore them on their shirts adjacent to name tags. Roman, famished for any kind of escape, read their names: GARCIA, SMITH, and SORENSEN.

They each flicked back open handcuffs.

Roman and Alex were staggered like lost children looking for a grown-up. Todd arose with a calm demeanor, turned his back to the officers, and folded his wrists inwards over his ass crack before he was even ordered to.

"Your friend's setting a good example," Leland told Roman and Alex. "Up and hands behind your backs, boys."

Alex started panting.

"You have the right to remain silent," Leland said. He droned on, but Roman was deafened by the crystal ball visions of his parents screaming.

Alex shot up from his seat and pounded his chest several times. "It was meeeeee!" He shrieked. "It was me! Leave my friends alone! They didn't do anything!"

"Don't say anything," Todd said without moving a muscle. "We'll get lawyered up, and we'll be fine."

Smith, the tallest officer, looked down at Alex and spun him around by the shoulder like he had slapped a tetherball. As Smith applied the handcuffs, Alex winced and sniffled.

"Don't say anything," Todd said, who also grimaced when he was cuffed by Sorensen.

"I didn't!" Alex replied, his voice cracking. "Just like you told me."

They both turned to Roman. The officers held them by their wrists. They looked like they were about to be pushed around like vacuum cleaners.

"Wait," Alex asked Roman. "Did you tell them something?"

"What? N-n-no," Roman replied. "Not really, anyway."

"The hell does that mean?" Todd asked.

Roman was saved by Garcia clasping metal around his twiggy wrists, ripping a few arm hairs out in the process, which made Roman tear up a bit as if he had stared straight into the sun.

Leland held the door open. "I said it's time to go, boys."

"Go where?" Alex asked with frightened puppy dog eyes.

"Don't worry. You'll be with your parents again very soon."

The cops steered the boys into the hall. Roman's senses were suffocated, but he managed to spot the classmate he saw go to the bathroom, gawking at him.

"Get back to class!" Grubner shouted, shooing away the boy, who ran into the main wing of the student body with the juiciest of gossip.

One person was all it took.

The boys walked in a single file line—an officer behind each of them—out past the school's front doors. Their apparent destination was three squad cars lined up in the bus drop-off lane. Blue and red lights flashed without sirens.

"Don't hurt them!" Grubner shouted from the school's front

steps. Roman peered over his shoulder to see the principal face-palming.

Roman looked over his other shoulder to see nothing but faces glued to the street-facing windows, all the ones Roman had never spoken to. The entire student body and faculty must have been pressed against the teal-tinted glass like a collage of Garfield window clingers.

"Do you see Lucy?" Todd called out from the front of the line.

"Shut up," his brooding escort commanded.

"Hey, come on," Leland told the officer in a reprimanding tone, then addressed Todd. "Sorry, son. Best to keep quiet for now."

But Roman couldn't help one last squint back at the windows. He didn't know many of them by name. He recognized Sako first because of his height and mass. Sako was pointing and laughing at Alex's trajectory. Next was Jared, who shoved his bangs deep into his scalp, likely wondering why he wasn't part of the lineup. Roman then saw several Armenian girls rubbing a pair of arms up and down—Lucy's arms. She buried her face in a pallet of tissues.

"Um," Roman said back to Todd. "Don't see her."

Next to the Armenian girls stood Eunice, unfazed, and Joy, who smirked. Her hands behind her back, she looked unamused, but still somehow entertained.

"That stupid bitch!" Todd shouted. "It was her!"

His words mashed into a roar. Roman looked to the front of the line and saw Garcia, his own escorting officer, trying to help Sorensen restrain Todd as he kicked the air toward the row of spectators.

"That goddamn bitch!" Todd continued. "That goodie-two-shoes, cock-sucking bitch! She told on us! I'll get that goddamn bitch!"

"Hey! Hey! Hey!" Leland exclaimed, rushing up. "Calm down, son!"

"It wasn't Tamar!" Alex said, hopping up and down in place. "It wasn't Tamar! No way!"

"Don't you think I know that?" Todd yelled back.

"Guys, guys, take it easy!" Leland shouted. "You were doing great! Just take a few deep breaths. I know you're scared, but like I said, you'll be back with your parents soon."

Roman just stood there—a newfound fan of nihilism—and observed. Sure, he was curious who ratted them out, but it didn't matter. Someone found out. That is all. He had failed.

Despite a crimson demeanor, Todd had otherwise cooled down when he was let into one of the squad cars. Alex hit his head trying to get in, but unable to massage himself at the moment, he leaned his forehead into the headrest.

Garcia opened a car door for Roman like a chauffeur, except there was nothing luxurious about the hard plastic seats within, which, combined with Roman's flat ass, felt like bone grinding on bone. Garcia got behind the wheel, and Leland took the other front seat.

The squad cars started within seconds of each other and pulled away from the curb. The convoy passed through a few local streets before hopping onto the eastbound Foothill (210) Freeway.

"Wh—where are we going?" Roman asked Leland.

"Like I said, son," Leland replied. "We're going to get you back with your parents. That's what we normally do in juvenile cases where no one's been hurt. So yes, you should be happy about that."

But Roman could only imagine his mother's glass-shattering cries and hardwood-warping tears, followed by quadruple-down enforcement of his curfew or an all-around demotion to eight o'clock to be served concurrently with severely reduced computer access.

Despite a mountain of potential consequences, a faint voice spoke from the shattered pile of Roman's hopes and dreams.

Does this mean . . . I'm not good enough?

After ten minutes, they exited onto the main Glendale thoroughfare and, not much after, arrived at a monolithic structure he'd passed by countless times, but was never curious enough to imagine what went on inside.

GLENDALE POLICE DEPARTMENT, engraved in a stone portico, read like it was an airplane banner nailed in the sky. An inexplicable G-force greyed Roman out for a few seconds.

The squad cars pulled into a gated parking lot where the boys were let out, then brought in through a heavy metal door where Roman heard a bunch of radios blaring distorted numbers and letters. From here on out, everyone wore a police uniform or was dressed like Detective Leland, business casual with a badge and gun at the hip. Alex flinched each time someone got too close. A few passing officers smiled at the boys, which confused Roman. Given his unnatural stance, he waddled like he had a giant turd stuck dangling between his legs.

Finally, they came across a short, darker-skinned female police officer who freed the boys from their cuffs with a tiny key and led them and their armed chaperones to another room with three booths protected by what looked like bulletproof glass. Someone on the other side fingerprinted the boys.

What awaited next door reminded Roman of something out of the movies.

The most muscular officer of the day—the barbed tribal tattoos on his biceps were ripping his uniform at its short sleeves—stood behind an old-school film camera. Ironically, he had the least intimidating demeanor of the day. His badge read RODRIGUEZ.

"Could you please remove your glasses, young man?" He asked Roman.

Roman secured his balance before handing his spectacles over to an out-of-shape cop. He was quick with jokes. His badge read HENDERSON.

"And if you can do it without falling over on me, stand up straight," he said, thumbs over his belt.

Roman stood upright against a height chart. His afro soared above where his head ended.

"So, are you six feet even or six-foot-five?" Henderson quipped. The armed chaperones laughed together.

"Hey, relax, kid," Henderson continued. "I'm just messing around. You don't have to smile if you don't wanna."

"Here we go. One, two . . ." Rodriguez said.

A cartoonish flash was the final blow to Roman's poor eyesight as he almost turned into a wall once they took his mugshot.

"Easy there, kid, easy!" Henderson said and handed back Roman's glasses. "You don't wanna get the paramedics in here, too, do ya?"

Everyone in dark blue laughed again. Roman was unaware that more people had entered the room. When his corrected vision recovered, he waited in the hallway for Alex and Todd. Leland led the three to what Roman expected would be the most traumatizing moment of his life: a jail cell. Instead, they ended up in another boring room decorated with a small table and chairs.

"We call this the playpen," Leland said before flicking on the light switch. "Even though you're all big enough to be in the academy, you're still minors. Take a seat, and we'll get you home soon."

Roman, Todd and Alex converged on the barren table.

"Who the hell told on us?" Alex asked, wasting no time with a stream of consciousness. "I can't believe this! My picture's gonna end up everywhere! Like they do at the post office! Everyone's gonna know! Our lives are ruined!"

"Calm down," Todd said, looking his friends over.

"Stop always telling me that!" Alex said.

"We're minors. Our cases are confidential."

"It's not gonna be confidential to our parents! They're gonna kill us!"

"I said, calm down."

"You were the one who snapped and started cursing out people back at school!"

But Todd stared straight ahead, emotionless.

"Fine," Alex said. "Rome, did someone turn us in or not? I thought you had our asses covered and shit."

"Al," Todd interjected.

Roman, who's never been less of a fan of speaking, doubly knew he could never handle the public relations branch of his "H-wording" corporation. "Uh, I um . . . I don't know." He truly believed that.

"I couldn't understand what that detective said," Alex said. "What were we arrested for?"

"I'm not sure either," Roman said.

"I didn't know they had laws against changing grades."

"You can both stop now," Todd said.

"Why?" Alex asked. "What am I gonna tell my folks?"

"You know they're probably recording us, right?" Todd said, hinting the Chin toward the sprawling wall mirror across the room.

Roman and Alex scratched the backs of their necks and looked away from their reflections.

After a half hour of silence, Leland stuck his head in the room and gestured for the boys to follow. Roman wished he'd be led to a firing squad, but the maternal cries he heard on the way gored his flesh more than any wartime caliber.

Audrey ran to him in the police station lobby and hugged him. She was still wearing her work clothes. The same went for Seda and Todd, and Alex and his mom, who Roman always called Mrs. Ter Alaverdian. Roman embraced his mother like he was five years old and had fallen off his bicycle. She was still his protector from the big, bad, ugly stuff.

"Are you okay?" Audrey demanded, almost out of breath. She gripped her son's cheeks and inspected him for contusions.

"I'm sorry," Roman said with squished cheeks, some of the rare graspable fat on his body. After she let go, his forehead landed on her left shoulder pad. "I'm so sorry, mom."

Roman turned his head to see Todd and Alex crying into their mothers' shoulders and begging for forgiveness.

"I spoke with your parents," Leland said.

Roman didn't notice the detective reenter the picture.

"You're all free to go," Leland continued. "Expect to hear from the court very soon. Have a good afternoon."

Roman's ears pricked up at that last part, but Audrey was too busy combing knuckles through the dunes of knots across his back.

This wasn't a regular hangout, so without parting "laters," the boys' paths diverged silently from the top of the station's front stairs.

Roman was baffled by how his mom wasn't berating him and making a scene, even if she wasn't one for public displays. He wished the ordeal would end with a cold shoulder for months.

To maintain the delicate balance, he didn't dare look her in the eyes as they headed toward her car. The passenger seat in his mom's Honda Accord was like a powder keg.

"You really didn't do that well last semester, did you?" Audrey asked out of the blue a few blocks into the agonizing drive home.

Roman looked out the window with shut eyes. If anyone could interpret his body language, it was his mother.

"So not only did you lie to me and your father, you also broke the law," Audrey continued.

"I . . . I didn't think we'd be doing something that bad," Roman said.

"Oh, come on. You knew it felt wrong. You knew it."

A mile or so from home, they slowed to a stop at one of Glendale's busiest intersections.

For a split second, Roman looked at her. Mascara snaked down her cheeks, and he wanted to kick himself in the nuts.

Audrey grabbed her sunglasses from the tiny compartment above the rearview mirror and put them on. "I told you; you are addicted." Her voice cracked. "I told you to stop wasting so much time on that stupid thing, and you didn't listen." She sounded out of breath. "You didn't listen!"

Audrey shook her head at the cross traffic and heaved between bawls while Roman wanted to rip his own balls off. But if Southern Californian earthquakes and their diminishing aftershocks have taught him anything, he'd hopefully seen the worst of it.

Turning onto their street, Audrey wiped her face with a Kleenex from a box she always kept tucked next to the parking brake. Roman was ready to sprint to his room after they parked in the driveway to ground himself and promise to stay clear of his computer for at least two hours before making a grand entrance on #xwarez to chug all the leak news he'd miss.

At least that was the plan until the worst surprise of the day, the most perturbing sight one could witness involving their home:

a stranger walked out the front door with what Roman believed was the living room television. A home robbery? What were the odds of it happening that day?

Another big-shouldered man emerged with a different boxy possession.

Just don't hurt me or my family, Roman thought.

He wanted to roll down the window and shout the secret location of the family jewels if it meant the alleged robbers would leave sooner. Based on childhood cartoons, robbers all wore the same masks and dark clothing, but the faces of these thugs were naked. The only wardrobe they had in common—their uniforms.

Roman noticed three more of them loitering by a parked van near the front lawn. Something tiny glinted from their chests. Another stranger lugging something out of the house almost tripped over himself. A glare of the sun's reflection sliced Roman's eyes, a glare that bounced off something that reminded him of a custom-cut piece of Plexiglass.

Wait.

Roman unbuckled and sprang from the car.

"They're gonna break it!" He cried, slamming the door behind him. "They're gonna break my computer!"

Audrey got out and followed, proclaiming a similar concern for more Maslowian reasons.

"What are you all doing in my house?" She asked, sounding demanding yet terrified.

Roman lunged toward the front steps.

"Wait, Roman, wait!" Audrey called out. "Stop!"

One of the officers near the van that Roman suspected was the scene's supervisor because he wore a tan trench coat rocketed up his hand and issued the same command. "Stop!"

The ones with free hands reached for their holstered guns.

"No!" Audrey shouted. She leapfrogged onto Roman's back. One of her high heels slipped off.

"Who's that?" An officer standing behind the suspected supervisor of the scene demanded.

Even with his mother hanging from his shoulders, Roman shuddered to a standstill like a wall door stopper.

"He's the kid," the suspected supervisor said. "This is all his stuff."

The rest of the officers resumed chatting or walking back and forth between the house and the van. Audrey slid off Roman's back. The suspected supervisor whipped out a small bushel of white and yellow papers from a folder he kept at his waist and handed them to her.

"This is all evidence," he said, waving an all-encompassing finger at the scene.

Roman remained cemented in place as the officers made a few more laps that ended with the confiscation of additional hard drives, monitors, towers, patch panels, and routers. Not long after, he heard the van's doors slam before it drove away.

Audrey picked up her shoe off the lawn and nearly lost her balance trying to put it back on. Her hair was frazzled. She walked past the front doors, which the police had left open.

Roman stumbled behind her, expecting more wailing reprimands, but in the kitchen, he was greeted by the back of Audrey's head and her elbows absorbing the kumquat countertop. She stared out to the backyard through the small window above the sink. The neighbor's hammock wafted in the breeze.

"M-mom," Roman mumbled.

Audrey didn't turn around. She intermittently sniffled.

He didn't want to break the dike holding back further tears, so he went upstairs to his room, which was nearly empty as the day they moved in. Among the few things left untouched were his bed, nightstand, dresser and hamper. He had flashbacks of how his voice echoed through the naked halls years ago.

For some unknown reason, Roman believed he'd be back on #mswarez later that evening; he could almost feel the resistance of his mouse across his desk surface like it was a phantom limb. But when he didn't stub his toe against the computer tower, he fell to the ground in an Indian-style position and whimpered.

"Shit," he said. He stuck his foot out again and got nothing but air. "Shit, man. Shit."

All he wanted now was a lifetime to mourn, but a car screeched to a halt in the driveway. Roman wondered what the police could have forgotten. But then he dashed to his bedroom window.

Wait. That's not the cops.

"Where is he!" Felix yelled from downstairs.

He barged into the house and howled up the staircase. It was one of the few times Roman felt threatened by his father's French accent.

"What did you do?" Felix thundered.

Roman knew this wasn't the time to contradict. He sprinted to the top of the staircase.

"Get down here!" Felix commanded. He was wearing a buttoned navy blazer and beige Dockers.

"I'm sorry, dad! I'm sorry!" Roman pleaded as he descended with caution.

"Sorry?"

"Dad, I'm . . ."

Felix grabbed him by his polo collar when Roman was a stair or two from the ground floor.

"Who's going to do business with me if they know my son is a criminal?" Felix continued. "Go hang with the gangbangers and rapists! You won't last a minute!"

Felix reeled in a fist, but converted it into an open palm that he slammed against the wall.

Roman flinched hard and swung his glasses off. He dropped to his knees to feel around for them.

"I left everything back home for you to ruin our family like this?" Felix said while his son pawed around his feet.

Audrey encroached on the scene, breathing through her mouth. Felix grabbed a small glass flower vase sitting on a nearby shelf and wound a pitch toward the kitchen.

"That's enough!" Audrey yelled as she grabbed Felix's arm and pinned it against the wall.

He stamped the vase back down in place, rattling the flowers and shaking off a few petals. He straightened his coat and looked again at Roman, still on all fours.

"I'm even happier now I didn't give you my name," Felix said.

That didn't hurt Roman as much as seeing his mother cry.

Felix pointed at Audrey. "This is your fault too!"

"Me?" Audrey replied. "It's both of our jobs!"

"You should have paid more attention to what he was doing in his room!"

"I'm checking in on him when I'm doing housework. When was the last time you even stuck your head in his room?"

Like other rare occasions that they argued, they did so away from Roman, this time deep into the recesses of the kitchen.

Roman found his glasses, or what was left of them, after his finger was pricked by a shard. No stranger to having his toe serve as a seeing-eye dog in the dead of night, Roman flung his foot around until he found the staircase and clung to the handrail and took the broken glasses up with him.

The volume of his parents' arguing toned down when he made it upstairs.

Since his room was now a dystopian landscape, Roman needed a new arena to think on things. The only other private space he could think of was his shower, so after dropping his clothes to the ground, he wrapped a towel around himself and felt his way to the bathroom. The downpour drowned out the yelling from downstairs. He hung his head and let the hot, therapeutic stream cascade onto the back of his neck. His afro was soaked and sagged like the shape of a traffic cone toward the shower floor. But the first-world privilege made him feel poor.

This is all I have now? Hot water?

He slammed a fist against the hollow, plastic wall attached to the shower head, an act that surprisingly didn't hurt much.

Good!

Roman punched it again, but the wall countered with a jab of harsh truth.

My friends! What's gonna happen to them? I've destroyed their lives!

Another punch.

They're gonna kick me off the channel! Everything I worked for! I'm just gonna disappear!

This time, he wound his entire torso and banged his head against the wet barrier.

"My parents," Roman said under his breath.

At moments like this, he recalled how his folks gave him everything and all the opportunities to thrive—granted, only what they *wanted* him to be good at, but would it have been so hard to have tried a little harder? For a little longer? Did he always have to lazily rebel and despise every sport he was forced to play?

Roman wound his head again and crashed it.

Gompf.

All my work! Erased! How am I going to prove myself now? I hate everyone!

Gompf.

My dad hates me.

Gompf.

I'll never have a computer again!

Gompf.

Faint shouts from the other side of the bathroom door interrupted the rhythm.

"Roman!" Audrey called from the hallway. "What are you doing? I don't care if you're naked!"

He was still banging his head when she barged in.

"Roman! Please! It's not the end of the world!" Audrey pleaded.

"I let dad down!" Roman yelled. "I let you down! My life is over!"

"Stop!"

She reached into the shower, wrapping her arms around her son's gaunt torso without trouble. Roman kept his eyes closed out of embarrassment. Audrey got a towel around him. His forehead was hot and red. She helped him back to his room, water dripping everywhere along the way. Roman let go of her when he was confident that he'd fall onto his bed without missing.

"You're not going to dry off?" Audrey asked.

Face first in his pillow, Roman slowly shook his head. Losing his lifestyle rendered his limbs immobile. Like the lost Wonders of the World, his sanctuary was burned into legend.

"I just want to sleep," Roman said.

Audrey looked at her watch. "But it's only four o'clock."

"I just want to sleep."

Roman heard French profanities from downstairs. Audrey left, presumably to calm Felix down, but soon returned with a glass of water and a small white pill.

"This will help," Audrey said.

More than willing to appease, Roman gulped down the pill. Felix eventually stopped yelling. Roman felt like a stopwatch had started.

The last thing he remembered was the home's smallest cranium inserting itself into his room.

"What did you do?" Leon asked.

Roman dignified his sibling with a polite descent into nothingness.

Next thing he knew, it was morning. He enjoyed a few blissful seconds as he read 8:09 a.m. on his alarm clock before remembering why he was home from school. Then his body ached like he had dozed in the wrongest ways possible, but it didn't stop him from jumping out of bed to peer out his window. He couldn't make out much, but could tell the black blob—his dad's Lexus ES350 to sighted people—was absent from the driveway. He put on a t-shirt and Lakers jersey shorts.

Roman, reliant on the handrail again, went downstairs and thought he was home alone.

"I called in sick," Audrey said.

The direction of her voice drew his attention toward the dining room table, where he could barely make out his mother's seated figure. He heard the turning of a page. She must have been perusing another department store catalog.

Roman didn't know whether to say good morning or start with another apology. Audrey got up and blurred into the distance before returning with something that smelled good.

Roman sniffed, and given his near absence of sight, his elevated sense of smell detected pancakes without fail.

"They've been ready since seven-thirty," Audrey said.

"Th-thanks," Roman said. He sheepishly walked toward the cold breakfast.

"I'm going to get a head start on this week's shopping," Audrey said. "I'll be back in a little while."

There was no goodbye, just the shutting of the front door, which provided Roman some much-needed perspective on his placement in the house. With his right toe leading the way again, he navigated back to his room without tipping over his short stack and turned on his alarm clock radio, now second only to the thirteen-inch television on his dresser in terms of state-of-the-art tech in his room.

Back in bed, he set his pillow upright and against the wall. He totally didn't mind the fact that he forgot to bring up some syrup. He was already full after the first bite.

KROQ's morning show, *Kevin and Bean*, kept him company until ten o'clock. Fond memories of sick days spent watching *The Price is Right* mustered up the energy to get out of bed and flip on the television, but he nearly tripped over himself when his phone rang.

Roman answered it on the third ring. "Hello?"

"Check out today's paper," Todd said.

"W-wait, did they take away your . . ."

Dial tone.

The Vallancourts weren't subscribed to the *Glendale Leader*, but he was certain some of his elderly neighbors were. He felt his way downstairs again, spent six minutes finding his shoes, and went outside. He took an unconfident blind leap between property lines and landed his right foot on a sprinkler, but miraculously kept his balance this time around. He smelled damp newsprint and dropped to his knees to claw around until he was hoisting the daily. After a stable journey back to his room, he dove face-first into the paper. A little ink rubbed off on his nose. Given his vision, it was a slow process, but Roman grasped the gist of the story.

3 Students Arrested for Computer Hacking

By Chris Beckett

Three H.L. Wright Magnet Students were arrested Monday for hacking into the school's computer system and altering their grades. The students, all juniors, were immediately released into the custody of their parents.

Roman's eyes skipped a few paragraphs.

"The hacking took place over several months," said Det. Derek Leland of the Glendale Police Department.

Their names were withheld because they were minors.

Roman heard the front door unlock. His instincts tossed him back into bed, where he kept quiet until Audrey walked in to check on him.

"No one's gonna know it was us if that's what you're worried about," Roman told her. "The paper didn't print our names because we're underage. None of dad's business partners will know."

Her response was to place a small pharmacy bag on his nightstand.

"They're contacts," Audrey said. "I know you're scared of using them, but this is the first of many things you won't have a choice in from now on."

Roman sighed and gave in with a few light nods.

"I also went to your school today," she said. "Your expulsion hearing is tomorrow."

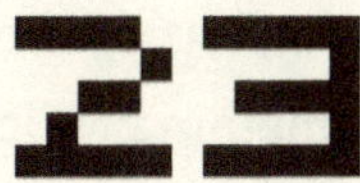

"We were tipped off," Grubner said to the five-member school board.

The principal and his co-prosecutor, Vice Principal Leininger, rested their elbows across a table before a winding dais.

Roman, Todd, and Alex folded their hands under the defendants' table, one over from the administrators. They wore suits traditionally reserved for family gatherings. A wide wood slat against the wall clipped together the seat arrangements like a binder ring.

"It had to be that bitch Eunice," Todd whispered to his friends. He had slicked back his hair instead of spiking it, but it still looked pretty hard to the touch.

"But why?" Alex asked. "I thought you guys were on the same page or something."

"Search me, bro. She probably had no idea how well we were really doing."

"I just don't get why."

Thermometer-popping rage surged up Roman's body at the mention of Eunice's name. Still, he occasionally zoned out, drugged by the satisfaction that it wasn't his lack of computing skills that led to the closed school board hearing an hour before the scheduled, open-to-the-public dusk meeting—just the absence of any competent leadership. He bowed his head.

"We knew this wasn't something to be taken lightly," Grubner said into a bendable microphone. "We vetted the tip and found inconsistencies in the grade book. We couldn't tell right away who was making changes, but we went back as far as we could and linked it all to these three students in front of you today."

Roman regretted not spending the whole damned party at Alina's changing grades as far back as when he started all this. Procrastination was always the villain in the end. He was stoned by the surrealness of all the attention.

"Our system makes a record of every change to a grade, and we're confident that at least a hundred grades were inappropriately altered," Grubner said.

The sparse audience gasped. Only the boys' parents were allowed to attend the hearing—standard procedure for expulsion reviews.

Roman sank down in his seat. It was one of the few times Todd followed his cue.

"Based on what we've gathered so far, the students obtained teachers' passwords," Grubner said. "The police informed me that the boys used a device called a keylogger to collect the passwords."

"Pervs went through my underwear drawer to get it," Todd whispered to Roman.

Grubner brushed his nose with his index finger and then cleared his throat.

"I know I run a new school, but I've been running schools for almost twenty years," he said. "I've witnessed students cheat on tests and even steal them, but this is the most pervasive instance of academic dishonesty I have ever seen."

Todd ran a hand over his stiff hair a couple of times and whispered to himself. "Oh, get over it. They're making such a big deal."

Alex leaned toward Todd.

"I think they'll go easier on us if we look sorry," Alex said.

"We'll be fine in the long run. Trust me."

Alex let out a slow exhale.

Grubner adjusted his bendable mic. "Now, granted, these boys never had any major disciplinary issues, but their blatant disregard for the integrity of what my colleagues and I strive to achieve every day solidifies my recommendation of expulsion from H.L. Wright Magnet School for all three students."

More parental gasps from the audience.

Roman twitched hard, like he had rudely awoken himself from one of those falling dreams. The school board's president, a woman of about sixty, wore a smile adjacent to a rose-shaped brooch. Her nameplate on the dais read "Dottie Shapiro."

"At this point, the board will take a few minutes to deliberate," she said. Dottie and her colleagues arose and retreated out a back door.

Roman heard the hearing room door whoosh open and peered over his shoulder, making eye contact with his parents' death stares for a second, which felt like nine years. Then he was drawn to a young blonde woman by the door. An aging officer on loan from the Glendale Police Department waved a finger at her and moved to close the door.

The girl had a college-ruled notebook pinned to her chest and a tape recorder that looked like a king-size Hershey's bar. She was short, but tenacious. "I'm here for the follow-up story."

"Now, Chris," the officer said. "You know this is a closed meeting. You want more information; you need to call the PIO."

"I need more than three-word quotes from the public information officer."

"Not my problem. Call him."

Roman took solace in knowing he had evaded a potential front-page picture.

"No matter what happens," Todd said.

The officer closed and locked the door.

"Hey!" Todd said.

Roman spun his focus back to his friend.

"Uh . . . sorry," Roman said. "I was—"

"No matter what happens," Todd continued.

He eked out reflective tears paired with a squished frown. Roman gave a few weak nods, unsure of what his friend meant.

Dottie led the pack out of the closed session. She took her seat and cut right to the chase.

"Student A," Dottie said into her microphone.

The school district didn't announce the students' names during expulsion hearings, so they used assigned letters. Ironically, Roman was "Student A."

"We affirm expulsion from the Herbert Lowell Wright Magnet High School," Dottie continued.

Roman heard Audrey start to sob. He couldn't bring himself to turn around again.

"Student B," Dottie said. "We affirm expulsion from the Herbert Lowell Wright Magnet High School."

Vigen barged out of the hearing room, pounded the doors open with his meaty fists, and belted Armenian obscenities from the hallway. Dottie gave him a few moments. Vigen, soon after, returned quietly and composed and sat next to his wife again.

"Student C," Dottie said. "We affirm expulsion from Herbert Lowell Wright Magnet High School."

Alex hunched and leaned forward, his fingers tapping on his thighs as he rocked back and forth.

With the matter settled, Dottie adjourned the hearing. Roman led the boys as he filed out into the hall, trying to avoid eye contact with his parents for a little longer. Outside, he heard unintelligible words from the hearing room, perhaps the parents cursing out the school board or, more realistically, asking about what to expect next.

The boys seized the brief limbo to catch up in front of a display case housing prism-shaped awards that Roman discredited with prejudice.

"How are you guys doin?" Todd asked.

"I don't know! I don't know!" Alex said with desperation. "What does this mean? What's gonna happen to us now?"

"Don't you know where all the bad kids go? Harding High."

"Ah, shit! Really?"

"Yeah, lots of assholes there, but don't worry . . ."

"I'm not worried about that. My parents already told me no more Blockbuster rentals ever again. And no more fast food either! No way I can eat khoresht every night!"

"That's all you care about?"

"Come on, Todd. I told you a million times, let's stop. Now listen to me for once. Why aren't we going after Eunice? Why aren't you ten steps ahead on that, huh? They were using us. They should be here getting their asses kicked out of school like we are or at least maybe they'll go easier on us if they find out we weren't the only ones involved."

Roman wanted to charge full steam ahead with Alex's plan. It made no sense: why would an overachiever get in the way of another's earnest effort toward their life's goal? There must have been some mutual respect. It all seemed so petty to Roman, who swore he'd curse Eunice out if he ever ran into her in public. The lust for revenge inflated his balls a little.

Todd massaged the bridge of his nose and groaned. "Don't you get why we weren't charged with breaking and entering?" He told Alex. "She's got to be holding that over us, so we don't turn her in either."

"Goddamn it! She's an evil genius!" Alex said. "Why does every girl in my life have to be smarter than me by like five years?"

Felix pushed the hearing room door open and held it for the other parents. Vigen was the last to walk out.

"Great job raising your son," Felix uttered to him with a sarcastic bite.

Running low on time, Roman wondered if his friends were getting the same shabby treatment. "Did they take your computers too?"

"This guy's still thinking about his computers," Todd said. "Yes, Rome. They took mine, as in one, because I only had one, like a normal person."

"Same here," Alex said. "But on top of that, my folks took away my PS2, but they let me keep my old systems cause my dad was too tired to move all of them."

"My dad said I could use his laptop for homework when I start school again," Todd said. "And if I need porn, I've got some old *Playboys* from like eighth grade that my older cousin gave me."

The parents inched closer.

"My folks said I could use their computer for homework too," Alex said.

Roman's friends may have just proffered the answer he was waiting for—Felix would have to allow him to use his laptop for school, so after a few heartfelt attempts at becoming a good student, he'd sneak a peek at #mswarez.

"What's going on with Lucy?" Alex asked Todd.

In an unprecedented move, Vigen yanked Todd away by his shoulders. Felix got in Vigen's face, nearly stabbing his nostril with his own index finger. "This is all your son's fault!" Felix yelled.

"My son?" Vigen shouted back. "This is all your son's fault, *eshi mek!*"

"You goddamn Armenians! You're all criminals!"

"You're the one bribing city officials!"

"How dare you! I would never do such a thing! I revised that project to comply with your stupid standards!"

"They're not stupid! Your project is too close to residential!"

"The residents will appreciate nearby retail much more than an insurance office!"

The face-to-face fathers repelled each other with shoves.

"*Mamat koonem!*" Vigen yelled.

"*Va te faire enculer! Fils de pute!*" Felix said.

The lent officer ran to disarm the scuffle, holding a dangling flashlight on his belt in place. Todd tried pulling Vigen away, but took a backhand—most likely an accident—to the face. Todd nursed his cheek for a moment and tried to hold his father back by the shoulders.

"I never want your son around mine again!" said Vigen, self-restrained.

"Same to you!" Felix said.

It didn't matter if it was partying douchebags grinding their antlers together or his father entwined in battle, Roman stood there and spectated. In fact, his attention was more drawn to the backs of Alex and his folks, who had cold-shouldered the fight like a trio of action heroes, leaving a fiery climax in their wake. Alex's dad had a hand on his shoulder and his mother on the other.

The officer bridged the dueling dads, then pointed at Todd's family. "You guys leave first. You all need to keep calm for your kids!"

Roman noticed Todd was missing. Seconds later, he was spotted by the building's entrance. Lucy appeared next to him, spaghetti straps and all. Roman couldn't hear them, but their fluttering hands were just as loud. A few people slithered past them to get in or out. Backlit by the sun, Todd and Lucy transformed into a slideshow of impassioned silhouettes until she flickered out of frame.

Felix and Vigen adjusted their respective belts and shepherded their families toward the exit.

Todd looked puzzlingly pale, like he was tapped of blood, but by the time he plodded back to Roman, he shrugged like his old self, then grinned like a ventriloquist dummy.

"Go Cyclones, I guess," Todd said, giving a shout-out to Harding High's mascot.

The drive home with Felix at the wheel was the longest, and amid the recent meshugas, it struck Roman that he hadn't sincerely apologized other than panicked sorries right after his arrest. He knew those didn't mean squat in the moment, but enough time for reflection had passed. Even if a sincere apology fell on deaf ears, it'd still be on the record for tax purposes. A warm nuzzle ran up the back of Roman's neck when they drove by a Thrifty ice cream sign.

"I'm . . . I'm really sorry, you guys," Roman said. He braced himself for harsh sonic waves, but Felix was concentrated on the road. Even Audrey had to pinch her husband's elbow, though to no avail. Roman noticed his dad fixed on him through the rear-view mirror for a second, but it might have been more related to gauging how far back that F150 was. Roman, like most kids his age by now, was beyond used to a bit of silent treatment after a domestic infraction, but there was a fine line.

Audrey looked over her shoulder at Roman. "He heard you," she said.

Roman was the first to get out of the car when they made it to their driveway, but spun back around when someone broke the silence.

"I'll take you to your new school for now," Felix said, still seated. "But hurry up and get your driver's license."

—

Audrey shaved Roman's head later that night. What took years to grow, she mowed down in minutes.

"Finally, you won't look like a bum anymore," Audrey said as she did laps across her son's scalp with an electric razor, leaving behind a thin veil of fuzz. "You will start your new school looking clean."

Roman had no choice but to sit quietly and watch his persona circle the drain. Every now and again, Audrey scooped a chunk of hair from the sink with a paper towel.

"Can't let it all go down the drain," she said. "It'll ruin the plumbing."

The razing of Roman's bush revealed another anatomical shame: his big ears. Well, they weren't so much as big as they weren't folded back as far as the average person.

When he woke up the following day, hundreds of loose folli-cles had pooled in the middle of his pillow. Then, he got a ran-dom idea after realizing he was home alone.

The library! The library has computers!

Roman flipped on *Regis and Kelly* for background noise, changed into his clothes, turned the television back off, and dashed out the front door.

He ran for the first half mile until his sides hurt. He walked the rest of the way to the Glendale Central Library. The oncoming wind was like kindling for his already burning eyes, thanks to his new contact lenses. He had already run more than the past two years of P.E. combined—at least six blocks—the morning after he became academically stateless. But an even weirder sensation was the cool air scraping his scalp.

Past a homeless man asleep on a reading chair and an elderly woman alone at a round table, thumbing through a newspaper, Roman saw two rows of computers. He sat by the last one by the window, shook the mouse, and waited excruciatingly long for things to boot up—about forty-five seconds.

He bet his fellow operators and fanbase were investigating his whereabouts by trying to track his IP address. After all, a few days' absence of one of the forum's most prominent members was not unlike the disappearances of Jimmy Hoffa and Amelia Earhart.

Once the web browser loaded, Roman logged onto #mswarez and saw several messages in his inbox. Some were from fellow ops, asking where the hell he had been. However, Roman's main worry was getting a message from Harry Link, a dis-invite to attend the Professional Developers Conference on the forum's behalf.

[20:36] 01(+HarryLink): hey man, is everything ok? You've been gone for a while. If you're sick or something it's cool. just lemme know

Roman typed.

[11:23] 01(+JaYnus): Yeah, I'm sorry. Just got caught up with a few things at school.

But he hesitated before pressing send. It was a lame excuse. But what would happen if he told the truth? He didn't know if he'd be deemed an unworthy amateur, demoted and ultimately blacklisted. So Roman backspaced and chose to play it safe for now. But what else would there be to do except not be on a computer if he were sick and bedridden?

[11:23] 01(+JaYnus): I'm sorry man, yeah really bad appendcitis. had to be in the hospital for a while. i'm back now.

Sent. But in typical Harry Link fashion, he didn't respond right away since it was daytime, and was likely at work. Roman hung around to visit other old haunts like *IGN*, *WIRED*, and AIM. The second he signed onto AIM, he got a message from Alex.

S0lidsnacK85: hey man, you got another computer?
S0lidsnacK85: how are you?
JaYnus: i'm ok
JaYnus: i'm at the library
S0lidsnacK85: haha i knew you'd figure out something quick
JaYnus: lol i guess
JaYnus: you ok?
S0lidsnacK85: yeah, folks are still a little pissed but whatever, they've done what they said they're gonna do.
JaYnus: so see you at harding next week?

S0lidsnacK85: yeah. maybe chill soon somehow too?
JaYnus: i dunno. can't really leave the house
S0lidsnacK85: except for the library apparently lol

Alex's ability to still laugh out loud injected Roman with guilt. His friend didn't ask to be dragged into this mess.

JaYnus: i'm really sorry the way things went down man. I didn't think this was gonna happen
S0lidsnacK85: dude, it's ok
S0lidsnacK85: something like the shit we went through im' sure we're gonna laugh about it someday
JaYnus: really? you're not traumatized?
S0lidsnacK85: well, i dunno lol. but everyone back at school is talking about us.
JaYnus: really?
S0lidsnacK85: oh shit, my mom's back from the store gotta go.

Alex went idle.

Roman thought it wise to do the same in case his parents called home to check on him, but he couldn't help marinating in the posthumous fame. Too bad it was as valuable as the empty shoebox in his closet. He logged off and left the library, but oh, did he plan to make a grand return. On the way home, he tried to think of excuses: an evening walk after dinner to clear his mind or just for good old exercise's sake. His website, irc.xwarez.net, was in desperate need of updates.

But that evening, a suited woman joined the Vallancourts at the dinner table all the way from the Yellow Pages.

"Don't post anything online," she said. "In fact, abstain from the Internet altogether."

Roman dropped his spoon next to his bowl of French onion soup.

Her name was Sasha Goldfarb, a clean-cut juvenile defense attorney who wore thick glasses like Roman and styled a bun streaked with various grays. Despite Audrey's offering of food, Sasha didn't eat. Instead, her main course was a pile of papers.

"Unauthorized access of a government computer," she said. "Hasn't really come up since I came to juvenile, but pretty black and white. Intent is there in the data."

Unlike all the pediatricians, nurses, and dentists who were all smiles and lollipops, Sasha was frank and drank black coffee at six-thirty in the evening.

"Are there any more computers in the house?" She asked.

"Sure," Felix said. "I have one, but our son doesn't have access to it anymore."

"Good. Make sure he doesn't."

Roman wasn't sure how many more daggers through the heart he could take. What kind of universe would strive to keep him from working toward his life's goal of getting rich off his acumen? He had no qualms about going white hat and abiding by Boy Scout ethics.

"Well, you don't have to worry," Felix said. He sounded proud about it. "The police took all his computers."

That didn't sound convincing enough for Sasha, who looked Roman dead in the eye.

"You're not doing anything else illegal, are you?" She asked.

Roman swallowed the iced tea he had held in his mouth for several minutes. He didn't understand. Kids today were downloading movies! How could something as benign as computer geeks sharing pirated software . . . The answer leaped to the front of his mind. He knew there was no other option than to hit the kill switch, the saddest of all prospects, but there was no other choice left.

"Roman?" Felix asked.

"Yeah?" Roman said.

"I want you to hear you say it."

For once, Roman was glad his folks had no clue what #mswarez and his website were all about. He shook his head like he was trying to appease an armed gunman. "I'm not doing anything else."

—

The next day was the same routine: Lucky Charms, *Price is Right*, and reciting, "Don't forget to spay and neuter your pets," as Bob Barker always did to close out the episode.

In the interest of time, Roman made for the library without showering, brushing his teeth or changing out of his basketball shorts—if anything, he'd blend in with the daytime regulars.

He split a computer screen between #mswarez and his website. He smiled with melancholic pride. It was still early afternoon, so the text on #mswarez flowed slowly.

Messaging Harry Link was the easy part.

[11:18] 01(+JaYnus): Hey, I'm sorry, I can't make it to PDC this year. I have to take a break from the channel.

Again, no response since it was the middle of a workday, which was Roman's preference.

Next was the website.

The closer the cursor got to hovering over the option to wipe everything clean, he started breathing heavily, almost dry heaving. This wasn't going to be easy, no matter how high-priced a lawyer advised him. He typed a message and sniffled when he made it go live.

"This site is currently down," it read.

Roman inhaled his snot, then coughed and screeched like a skipped record. A snot drip escaped his right nostril, but he shoved it back with his thumb. The homeless guy sitting across and a few computers over angled his head to see what was going on.

Roman clicked and typed away, pretending he was a law-abiding citizen utilizing a complimentary community resource.

"Hey, kid," the homeless guy said. "If they hear you acting all weird, they're gonna kick you out."

24

As if the "don't do drugs" style arrest in front of the student body and the movie poster mugshot weren't enough, Roman found himself in a long, imposing hall, dodging a tide of orange jumpsuits. He again wore a suit, the same for Todd and Alex, who, without words, elected him to lead the way. A few other teens also donned formal attire. Roman wondered how many collective bullying hours could be aggregated from the jumpsuits draped over mostly boys of various races. The scene made the bitter rivalry between the #winwarez assholes and the #mswarez noblemen sound like horseplay around a public pool.

A lot of minor defendants cursed and laughed together. A middle-aged mother slapped her presumed son on the back of his head for blurting the F-word. It was panoramic levity on such a heavy day, including the sight of a pig-tailed girl, skinnier than Roman, hugging a woman in a navy blazer and pencil skirt.

At least families were always there for each other, Roman thought.

"I've been clean for three months!" the girl wailed into the suit sleeve. "How can my mom miss this?"

Roman walked right on by. The gist of that moment would stick with him forever.

The brown and orange pebbled floor pattern reminded Roman of the linoleum from the kitchen of a great aunt who died in the mid-nineties. There was never a bad time for a nostalgic distraction. His expertise in eye contact evasion didn't matter, though, as a short boy in an oncoming single-file line of jumpsuits bumped shoulders with Roman. Despite his height, his vacant stare was icier than his parents' disapproving leers thus far.

The two overweight Los Angeles County Sheriff's deputies who walked by on the other side seemed like heroes.

All this because a stupid, over-achieving genius bitch couldn't deal with someone else earning a few more decimal points, Roman told himself.

The boys and their parents parked themselves by a courtroom door with a wooden plaque hanging above that read, "DEPARTMENT 4."

Todd gazed at Roman's head.

"I still can't believe that giant bush is gone," Todd said. "I was starting to think it was going to get you chicks. It was kinda getting cool as you grew into it, you know?"

"I should have told my mom that," Roman said. "Maybe she would have let me keep it."

The first joke he made in weeks was oh-so-freeing. He almost wanted to hug his friend.

"Did you lose weight?" Todd asked Alex.

Even Roman noticed Alex's suit appeared billowier than at the expulsion hearing—such unconventional reference points in time from here on out. Alex's chin looked sharper too.

"My folks haven't made burgers in so long," Alex said. "Almost two weeks."

"Tell the judge you're being starved at home," Todd said. "Maybe they'll go easy on you."

"If I can do that, Rome can get his folks thrown in jail," Alex quipped.

"Nah, he weighs the same as he did on his birth certificate."

They chuckled, perhaps the last opportunity to do so for the rest of the morning.

The Barry J. Nidorf Juvenile Hall was located in suburban Sylmar, about twenty minutes from Glendale and about half-way to Six Flags Magic Mountain. The campus was a sprawling network of brick buildings. None of it reminded Roman of the prisons he'd seen in the movies and on television, except for the winding barbed wire fences entrapping everything.

The boys stayed close to their mothers, who made small talk without coffee. Felix paced back and forth at the end of the hall, glued to his cell phone and occasionally intruded Roman's line of sight with disapproving head shakes.

When the time came, a bailiff led the families to a waiting room with steel benches lining the perimeter and a few down the mid-dle. Before Roman finished a visual survey as he sat down, a boy with a dark, gelled combover scooched beside him with a toothy smile.

"What did you do?" the boy asked.

What little energy Roman had left wasn't meant to be drained by a stranger. "Uh, it's kind of a long story."

"Where do you go to school?"

"I go to—I mean, I went to H.L. Wright Magnet . . . in La Vista."

"Never heard of it. I've always been homeschooled."

Roman couldn't fathom that such a concept was real. He

surprised himself with how he shed his introverted ways in an instant. He had to learn every smidgen about this kid's life.

"You mean you go to school at your house?" Roman asked.

"Yes," the combover boy said. "Since kindergarten."

Roman's taste buds salivated. "So, you can take naps whenever you want?" he asked with impatience.

"I guess, but I don't need naps."

"But like, you can grab a snack from your fridge anytime you want?"

Roman was asking the real questions.

"Yes, but I wait until my mom says it's time for lunch," the boy said.

Having never rapid-fired so many queries, Roman didn't know when he'd go too far. "So . . . so you've never had classmates? What about friends? How do you make friends?"

"Well, we get to go on field trips," he said.

"Field trips? . . . We?"

"Once a month . . . with other homeschool kids. It's part of our program."

"Wow," Roman said. "I had no idea that was a thing."

"We went to the aquarium once, and I got to pet stingrays."

"Yeah, cool, but then how did you end up here if you're homeschooled?"

"I stabbed a kid on one of the trips." His branching smile mirrored the pace of Roman's growing frown.

Roman tried to inch his flat ass away, and Todd's hand landing on his shoulder couldn't have had better timing.

"Remember, end of the day, we're minors," he whispered into Roman's ear. "They don't send minors to jail."

The waiting room thinned out as more people were let into the courtroom to see the judge.

When it was their turn, Roman, Todd, and Alex sat by each of their lawyers along a long brown table, a dozen or so feet from the judge's bench. They were represented by women. Roman's and Todd's parents paid for their lawyers, Sasha Goldfarb and another sharp-dressed woman, while a wrinkle-free and court-appointed deputy public defender was Alex's champion, which caused Felix to air some shit-talking from the audience upon finding out.

"I paid for one of the best attorneys in the phonebook, and that kid is going to get off for free," Felix said.

Roman spun around, certain his father meant to be heard. Audrey elbowed Felix.

Alex, who didn't appear to understand the insult, leaned to his right to ask one of his defendant tablemates a question. "Where's the jury?" He sounded like he was excited to ask.

"I don't know," Todd said, scratching his temple. "I'm just as confused as you are."

"There's no jury in juvenile delinquency," Sasha said while flipping through a small stack of papers. "Everything's up to the judge."

And that bench officer was Los Angeles County Superior Court Judge Maribel T. Espinoza, who clomped her way to the bench in thick heels, but stood no more than five feet tall. None of that mattered when she took the elevated bench. Roman thought about how he's been looking up to women all his life, and lately, he's had to tilt his head back further and further.

He expected the hammering of the judge's gavel to commence the hearing, but things got off to a very boring start. Judge Espinoza put on her bifocals and squinted at page after page of stapled documents. After a few minutes, she took her glasses and tossed them onto the dais. "I read this case file days ago, like how I always read everything before a hearing. But I had to read this one again. And again. I've never come across something like this."

She threw her hands up in the air.

"I don't know what to do!" Judge Espinoza said before cackling to herself.

She resumed rifling through more papers. "But at least I see here you're all enrolled at another local school already?"

Sasha stood up. "Yes, your honor."

"That's good, it'll save the education liaison some time," Judge Espinoza said. "Okay, well, just to be sure, prosecution, any objection as to why these young men should not be detained? To not remain in their parents' custody?"

Roman's heart started racing.

What? This is white collar! What custody? Slap on the wrist! I was told slap on the wrist!

The deputy district attorney was a tall man, standing at least a torso above the female attorneys, and with his baby pink cheeks, he could have been the youngest of the bunch.

"I have no objections, your honor," he said without looking up from the contents of a manila folder.

The relief after a near head-on collision with a semi-trailer truck coursed through Roman's nerves. Judge Espinoza ruled the boys could remain in their parents' custody since they didn't pose a violent threat to the community. But after all that waiting, the court hearing lasted ten minutes, and Espinoza ordered the boys and their parents back the following week.

—

They returned with the addition of a familiar foe's presence: Principal Grubner waddled up to the witness stand. Next to

Eunice, he was the second-most person Roman wanted to expunge from the earth.

"When did you first learn about the hacking that had taken place?" The prosecutor asked Grubner.

"We were tipped off by a student in confidence that something fishy was going on," Grubner said.

The principal regurgitated his testimony from the expulsion hearing, painting a portrait of students who weren't misguided, but instead had the most malicious of intentions.

When it was her turn, Sasha countered with what Roman dubbed the teddy bear defense because of how harmless he and his friends were to the physical well-being of their classmates.

"As it's been well solidified, these boys never had any disciplinary problems, let alone anything remotely close to bullying or physically harming any of their peers," Sasha said as she paced the well and turned to Grubner. "Is that correct?"

"I suppose so, yes," he said into a microphone.

"Did you even know any of these boys by name before the day you called them into your office?"

"Well, I recognized their faces," Grubner continued. "That's something that comes with the job."

"But they never set foot in your office for any disciplinary reasons?"

"No. Not as far as I could recall."

"But your honor, given all that, the principal proudly had the police waiting in the wings to arrest these boys without making a single phone call to their parents as a heads up or even to discuss working out a proper recourse for getting them back on the right track."

Grubner shook his head. "Look, as far as the police go, all principals throughout the district have been instructed to alert the authorities if there's an immediate threat."

"But didn't you say these young men posed no danger?" Sasha said with an accusatory shuffle toward the witness stand.

Roman wanted to pound his fist on the table.

Yes! Take that, you fat ass! he thought.

"So why did you think it necessary to call the police and have my client questioned by them?" Sasha said. "Didn't you think that would be a traumatic experience for someone who doesn't have a reputation for getting into trouble?"

"I consulted with my staff. They told me they must have broken the law," Grubner said.

Sasha pivoted, so one cheek faced him and the other, her clients.

"I see. So you, the principal, were unaware of protocol."

Roman had never heard anyone challenge Grubner's integrity like that.

"There's no protocol for something like this!" He pleaded.

Roman was about ready to kick his feet on the table and ask what's for dinner.

Then the deputy district attorney pulled up a chat log on an overhead display, a conversation between Todd and Alex from a random night. He referenced phrases like "what if we get caught," "this is wrong," "we're breaking the law," and "shut up, you idiot, don't say those words online like we've told you a million times."

Roman looked over the table at Alex and Todd, who both mouthed, "sorry."

Rather than any outward anger, Roman pitied himself. If he couldn't get his best friends to obey menial orders of avoiding H-wording talk online, how the hell was he going to convince far more powerful, wealthier, and influential people to take a chance on him?

Roman's focus dozed off for the rest of the prosecutor's spiel until he started wrapping things up.

"Your honor," the prosecutor continued. "The defendants are not lost boys. This was a calculated scheme, helmed by incredibly intelligent students who knowingly and willfully abused their talents. It may take some time to set them on the right path."

Time? Roman thought as he exchanged blank faces with Todd and Alex. *What does he mean by time?*

Sasha's retort was a prompt request for a sidebar. Unlike the ones Roman had seen on television, where lawyers approached the judge on the bench, they retreated to Espinoza's adjacent chambers. About half an hour later, they returned. But instead of proceeding with the hearing, Sasha and the other defense attorneys invited their clients out into the hall.

"We've reached a deal," Sasha said to the teens standing together with their parents. "It's up to you if you want to accept it."

Roman was puzzled. Were he and his friends guilty, not guilty or what?

"The good news is outside of high school, no one will ever know what you did," Sasha said. "Your records will be sealed."

Todd exhaled with such ferocity that his eyes rolled back into his head. Roman heard a couple of their parents sigh in relief, too, but not Felix, who emitted refund-demanding vibes.

"In exchange," Sasha continued, turning to Roman, "Mr. Ringleader has to do six months of community service." Then she addressed Todd and Alex. "While you two have to do just three months of community service. Trash pickup, basically."

"Absolutely!" Todd said without hesitation. "No juvenile camp? Let's do it."

"Yeah!" Alex said. "That sounds great! Whatever Todd said! I hate camping!"

They looked back at their parents and exchanged nods, but Roman didn't.

"So, it'll be like lunch detention?" He asked.

"Well, if picking up trash off the side of the freeway on Saturday and Sunday mornings is what you consider lunch detention, then yes," Sasha said.

Todd tugged at his collar and loosened it. "We have to sacrifice our weekends?"

"The most important thing to these judges is that you're in school and stay in school," Sasha continued. "Guess when that leaves you free time to pick up trash!"

"Oh man," Todd said.

"But rest assured, it'll be like nothing ever happened. Welcome to the juvenile justice system."

"Shit."

"Yes, there may be some of that to pick up while you're out there. But like I said: clean records when you boys are ready to apply to college."

Said boys exchanged begrudging looks.

"Okay," Todd said.

"Yeah," Roman said. "Fine."

The group dispersed, and Roman trailed behind his parents so as not to give rise to a public berating session. Suddenly, someone pulled him back and held him by his shoulders. It was Sasha.

"One more thing," she said. "And this part only affects you. The judge also wants to bar you from using a computer for a year."

Roman might as well have been sentenced to the electric chair. He had already made peace with running to the library to get his Internet fix, but to have zero access for three hundred and sixty-five days?

"Hey, are you still in there?" Sasha asked. "I know it's a lot, but it's the best offer you're going to get. This whole mess started with you, after all."

The bailiff started letting everyone back into the courtroom.

"I guess . . . I guess I have to," Roman said.

"Great!" Sasha said with the one smile she's cracked throughout the whole ordeal. "It won't be so bad, just find some other hobby. Go to the park and toss around a football, go kiss some girls, anything that's perfectly legal."

Back in the courtroom, the lawyers entered the agreed-upon disposition, but Judge Espinoza wasn't yet through with the boys.

"On occasion, probation officers will make surprise visits to your home to ensure compliance," Espinoza said to Roman, her hands folded and elbows on the dais. "Now, at this point, I usually make the joke that when a juvenile leaves this courtroom, I hope to never see them again. I mean that in a good way, of course, because I don't want you to get into any more trouble."

Roman heard his mother chuckle. It made him happy for a moment.

"I also talk about the importance of staying clean or emphasize the need to stay away from gangs, which fortunately have nothing to do with any of you," Espinoza said. "But that doesn't mean I don't have a message to share. You still did harm to society by cheating. Sure, grades might not seem like a big deal, but you shouldn't feel it's ever right to cheat people, not just your classmates, but anyone in any other stage of your life."

Todd let out an exaggerated yawn. "How many of these pep talks are we going to get?" He whispered to Roman.

Without taking her eyes off the judge, Sasha reached back, rested her fist on Todd's knee, and pressed down until he yipped. Espinoza paused to clear her throat.

"As I was saying, if you cheat others, you cheat yourself the most," Judge Espinoza said. "Good luck to you all."

But before she could declare the hearing over, a voice thus far unheard in the courtroom spoke up. "Um, excuse me, your honor."

Everyone's surprised glances were drawn straight to Alex, who was standing up from his seat at the defense table.

The one nonconforming mood was Sasha's, who ground her teeth and was a nanometer away from snapping a pencil in half.

"Yes, Mr. Alex?" Judge Espinoza said with a curious grin. "What can I do for you?"

"I'm sorry, I don't want to get into any more trouble," Alex said. He rested his fingers on the table like it was the back of a church pew. "I just wanted to make sure it's okay if I missed school on April 24."

Judge Espinoza raised an eyebrow. "Well, if it's for a medical reason like a doctor's appointment, of course. You just need to call—"

"It's just that April 24 is the remembrance of the Armenian Genocide," Alex said, cutting her off. "There's always a big march that day through Hollywood protesting the Turkish government and their continued denial of the Genocide. They killed over a million and a half Armenians in 1915. I—I go every year. Can I still go?"

Judge Espinoza ran her palms together up and down, but clung to her smirk. "I think I've seen something about that on local news before."

She jotted a few indiscernible notes on a piece of paper. "I'm not going to get in the way of someone's culture, especially of a young man like yourself who's in the midst of learning about it. Of course, you can go, and I'm sure your friends would want to join you as well."

Todd nodded frantically. So did Roman, despite the fact that he wasn't Armenian, but was willing to ride the coattails of his long last name and schnoz.

"Just be sure to remind your probation officer when it gets closer to April 24," Judge Espinoza said.

She then declared the hearing over and everyone carried on small talk back out to the hall. Roman felt an icy presence creep up behind him and Alex. Roman turned to see Sasha seething at his friend.

"Next time you want to put on the good Boy Scout act and talk to the judge, you talk to me first," she said.

"I did," Alex said, looking her dead in the eyes. "But you didn't ask for me."

While the reality of a computer-less life flayed through his meat, Roman was sure he'd find a workaround. But having to get up at the butt crack of dawn on the weekend—he loved sleeping in. Although he was almost seventeen, he still needed as much rest as his immediate post-gestation required to acclimate to sharing a dimension with people. How wasn't this child abuse? Bottom line, and he didn't mean to sound like a spoiled brat, he wasn't sure what the hell his dad paid for. Was that the best Sasha could do?

"There's no afternoon shift for the trash pickup?" Roman asked Sasha, who finished shaking her co-counsels' hands.

"What?" Sasha replied with a bewildered expression.

"I have to go super early on weekends?"

"Well, you don't have to go if you don't want to," she said, sliding her glasses down her nose.

"I don't?"

"Absolutely not. I can go right back in there and tell them you'd like to reject the deal because the prosecutor originally wanted to try you as adults."

—

Roman wormed out of his dad's car into unfamiliar darkness that sent a shiver down the back of his neck. The juvenile hall complex stood more brutalist in the hour leading to daybreak. Felix didn't bother getting one last look at his son.

"Hurry up and get your license," he said, speaking over a radio ad for Fletcher Jones Motorcars on Jamboree at the 73 before slamming the passenger door and driving off.

After the heat from the car's exhaust dissipated, Roman wrapped his jacketed arms over his torso and spotted Todd trembling in the same temperature-conserving pose by a flagpole and a small cluster of non-violent offender teens. Alex, dropped off by his dad, showed up last and scarfed down the last third of a breakfast burrito with one hand and fist-bumped his buds with the other.

Todd scoffed at him. "Never thought I'd be saying this to you, but smart."

"Not fast food either," Alex said after his last gulp. "Finally learning how to cook."

Roman smiled for a second. "Nice."

"By the way, did you hear Grubner got transferred to another high school?"

It was news to Roman. Even if Grubner led the investigation that got him expelled, he didn't want to ruin anyone's life and have them fired or something like that.

"He didn't get transferred, bro," Todd said. "He just took a job in the 626. Pasadena, from what I heard."

"Do you think he got fired?"

"I dunno, bro. Maybe he left in disgrace because of the shit we pulled on his watch."

Todd delivered a spirited slap against Roman's shoulder, who didn't feel any better as he hunched, now with both hands tucked into his pockets, but at least his nemesis wouldn't end up homeless.

A few minutes later, bulky and towering orderlies scanned the teens over with handheld metal detectors. Some minors had to fork over keys and belts and even a metal tongue stud before they were disproportionately shoved into five vans that whisked them away to a city called Newhall, according to an offramp sign spiked by the dawn.

The cleanup chaperones handed everyone lime-green safety vests, helmets, and thin wooden rods with needles tied on one end for picking up trash. The monitors surveyed the scene while cradling clipboards.

Bottles, cans, empty bags of chips, candy bar wrappers, cigarette butts, sunflower seed shells, and you name it dotted the off-ramp. The teens self-segregated into squads based on race. Roman stuck by Todd and Alex. They drew their backs close together to form a spherical trifecta for some sense of security. While some of their peers were intimidating, the smaller kids made up for size with a panoply of tattoos and slang in different languages. One of the smaller ones caught Alex scoping them out and sprang forth with open arms like a bat. Alex flinched hard and fell on his ass. The threatener recoiled to a brood of laughing homies.

"I told you don't stare and mind your business, bro," Todd said.

Alex dragged himself back up. "Man, I really hoped I'd never have to pick up trash again."

"Look at it this way. After some practice, you're probably more efficient now and will leave less crap for me and Rome to take care of."

Alex shook his head. "I can't believe we have to do this for three months."

"*This* guy, thinking it's a life sentence," Todd said. "One summer out of our lives."

Alex stomped on an empty, freestanding can. "I don't get how you're chill or joking about this. I thought you guys said we weren't going to get caught."

Todd shanked his trash javelin into the dirt and let it stand. "Well, what the hell do you wanna do, bro? Plan a revenge heist against Eunice and get in more trouble?"

"It's not that," Alex said. "I can't believe I let you guys get this far."

"Bro," Todd said. "Are you kidding me?"

"I should have tried harder to stop you guys."

"Simply chickening out every step of the way wasn't gonna do that."

An eastward breeze slapped Alex's safety vest against his armpits. He swerved his attention at an oncoming big rig on the highway that almost blew everyone's helmets off.

"You could have just walked away," Todd continued. "But you didn't. How come? Because you knew you could get something out of it too. You don't have to see her ever again, right? Jesus Christ, you're the one who was chasing a nerd who you coulda made wet with the hacking, but you didn't."

Alex stayed fixed on Todd, who went back to uprooting trash.

"I didn't because I didn't want to get my friends in trouble," Alex said.

"Well, it happened anyway," Todd said.

"I'm right. Just let me win."

"Sorry, bro. Game over."

Not wanting to have to pick up any emotional trash, which

was much more difficult to abate, Roman interrupted. "Um, I was the one that dragged you guys into this shit." Todd and Alex looked at him. "I didn't mean for all this. I'm really—"

One of the monitors called from atop a boulder of dirt doubling as a lookout post. "Stop talking and get back to work!" he shouted.

The boys resumed tending to their respective quadrants. They kept quiet until they sensed they weren't being watched anymore.

Todd stabbed a skewer of crushed soda cans into his trash bag. "Lucy broke up with me in case you guys were still curious."

Roman and Alex glanced over their shoulders.

"You guys aren't the only ones that lost something," Todd continued.

"Oh, man," Alex said. "I'm sorry." His de-littering stick in one hand, Alex went in for a handshake and a hug, but Todd waved him off.

"Don't worry about it," Todd said. "But yeah, it sucks."

"She was cool," Alex said. "Like how she knew a lot about cars."

"That's like one of the last reasons why I liked her, bro."

"Well, I think you'll have an easier time finding another chick who knows a lot about BMWs than one who's played *Final Fantasy VI*."

"Bro, that stuff doesn't matter," Todd said. "Jesus Christ. Haven't you learned anything from all this? Not just the hacking, but from the whole Tamar thing?"

Roman poked away at the dirt with his stick, pretending he didn't hear that, but not for long.

Alex, in one of his rare flashes of maturity—some patchy stubble helped too—didn't have a knee-jerk response. He just kept picking up trash.

"It kind of matters," he said. "But I know it's not everything."

Roman caught a side view of Todd's smirk. "So, are you gonna keep in touch with her or what?" Todd asked.

Alex dropped to one knee, making Roman nervous, but it was for shoe-tying purposes.

"I dunno," Alex said as he popped back up. "Maybe. Maybe this whole thing was meant to give our love lives a fresh start."

"Hey, I think you've gotta start a lot further back than me."

"True, but at least I wasn't the one taken down by a two-foot-tall robot."

Roman snickered.

Todd did the same. "Alright, alright. You've got me there, bro. I got that thing good, too, though."

"Imagine if this was the future and robots had rights and shit," Alex said. "You'd get the death penalty for what you did to Timmy."

Todd replied with an unamused chuckle.

Roman was relieved. His computers were long gone, but laughter with friends was a surprisingly effective backup.

"Like I said, guys," Todd said. "I told you we're gonna be fine. You guys were gonna go to GCC anyway."

Alex sounded like he was stirring something. "Right as always, huh, Todd?"

Alex stuck his pole into something on the ground. "Congratulations. Now, here's your prize." He undulated his de-littering stick and waved a flaccid magnum condom around, hanging from its tip.

"Ah, sick!" Roman said, spasming a few steps back. "Get that out of here!"

"Gross, bro!" Todd said. "Look! I think there's some shit on the end of it."

Alex swung his pole at the highway, flinging the condom onto the windshield of a white Ford Mustang. The boys, plus a few other delinquents in the immediate vicinity, started cracking up.

"Do you all need a write-up?" One of the monitors exclaimed after he swept himself into the only fun moment of the day so far.

By high noon, the boys cornered themselves into an oasis under the shade of a sycamore tree. Alex took off his helmet and wiped the sweat off his forehead. "How have you been, Rome? How are you getting by without computers?"

Startled by the question, Roman pricked a rock with his trash stick, bending its needle. The truth was he feared his empty bedroom more than forced volunteerism. At least the physical activity and his friends' company somewhat kept his screen-starved mind occupied.

"I dunno," Roman said, straightening the needle. "Watching T.V., movies. Might hook my GameCube back up. Got anything I can borrow?"

"Of course, dude! Anything but *Metroid Prime*, still haven't beaten that one yet, but may I interest you in *Super Monkey Ball 2*, *NBA 2K3* or *Tony Hawk's Pro Skater 4*?"

"As sequentially high as you can go, bro," Todd said, butting in. "Gotta keep this guy busy, so he won't come up with another master plan."

Roman didn't know it was possible to feel flattered and useless at the same time. "Uh, no more master plans without a computer. I don't even know where to find porn."

Todd and Alex both winced.

"Yeah, that's a tough one, bro," Todd said. "Thank god for my nest egg of *Playboys*."

Roman smirked and shook his head.

"And by the way, when I say master plan, I mean behind the scenes," Todd said. "*I* was the captain on the ground."

"I think a general is higher than a captain," Alex said.

"Whatever, man! In that case, you were a private pussy! You know what I meant."

"Well, Rome's mom probably thought he was the commander or something. Remember what she was saying in court?"

On purpose, Roman sat as far away from his parents as possible during the proceedings, so he didn't hear much from them.

"Yeah, Rome," Alex said. "I love your mom, but she was all like, 'I'm sorry my son led your boys down such a troubled path.'"

Todd air-quoted with his fingers. "I knew he had the 'fire in him,' or some shit like that."

Roman raised an eyebrow and an empty Coors Light can that he shoved into his trash sack. "She said that?"

"Yeah," Todd said. "Like she's known me for how many years, and she discredits how smart I am? Come on, bro."

After a lunch of pre-made ham and cheese sandwiches and Hi-C, followed by a few more hours of trash pickup, it was time to head back.

Alex and Todd passed out in the van, whereas Roman was wide awake. Alex sat next to him and snored the whole way. Roman was physically spent, too, but his brain raced faster than the red Corvette speeding past the convoy of vans.

He didn't think he'd get any kind of gift for a long time, not even a Christmas gift, but hearsay of his mother's pride would gladly do. Roman needed to prep for his own trial to get her to confess her admiration for her son's brilliance—or just plain old, blanket potential. Just for once.

—

Roman waited a few days to refine his argument. One afternoon, while his dad was still at work, he built up the courage and treaded downstairs. With each step, the sound of the four o'clock news grew louder.

He crept up behind the couch with the burning question, but Audrey was napping on her side. She was enshrined by the knick-knacks she displayed around the living room—a seasonal teddy bear here, a vase of tulips and baby's breath concentrically placed on a wooden stand there. The walls and floors rewarded her tender upkeep with quality slumber.

The question vibrated Roman's teeth, which served as a temporary blockade.

Mom . . . are you kinda impressed by what I did? he thought.

Even an inch of leverage was enough to eternally prove he had some degree of talent.

Audrey had already slipped into her pajamas. She'd wear them early on stressful days because she claimed it conditioned her mind for bed. Roman crinkled a rug with his toes. Audrey heard it drag across the floor and awoke.

"Something you need?" she asked, sounding groggy as she stretched.

Roman hesitated long enough to notice the endearing attentiveness in his mother's eyes, even if they were half closed. She didn't seem mad at all about being woken up.

"Uh, is there . . . are there any leftovers from last night?" Roman asked.

"Plenty."

"Thanks."

He went back to his room without grabbing any food.

Getting used to a life without computers never got easier. Roman just got better at warping the spacetime in his room, so he could fast forward to dinner and, eventually, the early bedtime his parents always wanted for him. After learning one couldn't be bored if asleep, he was fine with it too.

He savored every menial task in his minimalist room. He broke them down into blocks of seconds. Changing into his home clothes while imitating a sloth, a thick ninety seconds. Even emptying the contents of his backpack, textbooks and all, and arranging them horizontally flat on his desk in a style he assumed was some form of academic Feng Shui, ate up a juicy one-hundred-and-twenty-two seconds. As a bonus, it kept up studying appearances to his folks. Each block brought him that much closer to dreamland.

One afternoon, he bent over to retrieve his CD player from his backpack. A few pieces of paper got tangled in the headphone cord. Roman correctly sensed he was being watched and looked to the hall where Audrey stood with a sheepish grin. Of course, she was reacting to the A- penned across a recent math quiz.

"See," she said. "I knew you'd do better without any distractions."

Out of politeness, Roman responded with a faint smile, but on the inside, he retched at becoming the happy ending of an after-school special.

Sure, with ample free time, he did some light studying because, like any other verb, it killed time, but the ethically acquired knowledge left a more immense void than the stripping of his techie rights.

At that moment, Felix came upstairs, coat over his right shoulder, and dragged a rolling suitcase at a rushed pace like he was still trying to pass idlers on a moving walkway. Just a simper aimed at his wife, and into the master bedroom he went.

The silence between him and his father spoke volumes more than a gossiping aunt.

Killing time took the form of leaving Roman's T.V. on all the time. Even infomercial voices passed the hours faster than an intimate dinner with his thoughts.

Boredom kept tugging at his medulla oblongata. He insisted on staying out of bed unless it was time to hit the hay to ensure a quality night's sleep.

No duh he'd trade in all of his mother's love for a computer. He didn't even know anything about the latest leaks, let alone the latest drama with #winwarez. Oh, how he'd gladly pay to be a fly on the wall to Todd's and Alex's arguments at this point. For now, Roman settled for a blank stare before a segment of *The Screen Savers* about ripping audio without data loss—a new episode, but the pedestrian subject matter allowed Roman to drift off to sleep like his head was resting on the homely lap of a rerun.

—

Roman nearly fainted from his minute-long piss into a cracked urinal, a pleasant top-off to another exhaustive day of punitive labor. After the last drip, he stood still and let the serotonin paddle through his cheeks.

He dragged the tranquility en route to meeting Todd and Alex in the parking lot until it was shattered by shouts near the entrance of the juvenile courthouse. Roman turned around to see a bald—presumably head-shaven—ox of a kid propped up against the reception desk, lifting begging hands up to a landing strip spanning his lower lip and chin. "Please fix it!" He cried. "You have to help me!"

Roman had grown indifferent to such outbursts in an institutional setting by now, so he intended to remain unfazed.

"Please, Ms. Ambrose!" The bald kid begged in a Latino accent. "I need to print this, so I can turn it in or else I fail! Please, Ms. Ambrose!"

Roman wasn't sure what the woman's job was, but she stood over a computer, a badge hanging from her neck atop a civilian's striped button-down with rolled sleeves. She was unmoved by the pleading. Typical adult.

"I shouldn't have even said I'd let you, Hector," Ms. Ambrose said. "The printer doesn't seem to be working, anyway."

"Is it out of ink?" Hector asked.

A deputy down the hall scoped the commotion and started making his way over.

"I don't know. I'm sorry," Ms. Ambrose said. "I can't do anything about it right now. Next time, don't leave things to the last minute."

It was no front row to a brawl between #mswarez and

#winwarez, but hearing of a device tangentially related to his passion piqued Roman's side-eye.

"Everything okay?" The arriving deputy asked. He had a blonde buzz cut.

"Yes, yes," Ms. Ambrose said. "We're fine."

"I need to print my essay," Hector told the deputy. "I don't have a printer at home. I thought you guys would let me do it here."

"Look, I tried to help you, but there's clearly something wrong with the printer. It might be something to do with the updates."

"Why don't you head to a library?" The deputy asked.

"It's Sunday!" Hector exclaimed. "They're all closed!"

The deputy shrugged. He kept one hand on the two-way radio strapped to his chest.

Like the end of all previous days from his youth spent as a spit-shiner for Caltrans, Roman wasn't fulfilled. It puzzled him how a rehabilitative system flush with resources for the municipal good couldn't help a kid with his essay. So, in a way, doing the right thing could still be an act of rebellious mischief.

"Um, I think I know what's wrong," Roman said.

But no one heard him.

"I can help," he tried again in a louder voice that echoed down the hall and frightened him.

The involved parties looked his way.

"I can't let non-staff touch the computers," Ms. Ambrose said.

Hector pogoed his body like a saltshaker. An unknown number of chains shook beneath his oversized t-shirt. "Please! Please!" He foamed. "Let him try!"

"I might have to connect the printer to the network again," Roman said.

A sampling of his acumen in the ether, Ms. Ambrose and the

deputy looked at each other, then back at Roman, who picked up on their implied permission. He invited himself behind the counter and sat on the very warm rolling chair.

To start things off, Roman opened a browser window, which led to an intranet homepage. Not surprising, given he was seated at a government computer. Roman prayed there wasn't a secret webcam with a live feed to Judge Espinoza's courtroom.

Next, he opened MS-DOS, since this would have to be an inward operation. He typed in the command *C:\>arp* and generated the printer's IP address, 128.96.24.33, onscreen.

"See how I got the IP address?" Roman asked as he copied it.

"The computer's IP address?" Ms. Ambrose asked.

"Uh, no. The computer knows its own IP address. I mean the printer's IP address."

Roman moved the cursor over to the control panel. "Then you copy the IP and you go here." Next, he opened the device drive so he could paste in the printer's IP address.

"Uh, where's the paper?" Roman asked.

"I pasted it to Word already, so it's ready to go," Ms. Ambrose said. "Hector emailed it to me earlier."

Roman clicked print and gave the job a fifteen-second grace period. The longest sixteen seconds of his life later, he heard a whirring. Ms. Ambrose retrieved the essay from the printer tray and presented it to Hector, who snatched it.

"Thank you! Thank you! Thank you!" He proclaimed. "Thank you so much! Can I use your stapler, too, Ms. Ambrose? Thanks again!"

Roman responded with a modest smile and a few birdlike head bobs.

"Well, that seemed pretty easy," Ms. Ambrose said. "I think I can handle that if the issue comes up again."

Roman got up from the chair.

After Hector stapled his essay together, he nearly hurdled over the counter for a bear hug. "Bro, anyone messes with you here, I've got your back," he told Roman.

"Alright, alright," the deputy said, resting an arm on Hector as a means of pulling them apart. "No need to get into any more trouble."

The proposed protection didn't trigger the warmth of a wrapped Christmas gift, but the all-around smiles were nice. No, on second thought, screw that shit. All of this pre-loaded knowledge was ready at the drop of a hat. Of course, Roman hadn't forgotten it and how useful it could be. There had to be a price tag.

The reception desk group dispersed, and Roman thrust the entry doors open, the sun pinking his forehead, but what burned more were all the times he tried dodging requests for help when he could have charged for his services. As a bonus, positive reviews could have translated to word of mouth. There must be a related job, he thought.

"Hey!" A disciplining voice called from behind.

Startled, Roman twirled.

It was the same deputy from moments ago holding the door open. "I know what you're in for. But I won't say anything about helping that kid."

Roman waved like a moron until the deputy re-entered the juvenile detention center.

Until now, Roman never knew regurgitations of his P.C. knowledge could be worth anything before an eventual debut patent. He smiled at nothing, possibly because of acute heat delirium or a mental flash of himself standing in front of a chalkboard. The bewildering fuzzies evaporated when Roman made it to the parking lot, where Todd and Alex sought shelter under the temporary shade of a disabled-only parking sign.

"Bro, was that the longest shit of your life or what?" Todd asked.

"Uh, sorry," Roman said.

"It's not like we don't spend enough time under the stupid sun."

The boys low-fived before splitting apart toward their respective cars.

"See you guys tomorrow," Alex said. "I'm gonna go pass the hell out."

Alex, the last of his friends to earn his driver's license, flopped into a 1997 Mitsubishi Mirage and drove off. Roman, by now, had earned his driver's license as well. In return, his parents bought him a 1987 Mazda 626 for five hundred bucks.

Exhaustion around quitting time used to repress all of Roman's carnal urges save sleep. But for the first time in months, he felt like treating himself, maybe because he did a good deed without a room of joyless adults forcing him to.

Before subjecting himself to an afternoon of parental shunning and boredom, he stopped by the Rite Aid a few blocks from his house. Inside, parallel to an extensive display rack of greeting cards, he got in a short line by the Thrifty ice cream counter. Rite Aid bought out Thrifty a few years ago, but the new owners were smart enough to cling to its locally revered brand name of budget-friendly scoops. An air-conditioned breeze tickled Roman's nose hairs, still a far more natural climate than desaturating highway smog out to the horizon.

A pair of parents was just ahead of Roman. Their young son skipped across every other floor tile with his toddler sister stumbling in tow. Roman didn't mind their obnoxious jabbering while he waited.

"Uh, mint n' chip on a sugar cone, please," he told the cashier when it was his turn. He wondered what Alex would think of his order. He couldn't believe they hadn't discussed ice cream flavors. Roman looked forward to it.

A twiggy girl around Roman's age returned with his order and a smile.

Nothing beats that first lick of a cone after stepping back into the scorching sun, Roman thought to himself as he left the store.

Some of the ice cream streaked onto his wrist, a minor inconvenience surpassed by a sudden, trembling tap on his shoulder.

Roman spun around to see that it was Lucy. He hadn't seen her since he and his friends were expelled. A cup bearing an unidentified ice cream flavor rested in a sugar cone in her left palm. Her lips had shriveled like a raisin.

"Hi," Lucy said.

"Uh, hi," Roman said.

Two of Lucy's girlfriends stood behind her with judgmental glares. That didn't bother Roman. If the stigma of being a criminal rendered him less approachable than usual, it'd be H-wording's door prize.

As for the one girl who wanted his attention, Roman was clueless about what to say to Lucy.

"I'm so sorry! I'm so sorry!" She cried while proceeding to squeeze him.

Roman didn't have an ice cream topping bias, but a wailing Armenian girl was too rich for his inexperienced palate.

"I didn't mean to," Lucy continued.

Roman looked down at her.

"I just told Marina, that's all!" Lucy muttered before curtsying her head.

"I, um, I'm not sure what you mean," Roman said. "You told on us?"

Lucy let him go and backed off. "No, no, I'd never do that! I just told Marina because I didn't know how to react when Todd told me, and I think she told another friend. And then word got out and I think Joy told on you guys to the principal. I didn't think it would get out of hand!"

Of course, Roman thought. *It had to be Joy.*

She probably took her namesake emotion in ratting him out.

"I even think I saw her walk into Grubner's office," Lucy continued. "She looked so goodie-two-shoes."

Even if it was Joy who had ratted the boys out, Roman was in the presence of his ambition's *true* downfall, the wrecker of his some-day ginormous home. He felt his heartbeat in his knees. He covertly started grinding his teeth. A succubus . . . in . . . spaghetti straps!

"I think a few people at Alina's party knew because of her," Lucy said. "Is that why you were acting weird?"

Roman ground his molars together. Despite her apologetic state, Lucy looked like she was waiting for an equal to or greater than reaction.

"I didn't know you guys would get arrested!" Lucy said. "And that . . . that he'd break up with me."

A tear streamed down past her right sunglass lens.

Roman glanced at his hand, now covered in melted mint 'n chip. "He . . . broke up with *you?*"

Lucy bobbed her head a few times and sniffled. No one ever looked sadder holding what Roman had visually confirmed was a scoop of Chocolate Malted Krunch. She conducted her own visual inspection of Roman.

"Um, what happened to *you*?" she asked.

Roman bent his chin toward his torso and finally noticed the sash of dirt over his white t-shirt.

James F. Harding High was the third-removed cousin whom hardly anyone remembered to invite to family reunions. Compared to other area schools, its only leading statistic was its imports of expellees.

The omnipresence of ripped arms and threatening stares from the forced community service detail had the unintended benefit of toughening up Roman, Todd, and Alex a bit. They'd walk down the hall crammed with prodigious lockers and low ceilings, never reciprocating side-eyes trying to establish dominance.

Roman also swore he once heard Alex bark at someone.

Most of the time, however, it was Lakers talk.

"It's not even exciting, bro," Todd said. "It's gonna be another postseason of sweep after sweep."

"I dunno," Alex said. "Sacramento's looking damn good again."

"Yeah, right, bro. Wake me up if the league lets a team from a city nobody cares about make the finals, especially over L.A."

"Or maybe we're just saying that cause we're biased."

"I don't think anyone cared in the eighties when it was always Celtics-Lakers. Everyone just wanted to see Johnson and Bird."

Roman was also happy he no longer had to wear collared shirts and khakis—he went to school every day in blue or black jeans. Who would have thought getting arrested would result in a less stringent dress code? Since then, his skin hasn't been touched by khakis. Alex wore jeans, too, the same black ones every day. He also still wore his old polo shirts because he said his parents hadn't taken him clothes shopping in a while.

The boys' leveled-up confidence carried over to lunch as they now sat at actual lunch tables out in the open rather than taking refuge in shadowy corners, although Roman wasn't any better at dealing with new people.

One lunch break, strangers' elbows at a neighboring table were too close for comfort. So, naturally, when one of them bumped into Roman's, it belonged to a girl. Thank God she just twitched away.

Alex was preoccupied with cradling a spicy chicken sandwich. "At least this place contracts with the same food vendor." He sat across from Roman and Todd.

Although the girl's attention to the joint collision was gone, Todd scooted toward her and her friend. "Sorry, my bros a klutz," he told them.

"That's okay," the impacted girl said. She paired a chin-length bob with a black choker necklace and a rugby shirt.

"So," Todd said. "Do you guys . . ."

"We're new here," Alex said, sticking his head into the middle of the introduction. "Did you hear about what happened at Wright Magnet?"

The girls looked at each other.

"Um, no," the girl in the choker necklace said.

Roman bet he could master anything from archery to zebra grooming with all of this new free time, except for talking to girls. It didn't bother him that that didn't bother him.

Alex bent up a side of his semi-unibrow. "Want to know why we're new faces around here? It's a cool story."

"I don't know. Did you guys kill someone?"

The choker girl's friend laughed and almost blew Coke out of her nose.

"Damn it, why does everyone say that about me and Rome?" Alex asked as he scratched the back of his head.

The girls laughed harder.

"No, wait!" Todd interjected. "We didn't actually hurt anyone."

"We did have good lawyers, though," Roman said, not as a means to impress, but shoo. Then, as he had hoped, the girls, aghast, left the table with their trays of half-eaten lunches.

Todd darted a critical glance between Roman and Alex before shaking his head. "Why the hell do I keep thinking you guys can be good wingmen?"

"I was just trying to tell them our story," Alex said. "We'd look like badasses."

"You can't just dive into it that fast, bro. You gotta build up to it. No matter how cool something is, it can be killed by sounding desperate."

"Then just let me lead next time," Alex said. "I've been a bachelor longer than you."

He surely meant that as a joke, but Roman turned his head away in favor of the sight of flies lapping a trash can's air space. The table fell quiet. Roman waited a few seconds before looking back at Alex, whose expression was that of a LEGO-stepping victim. Todd picked at his palm.

Alex got up and fumbled with his belongings. "I'm still kinda hungry. Gonna grab some Funyuns before lunch is over. I'll see you guys later." He tossed his backpack over one shoulder and took off.

Todd spun himself to the top of the table in a thinker's pose. Roman copied and waited ninety agonizing seconds to capitalize on this brief window of one-on-one time. "Uh, by the way, I kinda ran into Lucy over the weekend."

Todd spoke while gnawing on a hangnail. "Oh, yeah? With another dude?"

"Uh, yeah. At Rite Aid," Roman replied. "But not with another dude. I wanted to get some ice cream, and she was there too."

"I know, bro. I'm kidding. Was she there with anyone, though?"

"Just some girlfriends. I didn't know any of them."

"Awesome, bro. I'm guessing she said 'hi' first while you waited in line or else nothing would have happened."

"Uh, actually, I already had my cone of mint n' chip when she came up to say hi."

"Oh, nice. Hope it was yummy as hell, bro."

Roman cleared his throat. "Then she told me everything."

"About what?" Todd asked. "A new boyfriend?"

"No, uh, about us being arrested."

"Wow, bro. I didn't think we'd become legends that fast. Too bad you can't make billions off that, but at least you've got a good intro for your memoir. Maybe that'll make you rich down the road."

"She, uh, talked about how it was all her fault."

Todd cut the quips.

"I'm . . . I'm not mad at her," Roman said.

Todd ripped off the hangnail and, with it, a longer band of

skin than he probably expected. He started bleeding lightly and grunted. He grabbed a used Kleenex from one of his pockets and started putting pressure on the minor wound. Todd sucked on his afflicted finger. "After we got kicked out, I knew my parents would get super strict and shit and make me stop dating her. I just wanted to get ahead of it—on my terms. I don't remember what I said exactly; I was too in rage mode. I haven't spoken to her since then."

The concept of romance was as confusing as ever. Roman never planned to undertake a skincare routine, so straying from love and its byproducts, like wrinkle-inducing stress, would be his preferred method. That's ultimately why old people looked that way, he thought, they had had enough of people's shit. Beyond that, he couldn't think of any more philosophical tandems to better prepare his pending statements.

"Or maybe I need to stop losing my cool," Todd continued. "I mean, what kind of lawyer am I gonna be if I snap at the judge or something?"

Out of nowhere, Alex returned with his promise of munching on Funyuns. "Or maybe you should just shut up and listen to us for once."

"What is this?" Todd said. "You guys ganging up on me now?"

Yes, Roman thought. *I'm ganging up on you, and I'll take anyone as a teammate.*

He didn't care about himself, but he knew by now most guys, his friends included, go nuts without chicks—at least starting around this age.

"I'm not trying to do that," Roman said. "I was just gonna say, if you want to, you know, you can, uh, go for it."

"So, I've got your permission, bro?" Todd said in a sarcastic tone. "Gee, thanks."

"That's not what he meant," Alex said.

Todd blanched, palms stretching out from his shoulders. "You think it's that easy, bro? I can just flip a switch, and we're back together like that? Like she's gonna forgive me for breaking her heart or whatever so quickly?"

The trajectory of Roman's good intentions took a nosedive.

"After all this time," Todd said. "Especially after all this free time you both have now. You guys still don't know anything about girls."

Roman sulked in the truth, but didn't let it get to him—it couldn't get to him.

Alex, on the other hand, kept an upright posture. "I know that if you let it go for too long, you're gonna lose her for good."

"Oh, snap, you're gonna win a Pulitzer in no time with introspective questions like that, Al," Todd said. "You're so wise now, master . . . master . . . Who's that green puppet from that space movie? Not Kermit, right?"

"Yoda. Come on, man. I'm not even that much of a *Star Wars* fan."

"Look, let's just drop it."

But Roman had one last variable to insert into the equation. "Uh, she cried."

Todd turned his head a little his way.

"Who cried?" Alex said.

"Lucy," Roman said.

Todd didn't move another millimeter.

"You made her cry?" Alex exclaimed with a wide-open mouth full of pulverized cornmeal.

"No, no!" Roman said. "I was telling Todd that uh . . . ugh. It's a long story. I'll tell you later."

"I don't need to hear more," Alex said. "Well, there you go, Todd. John Stockton couldn't have given you a better assist."

Todd elevated the Chin and spoke smugly. "We also don't speak of the Jazz here. I'm still pissed about the '98 sweep."

He started swaying his torso back and forth at a developing pace with interlocked fingers until he stopped moving. "She was the best sleeper."

Roman, caught off guard, shared the same perplexed look as Alex.

"Funny how she always looked tired, right?" Todd said. "It surprised me too. I didn't think it was possible to have a great time with someone when you're awake and knocked out."

Alex waited a few moments. Seemed like he was processing a question. "Are you saying . . . are you saying you watched her sleep?"

"No," Todd said with a reminiscent smile. "I always woke up before she did. And I didn't care."

Then, he quickly changed his mood. "I'm just messing with you pathetic freaks. So . . . Yankee Doodles?"

Alex chuckled. Roman didn't.

"Right now?" Alex asked.

"Yeah, screw fifth period, bro. We haven't gone this week anyway."

Alex took in a deep breath and beamed from ear to ear. "Screw it." He even took point toward the student parking lot.

Senior year came with one less period for each of the boys. Their school days ended earlier than their underclassmen—one-thirty in the afternoon.

Despite the sanctioned half days, it wouldn't be the last semester of high school without succumbing to at least one symptom of senioritis. Luckily, most teachers at Harding High didn't bother to take roll, so once or twice a week, the boys took advantage by skipping fifth period after lunch.

Roman expected some kind of disciplinary risk, only to be comforted by the sight of other wayward seniors along the way to the parking lot, one of the rare real-world occasions in which he believed in the strength in numbers. It was all too easy. The absence of everyone's shadows made things even less sinister. He supposed he was happy to carry on a tradition of harmless fun from prior generations, from doo-wop curls to grunge split ends and ethnic spikes.

Roman, Todd and Alex would chauffeur themselves across a boulevard of fast food franchises and real estate offices. Roman always blasted KROQ along the way to Yankee Doodles. It was a sports bar in neighboring Tujunga that, for some reason, opened at noon every day, so the boys always had first pick of pool tables, but it came with the drawback of musty Clorox bleach aerating from the bathrooms to the kitchen. It took just a game or two of cutthroat to get used to it. The boys divvied up an eight-ball rack to five balls a person and whoever knocked in their assigned quintet plus the eight ball won.

If Todd were the victor, he had a patented catchphrase. "Rack 'em, bitch."

Alex tried to be cool and unceremonious with his wins but couldn't repress the sides of his lips curling up to ninety-degree angles.

The three, however, were equally bad at pool, so the only pocket they called was for the eight ball.

A pair of jukeboxes acted as monoliths welcoming people to the adjacent restrooms. Roman's parents gave him three dollars a day to legally nourish him. It was also enough to cover a few games' worth of pool in quarters—the tables were coin-operated—and help pay for a small basket of fries, which never lasted past the first game.

After his last bite, Todd wiped his hands on his pants and proceeded to a lucky shot that bounced the cue ball off three side rails and struck two others before knocking one of his in, the eleven ball. He shrugged and proceeded to the last shot, the eight ball, which was a successful straight-line drive.

Todd didn't egg on Roman for another game, however. Instead, Todd grabbed his stuff and saluted his friends.

"Sorry, buds," he said. "Gotta bounce early today."

"What? Why?" Alex asked.

"Doctor's appointment."

"You'd seriously schedule an appointment on one of our pool days?"

"Yup. But don't worry, I'll save you guys a trip and ask him if he thinks you're both jerking it too much."

Roman and Alex watched him power walk out of the pool hall, then they looked at each other.

"I've got a few more quarters," Alex said, fishing them out of his pocket and offering them to his friend.

"I'll rack," Roman said.

He spent a solid two minutes making sure the balls were in the correct order and packed them in as tightly as possible, only to be disrespected by a lame break by Alex, one that decomposed the triangle into the shape of a fried egg.

"Sorry," he said. "This is gonna be a long game."

But Alex seemed more bothered when "Black Magic Woman" by Santana played on the jukebox. "Ugh. This is the crap my parents listen to. Oh well, at least we get to kill these last few fries."

"Yeah," Roman said.

"Wait," Alex said. "Before we start, I forgot to show you guys something, but I can at least show you for now."

Alex leaned his cue against a wall, but it rolled over and fell anyway. He didn't give it a second thought. From his backpack, he pulled out what appeared to be a newspaper that he flipped through at a manic pace before shoving it in Roman's face.

At first, Roman thought it was a newspaper clipping of their H-wording heist and that Alex was once again overly nostalgic until Roman was up close and personal with an artsy snapshot of a glistening cut of steak. Next, he noticed the masthead, the *Glendale Gem*.

"It's my first review for a new independent paper in town!" Alex said. "You know Manny's? That place on Brand we always thought was for old people? Turns out they make bomb steak! Especially rare steak. You ever try a rare steak?"

"Um," Roman said. "I don't think so. You mean like raw?"

"Well, not really. It's just cooked less. It's the best. You don't need any A1 sauce or anything. I can't believe I was eating well-done steak my whole life. Well, it's basically what my mom orders for me and her all the time. Eating rare steak is like the most mature thing I do now."

Roman focused back on the restaurant review. *The Fairest Rare*, the headline read.

"I didn't write that, the editor did," Alex continued. "I didn't like it, so don't pay attention to that. But this is a brand-new weekly that just started a few months ago. I haven't made the *Glendale Leader* just yet."

"I think it's good," Roman said. "This is . . . really cool."

Alex's eyes lit up as he folded the article into a neat rectangle and slipped it back into his backpack. "They said they're going to pay me fifty bucks for each one I do and my meal too! That's almost a new game every time I eat at a restaurant!"

"That's awesome," Roman said.

And he meant it. He was elated for his friend. Alex reminded Roman of a younger version of himself.

"And imagine when I'm ready to apply to USC from GCC," Alex continued. "I'll have a portfolio to submit with the application. Their journalism school's gotta be impressed with that, right?"

Roman shifted his concentration toward the legs of the pool table. "Right. Totally." He wondered if they had to be lifted up each time it's time to vacuum and whether it was some big, buff dude's job. It definitely was a crappy job, but at least he was earning a little money.

"Best part is all I do is email them the reviews," Alex continued. "I can work from home, but it's a lot better than doing homework. And they're starting me off with two articles a month, but if the readers like it, I guess they'll let me do more."

"That's great," Roman said. "Congrats. It all sounds great."

"Thanks!"

Their game continued with Alex doing a live reading of his review in between turns and he went into great detail about his favorite style of potatoes—scalloped.

Roman was surprised when he found himself a shot away from victory and kissed the eight ball into a called corner pocket.

"Sick," Alex said. "I think that's the fastest I've ever lost."

"Let's go again," Roman said, already sharpening his cue.

He wanted many more games.

"Uh, sure," Alex said. "Just gotta run a few bucks through the change machine."

But the next two games went by even faster, with Roman

winning by greater and greater margins. It was a relapse into mastery.

"One more," he said as he chalked his cue with vigor.

"I'd be down," Alex said, tapping on his pockets with his palms. "But I'm out of quarters."

"You sure?"

Roman bounced the base of his cue on the floor to shake off the excess chalk from the tip, and just before stopping, he decided it doubled as a taunt.

"Plus, maybe we should start heading home soon," Alex said.

"Oh," Roman said. "Yeah, maybe."

But he jonesed for a moment that he could live in forever like some kind of *Twilight Zone* episode. Of course, neither Alex nor anyone could have picked up on this, maybe except for Todd. Roman didn't need more than the flimsiest of firewalls to back up from the cusp of a deep conversation, especially about himself.

The non-playing reminded him of why he tried so hard to keep his mind busy. He kept having flashbacks of helping that kid at juvenile hall with printing his essay.

"I don't know what I'm gonna do," he uttered, gazing up at the sports bar's rafters like they were holy.

"Huh? It's alright," Alex said. "If you got a buck or two, I can go get change."

"What?"

"I said you got a buck or two?"

In the span of a benign heart murmur, the sight of Alex and his eager eyes helped Roman remember what was the most productive distraction of all. "No, I mean, I don't . . . I don't know where to go from here."

"You mean you don't wanna go home?" Alex asked.

Roman scratched the back of his head. "I thought for a sec . . . that I could be a teacher."

"What?" Alex asked.

"Teach . . . teach computer classes and stuff, you know? Can you believe that?"

Alex raised his chin like Todd. "Hell to the no."

Alex laughed.

Roman replied with a few melancholic cracks to his delivery. "I researched it one day at the library. I need to get a master's degree and shit. That's gonna take years."

Alex placed his right hand on Roman's shoulder, presumably with more confidence than attempting such a move with a girl. Roman didn't object.

"I wanna be big *now*," Roman said.

"Dude," Alex said. "You're gonna be fine."

Roman debated whether he regretted bringing all this up, but this persistent absence of the Internet metastasized into such unnatural desires.

"Really?" he asked.

"Seriously. You're the person I'm least worried about."

"Why?"

Alex pulled his hand away and erupted with more conviction than for any other video game or delicacy. "Do I really have to spell it out for you? Look at all you've done, man! Who else has ever hacked into their freaking school and changed their grades? Who else figured out the shit they do in movies and actually did it in real life?"

It was the assurance Roman wanted to hear, from his parents or not, but it still didn't solve anything.

"Who knows what the hell else you've got up your sleeve?" Alex continued.

But Roman felt like he was wearing a wife-beater. No ideas were coming as of late, pretty much since his downfall. So, betting on a light switch-flipping moment wasn't looking like the surest investment anymore.

"Plus," Alex said. "How do you think I felt when I realized I didn't want to be a game designer anymore? I got lucky, now that I think about it. If anything, you're gonna be at GCC. You think everyone knows what the hell they wanna do with their life when they start junior college? I'm not even sure if this journalism stuff is going to work out for me."

Still, more education.

Great, Roman thought.

"You're gonna be able to use computers again soon anyway," Alex said.

"Yeah, I know."

Alex gripped Roman's shoulder again. "Rome. Trust me. You're gonna figure it out."

They closed out and parted ways. Alex's spiel, a predictable last resort, didn't trigger an epiphany on what to do, but who cares? Roman was just happy to have a steady lunch partner for another year or two. Plus, they still had several months to go before graduation.

When it came to prom, he didn't give two shits, but he looked forward to grad night, a twilight trip to Disneyland from 9 p.m. to 2 a.m. for high school students. That was perhaps the one silver lining to expulsion from the joyless H.L. Wright Magnet High School, which didn't even have a sports team and did not partake in grad night.

Losers, Roman thought.

His parents took him to Disneyland once or twice when he was much younger, so outside of waving cast members, he didn't remember much. He wasn't even a huge fan of the theme park, just the opportunity to perturb a bedtime.

—

"What!" Todd shouted in the school hallway at the apex of a student bunching.

Roman slithered his way through the crowd to a bulletin board. After taking a mob shoulder to his cheek, he tried to readjust his glasses, then remembered he'd been wearing contacts for months. He glazed over the message until a key sentence that everyone seemed to gawk at in horror.

As of today, grad night is canceled.

This must have been the so-called senior prank, far evolved from the old days of streaking—a more psychological shenanigan to strike terror in hearts and minds.

Too many unexcused absences . . . Roman continued reading . . . *committed by the majority of the senior class.*

But so what? Roman thought. After all, he and his friends were merely keeping up the tradition.

"Hey!" Alex shouted from the back of the crowd.

Roman could recognize that bobbing unibrow anywhere.

"What's going on?" Alex said. "I can't get through!"

Roman turned back to the pinned announcement, which concluded with a signature at the bottom.

—Sincerely, Principal . . .

But Roman twirled away in rage before he finished reading the head of the school's name.

The doctor's order was a heavy dosage of commiserating with his friends. Roman saw them gather at the rear of the crowd. On the way, Roman heard an outsider's voice in his head, one from juvenile hall belonging to perhaps the only kid weirder than himself within California.

We get to go on field trips, that kid said once.

Roman slightly altered his trajectory.

"So, God hates us," Todd told Roman, who passed him by. "Hey, where are you going, bro?"

"Oh, jeez," Alex said. "I know that look. What's he gonna do now?"

"I'm gonna go to the library," Roman said.

"Sounds good, bro," Todd called out from behind. "Just make sure we don't get life sentences this time."

Roman was lucky that Harding High's frumpish librarian had the same loser habits as H.L Wright Magnet's, as she ate her lunch in the library alone—it must have been a universal job requirement. He sat down at one of the computers in a row and Googled the phone number for Disneyland and, in the process, learned his first Orange County zip code—714. Then Roman approached the librarian, who munched on homemade tuna salad out of Tupperware while the day's newspaper was splayed next to her on her desk.

"I'm sorry to interrupt, but I need to call my mother," he said.

The cud-chewing librarian studied him.

"Uh," Roman said. "I need to tell her where to pick me up from before she leaves work."

Still chewing, she gestured her head to the courtesy phone at the edge of her desk. Roman sprinted and dialed the number he had just memorized, fingers crossed for what seemed like an eternity until a woman answered.

"Yes, of course, we allow homeschooled children to attend, but the same chaperone rules apply," she said. "I'm assuming you're all registered with one of those homeschool programs?"

"Uh, yeah," Roman lied. "Homeschool program, you mean like . . ."

"The homeschooled students that come visit us are usually part of a network that allows for group gatherings since some parents prefer shared experiences."

"Right, right."

Then Roman drew a massive blank, hung up and dashed back to the computer for a few rounds of research. It had to be so believable—three homeschool friends seeking to enjoy the one senior year experience their parents had castrated from them.

Roman got up and jogged to the phone again before the librarian could protest. "Sorry, one more time, one more time," he said and caught a skeptical, yet fatigued side eye from her.

He re-dialed Disneyland again and was reconnected to the same woman he spoke with moments ago. "I'm sorry, I was on my cellphone. Bad reception. We are all part of the National School of Correspondence of Kenosha, Wisconsin. We'd like to attend on uh . . ." He tried to remember the available dates, but remembered only one. "May 20. We'd like to come on May 20."

"Sounds great," the Disneyland employee said. "All we need now is payment and a waiver."

"A waiver?"

"Yes, just print it off the grad night website and fax it to the number on the form. But you've got to hurry. There's less than two weeks before the deadline."

"Sure, sure. And payment?"

"It's standard to mail a check or money order, but if you need more time to sort things out, you can pay at the gate."

"Sure, sounds good. Thank you."

But it didn't sound so good in his head as he pulled into his driveway in his decrepit Mazda.

I'm already in hot water. Maybe more assurances just needed to be investigated.

Inside his house, he was greeted by a stiff Audrey in the kitchen.

"Your grad night was canceled?" She asked with arms crossed over a scornful gaze.

Roman couldn't believe it. The shit storm had gotten worse already. This half-pincer attack didn't even afford him a few minutes to rehearse bullshit lies.

"Um, yeah," Roman said. "How did you know?"

"I just got off the phone with Todd's mom."

"You . . . you guys are talking again?"

"She said it's because too many students have been ditching this year."

Cold sweat flushed to Roman's pores.

"But not you," Audrey said. "Right?"

Roman long ago made peace with never becoming adept at improv, but he knew a divine upper hand when he saw one. "I mean, yeah. How else . . . how else would I be doing better in my class if I was ditching, you know?"

Audrey nodded as she did a quick scan of the kitchen. "This isn't fair. It's not fair to you or your friends!"

Roman had to unnaturally repress his "but mom" instincts.

"Um, yeah. Definitely not," he said.

Audrey moved some plates and cups from the kitchen counter to the sink. "Grad night was one of my favorite high school memories," she said as she soaked the dishware.

"You went?"

"Sure, I did. Me and my girlfriends skipped up and down Main Street U.S.A. and rode the teacups until the sun came up or our dinners, whichever was first."

"That's really cool, mom," Roman said.

He was further startled when Audrey kicked the trash can back into its slot by the sink.

"Those sons of bitches!" She shouted. "They're not going to take this away from you too."

Audrey grabbed a cordless phone off the kitchen counter and dialed. Roman heard a few faint rings.

"Hello, Mrs. Tovmasian," Audrey said. "It's me again. We have to do something for our boys. They don't deserve to be robbed of an experience like this right before they graduate . . . Right? They're still kids for a few more months!"

Roman was dumbfounded. He expected a swarm of cameras to invade the kitchen, all pointed at him, as a parental prank gotcha moment for a low-grade, mid-season reality show.

Instead, Audrey pounded the kitchen counter with her fist like an impassioned tyrant at the United Nations protesting sanctions.

"Right?" she said into the phone. "What can we do? . . . Hmm. Maybe we can organize our own trip for the boys."

Roman's cheeks turned red, humbled by a type of gesture he never expected from either of his parents ever again.

"Some schools let you bring your girlfriend or boyfriend," Roman said. "We just have to pay at the gate."

"Okay, okay," Audrey said. "You guys handle that while we think of a safe way to get you there and back."

"Will do," Roman said. "I'll be right back." He ran to his room and called Todd's new cellphone.

"Bro," Todd said. "Are our moms serious?"

"Uh, yeah, seems like it," Roman said.

"This is crazy. I know like twenty or thirty people who'd want to come too. Even some friends from Wright Magnet, since they don't get a grad night either."

"I'll get our moms to line up a tour bus or something."

"What about the tickets, bro? And you think our folks will just pay for a bus for so many people?"

"Um, just tell everyone to bring money for the ticket the day of. I called Disneyland today and they said we can pay at the gate. Then, we'll tell our folks we can charge twenty-five bucks on top of that for the bus, but we'll actually charge them fifty."

"This guy. Haven't picked up enough trash off the freeway?"

"No. Uh, I'm just gonna need to buy some new computer parts in a few months."

"Awesome. You're nuts, bro. I'll talk to you later."

Roman ran back down to the kitchen, where his mom waited with a game face. "Mom, Todd and stuff wanna go and a few other friends are down. We'll probably need to rent a bus. Could you do that for us, and I'll get the money from everyone who comes, then we'll reimburse you." Roman spat that all out in a single breath, gripping both sides of the kitchen island as he almost passed out.

Audrey beamed like he had brought home a 4.0 report card for the first time, or that's how he assumed she'd react.

"Then that's what we'll do," Audrey said. "I'll look through the Yellow Pages and find a good deal."

A flood of emotions warmed Roman's soul. He didn't care if he was in the middle of a crowded mall with everyone aiming judgmental leers and laughs as he proceeded to hug his mother.

"Mom," he said. "I . . ."

The front door to the house opened and closed.

Felix passed through the kitchen, dress shoes tapping like high heels.

"Hello," he said in a melodic tone, then tossed his suit coat draped over his arm onto a dining table chair and his briefcase onto the couch.

"Hi, hon," Audrey said.

Roman stood in place, waiting for his parents to start a conversation so he could duck out back to his room.

Felix returned to the kitchen and started flipping through the mail. He said nothing and went to the bathroom, keeping quiet.

Audrey tossed a few veggies into the blender and turned it on.

—

A warm evening gust tussled Roman's sprouting locks. He was the first to step onto a repurposed school bus, painted charcoal, that pulled into a vacant quarter of an Albertsons parking lot.

He readjusted a fanny pack around his waist and reminded himself he had indeed faxed the waiver after Todd coaxed his twenty-six-year-old cousin to sign it. Roman shook hands with the driver, a safety vest-wearing middle-aged woman.

"Uh, sorry to make you work this late," Roman told her.

Her eyebrows shot up past her reflective visor. "Are you kidding me? This is easy overtime."

Roman stuck his head outside the bus. "Uh, let's go," he said to the still-growing crowd.

Roman hung out up front as he watched people board, mostly Todd's old friends from Wright Magnet, his basketball buddies—the Arbis, Artins, Gohars and Anis of the world—and a few casual friends they've made at Harding High. Some of the dudes high-fived him, but the girls offered no greeting.

He saw them as dollar signs anyway until Alex boarded by himself. He was wearing a Blockbuster employee uniform.

"They wanted me to do a longer shift, but I got out of it," Alex said. "And I got the deadline extended for my next review."

"You're gonna get rich before all of us," Roman replied.

They smiled at each other. Alex took a seat midway toward the back. Not wanting to sit with a stranger for the trek to Anaheim, Roman sat next to his friend.

"Todd didn't invite Sako?" Alex asked.

"If he did, I would have said something," Roman said.

Todd was one of the last to show up. After getting on the bus, he made eye contact with his friends. Then he looked down toward the asphalt as Lucy climbed up with pattering flip-flops.

She surveyed the passengers until she saw Roman and greeted him with a jubilant wave.

Alex leaned over as she made her way down the aisle. "He better not mess it up this time," he told Roman. "Lucky asshole."

Roman smirked.

Lucy lunged down the aisle at Roman and gave him a bear hug.

"So good to see you again!" She said, squeezing him and making him look like a nearly empty tube of toothpaste.

Roman let the petite girl have her way while Todd snickered in the background, a hand pressed against a vertical rail. Since he was kind of blocking the way, a girl shorter than Lucy snuck by under his arm.

In addition to a modest crop top and white jeans, she had styled a ponytail held together by a green scrunchy.

"Hey! So, is Tamar coming?" Todd asked scrunchy girl.

Mouth slightly agape like a fish, scrunchy girl looked over her shoulder. "No, she's with her new boyfriend tonight."

Roman glanced at Alex, who stared out the window. It was quite perplexing when what looked like rainwater splashed onto the window, but it was just sprinkler splatter.

"Oh, okay," Todd said. "Well, do you know my friend, Alex? He was one of the guys that was part of the hacking."

Alex jerked his head toward the introduction at the front of the bus.

"Oh, really?" Scrunchy girl said while looking his way.

"Yeah, but I was more boots on the ground," said Alex promptly, who then aimed his thumb at his friend. "Rome here was the one who did the actual hacking."

Scrunchy girl lit up with curiosity while walking down the aisle. "Really? You were the hacker?"

"Uh, yeah," Roman said, caught off guard.

"How did you learn to do that?" Scrunchy girl asked.

Roman wasn't sure whether to dive to the bottom of the iceberg that was #mswarez or perform a layman's breakdown.

"Just trial and error, I guess," he said.

"You mean you got caught a couple of times?" Scrunchy girl asked.

"No. I just practiced. I had to guess the right IP addresses randomly. I also picked up a few things from this forum I was a part of."

Roman spotted Todd looking over his seat, the Chin up in the air.

"Oh, and we used this thing called a keylogger," Roman continued. "We used it to record keystrokes. That's how we got the teacher's passwords."

"Weren't you scared?" Scrunchy girl asked as she took a seat across the narrow aisle. Their conversation carried on between bodies passing by.

"I didn't give a shit."

Her glow. The way she cupped her own chin with her fingers. It was a type of social engineering he had never prepared for or even imagined.

Scrunchy girl shut her fish mouth and then formed a modest smile. "I'm Arax, by the way."

Roman extended the type of handshake he's only known, meaning just for guys.

"I'm Roman," he said.

"Yeah, I know. I think everyone in the school knew after you guys got kicked out. Do you think you'd do it again knowing what would happen?"

Roman grinned. The bus engine cranked like an aging beast.

At this time of night, the heart of Orange County was just under an hour's drive away. Roman fielded a barrage of questions from Arax, but didn't take the initiative to tease the next chapter, allowing for some occasional dead air. Todd turned around from the seat directly in front of Roman and filled those gaps with anecdotes about his best friend's clumsiness or nocturnal misadventures with Alex, whose expressions played along with the mood, though he didn't add much.

Despite the color of their bus sticking out like a sore thumb compared to the school of yellow student-transporting vessels when they arrived at Disneyland, no one really batted an eye when Roman stepped off. By then, the conversation with Arax fizzled as she had some girlfriends to greet and catch up with from the back of the bus. But the timing was fine as Roman had to don the leadership cape for the evening.

Teens raced to the turnstiles, chaperones dangling behind, urging everyone to stay together. Just past the security station and a minimal gate, Roman spotted Mickey Mouse's face composed of hundreds of Nemesia flowers.

"Come on," Todd called out to the group. "I hate to be that guy, but let's stick together."

Roman unzipped his fanny pack and pulled out a thick wad

of cash worth several thousand dollars, which would have hypnotized every human except for an aging Disneyland employee standing behind the glass of an entry booth. She wore a blue t-shirt, had walkie-talkies strapped to both sides of her waist, and donned the horn-rimmed glasses Roman used to wear. She's likely seen her fair share of vomiting over the decades, but never akin to the monetary spewing of this caliber.

"You want to pay in cash?" She asked.

Roman held out the money and spread the bills apart like he was posing for a rap album cover. "Uh. When I called, someone said it'd be okay."

"But everyone has paid online."

Roman looked over his shoulder and saw everyone's frozen stares.

"Just one moment," the employee said.

Before Roman knew it, a squadron of workers in identical t-shirts stood behind the entry booth glass, counting the bills.

After a quick security screen, everyone was rushed in and handed their tickets, but Roman was given three extra items: red paper bracelets, which Roman deposited into his fanny pack.

"Those are for the buffet," the employee said once the counting was done. "Give them to your chaperones. Now, please, we've got tons more kids to process."

Everyone was carefree again once the bells of the Disneyland railroad chimed from the track above Mickey's floral grin.

Todd, his arm wrapped around Lucy, led the tilting back of heads as the vintage gas lamps and ragtime tunes welcomed them down Main Street, U.S.A.

The group broke apart, leaving Roman with Todd, Alex, Lucy, Arax, and a few other girlfriends to stroll down the sendup of small towns inspired by the turn of the twentieth century.

Sleeping Beauty Castle, traced with a majestic corona from the moonlight, perched a few hundred yards ahead. Roman wouldn't have known the names of any of these places if it weren't for the map he carried.

Some high school seniors skipped like first graders; girls, arms interweaved with their friends', while their boyfriends in backward baseball caps treaded with unimpressed faces.

"Uh, Rome," Alex said. "I forgot to mention, 'cause I rushed here right after work. I didn't get a chance to grab a bite. Think we could do a quick detour for some food? Gonna need energy for the night."

Roman reached into his fanny pack and retrieved the wristbands. "Uh, I got these. They told me I could take two other people to a free buffet for chaperones."

"Sick!" Alex said. "Where is it? I could *so* destroy a buffet right now."

His reaction caught Lucy's attention, who said something to Todd that was drowned out by the parkgoers.

She and Todd walked over. "How about you three go get something to eat?" Lucy said.

"Are you sure?" Alex asked.

Lucy lightly pressed her elbow into Todd's stomach. "Of course! I told him me and my friends can get some of our shopping out of the way for now."

The boys exchanged nods and glances. Todd kissed Lucy on the forehead and started departing with his friends.

Roman turned around and spotted Arax, who waved, but he wasn't sure if it was meant just for him.

"Have fun!" she said.

Roman, Todd, and Alex didn't know where to go until they simultaneously pointed at their red bracelets to a helpful worker, who told them to line up under a striped awning shielding dozens of adults, most of whom raised eyebrows at the boys since they were likely at least half their age.

The line eventually led to a stuffy cafeteria with peach walls and booths. They met a cross-pollination of pasta and lukewarm fish in the air. They were the youngest there by many years, but they had bracelets on, so no one gave a shit.

The boys grabbed their trays and got in the fast-moving buffet line. Alex loaded up a pile of spaghetti from the get-go, then held his breath past a few more carb options until he arrived at the carving station. Alex exhaled. "Buffets try to screw you with having carbs at the start of the line, so you get full and don't have too much of the good stuff," he told his friends.

Then, he directly addressed the man with the giant knife. "I'll take three slices of your finest ham," Alex said.

But Roman didn't heed the advice. He stocked up on spaghetti and penne with marinara, a croque monsieur, and a few dinner rolls. Todd kept things simple and snatched a personal-sized pizza.

After, they occupied a booth. Todd took in the scenery and asked a question sarcastically. "Where the hell *are* we, bro?"

Roman and Alex couldn't help but crack up a little, but didn't say a word. They started eating.

"So, what'd you think of Arax?" Todd asked Roman.

Roman swallowed a big gulp of iced tea. "Um, she's cool. I didn't think she'd be that interested in the shit we pulled."

"Jesus Christ, bro. Do I have to spell it out for you? People are gonna be hooked on our story. Use it to your advantage from now on."

"I guess we're just used to doing all the legwork for him," Alex said.

Todd raised the Chin once again. "*Hundred* percent."

"You're the skinniest person ever to be a lazy ass," Alex quipped at Roman.

This time, all three chuckled at the harmless punchline.

Then, Todd meticulously peeled the tomatoes off his Margherita pizza. "I think now I just hate tomatoes on things altogether."

"It's okay," Alex said. "Everyone has foods they hate. I hate olives."

Roman enjoyed the banter in his favorite way, silently, until his right contact lens fell out. His fingers scampered around the table.

"What's wrong, bro?" Todd asked. "You okay?"

"Yeah, yeah," Roman said. "They fall out sometimes." He found the stray contact, but before popping it back in, he glazed over the four corners of the dining hall until he detected a familiar figure.

The one eye still affixed with a contact lens twitched.

The figure was seated at a booth across the room that he shared with three other adults. Short and bald save for a horseshoe. Glasses. A huge gut. A dubious glare.

It can't be him, Roman thought.

He snapped his attention back to his friends.

"Should we get going?" Roman asked Todd and Alex. "Got a long night ahead of us, no?"

"Why?" Alex asked. "I'm just about ready for seconds."

"Maybe we don't want to fall too behind," Roman said.

"What are you talking about, bro?" Todd asked. "I'll call Lucy, and we'll find them."

Roman's eyes darted the figure's way for a split second and saw it exchanging pleasantries with his tablemates.

He didn't know what to make of that. His friends munched on, but he was grossed out after shoveling a portion of his penne into his mouth. He must have accidentally scooped some of the white cream he's always hated.

"Yack," Roman said. "What is that?"

Alex inspected his friend's plate. "Is that Alfredo sauce? Don't get me *started* on Alfredo sauce."

ACKNOWLEDGMENTS

This story was inspired by my friends, Shaunt and Ara, who I can't thank enough.

I'm surprised they still want to know me after how often I cajoled them for minute details while we were out for beers.

I'm also grateful to my mother, Nelly, for her unwavering support and encouragement ever since I announced this project.

This took six long years, but you know what? I can't wait to do it again.

Arin Mikailian is from Glendale, California, where he still resides. He had to unlearn years of journalism to take a stab at fiction. He also wrote most of this book at a local craft beer bar.